READERS ALSO LOVE BRYAN'S DRAGONS IN OUR MIDST SERIES

As parents of boys who are avid readers, my wife and I struggled to find reading material that fed their appetite while reinforcing the virtues we value. Bryan Davis is a good man and a great storyteller. And this series is an all-time favorite my sons still speak of, even now into their college years!

MARK T. HANCOCK, HUSBAND AND FATHER, CEO OF TRAIL LIFE USA

One of the best blends of contemporary fantasy and allegory that I have read, Dragons in Our Midst will have you hurting and rooting for Billy and Bonnie. If you love fantasy, King Arthur, and hopeful adventures, this is the story for you.

SCOTT APPLETON, AUTHOR OF THE SWORD OF THE DRAGON SERIES AND THE NEVERQUEEN SAGA

It all started with a boy who could breathe fire and a girl who had wings. Dragons in Our Midst invites readers to lift up their swords and join Billy Bannister and Bonnie Silver as they battle dragon slayers, uncover ancient legends, and—of course—come face to face with dragons. Bryan Davis delivers a clean, complex series that challenges and uplifts its readers. When I was a teenager, Billy and Bonnie's story captured my own heart and imagination. And today, its poignant messages of faith, sacrifice, and courage endure and stand ready to inspire the next generation of young readers.

JESSICA SLY, AUTHOR OF *THE PROMISE OF DECEPTION*

WHAT READERS ARE SAYING

Raising Dragons is an excellent start to a thrilling, inspiring, and faith-building series. Bryan Davis's unique meshing of legends, myths, and truth is incredibly creative. Together with his strong storytelling and thought-provoking themes it makes for an unforgettable ride. Bryan Davis's books exceed any others in the genre for thematic depth and yet are just as gripping and exciting story-wise as other books of the genre (or even more so). Bryan Davis is my favorite author, and I hope he will become yours too when you dive into the fascinating world of dragons and slayers, of light and darkness, and of truth and deception in *Raising Dragons*.

JOSEPH B., AGE 17

If you love fantasy, you NEED this book! You won't be able to put it down! If you love dragons, you'll love this book! Dragons aren't just portrayed as big bad beasties, as in other books—they're actually heroes! Are you a Christian who wants a deeper relationship with God? This book models that too! Are you seeking God, but always afraid of committing? This book models what true faith looks like and shows that you can love and trust God through everything!

NICK B.

Absolutely brilliant. This is not your typical dungeons and dragons book. Even at 28 I find this book/series addicting. Mr. Davis combines faith and fantasy flawlessly. There are books about King Arthur, Merlin, and dragons aplenty, but to find one whose story line spans centuries and also teaches modern Christian values, that is rare. Mr. Davis includes many unexpected twists and turns and a story line so unique it simply cannot be rivaled. *Raising Dragons* is guaranteed to pique the interest of readers of all ages.

LORI W., AGE 28

Bryan Davis tells a terrific tale teeming with perilous predicaments, fascinating fantasy features, and likeable, charismatic characters who grow in their faith. The engaging writing style captivates the mind and the Christian themes captivate the heart. This epic novel is a superb start to a sensational series.

SHANNON, AGE 24

When I first picked up this book, I didn't know what to expect. By the time I finished the first chapter, I couldn't put it down! I love the way Bryan Davis mixes dragons and faith. It is a very touching experience.

ANNABETH, AGE 13

Bryan has a natural flow in his writing that make his characters come to life through his in-depth description of each character and the way the narrative evolves. I would heartily recommend this book to any fan of the genre regardless of age as the book has a broad appeal to all ages and all walks of life.

JOHN B., AGE 59

I recently reread the Dragons in Our Midst series and fell in love all over again, probably even more so than the first time. Bryan Davis's writing really makes the story and characters come alive. The Dragons in Our Midst series is a fresh take on the fantasy adventure genre, mixing dragons, knights, and the Arthurian legend with modern day. Even a reread makes you want to keep coming back for more.

MADI T., AGE 20

Mr. Davis's work *Raising Dragons* and the series that follows are some of the best Christian fantasy I have ever read. They are the perfect example of an author's work that challenges his readers to learn and grow. He also has a great way of leading his readers to Christ and to become more mature Christians. The series is great fun to read, no matter your age.

JEREMY D.

OTHER BOOKS BY BRYAN DAVIS

DRAGONS IN OUR MIDST

Raising Dragons
The Candlestone
Circles of Seven
Tears of a Dragon

ORACLES OF FIRE

Eye of the Oracle
Enoch's Ghost
Last of the Nephilim
The Bones of Makaidos

CHILDREN OF THE BARD

Song of the Ovulum
From the Mouth of Elijah
The Seventh Door
Omega Dragon

THE REAPERS TRILOGY

Reapers
Beyond the Gateway
Reaper Reborn

TIME ECHOES TRILOGY

Time Echoes
Interfinity
Fatal Convergence

DRAGONS OF STARLIGHT

Starlighter
Warrior
Diviner
Liberator

SEARCH FOR THE
ASTRAL
DRAGON

ASTRAL ALLIANCE SERIES

BRYAN DAVIS

wander™
An imprint of
Tyndale House
Publishers

Visit Tyndale online at tyndale.com.

Visit the author's website at daviscrossing.com.

Tyndale and Tyndale's quill logo are registered trademarks of Tyndale House Ministries. *Wander* and the Wander logo are trademarks of Tyndale House Ministries. Wander is an imprint of Tyndale House Publishers, Carol Stream, Illinois.

Search for the Astral Dragon

Designed by Jennifer Phelps

Edited by Deborah King

Published in association with Cyle Young of the Hartline Literary Agency, LLC.

For information about special discounts for bulk purchases, please contact Tyndale House Ministries at csresponse@tyndale.com, or call 1-855-277-9400.

Library of Congress Cataloging-in-Publication Data

A catalog record for this book is available from the Library of Congress.

ISBN 978-1-4964-5179-8 (hc)
ISBN 978-1-4964-5180-4 (sc)

Printed in the United States of America

28   27   26   25   24   23   22
7   6   5   4   3   2   1

To all who long for justice, strive for freedom,
and pray for enlightenment:

Like a tireless warrior, fight injustice, shatter
the oppressor's chains, and persevere on your
knees. Someday a morning will dawn when
Light will chase away darkness, and all of God's
people will be set free in body, mind, and soul.

PART

01

ESCAPE

The spaceship shuddered with a telltale rattle. We were nearing the end of the wormhole, and time was running out—probably less than an hour left until we landed. I pulled the chain attached to my shackled ankle, holding the hefty links with both hands and pushing with my legs against the wall with all my might.

As I strained, something creaked. I stopped tugging and crawled close to the wall next to my flimsy cot. Barely visible in the dimness, the chain's wall bracket was slightly bent, maybe a couple of millimeters more than yesterday. I was getting closer. But how much longer would it take? This morning might hold my last chance to escape execution.

At the ceiling, the tiny spy camera's flashing blue light rotated toward me, silent compared to the ship's gravity-engine hum. I released the chain and reclined on my cot, stretching my arms as I pretended to be waking up.

A half-dozen lights blinked on the opposite wall, some red, some green. Apparently my wakefulness had been noticed by the ship's computer. "Emerson," I said as I sat up on the cot and blinked, feign-ing bleary eyes, "what time is it?"

Emerson replied from speakers embedded in the ceiling, his voice realistic in cadence, though still somewhat mechanical. "It is five twenty-eight, Megan. You are not scheduled to awaken for thirty-two minutes."

I shook the chain's links. "Tell the captain *he* should try sleeping chained to a wall."

"Captain Tillman's habits are not relevant. According to my data-base, a girl your age needs at least eight point two hours of sleep. You should—"

"To blazes with your database!" I touched the two-inch-wide metal collar that encircled my neck and slid it off the burn inflicted by the court's interrogator, still sensitive even after five months. "Does your blasted database say to put a dog collar on a girl my age and zap her with electric shocks? Does it say to work her fourteen hours a day like a whipped mule and then chain her to a wall at night? Does it say to feed her barely enough pig slop and dishwater to keep her alive for another day of slave labor?"

"Negative. But my database does indicate that your vocabulary level and oratory skills are greatly advanced for a teenager who was reared by pirates."

I scowled. "Freedom fighters, you mean."

"I am merely using the terms provided by—"

"Oh, go reboot yourself." I let out a loud huff and sat on the cot with my sock-covered feet on the metal floor, the shackle chafing my ankle. Some freedom fighter I was. I couldn't even free myself. Instead, death stalked ever closer. In a few hours, the captain would leave the *Nebula Nine* to search for his kidnapped son, following up on a report that Oliver might be on Delta Ninety-eight as a prisoner of slavers there, members of a race called Jaradians. Landing on that planet would offer my first opportunity to escape since I'd been cap-tured. But if the captain decided to follow the judge's orders to the letter, he might execute me before setting out to find Oliver, probably using his remote to deliver a lethal shock to my collar. To save my life, I had to get off the ship as soon as we landed.

Thinking about that awful shock made me cringe. The pain would be horrible, ghastly. Yet, the shock would finally end my torture, and I could join my father in the heavens, living in eternal comfort with the Astral Dragon, the deity he believed in with all his heart, the one he had even named his ship after. At least I hoped I would go to such a wonderful place. If my parents' beliefs were true, and an afterlife really existed, maybe there we could find justice. This galaxy was surely void of it.

Tears crept to my eyes. A sob threatened. Fighting it off, I took a deep breath and steeled myself. I couldn't give up. I had to be the fighter my parents taught me to be. I had to escape and find my mother. Yet, to do that, I needed to know the captain's plans to the minute—and I needed to get my hands on that remote. Maybe I could trick Emerson into giving me a clue.

I looked at the flashing lights on the wall. "Emerson, what's on my chore list today?"

"Nothing. The list is empty."

"Empty?" Hot prickles ran down my back. Trying to shake them off, I laughed under my breath. "Um . . . Emerson, that's impossible. After a planet landing, there are tons of maintenance checks to do. Lots of stuff can shake loose during atmosphere entry."

"Dionne and Dirk are scheduled to perform routine maintenance duties."

I furrowed my brow. "Dirk? Why him? He's just a scullery boy."

"He is also listed as a computer technician. He will be helpful to Dionne."

"But *I'm* her assistant. Does the duty list say anything about me at all?"

"I am authorized to give you public postings. Nothing more."

"What? You can't even tell me my own assignments?"

"Negative. Your security access has been terminated."

"Terminated?" Like a cold wind, the interrogator's threats returned to mind. *If you don't tell us where it is, you will be terminated.*

Captain Tillman is under strict orders to execute you if you refuse to reveal your secrets.

I swallowed hard, feeling the collar's pressure against my throat. "Why was it terminated?"

"A reason was not entered in the termination record."

"So I just sit here in the dark all day?"

"Negative." Shielded bulbs in the ceiling flashed on, giving light to my little corner in the bowels of the ship. The cot with a tied-down pillow against one wall served as my bed, and a shower and vacuum toilet against another wall gave me a place to do my personal business. Removable panels filled most of the remaining wall space, providing access to storage or to shafts that led to nearly every part of the ship.

A slight stinging sensation ran along my arms and calf muscles. I looked at the network of conductive ink on the inner portions of my forearms and legs, surgically imprinted parallel to the nerves underneath. Electrical fields from the lights had activated the ink, causing the sting. Not bad. No more than a tingle that I barely noticed anymore, as long as the captain wasn't wielding his remote.

My full bladder gave me a hard pinch. I glanced again at the still-blinking, still-rotating camera. "Emerson, I need some privacy."

"Acknowledged." The camera's light turned off.

"Thanks, but I can't get dressed yet. Is someone going to unlock me at six like usual, even though I'm grounded?"

"I cannot answer that question. Your security access has been—"

"Terminated. Yeah. You said that. I'm not deaf."

"Then simple logic should have instructed you not to ask the question."

I heaved a loud sigh. "Listen, genius. The chain's long enough for me to do my business in the pot, but I can't put my pants on. Do you get that? It's simple human anatomy."

"Acknowledged. You have fifteen minutes of privacy."

"Great, but I still can't put my pants on." Grumbling to myself, I focused on a wall panel that led into the ship's hull space. The shaft the panel concealed might be my best chance to get away and hide, but it was useless until I could get the ankle shackle off.

After using the toilet, I sat on the floor with my feet braced once more against the wall and both hands again clutching the chain. I pulled and pulled while glancing at the ladder leading up to bridge level, hoping not to see the captain's shiny black boots tromping down the rungs and my collar's remote-control unit in his hand.

As I pulled, the bracket bent a millimeter farther, though still not enough. I kept pulling. What choice did I have? It was either break free or die.

Footsteps sounded from the level above. I let go of the chain and sat on my cot, trying to settle my racing heart as I stared at the ladder. Yet, no one descended.

Breathing a sigh of relief, I stood and looked at the dormant camera. Wasting my privacy time on a stubborn bracket probably wasn't the best idea. I stripped off my knee-length night jersey, exposing a pair of loose shorts, a white singlet undershirt, my locket at the end of a leather cord, and the brand on my upper arm—a fierce dragon, the Alliance's symbol for piracy, infused with purple ink to make it show clearly. The ugly scar always drew my eyes toward it. Even after five months of healing, I could still hear my skin sizzling as the red-hot iron burned into soft flesh to make its court-ordered mark.

Wincing, I tore my gaze away from the brand. Those monsters would pay for their cruelty . . . someday.

I set the locket on my palm and opened the clasp for the thousandth time. My mother and father, Anne and Julian Willis, gazed at me from a browning, wrinkled photo taken four years ago. They were happy then. So was I. But now? How could I be happy? My father was probably dead, and as far as I knew, my mother was imprisoned or awaiting execution somewhere. It was always risky to check on her. Yet, today I really needed to know.

After glancing at the dormant camera once more, I snapped the locket closed and set my thumb against the locket's back. Its embedded thumbprint reader activated, and the secret lead-lined cover popped open, revealing a tiny ruby—a dragon's eye. The gem glowed red.

Fresh tears blurred my vision. My mother was still alive. But for how much longer? Prisoners found guilty of piracy rarely survived long enough to complete their sentences.

I closed the locket and whispered, "Mama, somehow I'm going to get you out. I just have to find where they're holding you."

"What's that?"

I spun toward the voice. First Mate Gavin Foster stood at the bottom of the ladder, a computer tablet in hand.

I gasped, stuttering, "Just . . . just my locket. My parents gave it to me. The captain knows about it." Feeling naked with just a singlet covering my torso, I hugged myself. "I was getting dressed."

Gavin stared at me with his ratlike eyes. Even the long-sleeved blue shirt with the *Nebula Nine* eagle logo on the breast pocket couldn't make him look like anything but a weasel. "Sorry about that. I would've knocked, but you don't have a door."

"You could've called." I scowled at him. "How long have you been watching me?"

"Why? Got some secrets you're hiding?" He huffed a laugh. "Don't worry. I didn't see anything. And I'll just be a minute."

"Doing what?"

He opened a panel next to my cot. "Checking your suit. Routine inspection."

"Why you? Kind of below your pay grade, isn't it?"

"Landing day is always busy. We all have to wear multiple hats." He withdrew my pressure suit along with its attached air tank from behind the panel, hung them on a wall hook, and squinted at the tank's meter. "Ninety-four percent. That's plenty."

"If everyone's so busy, why is my duty list empty?"

"What?" He looked at me, his thin eyebrows bending low. "Are you sure?"

I nodded. "Emerson said my security clearance has been terminated."

"Terminated? That's rather ominous." He glanced at the inactive camera before whispering, "If I were you, I'd make myself scarce for a while."

I tensed. "The captain's going to kill me today, isn't he?"

"Most likely. You've been living on borrowed time. According to the court order, he could have executed you on your thirteenth birthday, and he won't want any contraband inspectors seeing you. Either you spill your secrets, or you'll be dead before we land."

"I already told him I don't know where my parents' cache is. They got someone to move everything, and they didn't tell me where. And I have no clue where that dragon eye thing is. I never even heard of it till the captain mentioned it."

"And those lies didn't convince him, did they?"

"They're not lies."

"Cut the crap, Megan." He gestured toward the collar around my neck. "I'll bet the remote's light is blinking red right now."

I tugged at the collar. "Lie detectors aren't always right."

"Maybe not, but, like I said, I'd make myself scarce."

I glared at him. He knew as well as I did that escaping was point- less unless I had the collar's remote. I would get fried to a crisp before I could run out of sight of the ship. "You know why I have to stay on the *Nine*."

"Yeah, I know." Gavin crossed his arms and looked me over, but not in a creepy way this time. "Listen, Megan, I'm as anti-pirate as any Alliance officer, but I draw the line at killing a kid. That's worse than being a pirate."

"So you'll help me?"

"If I can." Gavin stroked his chin. "Tell you what. Emerson's showing a possible hull-integrity anomaly. No air loss, so it's probably nothing. I was going to check on it in a minute, but I'll assign it to you. That'll give you an excuse to hide in the hull space while I look for the remote. From that point on, we'll play it by ear."

I pursed my lips. What was Gavin's game? That line about not killing a kid sounded hokey, maybe a scam, but his offer might be my best chance to survive. I put on a thankful smile. It fooled most adults into thinking I believed them. "Great. Thank you. But you'll have to find the remote in a hurry. Hiding in the hull space won't work for long."

"Don't push me, Megan." He wagged a finger. "Listen. I'm really sticking my neck out for you. If you get caught, I'll deny I had anything to do with this, and the captain will believe me long before he'll believe a pirate."

I nodded firmly. "Right. I get that. No problem."

After tapping a few times on the computer tablet, he attached it to his belt and withdrew an electronic key cylinder from his pocket. "I'll unlock you."

Crouching, he set one end of the cylinder against the shackle. A moment later, the lock clicked, and the shackle popped open. I pried it off and dropped it to the floor. "Thanks again, Gavin."

He straightened and pointed at my suit, still hanging on the hook. "Don't forget to attach your harness. The wormhole exit will shake this ship like a rag doll."

"Yeah. Sure. I've been through it before. It's almost like an earthquake."

When Gavin climbed the ladder out of sight, I pulled my storage box from under the cot and withdrew my maintenance-duty clothes—khaki cargo pants and a long-sleeved, button-down work shirt, an outfit similar to what I'd worn while working on my parents' ship, the *Astral Dragon*. Fortunately, the court official didn't give me a hard time when I refused to wear a prisoner's dress to board the ship. I told him I'd never worn a dress in my life. No one bothered me about that again.

After putting the clothes on, I grabbed the suit and helmet, slid them on, and added my magnetic shoes to complete the safety requirements. I then clipped my flashlight to the suit's harness, a series of straps that wrapped around my shoulders, chest, and waist. The harness also fastened the air tank to my back.

Looking at the wall panel leading to the hull, I took a deep breath. Trusting Gavin felt like a fly trusting a spider inviting it into a web, but I didn't have any other way to get the remote. He had to come through. I whispered, "Let this work," not really sure if the Astral Dragon was listening, but a quick prayer couldn't hurt.

I tugged on the wall panel. Dirk toppled out of the dark shaft and tumbled to the floor. He blinked at the light and spoke in a hushed tone. "I think we're in trouble."

"In trouble?" I asked as I grasped Dirk's wrist and hauled him to his feet. "Why?"

"Wait. How'd you know I was in the hull shaft?" He looked at me with wide brown eyes that matched his coppery skin tones, though not as dark as his mop of unruly hair. "I didn't knock yet." His safety pressure suit tucked under an arm, he pointed at my helmet. "And why are you wearing that in here?"

I whispered, "I'm going to the hull space."

He stood nearly toe to toe with me, his eyes a centimeter or two lower than mine, normal for a ten-year-old, though his nearly equal height always reminded me of how small I was for my age. "Why?" he asked. "And I can't hear you very well."

I unlocked my helmet's glass shield and lifted it. "No time to explain. And you didn't answer my question. Why are we in trouble?"

"Gavin told me to keep my suit close. He usually doesn't even notice me, so he must have meant it."

"Yeah, don't worry about it. He's just acting weird today." I looked into the low, dim shaft Dirk had come through and imagined the path he took from his quarters to mine, a crooked, air-filled one. "Have you ever been to the hull space? There's not much oxygen. It's like being on top of a super-high mountain. It's hard to breathe without an air tank."

"Nope. Never been. But I know how to use my suit. We drilled so many times."

I glanced at the ceiling camera, still dark, probably less than a couple of privacy minutes left. I whispered to Dirk, "You climb like a monkey. See if you can disable that little spy while I get what I need."

"Sure thing."

While Dirk used wall brackets to climb toward the ceiling, I grabbed a rivet gun from a drawer under my cot. After fishing a handful of rivets from a jar, I loaded them into the gun, then slid it into a belt holster. With every passing second, the captain's shadow seemed to lurk nearby. A phantom pain clutched my throat, and a real one stung my forearms. Fear often triggered the conductive ink.

When I finished, Dirk displayed the camera in his palm. "Someone's bound to notice soon."

"Yeah. We need to hurry." I took a deep breath. "I'm going in. Get your suit on. I'll see you there." I opened the panel and looked back. "Don't forget to fasten the air locks as you go. They're not automatic."

Dirk nodded. "Got it."

I unclipped the flashlight from my harness, turned it on, and walked into the corridor. After about ten steps, I passed the shaft to the right that Dirk had used to come from his quarters. Another four steps brought me to the air lock door. I pushed the pressurize button on my harness and waited as air flowed throughout the suit and into my helmet. When it finished, I opened the door, entered the cramped transition room, and locked the air-safety mechanism behind me. After going through the second door and locking it from the other side, I walked on.

As the passage narrowed and its ceiling lowered, I scrunched down more and more until I had to crawl on my hands and knees, the only way to navigate the passages that zigzagged through the ship's innards. Yet, the going was easy. Since I was now far from a gravity-enhanced floor, my body nearly floated.

When I reached another intersection, I cast my light down a shaft to the left and followed the beam to the hull's main access hatch, a door in the shaft's ceiling. I opened the hatch and crawled out on top.

As I stood in the dark expanse, a strange sensation surrounded me. Since there were no cameras in the hull space, a security-design flaw in the Nebula series, I was alone, hidden from prying eyes, unchained to walk where I pleased within the ship's skeletal structure, or even leap from rib to rib in the low-gravity environment. For the moment, I was free, just me and the ship—my prison. And my responsibility. I had a job to do, and self-preservation instincts kept me honest.

I guided the flashlight beam from place to place until the light revealed an oddity. Straight ahead, a metal girder rested on top of the shaft. I swept the light along the girder. About ten paces away, the other end was still attached to the ship's central support column by an elbow joint.

I squinted at the joint. Strange. It should've been locked in place by a bolt with an attached cotter pin, unable to swivel. The bolt must have broken or fallen out, which can happen during a landing but not likely while cruising through a wormhole.

Bending my knees, I lifted the girder and shoved it upward. The loose end floated toward the spot on the curved hull where it was supposed to be attached while the joint pivoted to allow the motion. I jumped down onto a metal catwalk bridge and hustled across to a meter-wide metal platform that surrounded the central column. I grabbed a redundant cotter bolt assembly from a nearby joint. When my girder rose to the proper angle, I shoved the borrowed bolt into the elbow, locking it into place.

With the flashlight still in hand, I climbed onto the girder and trudged along its upward slope toward the ceiling, slowed by the clumsy suit. When I arrived, I used my big toes to activate the magnets in my shoes. I planted my feet against the hull, locking myself in position near the end of the girder.

A few steps away, the emergency escape hatch's wheel protruded from the hull wall with a rolled-up tether line attached to it. Just a couple of turns of that wheel would open the hatch and lead to the top of the ship, another interesting design in the Nebula series—a primitive way to escape in case the ship lost power.

Turning back to my work, I inspected the holes where the rivets used to be—no sign of fractured connectors. How could the girder have broken every rivet and the pivot elbow lost its locking bolt at the same time? It seemed impossible.

Casting the thought aside, I pulled the rivet gun from my belt and shot eight rivets through the flange and into the airtight catch sockets mounted on the opposite side of the wall. The moment I finished, a tremor shook the hull. Vibrations ran under my shoes, as if the ship were shivering. Clutching the girder tightly, I whispered, "Steady, girl," as much to myself as to the ship. Tremors happened every day in the wormhole, more frequent near each end, but standing with only a sheet of metal between me and death made me shiver along with her.

When the tremors settled, I deactivated the shoe's magnets, walked back down the girder to the central column, and sat on its surrounding platform, my legs dangling over the edge. After setting the rivet gun at my side, I pulled a meter of safety line from my harness spool and attached the carabiner to the platform.

Now that I was no longer too busy to think, reality returned. Like I told Gavin, if the captain planned to execute me, sitting in the hull space was just a temporary reprieve. He would eventually find me, and he could always shock me from a distance with the remote-control unit. If Gavin couldn't get his hands on it, I was doomed.

Feeling lonelier than I had ever felt in my life, I aimed the flashlight at the access shaft. "Come on, Dirk," I whispered. "It's not that hard to put your suit on."

Soon, Dirk appeared in the flashlight's glow as he climbed out of the shaft. Wearing his pressure suit, air tank, and helmet, he shuffled toward me along the catwalk.

I touched the commlink button on my helmet and opened a

channel to him, a safe move since local transmissions were private and needed no authorization. "About time you got here."

He sat next to me on the platform. "The captain came right after you left. I barely made it into the shaft in time."

I stifled a gasp. The captain was searching for me, probably to execute me in person. He would have no other reason for showing up at my sleeping quarters. Trying to keep my voice steady, I probed further. "Do you think he saw you?"

"I doubt it. I know how to be a ghost."

"True." I imagined Dirk peering out of the shaft through the tiniest of gaps, but I couldn't picture what he was wearing. "Did you have your suit with you when you hid?"

He shook his head. "I hung it on your wall hook while I took my shoes off. No time to grab it until after he left. Sorry about that."

"No, no. That's good. He probably thought your suit was mine. He won't think I'm here in the hull space."

"Then he's probably still looking for you."

I sat quietly for a moment, then sighed. "I think he wants to kill me."

Dirk's brow shot upward. "Really? Because of the pirate thing?"

"Yeah." I resisted the urge to frown. "The pirate thing."

He waved a hand. "That stuff never bothered me. I know what it's like to get arrested for something you didn't do. I mean, not me. My father did. I saw it happen."

"Oh? What did they accuse him of?"

He fidgeted. "I . . . um . . ."

"Never mind." I patted his knee. "Thanks for coming. You're a great friend."

"No problem. We kids have to stick together. That's why I came to see you this morning." He opened his gloved hand and showed me a microscreen that fit on his palm. "Check this out. I saw Gavin looking at it like it was really important. When he came to my room, I picked his pocket to see what it was."

"You picked his pocket?" I grinned. "You little sneak. And they call *me* a pirate."

"Yeah. I was gonna give it back, but then I saw—"

The ship's framework quaked, making us bounce. Dirk nearly toppled off our perch, but I grabbed his arm and pulled him back to his seat. "You should lock in. When we shoot from the wormhole, the *Nine*'ll shake like a wet dog. And you don't even have magnetic shoes."

"My suit doesn't have a line. I guess it's 'cause I never work in the hull space."

"All right. Just stick close to me. I've got loads of experience, which reminds me . . ." I checked his air tank meter—10 percent. "Dirk! Your air's way too low!"

"Oops. I told Gavin I would check it. I guess I forgot when the captain showed up."

I squelched an urge to scold him. Checking the meter was second nature to me but not to him. "No worries. I have plenty. We can swap my air line between us."

"Great. Thanks."

"Now let's see what you've got here." I took the microscreen and held it on my palm. "It looks like the kind of video receiver my family used for spying."

Dirk's eyebrow twitched. "Really? You know about stuff like that?"

I laughed under my breath. "And a whole lot more. My mother never taught me how to knit socks or decorate a cake, but I could ride a horse by the time I was three, shoot a gun before I turned five, and fly our family's ship by myself on my eighth birthday. I was the main pilot most of the time after that. And I was the ship's mechanic. My father taught me about every bolt and button on the *Astral Dragon*, and everything he knew about communications and surveillance equipment." I lifted the receiver a notch higher. "Like this little gem."

"Since you're an expert . . ." Dirk pointed at the microscreen. "Check out the angle. It looks like the camera's somewhere inside Emerson."

I leaned closer to the image. "I see what you mean."

On the screen, the captain sat at his control console, the massive viewing window in front of him, the first mate's empty seat to his left. The side of his face in view, the captain spoke softly into his handheld computer tablet. "If my suspicions are correct and the SS Squad is real, the mass-murder plot must be squashed. Except for finding my son, there is nothing more important."

I furrowed my brow. SS Squad? What in blazes was that?

"To succeed," the captain continued, "I must have complete secrecy. If anyone knows I'm coming, all could be lost. My only recourse would be to have the dragon's eye in my possession."

I sucked in a breath. So that was why he'd been grilling me about the dragon's eye. But how could it help him? Other than indicating whether or not my mother was alive, it had no other power that I knew of.

"I have to find it," he continued, "no matter whom I have to hurt, though it pains me to make anyone suffer . . . especially Megan."

"He's talking about you," Dirk said. "Why would he make you suffer? And what's a dragon's eye?"

"Shhh. Keep listening." I clutched my locket through the front of my suit. I couldn't let anyone know about the ruby, not even Dirk. Fortunately, the captain's suspicions about the locket hadn't lasted long, especially after an X-ray couldn't see anything inside.

"Although she didn't choose piracy," the captain said, "I make no apologies. If I must, I will make her suffer again. Her pain will be short-lived, and the long-term benefits for billions of people out-weigh that pain."

Dirk shook his head. "The captain's a psycho. A real nutcase."

"Yeah. It's like he's trying to convince himself that killing me isn't bad."

Captain Tillman took a deep breath. "I will make one more effort to convince Megan. This will be her last chance. I have no choice." After a deep sigh, he added, "Personal log complete. Encrypt message." He looked toward the ceiling. "Emerson, turn the bridge's audio logging back on."

"Acknowledged."

Dirk and I stayed quiet. I didn't know what to think except that the captain really was planning to kill me, probably whether I handed over the dragon's eye or not, and I had no way to escape. Gavin was my only hope. Yet, it seemed like he was spying on the captain, which meant that Gavin probably wasn't trustworthy either.

The captain fastened the computer tablet to his belt and gazed toward us—that is, toward Emerson's console. His brow low, he was obviously deep in thought, maybe thinking about his missing son and wife, who had died a few years earlier. Knowing how much it hurt me to lose my own family, I understood his pain, but not enough to sympathize with his murderous rage.

"I think he's finished talking," Dirk said.

I let my shoulders sag. "I noticed."

"The captain wouldn't want his secrets recorded. That means he doesn't know the camera's there."

"Good point." I ran a gloved finger along the edge of the micro-screen. If the hidden camera was the same size, it would be easy to hide, though not much escaped the captain's notice. "I wonder what Gavin's up to."

Dirk pointed at the screen. "Speak of the devil."

Gavin walked onto the bridge. When he sat at his station, the captain spun toward him. "Anything to report on the hull?"

Gavin nodded. "All systems are now nominal. I sent Megan to check the integrity. She's more thorough than a camera droid."

"No wonder I couldn't find her." The captain narrowed his eyes. "But I saw her suit. She wouldn't go in the hull space without one, would she? The air's so thin and bitter cold."

"No idea." Gavin half closed an eye. "I didn't know you cared about her."

"I don't. I mean, not personally. She's valuable until I get the information I want. I need her alive, at least for now."

"Whatever you say." Gavin shrugged. "None of my business what you think of her."

The captain looked away. "Where is she now?"

"I don't know. Hiding, probably."

"Hiding? Why?"

"Scared to death you're going to kill her. She knows someone terminated her security access. That girl's far from stupid."

The captain unfastened the remote-control unit from his belt and showed it to Gavin. "How smart is it to hide when I could shock her from where I sit?"

I squinted at the remote. Normally he hid it out of sight, ensuring that I couldn't find it and escape, which meant that he had probably been planning to use it on me when he showed up at my hovel, just as I thought.

Gavin extended a hand. "Let me give it a try. Maybe I can convince her to spill her secrets."

"Maybe." The captain refastened the remote to his belt. "I want to give it one more try myself."

"Whatever you say." Gavin rose from his seat. "Shall I gather the troops?"

The captain nodded. "Wormhole exit is in ten minutes. Everyone at their stations in five."

When Gavin walked out, the captain rose and looked through the front viewing window again, his back toward us and his hands in his pockets. "Emerson, verify the hull readings."

"Hull integrity is at one hundred percent."

"Good. Do you have anything else to report?"

"Affirmative. Security protocol seven."

"Seven?" The captain pivoted toward Emerson's console and walked closer, his forehead deeply creased. "Show me the protocol data on your local screen."

The captain's eyes moved back and forth as he read Emerson's console screen, just above the camera in our view. He glanced straight at us for a microsecond before taking a step back.

Dirk whispered, "He spotted the camera."

I nodded. "But he can't risk saying anything about it. He doesn't know who's watching."

"Thank you, Emerson," the captain said as he set his hands on the console. "You can restore Megan's security clearance."

"Understood, Captain."

Keyboard clicks sounded. Apparently the captain wanted to give Emerson a command no one could hear. After a few seconds, he backed away and returned to his seat. "Emerson, open all speaker channels."

"Speaker channels now open."

The captain leaned back in his chair and spoke toward the ceiling. "Megan, I know you can hear me." His voice came through the tiny monitor as well as through a speaker somewhere in the hull space, though it sounded odd in the thin air. "I understand your fear. You think I'll execute you if you don't tell me your secrets and that I'll probably kill you anyway if you do." He breathed a long sigh. "Megan, you think you're protecting something—your family's honor, their wealth. I don't know. But my need for information is far more important than you realize.

"I know your mother had what is called a dragon's eye. It is powerful, far more powerful than even she realizes. If your mother's gem gets into the wrong hands, entire planetary systems could fall under tyrannical rule. Already countless children are enslaved in horrific conditions to serve an expanding evil influence, and if that influence comes to power, billions will die."

I stared at the screen, trying to stay calm. This was a new tactic, maybe related to that SS Squad he mentioned earlier. But I couldn't trust this psycho. Never.

"Megan," he continued in a pleading tone, "don't let your pride get in the way. I have to find the dragon's eye. I can stop the tyrants. Just give me the tools I need to save the lives of countless innocent people, including my son's. If you do, all will be forgiven. I will make sure your sentence is annulled, and the collar will come off forever."

I swallowed, pressing my throat against the collar. Stop the tyrants? Who but a tyrant would imprison a girl, shock her senseless when she tried to go home, and threaten her with torture to get what he wanted? Maybe the captain was just one insane tyrant trying to stop another. Why should I give him information when other tyrants didn't have it? I would never let the dragon's eye get into the wrong hands, certainly not his. I had made a solemn promise. Breaking it would be worse than dying, especially since the eye could be used to kill my mother.

"Megan, I restored your security clearance. Emerson will grant you a voice channel."

"Don't," Dirk hissed. "He'll find you."

"He'll find me anyway." I switched my helmet's commlink to Emerson. "This is Megan. Patch me to the bridge."

Emerson's voice came through my helmet speaker. "You are now connected."

After taking a deep breath to settle my nerves, I cleared my throat. "Captain Tillman. It's Megan."

The captain rose from his chair and looked at the ceiling. "I assume you heard what I said."

"I did."

"And will you tell me where the dragon's eye is?"

I inhaled again and squared my shoulders. "No."

"No?" The captain unfastened the remote-control unit from his belt and set his thumb over the trigger. "You know what happens when you defy me."

I shuddered, but I couldn't back down. "I said—"

"Captain?" Dr. Cole—the ship's doctor—walked onto the bridge, a squint wrinkling his elderly face. "Don't do this. Please. Maybe she really doesn't know where it is."

"She knows. I'm sure of it." The captain looked upward once more, again ready to press the remote's trigger. "Last chance, Megan. Where is it?"

I steeled my body. Lying wasn't an option. That blasted light on the remote would flash red. My only hope to avoid torture was to reveal the secret, but I couldn't. Not now. Not ever. If I was going to die, at least I could go out in a blaze of glory.

I spoke with a firm tone. "Stuff it, Captain. I'm not telling you anything."

Captain Tillman pressed the trigger. The collar sent a jolt into my neck. Conductive ink on my forearms and calf muscles energized. The muscles knotted. Horrific spasms sent peals of pain down my spine and across my skull.

I leaned into Dirk's arms and cried as pain ripped through every part of my body. I screamed, "Please! Oh, please stop!"

My vision darkened. Every sound warped. Like a faraway echo, Dr. Cole's voice drifted in through the hull's speaker. "Captain! This is monstrous!"

As if spoken in a dream, my mother's voice entered my senses, quiet and far away. "Megan, come here, quickly."

In a dimly lit vision, I ran to the *Astral Dragon*'s bridge. My mother met me there and set a hand on my shoulder. A strange light made her easy to see, as if she glowed, though the rest of her appearance seemed normal—blue eyes, narrow face, and auburn hair.

"Megan, this is our riskiest mission yet. In case we get separated, I want to give you something I was saving for your thirteenth birthday." She tied a leather cord at the back of my neck. "If you want to hide something valuable," she said as she set a small locket on my chest, "sometimes the best place is in plain sight."

I looked down, crossing my eyes to focus on the locket. "Why do I need to hide it?"

"Because a dragon's eye is inside. Extremely valuable." She nodded. "Take a look. You can open the back clasp with your thumbprint."

I pressed my thumb on the back of the locket. The clasp popped open, revealing a tiny ruby glowing vibrantly, as if infused with scarlet radiance. "Why is it valuable? It's so small."

"The legends say it has great power, but I don't know what all it can do. My grandfather used an ancient ceremony to tie this one to my life force. If I were to die, it would stop glowing. Now that you have it, you'll always know if I'm still alive. Like I said, in case we get separated."

"We're not getting separated, but thank you." I snapped the back of the locket closed and opened the front clasp. "I have the perfect photo I can put in this side."

"Good. It'll keep suspicious people from snooping." She touched her chest where her own locket dangled. "I have a dragon's eye, too. My grandfather tied it to your life force when you were born."

I tilted my head. "I don't remember ever meeting him. Did I?"

"Long ago when you were maybe three." She laughed softly. "Whenever he kissed you on the forehead, you said he smelled like dirt."

I smiled. "I think I do remember that. Kind of a mossy smell."

"He was a farmer. Loved to dig his hands into the soil. Anyway, I haven't seen him since. One day he just left, and no one ever heard from him again." She caressed my cheek. "Someday soon I'll tell you more. For now, remember this. Don't ever let anyone have the dragon's eye, no matter what. Since it's connected to my life force, someone could use it to kill me."

I enclosed the locket in my hand. "I'll protect it with my life."

Blinding light flashed. My mother vanished, along with the blackness. Mind-numbing pain shot through my body again, though not as bad as before.

Dr. Cole called through the hull space's speaker. "Are you all right, Megan?"

As my muscles began to loosen, I sniffed hard. Tears trickled, but I couldn't take my helmet off to brush them away. "I think so."

Dirk took my flashlight and locked his arm around mine. "Just rest. Lean on me as long as you need to."

On the microscreen still in my gloved hand, the captain reattached the remote to his belt. "Emerson, close the speaker channels."

"Channels closed."

"You shouldn't have stopped me, Cole," Captain Tillman said, his voice now coming only through the microscreen in my hand. "We're trying to stop mass murder. She has to talk."

Dr. Cole pointed a finger at him. "Pardon my insubordination, Captain, but can't you see the hypocrisy? You're playing the role of noble warrior for the innocent while cruelly torturing a little girl. That's madness."

The captain clenched his jaw but stayed quiet. They stared at each other for a long moment. Finally, Dr. Cole set a hand on the captain's shoulder. "Use kindness. Appeal to her heart, to her sense of heroism and sacrifice. Let her know your alternative plans."

The captain sneered. "Pirates have no sense of heroism or sacrifice. Power is their only language."

"At her age, she might listen. Obviously threatening to kill her isn't working."

I stared at the microscreen without blinking. This conversation was getting interesting. Did the captain really have alternative plans or was he playing some kind of mind game?

After another moment of locked stares, the captain nodded. "You're right. You're right."

Gavin and Dionne walked into view. Whether or not they had heard the conversation, I couldn't tell.

The captain heaved a heavy sigh and looked at the ceiling. "Emerson, reopen the channels."

"Channels open."

"Megan," the captain said, "I'm sorry. Report to the bridge. I want to apologize in person and give you more information, something I haven't told you before."

Still holding to Dirk's arm, I whispered, "I'll come as soon as I can."

"Stay put for now and join me after we leave the wormhole." The captain waved to the others. "Everyone to your stations. Wormhole exit in three minutes."

"Emerson," I said, "cut off my commlink's microphone."

Something clicked. The bridge could no longer hear me, though I could still hear their voices coming through my helmet speaker and the microscreen.

"Are you really going?" Dirk asked.

"What in blazes do you think?" I extended my legs. Although my neck felt scorched again and my calf muscles still hurt, the spasms had stopped. "I'm staying right here. I don't trust Captain Tillman and his alternative-plans lie, or Gavin, or Dionne or anyone else. Except you, of course."

"And Dr. Cole?"

"He's okay. He stood up for me to the captain's face. Hard to argue with that."

"Good. I like him. He took me on board after my father went to jail. I have to work here, but it's better than getting stuck with my grandpa. He gets drunk and beats me with a belt."

I winced. "That's awful. No kid should ever have to suffer like that."

"Tell me about it. One of the reasons I went with Dr. Cole when he offered was to someday be an Alliance pilot. Maybe I can do something to help kids like me."

"I'm sure you will." I imagined a huge man with a belt whipping poor little Dirk. In my mental picture, no one else was around. "Where's your mom?"

"Dead. She killed herself. Went psycho, worse than the captain." Dirk shrugged. "That's all my father told me before he got arrested for killing her. But he didn't do it. I'm sure of it."

"If you're sure, then I'm sure." I looked at his face behind his helmet's glass shield. His sad expression told me not to pry any further.

I tightened my arm around his. "Well, I'm glad you're with me. I need a friend."

"Same here, and I'll stay as long as they'll let me. But we can't hide forever."

"I know. We'll have to come up with a plan." I again gazed at the microscreen. The control room's huge viewing window took up most of the screen. Crew members moved across it from time to time, their heads and shoulders in view.

The shaking worsened. I checked my carabiner and scooted hip to hip with Dirk. We were on this ride together, for better or for worse.

I checked his air meter again, down to 5 percent. "Your air's super low. Once we're out of the wormhole and the ship settles, I'll hook you up to my tank and give you more."

He nodded. "Sounds good."

In the viewing window, the wormhole's exit appeared, blackness at the end of the tunnel with multicolored sparks dancing at the outer edges. The sparks grew bigger, wilder, faster, converging toward the center of the exit as if spreading a web of electrified glitter across the hole's circular terminal point.

"Thirty seconds to exit," the captain said. "Emerson, shields up. Everyone on the alert. You never know what might be lurking out there."

"Shields are going up."

All around Dirk and me, the panels on the ship's hull began to glow orange. Their control boxes hummed, one for every thirty-two panels, each lead-lined box attached to the interior side of the hull.

Something crackled above me. The panel where I had refastened the far end of the support girder was still dark, and the surrounding glowing panels sizzled where they connected to the repaired one. Had I somehow damaged it with the rivets?

"Shields are at ninety-eight percent," Emerson said. "One panel is reporting a failure status."

"We'll be all right," the captain replied. "Shields are just a precaution. Hitting a ship that's blasting out of a wormhole is almost impossible."

A moment later, we burst through the sparkling web. Colors flew in all directions, like supercharged fireworks arcing at hypersonic speed. The ship rattled. Dirk and I clung tightly to each other. The second the sparks diminished, a new burst of light appeared. A photon torpedo zipped toward us.

"Evasive action!" the captain shouted.

Our ship dove out of the way. The sudden drop threw Dirk and me off the platform and sent us flying toward the hull's wall, my arm still locked with Dirk's. The safety line tightened, snapping me back, jerking hard where our arms joined and sending pain through my shoulder. An explosion ripped a hole in the hull. Air rushed out. An alarm squealed. The vacuum grabbed us and flung us toward the breach.

Again the line tightened. The outward suction pulled on our bodies. Dirk's arm began slipping out of mine. Frantic, I stuffed the microscreen into a chest pouch, grabbed Dirk's wrist with both hands, and hung on, digging my fingers into his suit.

Dirk's body stretched toward the hole, his eyes wide with fear. "Megan!"

I looked past him through the ragged gap in the hull. Stars dotted the two-meter-wide slice of outer space. Death awaited in the inky blackness. Sweat beaded on my forehead. If my grip failed—

Shouts burst from my helmet's speaker. "Engage air locks!" the captain yelled.

A garbled voice followed. "A maintenance hatch is open!"

I gulped. I had closed that hatch and engaged the air lock—I was sure of it. Had Dirk left it open?

"Air-containment redundancy measures failed, Captain," Emerson said in a calm tone. "I suspect sabotage."

The ship lurched again. The force tore Dirk from my grasp. He plunged through the hole and disappeared.

I screamed, "Dirk! Can you hear me?"

Only silence came through the link. As the vacuum rush eased, the breach alarm quieted, having no air to travel through. I settled to the catwalk more slowly than usual. The gravity engine was dying.

"Dirk!" I heaved rapid breaths. With his air under 5 percent, he couldn't possibly survive long. I had to help him somehow, maybe alert someone on the bridge.

I strained to listen to the helmet speaker. No sounds came through. All of the air in the ship must have been sucked out. I withdrew the microscreen and looked at it. The bridge lights had dimmed to emergency level, flashing in a frantic rhythm. No crew members were in sight. Nothing moved.

My body trembling, I whispered, "Emerson? Status report?"

No one answered. I had asked for my commlink microphone to be cut off. Maybe Emerson couldn't hear me anymore.

I looked at the maintenance shaft leading to my quarters. It would take way too long to try to get back to the bridge to see what was going on. I had to try to rescue Dirk.

After reeling out more line, I pushed off, floated to the fracture in the hull, and caught the edge of the hole, careful to keep from cutting my gloves on the jagged metal. One slice, and I would be as good as dead.

I extended my head through the breach and searched the pitch-black surroundings. A tiny white form flailed in the distance, maybe two hundred meters away.

I called into my helmet's commlink, "Dirk, I see you. Can you hear me?"

Again, no one answered. The commlinks in these maintenance suits were designed for short distances. Only the landing-party ear commlinks allowed for more.

"Dirk," I said, breathless, "I can't hear you, but maybe you can hear me. Hang on. I'll see if I can turn the *Nine* around to get you."

I looked at the microscreen again. Someone in a pressure suit walked past the camera and stopped at Emerson's control panel.

"Emerson," he said, his face now visible through his helmet's glass shield. "Are there any survivors on board?"

I sucked in a breath. Gavin. Was he the only one who had managed to put on a pressure suit in time? And his voice came through my speaker clearly. That meant Emerson's commlink to my helmet speaker was still open. I could hear the bridge, but no one there could hear me.

"Emerson," Gavin repeated, "this is First Mate Gavin Foster. Give me security clearance."

"Voice not recognized," Emerson replied. "Security clearance denied."

"What?" Gavin slapped the console. "I'm the first mate! As the only survivor, I am now captain of this ship. How can you not recognize my voice?"

"Your voice has no match in the security database."

"Stupid computer. I guess I'll have to do a life-form scan on my own." Grumbling an obscenity, he stomped out of view, apparently wearing magnetic shoes.

My heart thumped. A life-form scan? Gavin was going to use a portable heat sensor to search for survivors, and without Emerson's help, he would have to go to every compartment on the ship, including the maintenance shafts. If I stayed inside the hull, he would eventually find me.

But did I *want* him to find me? Obviously Emerson didn't trust him. And neither did I. Besides, he never cared two spits about Dirk. If I wanted a chance to rescue Dirk, I had to hide, but for how long?

I reeled out more line and pushed myself completely outside the ship. Now standing on the hull's exterior, I turned on the shoe magnets for extra protection and walked as far as the line would allow.

Over a silvery curve in the *Nebula Nine*, the top of a pitch-black ship came into view, illuminated by the *Nine*'s docking lights. I ducked low, rose slowly, and peeked at it. The foreign ship's observation deck sat atop a single lower deck, the engine chamber below that. As I continued to rise, the entire ship seemed to rise with me. Could it be? Yes! It was! The *Astral Dragon*! My parents' ship had docked with ours!

Just as I opened my mouth to shout, a sense of dread held my tongue in check. What if Emerson hadn't cut my commlink microphone? Gavin would be the only person who would hear me. Apparently he had spied on the captain and planned this attack, killing nearly everyone on board. How could I possibly trust him?

A light flicked on inside the *Nebula Nine*, visible through the hull breach. I crept back and peered in. Gavin swept a flashlight around the hull space, as well as a life-form scanner wand. When he saw the line leading from the central support to where I now perched, he looked toward me.

I ducked to the side. Had he seen me? He hadn't aimed the flashlight my way, so maybe not.

Two seconds later, the flashlight's beam shone through the breach. Something tugged on my line. I detached it from my harness and let it fly loose. It reeled into the breach and disappeared.

Now with only shoe magnets attaching me to the ship, I peeked into the hole again. The flashlight's aura provided a view of Gavin looping my line into a coil. When he finished, he returned to the maintenance shaft, crawled into the hatch, and disappeared.

His voice came through my helmet speaker. "I searched the entire ship. No survivors."

A female voice replied, "So they're all dead? Even Megan?"

The woman's voice sounded familiar, but I couldn't place it—too tinny and distant.

"I found her anchor line," Gavin said. "It led through the hull breach. She got sucked into space. I guess the force tore her from the line. It was hanging loose."

"Then we'll scan the area around the ship and find her. She was wearing her suit, right?"

My legs shook hard. The woman sounded like my mother. But that was impossible. She couldn't be in league with Gavin, especially not on a mission to kill so many people.

"Yes," Gavin said. "I assigned her a hull-space job and reminded her to suit up and fasten her line."

"What about her prisoner collar? Was she still wearing it when you last saw her?"

"Yes. I looked for the remote, but it wasn't on the captain's belt. I found a spare collar and remote, but they're not the right ones. Unless the captain disabled the automatic trigger, she might be far enough away to activate a shock."

"Then get in here on the double. We have to look for her."

"We can, but it's probably hopeless in the vast—"

"Don't tell me what's hopeless. I'll search for her to the ends of the universe and . . . Wait. Zoë says she sees something floating out there. Sending coordinates to you."

"Receiving now."

I peered at the microscreen. Gavin was sitting in the captain's chair, looking through the front window and manipulating a dial on the console in front of him. But I really wanted to see inside the *Astral Dragon*. And who in blazes was Zoë?

"I switched the front window to the aft camera," Gavin said. "I'm zooming in on the coordinates." The window warped and magnified Dirk's flailing body. "I see a human wearing a space suit. It must be Megan."

The woman shouted, "Get on board now. We're going after her."

I gasped. Yes, she was definitely my mother.

Gavin touched his helmet's commlink switch and hustled out of sight.

"Mama!" I called. "Wait!"

Holding to the edge of the hole, I turned off the magnets and propelled myself back into the ship. I floated toward the maintenance shaft but much too slowly. When I finally reached the shaft, I zipped through it and into my quarters. Still weightless, I bounded up the ladder and flew into the bridge area, floating alongside dead bodies, all the while grabbing anchored objects, propelling myself toward the docking station, and calling, "Mama, wait! It's me, Megan!" But no one answered. My commlink's external channel was still closed.

Just as I reached the docking door, the warning light above it flashed. A craft was moving on the other side. I set a hand against the wall and flung the door open. The *Astral Dragon* reversed out of the dock at high speed. Seconds later, it appeared in the front window as it flew toward Dirk.

I engaged the magnets, planted my feet, and walked toward the window, bypassing two corpses—Captain Tillman and Dionne. The captain floated, while Dionne wavered in place with her magnetic shoes locked to the floor. I shuddered for a moment, then moved on. I couldn't take the time to react any further.

In the viewing window, the *Astral Dragon*, easy to see with its lights flashing, hovered over Dirk. Although the *Nebula Nine* was still zipping through space, so was Dirk, keeping him within sight. Since his ejection from the *Nine* had slowed his momentum, he grew smaller in my perspective by the second. I checked the indicator light at the bottom-left corner of the window. It was still showing the view through the rear camera. We were heading in the wrong direction.

The *Astral Dragon*'s lower hatch opened, and a ladder descended, similar to the in-space collecting system on the *Nebula Nine*. Someone in a space suit, probably Gavin, gathered Dirk into his arms and rode with him up the ladder as it retracted.

Relief for Dirk flooded my mind, yet tears welled all the same. My mother had come here looking for me. I was so close to being with her again, but Gavin's search had come up short. Should I have trusted him right away? Emerson must have had a reason for refusing to give him security clearance. Was he a traitor who had made the *Nebula Nine* vulnerable?

Either way, I was helpless. As a prisoner, I had no clearance to operate any flight controls or command Emerson to do it for me.

"Megan Willis," Emerson said. "Can you hear me? I reopened your output commlink. You are able to respond."

Still staring at the *Astral Dragon* as its bottom hatch closed, I touched my helmet. "Yes, I can hear you."

"You are the only surviving crew member remaining on the ship."

"Crew member?" The *Astral Dragon*, shrinking more and more in the distance, flashed lights in every direction, apparently searching for me. Now that my mother had picked up Dirk, she probably thought my body was still out there somewhere. "I'm a prisoner, not a crew member."

"Prisoner or not, you are still a crew member. Regulations allow issuance of a pressure suit only to crew members, so the captain registered you as one."

"Yeah," I murmured, barely aware of the conversation. "I remember him saying that." I continued staring at the searchlights. I was alone . . . so alone. And soon I would die alone, deprived of oxygen when the available air tanks ran out.

"Megan Willis," Emerson said again, louder this time.

Now crying, I clenched my fists and shouted, "What?"

"If you wish to pursue the *Astral Dragon*, you must act now. I await your orders, Captain."

I squinted at Emerson's control panel. "Captain? What are you talking about?"

"As I said, you are the only surviving crew member on board, which makes you the captain. Therefore, I await your orders."

"Then why didn't you let Gavin—never mind." I jabbed a finger at the front window, the view still tuned to the rear camera. "Call the *Astral Dragon* on the hailing frequency."

After a moment of silence, Emerson's voice returned. "I am attempting to call, but our signal is not sending. Our ship's external transmitter might have been damaged. It is not responding to a system status check."

I drew a mental diagram of the *Nebula Nine*'s outer surface. The ship's transmitter was located at the exact spot where I had exited through the breach. The shield array for that panel was designed to protect the transmitter as well. The attack had probably been planned specifically to destroy the transmitter and disable calls for help. Considering the speed we had been traveling and the captain's quick order to evade, hitting that spot intentionally had to have been nearly impossible, but somehow my mother had done it.

I searched for the *Astral Dragon* in the window view. Only the slightest pinpoints of flashing lights appeared. I had to signal my presence here on the *Nebula Nine*.

"Make a one-eighty turn and approach the *Astral Dragon* at impulse speed with shields down, weapons unlocked, and the docking bay open."

"A surrender posture," Emerson said.

"Exactly."

"An excellent suggestion, Captain, but when I attempted to set the port thruster, it did not respond. I requested status checks on all of the thrusters and received no response."

"Damage from the attack?" I asked.

"Not likely. We suffered only one direct hit. Perhaps someone tampered with the thrusters."

I cursed under my breath. Gavin again. "Why didn't you recognize Gavin's voice and give him command of the ship?"

"Just before the attack, I noticed a camera mounted within my console and reported it to the captain. He instructed me to erase the first mate's security clearance."

"He figured out that Gavin's a traitor." I looked through the front window once more—no sign of the *Astral Dragon*. "I'll check the thrusters. Monitor that ship while I'm in the engine room."

"Does your suit's tank have a sufficient supply of air?"

"Probably, but I'll take a spare with me." I stepped over to the wall where the emergency-supply cabinet rested adjacent to Emerson's control panel. The door stood open with Dr. Cole's body hovering next to it. Inside, the space suits floated in a haphazard array centimeters above the floor, with no air tanks in sight. "Gavin sabotaged the emergency survival suits. I'll have to go to someone's quarters and look for a personal one."

"If Gavin took the time to dispose of the tanks on the bridge, he might have done the same to the personal tanks."

"He was inspecting all the tanks, but he didn't steal mine or Dirk's. So maybe some others are still around."

"May I suggest that the thrusters are a higher priority? The distance between our ship and the *Astral Dragon* is increasing."

"Yeah. You're right." I focused on the tiny digital meter at the corner of my face shield—52 percent. I lost quite a bit while trying to rescue Dirk. "I probably have about thirty minutes left."

"I suggest that you start the repair process for the thrusters while I use my sensors to search for an unusual weight reading on the ship. That is where the tanks will be, but I will have to turn on the gravity engine to check. I will also restore normal lighting."

"Good. Do that. I have to get some tools." With gravity returning, I switched off my shoe magnets, crossed over to the maintenance side of the ship, and shinnied down the ladder to my room. After grabbing my all-purpose tool kit and attaching it to my harness, I looked toward the ceiling. "Emerson, turn gravity off for two minutes. I'm going to the engine room through the shafts. If I'm weightless, it'll be faster than going through the main access."

"Acknowledged. Keep in mind that I cannot search for a weight displacement without gravity."

"Got it. Just two minutes." I walked into the access shaft until the gravity engine silenced, then guided my weightless body along with my hands on the sides, this time taking a right turn at the first intersection. When I reached a shaft-floor opening directly above the engine room, I pushed down through it and let my momentum carry me toward the floor of the circular chamber.

The engine room, about fifteen meters in diameter and brightly lit by fixtures on the ceiling, looked like a war zone. Two uniformed bodies hovered prostrate near the floor—"Rocket" Millhouse, the chief engineer, and Price Applegate, the junior engineer. A pair of tankless emergency space suits floated just above the waist-high engine control panels, likely thrown about the room by the vacuum suction.

When gravity kicked in again, my feet settled, and the space suits dropped to the control consoles while the corpses flopped to the floor. Straight ahead, the main fusion engine sat at the center of the room. Yellow and metallic, the cylinder spanned half the room lengthwise and about a third widthwise. Four control panels stood around the engine with gaps between each one, providing access to the engine.

Normally, I would have heard the engine's hum, but in this vacuum, no sounds emanated, though electrical tingles on the ink in my forearms let me know that it was running.

I pushed a space suit to the side and read the screens on the main panel's angled surface. The digital readings indicated that the central engine was operating at nominal levels, currently powering only the gravity engine and various electrical devices spread throughout the ship, including Emerson.

The screens for the four thruster engines, mounted on the walls at ninety-degree intervals around the room, indicated that they weren't running at all—not unusual. After we accelerated into the wormhole, we needed no thrusters, and when we exited, we continued traveling at a high rate of speed. Inertia would continue driving us ever forward until the captain activated the thrusters to turn the ship or slow it down.

I touched the port engine's control knob. It had been set to three out of ten. Yet, the output reading showed zero. I hurried to that thruster, opened a small red box on the side that gave me access to its emergency controls, and set my fingers on the power control knob. "Emerson, I'm ready to override the port thruster. What power setting?"

"Start at one point seven with an angle of thirty-eight and be ready to change those settings on my command."

I turned the appropriate knobs. The shift in gravity forced me to widen my stance to resist the pressure. "It's working."

"Captain, assuming that your estimate of thirty minutes of oxygenated air supply was accurate, I calculate that by the time we reach the *Astral Dragon*, you will have less than a minute of breathable air remaining."

"Did you locate any other tanks?"

"I found a weight aberration in Gavin's quarters. Assuming the tanks are the reason, if you try to retrieve one, you will not be able to manually operate the thrusters while you are absent from the engine room. Also, the *Astral Dragon* might leave its current location. Chasing it would take more time than you have remaining."

"Are any planets within reach? One that has oxygen?"

"Delta Ninety-eight is in range, the target of our original mission. Your only other viable option is to find the reason I cannot control the thrusters and repair it. Then I can guide our search for the *Astral Dragon* while you retrieve a filled tank."

I looked at the floor's removable panels, some of them covered by bodies. "Gavin probably cut cables under the floor. I have a splicing kit on my belt, but it'd take half an hour to do the job. And that might not even be the only problem."

"Then either we chase the ship and hope your oxygen lasts, or we fly to Delta Ninety-eight. With the turn we are currently making, even that will be out of range soon."

"If we change course, can you keep track of the *Astral Dragon*?"

"No, Captain. We are already almost out of tracking range."

My cheeks grew hot. I imagined my mother's face as she said, *We're going after her.* The last thing I wanted to do was to abandon my course, not now, not when she was so close. But since chasing the *Astral Dragon* might be a suicide mission, I had only one realistic choice remaining—land on Delta Ninety-eight. Maybe I could fix the transmitter there. Maybe the *Astral Dragon* was still nearby, and maybe Dirk could convince her that I was still on the *Nebula Nine*—that is, if he survived. Yet. even if I traveled to the edge of the galaxy, somehow my mother would find me.

"Captain," Emerson prodded. "In less than a minute, all of your survivable options will be gone."

I sniffed back emerging tears. "We're going to Delta Ninety-eight. What should I do with the thrusters?"

"Switch off the port thruster, go to the starboard thruster, and set it to three point four with an angle of seventy-two. I will try to minimize the amount of running between thrusters. Otherwise, you will expend too much oxygen."

I shut down the port thruster and hurried across the room to the starboard one. When I turned it on and set it as Emerson instructed, I again braced myself for the shift. "Starboard thruster online."

For the next ten minutes, I ran from thruster to thruster, following Emerson's commands. In the insulated suit, sweat dampened my hair and shirt. All the while, I kept checking my oxygen meter. It tumbled to 40 percent, then 30 percent, then 20 percent. As Emerson guessed, the effort was forcing me to use way too much.

Monitors on the control panels showed views of what lay around the ship, including a planet straight ahead, but while running I could get only passing glances as we drew closer and closer. I just had to trust that Emerson knew what he was doing.

Still following his instructions, I ran to the bow side and turned that thruster to nine out of ten to slow our speed for atmospheric entry. The sudden deceleration threw me against the curved wall and pinned me there.

I squeezed out my words. "Emerson . . . we're . . . braking . . . too . . . fast."

"An incremental slowdown would have forced you to run to the bow thruster several times. As I indicated earlier, I want to minimize your travel and oxygen loss."

I glanced at the helmet's oxygen meter again—2 percent. The reading flashed red. Emerson was right. I had to save every molecule I could.

"Great," I grunted, "but I'm stuck."

"You are experiencing an inertial shift and an increase in the planet's gravitational effect as we tilt toward it. You will be able to move soon."

An alarm in my helmet blared. The meter flashed 0 percent. I gasped for a breath, but nothing entered my lungs. I couldn't even call for help.

Closing my eyes, I prayed for relief, for the great Astral Dragon to help me out of this mess. It was all I could do. Seconds later, something hissed. Oxygenated air leaked in. I gulped it greedily. Apparently an emergency valve had opened, sending air from the pressurized suit into my helmet. At least I could breathe now, but depressurizing would kill me before long.

"Emerson," I said, coughing. "Oxygen is almost gone. I'll be dead soon."

"I am opening the vents. When we enter the atmosphere, you will likely notice air movement in your compartment and perhaps some shaking. Only then will it be safe to remove your helmet."

"When will that happen?"

"Approximately one hundred thirty seconds. Fortunately, the upper atmosphere of this planet has oxygen, though it will be thin and bitterly cold. The heater in your suit should protect you."

The inertial force eased. "Any more thruster changes?"

"Shut down the starboard and port thrusters on my mark. First the starboard."

I peeled myself away from the front wall and staggered toward the starboard side. My head pounded. My legs ached. My skin felt like it was on fire.

When I reached the thruster, I set my hands on the controls. "I'm here." The call rang painfully in my ears. Even my teeth throbbed.

"Countdown," Emerson said. "Four . . . three . . . two . . . one . . . now!"

I shut off the thruster and struggled across the angled room toward the port side, each step stiff and slanted as gravity kept pulling me toward the front. Pain spiked. My head felt ready to explode.

The ship bounced. I stumbled to the port thruster and grabbed it to keep from falling. "Emerson?" I called, my words barely escaping my lips. "I'm here."

"Shut it off."

I flipped the switch. "Done."

"The timing was a few seconds too late, but we can compensate with the landing thrusters. I tested them earlier and found that I can still control them. Apparently no one tampered with them."

"Good." My legs buckled. I collapsed and sat down hard. Pure torture throttled every part of my body. Without a doubt, I would be dead in seconds.

An emergency suit hanging over a control panel swayed. Could it be from gravity? Or air?

I unfastened my helmet and carefully lifted it. Frigid air seeped inside—bitterly cold and thin, but still—breathable air! Gritting my teeth, I continued prying the helmet off, letting air in a little at a time. As I sucked it in, my lungs ached, rebelling at the freezing bitterness but still begging for more.

Dizziness swam through my head. My entire body shivered. I whispered as I dropped the helmet to the side, "Emerson . . . not . . . enough . . . oxygen."

His voice emanated through a control-panel speaker. "Oxygen percentage in the air is eight and increasing rapidly. Your bigger problem is cold and lack of atmospheric pressure, but both of those will alleviate soon."

"Okay." I licked my dry lips and heaved for a breath between each word. "What . . . do . . . I . . . do . . . now?"

"If you are able, come to the bridge and take the helm. I am not authorized to land the ship."

"I'm . . . coming." Summoning every remaining ounce of strength, I climbed to my feet, staggered to the ladder, and struggled up the rungs to a corridor at bridge level. As I lumbered to the door at the end, I shed the space suit's cumbersome gloves but kept everything else on to battle the frigid air.

Walking on stiff legs, I came upon an open door leading to the ship's weapons room and paused to peek inside. Normally the door stayed closed, and Captain Tillman and Gavin had the only keys. Maybe Gavin had broken in and taken some guns, but I didn't have time to check.

I entered the bridge and gazed at the front window as the ship flew through a cloud bank, covering the view with thick fog. I pivoted toward Emerson's main input/output interface where his monitor hung on a curved wall above his control console, directly opposite the ship's front viewing window. Emerson's screen displayed a checkerboard-like series of camera views that showed nearly every part of the ship. Vacant crew-member stations lined the rest of the wall. The bodies of their former occupants lay dead on the floor.

My chest ached—and not just from my recent lack of oxygen. The scene brought back a memory from when I helped my parents raid an ammunition storage facility. I had just turned ten the day before, and I was allowed to sneak into the building with them, packing an automatic rifle that matched theirs. Of course, I had practiced with the weapon for weeks and become a great sharpshooter, but I had never used one in combat.

After we climbed through a window that my father jimmied, we sneaked into the main storage room where several men were opening crates and unloading ammo. When they saw us, they dashed for their rifles. My father fired the first shot, killing one of the men. My mother did the same while I stayed hidden, as planned. Then one of the men grabbed my mother from behind, set a pistol to her head, and barked at my father to surrender.

I didn't hesitate. I shot the man between the eyes. He toppled forward and slammed his face against the concrete floor—dead. Trembling, I looked around the dim room. The men all lay motionless. And I was the reason one of them would never go home again.

My first kill. And not my last.

In the silence of the ammo warehouse, I dropped my rifle at my mother's feet, fell to my knees, and sobbed.

As I gazed at my dead *Nebula Nine* crew members, I cried with the little girl in my mind—for all the deaths, the loss of innocence, and for barely missing the chance to be rescued by my mother. That thought hit hardest of all. During the chaotic action, I didn't have time to think about it. Adrenaline ruled my body. Survival instincts reigned.

But now in the silence of the tomblike ship, the hole in my heart deepened, and the sight of the *Astral Dragon* shrinking in the distance pulsed in my mind. I was alone. And alone felt like the end of the world.

Nausea churning in my stomach, I brushed tears from my cheeks. If I wanted to find my mother, I had to forget about the past and get to work. I sniffed hard. "Sorry, Emerson. I'm ready now."

"No apologies necessary, Captain Willis," Emerson said from the speakers in his control panel behind me. "I have been fully informed about human emotions."

I brushed another tear from my cheek and released a final spasmodic sigh. "Okay. Let's land this ship."

"First, you should sit at the captain's control console."

I looked at the seat. The captain lay behind it. Close. Too close. And way too soon. "The first mate's station will work, won't it?"

"Affirmative."

I slid into Gavin's chair, strapped in, and surveyed the controls on the console's angled surface. Some of the dials and meters seemed familiar, like the landing-thruster sliders and the altitude and angle indicators, but several others were foreign, much different from those on my parents' ship. "Emerson, I've landed the *Astral Dragon* before, but it had a steering yoke. I don't see one here."

"Look for a large button at the center of the console and push it."

I found a fist-sized black button directly in front of me and pressed it with a thumb. A square hatch opened at that spot, and a steering yoke rose through the gap and locked in place. I grasped it with both hands. "Perfect. Almost exactly like the one on the *Astral Dragon*."

"Yet, you will have to learn the other instruments. You cannot fly blindly. This cloud bank might extend down to the surface."

"Oh, right. Good point. I've landed in bad weather before, but only a few times."

"I will check the conditions at the captain's proposed landing zone."

While I waited, I tested the yoke's feel by moving it slightly in each direction. It seemed tighter than the one on the *Astral Dragon*, but I could adjust without a problem.

"Scanners indicate that our landing zone is clear."

"Great." I inhaled deeply. The air was much warmer now and far more satisfying. It smelled old, like fungus-infested trees, the ones in Matherly Forest during decay season—musty, damp, mildewy. It smelled like my great-grandfather. It smelled like home.

I allowed myself a smile. Landing on a new planet was always thrilling. Exotic plants. Strange creatures, some intelligent, some bestial. And always a treasure trove of new adventures. Not only that, since Gavin knew where the *Nebula Nine* was heading, then maybe my mother did as well. This planet would be the obvious place to search for me. And Gavin knew how to locate the *Nebula Nine's* beacon, assuming he would tell her the signal's frequency.

"Emerson," I said as thick fog pelted the ship's front, "when we land, can you send a continuous beacon on two different frequencies?"

"Affirmative, but only a weak signal. The internal transmitter has a short range. The *Astral Dragon* would have to be within sight distance to detect it."

I heaved a sigh. "Right. You mentioned the external transmitter problem. But maybe I can fix it."

"It is a simple device. Perhaps it is merely a matter of a loose connection."

I raised a mental image of the transmitter—a single metal rod covering circuitry with six wires running from its base to the ship's electrical shafts. Since the transmitter had no moving parts, repairing it would probably be easy. "Okay. Suppose I can fix it. I want you to send one beacon on this ship's normal distress frequency and another on the *Astral Dragon's* frequency. My mother is more likely to find me that way."

"Do you have a plan for the other repairs?"

"After the transmitter, I'll work on the thruster link and the hull breach while you're sending the beacon."

"Acknowledged."

Soon, we dropped below the cloud bank. Trees and swamps covered every meter of land, giving us no place to set the ship down. "Emerson, did you choose this jungle area on purpose?"

"Captain Tillman chose it for our initial descent. Logical analysis provided an ideal landing location based on a need for secret arrival as well as ease of travel to the capital city of Bassolith."

I leaned forward and searched for the city in the distance, but at this low altitude, it wasn't in sight. "Is that where the captain's son might be?"

"Correct. Topographical maps of the planet show a mountain range to the east of Bassolith. Captain Tillman already had plans to land in a mountain pass out of sight of the city, and I am following his prearranged orders. I will pass full control over to you in a moment."

"What about the Jaradians? Won't they be expecting us? Maybe setting up an ambush?"

"Since the captain did not relay his reason for coming to this planet, other than searching for his son, Oliver, I cannot estimate the ambush potential." As we descended, a mountain range ahead loomed taller and taller. "It is well known, however, that Bassolith is a center for slave trading, including the buying and selling of children. The practice is officially illegal, but the Alliance has trouble enforcing the law on a planet that is so distant from headquarters. A greater danger for you than ambush is being kidnapped and sold."

In my mind, I pictured a dozen dirty children walking in a line, flanked by two fairy-tale-like ogres bearing spears. How could anyone, man or beast, believe that enslaving children was the right thing to do? Only the darkest of hearts could excuse making kids suffer. And only the coldest of hearts would leave them in their suffering. Captain Tillman's face replaced the image, his expression sad, the way it always turned downward whenever he thought about his son. The poor kid was still being held prisoner here somewhere. As the new captain of this mission, how could I abandon him? If Oliver was here, I had to find him. I couldn't live with myself if I didn't try. Maybe when my mother found me, we could search for him together.

A faint beep jerked me from my thoughts. In the front window a small red box hovered over the base of the closest mountain. "Is that our landing zone?"

"Affirmative. The ship is yours, Captain."

I grasped the steering yoke with both hands. As we closed in on the landing spot, the red target box grew. Using the controls built into the yoke's grip, I adjusted the power and angle slightly to get a better feel for how much a tweak would affect the ship. Each change made the box tilt with the ship's motion.

After a few seconds, I nodded and whispered to myself, "I got this."

Hoping to avoid detection, I descended to about thirty meters above the ground and stayed there as we approached the closest mountain. The target box was trained on a pass to the right of that mountain and to the left of a smaller one.

As I closed in on the site, I elevated over a ridge, bringing the landing spot into view—a grassy meadow with a nearby stream and surrounding woods. Now fifty meters higher than the target and a thousand meters away, I decelerated, easing the ship forward and down until we settled softly on the grass.

I shut off the landing thruster and pumped a fist. *Yes!*

"Captain Willis," Emerson said, "your landing was perfect."

"Thanks, but I couldn't have done it without you."

"That is a true statement. We all must do our parts."

I rose from the first mate's chair. "And now mine is to repair the ship, starting with the transmitter."

"According to protocol, your first duty is to burn the corpses of your shipmates and collect their ashes for the journey home."

Emerson's mention of the corpses slowed my rushed thinking. "No, there's something even more important." I tugged on my prisoner collar. "How do I get this blasted thing off?"

"Since you are the captain, you have access to all secure files in my database. I am now scanning the collar's specifications to locate relevant information." Emerson paused for a couple of seconds before continuing. "I located a document that appears to be important. If a prisoner wearing the collar travels more than one hundred meters from the remote-control unit, the collar will shock him and send a signal to the ink imprinted in his skin, which will induce muscle cramps in his arms and legs in order to incapacitate him and prevent escape."

"Yeah, I know all that. But what about getting it off?"

"The collar has an electronic lock that can be opened in two ways. One is to send an encrypted signal that the collar decodes. Another is to allow the collar's power to run down. When its internal battery dies or is shut off any other way, the collar will unlock and open on its own."

"A battery?" I ran a finger along the collar, searching for a compartment that might lead to the power cell. "I didn't know it had one. I wonder how long it lasts."

"The ship's power recharges it automatically, a feature in all Nebula-series ships, and it will also recharge when exposed to sunlight or any number of other light sources."

I imagined sitting in a darkened room. I could do that for a year if it meant getting the collar off. "So, let's say I leave the ship but not far enough to trigger the shock. If I go to a dark place, the battery will eventually die."

"Affirmative, but when the battery power decreases to a certain level, the collar will deliver a lethal shock."

"What? Are you kidding me?"

"Negative. I do not kid. The shock is a fail-safe to keep prisoners from draining the battery in order to escape. When the power level decreases to a critical level, the collar emits an alarm, indicating that it must be recharged within five minutes or it will use its remaining power to kill its wearer."

I swallowed, once again making the collar press against my throat. "Okay, but you can send the unlocking signal to the collar, right?"

"I could if I had access to the proper code, but only the captain had that information. Keeping the code in my database would subject it to hacking by a resourceful prisoner."

"What about using a bolt cutter to just snip it off?" I shook my head. "Too obvious. I'll bet it has another fail-safe for that."

"Correct. Any attempt to cut the collar will result in a lethal shock."

I kicked the base of the chair. "Blazes!"

"Captain Willis, I am programmed to remind you that coarse language is a violation of an officer's code of conduct."

"What? *Blazes* isn't a bad word. People say it in Alpha One and Humaniversal all the time."

"Perhaps those within your circle of acquaintances say it, but it is on a list of words for officers to avoid, no matter which language they are speaking."

I rolled my eyes. "Well, excuse me for being a potty-mouthed pirate. As long as I have this collar on, you might hear me say it a lot."

"Acknowledged. I suggest that you carry out your priorities while I search the communications archives for any correspondence the captain might have had regarding the collar. Since governing protocol states that the proper signal must be on file at the justice department, perhaps we can locate an official who has the information."

I raised a finger. "Wait. You mentioned the justice department. Do you have access to records about my parents?"

"Affirmative."

"What do they say about my father? And do they mention my mother escaping?"

"Records indicate that your father was executed, and your mother was incarcerated on Beta Four. There is no mention of an escape."

Heat surged into my face as my voice pitched up a notch. "Then the records are wrong—at least about my mother. She *was* imprisoned, but obviously she escaped. So maybe they're wrong about my father, too. Maybe he's really still alive."

"Inaccuracies in records are possible, but it is more likely that your mother's records are simply old. An escape from Beta Four could have been recent, and I have not received an update from the justice department since we left the Alpha system. Another possibility is that her escape has not yet been detected. The authorities on Beta Four do not make frequent prisoner checks. Many prisoners die in the frozen wastelands there."

I lowered my head. "Right. That makes sense."

"When I am able, I will send a request for a records update and for the collar code, but even after that it could take weeks to receive a response. In the meantime, for your safety, perhaps you should stay in the light to keep the collar's battery charged."

I heaved a resigned sigh. "All right. I'll burn the bodies."

"You will need the accelerant stored in the rover bay. Otherwise, the fire will not be suitably hot. And considering your size in comparison to your fallen crewmates, it will be a burdensome task, even with the gurney. Afterward, you can wash and refresh yourself at the stream."

I frowned. "Now you're my hygiene coach?"

"I am merely pointing out the availability of a water supply. Captain Tillman chose this place so he could refill the fusion engines with fresh water and because the water here is potable."

"What's *potable*?"

"Drinkable."

"Okay. I guess I'd better get started." After taking my pressure suit off, I collected personal items from all the bodies, set them in a box near Emerson's console, and pressed the front hatch button. Below the main window, a ramp descended to the ground in front of the ship, providing a view of the outside.

I blinked at the daylight streaming in. I was finally going to exit the *Nebula Nine*. Only hours ago, I imagined myself practically dancing down this ramp if I ever were to get ship leave, but now I had to wheel bodies while hanging my head. All joy had melted away.

Still, whether happy or sad, I couldn't leave without the collar's remote. "Emerson, do you know where Captain Tillman hid the remote unit?"

"I do not, but I can force it to emit an alarm. Sending signal now."

A high-pitched squeal came from the captain's station. I followed the sound to the chair arm, opened a compartment there, and grabbed the remote unit from inside. The moment I picked it up, the alarm silenced. After fastening the unit to my belt, I retrieved the wheeled gurney from sick bay, collapsed its legs, and rolled Captain Tillman onto it. Once I had settled him in place, I raised the legs and began rolling him toward the ramp.

"While you are gone," Emerson said, "I will make a list of repair duties and check inventory for necessary parts."

"Good. Thanks." I guided the captain down the ramp and across a grassy area to the stream and laid him near the bank. I then did the same for the other crew members, using the lower rear hatch to remove the men from the engine room.

After finding the accelerant, I aligned the corpses side by side, foraged in the woods for kindling, set some around each body, and doused the wood and the bodies with the accelerant. Now I needed a way to ignite everything. We had matches in the galley, but a flame-thrower would be quicker.

I hurried back to the ship, walked into the weapons room, and flicked on the light. The wall hangers that normally held all sorts of weapons were empty, and the drawers and cabinets were open, revealing no ammunition inside. As I had guessed earlier, Gavin must have taken everything before searching for me on the ship. And why not? He thought everyone on board was dead.

Still, one possibility remained—my welding torch. I hustled

to my room, found the torch and portable fuel tank in my box, and took them outside. Before lighting each pile of dried branches, I saluted the fallen crew members. Whether they deserved the honor or not, they were fellow human beings. Some had spouses and children who would miss them. Who was I to disrespect people I didn't know very well?

As the wood around Captain Tillman burned, the stench of scorched flesh reached my nostrils, noxious and irritating, somehow appropriate. Even when he appeared to be kind, it was just a mask. During one of our interrogation sessions, he mentioned that I looked like my mother. And it was true. My mother and I looked a lot alike—blue eyes, high cheekbones, narrow chin, and lightly freckled cheeks, though her auburn hair didn't quite match my brown locks. At the time, I thought he was being sympathetic, but now I realized that it was an attempt to soften me up, a way to get information. He was never anything but a self-serving rat.

For better or for worse, Captain Tillman was dead. And he died thinking me a rebellious pirate. But that was okay. I didn't need approval from a tyrant. Although he revealed a passion to save billions of people, that story might have been a trick to get me to give away my secrets. Now I would never know, either that or whatever his "alternative plans" might have been.

The flames raced across the captain's body, catching his uniform. I turned and marched toward the ship. It wouldn't be right to take pleasure in watching him burn.

After putting the torch away in my room and grabbing a bar of soap and my dirty clothes from the laundry pile, I returned to the stream. Although I had a shower stall, it was tiny, barely enough room to lift my elbows, and the water pressure was little more than a trickle. Enjoying my newfound freedom in the generous flow would be much better.

Leaving my shoes and the remote on shore, I waded into the knee-deep current. The cold temperature drew a gasp. I splashed water on my face and arms until I got used to the temperature, walked the rest of the way in, and submerged to waist level. I dipped my head just long enough to get my hair wet. I had learned long ago that water had no effect on the collar, so no problem immersing it.

While the fires continued burning, I scrubbed my entire body, including the filthy clothes I was wearing and the rest of my clothes in case I needed them. The frigid water raised a hard shiver. I finished washing in a rush, walked out of the stream, and, after retrieving my shoes and the remote, hung most of my clothes here and there on the ship's wings before returning to the fire with the shirt I planned to wear.

With a little time to kill while waiting for my clothes to dry, I foraged in the ship's galley for a few nutrition bars and returned to the flames. As I ate, I rotated slowly to expose each side of my wet clothes to the drying heat. Different angles of this new planet came into view—a huge, unscalable mountain; a dark, dense forest; and a stream that probably led toward an alien city. Eventually, I would have to search that city, pretending that I knew what I was doing. But I didn't know. Far from it.

As I imagined what the city might look like, Oliver came to mind. If he was there, how could my mother and I find him? Captain Tillman believed he was being held by slavers—but would they keep him in a prison? An institution for lost children? Or would he be working as a servant boy?

A shadow crossed the area. I looked up at a cloud drifting in front of the planet's binary suns, the orbs now descending in the sky. Evening would soon arrive. I had to hurry. I gobbled a second nutrition bar and got back to work.

As I wrung out my shirt's long sleeve, my hand came across a rip in the elbow, birthed by the many times I had belly crawled through maintenance shafts. An image came to mind—myself wearing a ragged shirt while wandering through the city. If my mother and I decided to go there in search of Oliver, she could follow in stealth while I probed the area as a slave. Although dangerous, pretending to be a slave felt right. I had been treated like one for months. And if I came across clues to Oliver's location, my mother and I could rescue him together.

During my time of pondering, the hanging clothes and the clothes I was wearing had dried enough to bring them inside. When I reentered the ship, I hung the still-damp items in my hovel and returned to the bridge.

Emerson spoke up. "Inventory check revealed that we have a hull panel in stock to replace the damaged one. Unfortunately, we are low on rivets. You might need to salvage a few from redundant areas."

I adjusted my shock collar to allow the skin underneath to finish drying. "No problem. I know where to find some."

"I have another lack of inventory issue to report. We do not have a spare external transmitter in the general parts storage cabinet."

I glanced at the portion of the ship where the transmitter protruded, though it wasn't in view. "It's just a metal sleeve wrapped around the circuits. I should be able to make a replacement."

"Affirmative, assuming the circuits are intact. If one or more has been damaged, then the difficulty will be much higher."

"I'll find out." I read the to-do list that Emerson displayed on his console screen. "First, I'll fix the transmitter, then while I'm working on the hull panel and thrusters, you can send a distress signal. Maybe my mother will find me right away, and then we'll look for clues to where Oliver might be."

"Captain Willis, your plan is excellent."

"Thanks." I couldn't help but smile. Captain Tillman hardly ever complimented anyone. I glanced outside at the still-smoking fires. "Could you send a droid to collect the ashes and crush the leftover bones? They'll be too hot for me to handle for a while, and I don't want the wind blowing the ashes away. They're in rank order—lowest on the left, highest on the right."

"Affirmative."

A cabinet door opened under Emerson's console. A dark-gray droid rolled out and scurried toward the galley, probably to get a collection jar. With tanklike tread for wheels and an oversized pair of claws and tiny cameras in front for eyes, it looked like a mutant praying mantis. Since we rarely used the droids, I didn't get to see them often, making it a treat to watch the nimble little machine rushing off to do its job. I had heard that we also had a flying drone, but I didn't know where the crew stored it.

With the corpse-burning job taken care of, I climbed onto the roof of the *Nebula Nine*, knelt next to the meter-long transmitter antenna, and wiggled one of the horizontal wings—far too loose. A crack at the sleeve's base had detached it from the ship, allowing me to slide the sleeve up and completely off the inner core, leaving a metal frame surrounding exposed circuitry. A quick check revealed the reason for the malfunction—a fried relay switch, easy to replace—but did we have one in inventory?

I called out, loud enough for Emerson to hear. "Emerson, look up the electronics parts in this transmitter. Do we have a spare relay switch? I can solder it on."

"Negative." His reply from within the ship sounded distant.

"Can I borrow one from another device somewhere?"

"Negative. That particular switch is not used in any other Nebula-series device."

"Blazes!" I needed that switch to have any hope of contacting my mother. I slid down to the ship's wing, jumped to the ground, and hustled up the ramp. "Are there any stores in Bassolith that sell the switch?"

Emerson's voice emanated from a ceiling speaker. "That information is not in my database, but I can send messages to the city to learn about inventory in the retail outlets. The process will take some time, but the switch is common. I should be able to locate one."

I halted at an access panel that led to the hull space. "Can the internal antenna transmit far enough to send messages to Bassolith?"

"According to the transmitter's specifications, I should be able to reach the closer side of the city. Perhaps I can find a parts seller in that area or boost my signal from a receiver and transmit throughout the city. One way or another, I expect a successful outcome. I will purchase the switch in Captain Tillman's name, and when you go there to pick it up, simply mention that you are there in his place."

"Okay. Good. While you're doing that, I'll repair the hull and take a look at the thrusters. Then we'll fly the *Nine* into the city to pick up the part."

"Acknowledged."

After finding the spare hull panel and attaching my tools to a work belt, I entered the hull space, riveted the panel in place, and checked it for leaks. Working in full gravity slowed the process, but it was still an easy fifteen-minute repair job. So far, so good.

I hustled to the engine room and began pulling up floor panels. Under the third panel, I found cuts in the lines to the thrusters and spliced them in about half an hour. They had obviously been cut on purpose. More of Gavin's work.

After finishing the splices, I ran a thruster test. The engines purred as I shifted from one to the other. I shut them off and brushed my hands together. Now to get the transmitter working.

I returned to my quarters, shed my tool belt, and sat on my cot to rest for a second. "Emerson, any luck finding the switch?"

"Affirmative. Bassolith has an ironworks factory with a parts department. They have the switch in stock there."

"Perfect. How can I buy it?"

"I can wire the funds and ask them to have it ready for you as an aide to Captain Tillman. Your bigger problem is how to travel there. I checked the city's docking schedule. The *Nebula Nine* has no landing authorization. Apparently Captain Tillman planned to stay here and proceed on foot or by rover."

"Stealth entry. That makes sense." I ran a tense hand through my hair. "I guess I'll have to do the same."

"The danger level will be extremely high. As I mentioned earlier, you will be a target for slave traders."

"I don't have a choice. I have to signal my mother. But I have a plan I've been thinking about. It should work."

"Very well, Captain. Let me know if I may be of any assistance."

"I will." I put away my clean clothes except for the ripped, long-sleeved navy polo shirt as well as my second pair of khaki cargo pants. I put them both on and hustled back outside.

Now that quite a bit of time had passed and the droid had collected most of the ashes and bone fragments, some of the remnants were cool to the touch. I smeared ashes and dirt on one cheek, the backs of both hands, and here and there on my clothes.

When I finished, I returned to the bridge, spread my arms, and turned in front of Emerson's visual sensors. "What do you think? Am I a convincing slave girl?"

"Your prisoner collar will give you away unless the citizens are unaware of its purpose, which is possible. The collar is not used outside of the Alpha system."

"Right. I could pass it off as a slave collar, you know, to keep me from escaping, which is why my master lets me walk where I want to go."

"Acknowledged. Yet, your hair is too even and clean. Unless you are a house slave, I think you would not be so well groomed."

"Good point. I'll rough it up on my way out." I lowered my arms. "Any last-minute instructions?"

"Just some weather data. Delta Ninety-eight revolves around Yama-Yami, an eclipsing binary star system. It is now early spring-time and warm enough during daylight hours for the clothing you have chosen, but by the end of the long night, it will be too cold. I suggest that you return before nightfall, which will be in about four hours. Although up to three of the planet's five moons will provide light, they will not heat the atmosphere."

"Don't worry. I hope to pick up the switch and hustle out of there. I'll take one of the rovers and hide it as close to the city as I can. That'll help me get there and back in a flash."

"I will program the rovers to accept your voice commands. You should also take the former captain's computer tablet. It will have photos of the sentient beings you might encounter in Bassolith and information about their habits. Your biggest obstacle is likely to be your inability to understand the language of each species."

"Don't worry. I've got that covered. But how will they understand me?"

"Do you speak Humaniversal?"

I nodded. "I'm fluent. I spoke it before I learned Alpha One."

"Good. Every species here understands Humaniversal, though most cannot speak it."

"All right. Anything else?"

"Affirmative. The computer tablet also contains the captain's log, which is valuable for posterity, though access to it requires a password that only the captain knew. Since precipitation occurs frequently here, I suggest you take along a protective bag in case you need to store it safely."

"Sure, once I get the tablet." I searched through the personal items I had collected from the crew earlier, found the computer tablet, and looked it over. No bigger than my hand, it had a belt clip for easy carrying.

I clipped the computer tablet to my belt. "I wish I could take a gun. I have a welding torch, but it would be pretty clumsy in a fight."

"You do need a suitable weapon, and it should be something you can conceal. The citizens of Bassolith would not like seeing an armed slave in their midst."

I gestured toward the weapons room. "But Gavin cleaned us out."

"Perhaps he missed something among the captain's personal items."

"Good thought." I rummaged through the pile and found a stun disk. Since it looked like a clamshell instead of a gun, no one would think I was armed. Although it wasn't lethal, pushing the button on top could deliver a jolt from several paces away. It would do in a pinch. "Found a stunner."

"Excellent."

I slid the disk into my pocket. "I'm leaving. I'll be back as soon as I can." I hurried to my quarters again, grabbed a pocketknife from my tool kit, and extended its serrated blade. I opened my locker door and looked at the mirror inside. Emerson was right. Although I kept my hair short for work—about chin length—it was too neat for a slave.

I chopped at my hair with the knife here and there, letting the shorn ends drift to my feet. When I finished, I studied my reflection. The ragged mop looked like it had gotten caught in a fan. It was perfect.

From the locker I withdrew my personal-items container, a wooden box. I flipped open its lid and pinched my wafer-thin translator—similar in shape to a hearing aid and small enough to hide completely within an ear. Invented by my father years ago, it could translate almost any spoken language to Alpha One. Although he could have sold it for a lot of money, he kept it a family secret, making one each for himself, my mother, and me. Since it didn't look valuable, no one ever questioned me about it, and I was allowed to keep it.

After inserting the device in my ear, I rummaged until I found a plastic bag for the captain's computer tablet. I then scooted to the cargo bay, climbed into one of three hovercraft that we called rovers, and closed the glass hatch over my head.

As I looked over the controls, an excited shudder ran across my body. Being a prisoner, I had never been allowed to sit in one of these before, much less drive one, though I had driven a similar rover my parents borrowed about a year ago. In spite of barely missing my mother's rescue attempt, maybe I could enjoy something for a change, knowing that the rover would help me get the relay switch so I could contact her.

"This is Megan Willis," I said to the console as I grabbed the steering wheel. "Give me control and open the bay door."

When the rectangular bay door slid up, I clicked the elevation switch on the dashboard. The whooshing engine shook the rover and lifted it several centimeters off the floor. I pushed the hand throttle forward and steered the rover through the doorway and over the grass.

At the remnants of the ash heaps, I stopped and climbed out of the pod. One jar remained, the captain's. Soon, the droid would return to collect it.

As I stood in front of the jar, the sight of the dark ashes drilled bitter pain into my gut. I needed to push away the torture the captain caused and focus on his good side. This man, at the risk of his stellar reputation, rescued me from the labor camp's execution row and trusted me to work on his ship. Me, only a twelve-year-old girl at the time. Although *I* knew I could do it, no one else did. He put the lives of the crew in my hands, which made some of them hate me and maybe caused them to disrespect him as well. His trust in me cost him a lot.

I laid an arm over my chest in salute and whispered, "Fair travels, Captain. Regardless of what you did to me, I hope the great Astral Dragon welcomes you into his celestial lair. Maybe those alternative plans you had would've shown me that you're not really as cruel as I thought." Not sure what else to say, I added a light shrug. "Anyway, I'll look for Oliver. I promise."

Stooping, I poured a handful of the warm ashes onto my palm, then rubbed them into my hair and left it mussed. I inhaled deeply, literally breathing in the captain himself. Although I despised his cruelty, I needed some of his courage.

After taking another deep breath, I squared my shoulders, reboarded the rover, closed the hatch over my head, and flew on. During missions with my parents, I had worn disguises while infiltrating high-security fortresses; faced gunfire and hails of poison-tipped arrows during wild, narrow escapes; and sprinted through dark forests while being chased by ferocious guard dogs.

I could do this.

I guided the rover down the slope leading to the city side of the mountain, hovering over the stream's winding path, the easiest way to avoid the massive trees that gave me cover with their arching boughs. The rocket booster under my seat sent tickling vibrations up my spine and water spraying to both sides and behind me.

Such freedom! With the remote-control unit attached to my belt, I could go wherever I pleased—no fear of the dreaded collar. I had finally flown out of the captain's cruel cage.

As I drove, I looked all around, including over my head, to take in as many sights as possible. At times, the trees above waved in a cyclonic pattern, blown about by a twisting wind. White sparkles often appeared within the swirling air, as if the air itself had come alive, ignited by glitter gathered from the sky.

Although I wanted to watch the display, I had to concentrate on the stream's snakelike path. The slightest deviation might send me crashing into a tree or a boulder.

Soon, the terrain leveled out. The trees thinned, and the stream's current slowed as it widened. Now I needed to park and figure out a way to peek into the city without being seen.

After steering the rover to a thicket and hiding it from view, I found what appeared to be an evergreen tree. With bluish needles that curled at the end, it wasn't like any tree we had on Alpha One, though its low branches resembled a fir's, making it easy to climb.

I scaled the tree as high as I could. Clinging to the swaying trunk, I looked toward the center of the city, now about a thousand paces away. Three-to-four-story buildings appeared to be made out of yellow bricks, maybe clay, all lined along the edge of a wide road that hugged the stream. Walking bridges spanned the stream here and there, and a few bipeds of some sort ambled across them in a slow shuffle, as if they were wearing anchors for shoes. Everything looked safe enough from here.

After climbing down, I unclipped the computer tablet, turned it on, and found the descriptions of the citizens of Bassolith. Nearly 80 percent were Taurantas—bipeds with armor-like scales in front, heavy tails in the rear they could use as a weapon, and horse-shaped heads with short, spiny protrusions running up the nose, over the head, down the back, and along the top of the tail, much like the spines of a dragon.

About 20 percent taller than most humans, they had hands with opposable thumbs, scaly on the back. Although friendly to outsiders, some were involved in the interstellar slave trade and used their reputation for kindness as a way to take strangers by surprise. As a result, it was best to trust no one on this planet.

Around 10 percent of the citizens were Jaradians, similar to Taurantas in every physical feature except that they lacked a tail, which made them faster. They were also more aggressive, less friendly, and not as smart, though they were just as strong, and they tended to be more distrusting of others.

For both Taurantas and Jaradians, the males were darker, either purple or black, while the females could be almost any other color, though usually a shade of blue.

The remaining 10 percent of the intelligent creatures were various birds and four-legged mammals, all of whom spoke their own languages, though most of them understood other languages spoken in the city, especially Humaniversal. They usually stayed to themselves in small communities here and there around town, though some birds were friendly to strangers. Since slave trading was a competitive industry on Delta Ninety-eight, birds were sometimes employed to scout for victims. Once again, their friendliness could not be trusted.

Although humans occasionally visited the city as merchants, some in the slave-trading business, none lived there. The winters were too cold and the summers too hot for their sensitive skin.

I looked through the tablet's other apps and found a photo icon labeled "Oliver Tillman." When I tapped on it, his image filled the screen, a blue-eyed boy with bushy, light-brown hair who appeared to be eight or nine years old, though he was probably eleven or twelve by now, based on conversations I had heard. With fair skin and rounded features, he didn't appear to be much like his rugged-looking father. Since he might be malnourished now, I had to keep watch for a boy with more sunken cheeks.

Looking ahead, I imagined myself walking into the city, trying to impersonate a slave as I searched for the ironworks factory, keeping an eye out for any sign of Oliver. No slave girl would have a computer tablet, and I couldn't risk getting it stolen. Not only that, my shoes were in nearly perfect shape, too new for a lowly slave, and the protective metal slowed me down way too much. Also, since the soles of my feet were hard and calloused from years of running barefoot, I could walk on the prickliest ground without much pain.

I took my socks and shoes off and slid them under my seat in the rover. Even if someone stole them, I could replace them somehow. I set the computer tablet inside the plastic bag, sealed it securely, and buried it under a leafy green bush that stood exactly ten paces from the stream, then set a large stone at the edge of the stream to mark the spot.

Standing next to the clear-running water, I looked toward the city again. Sudden fear raised a shudder. I told myself I could do this, but could I really?

I longed for help, a companion at my side, but that was impossible. I was truly alone. Yet, I could still get another boost. I set my locket in my palm and opened it, revealing the photo. What would my parents say in this situation? They often quoted proverbs, like "Killing the innocent is forbidden. Even in self-defense against evil, it is a last resort. Life is sacred." But they didn't always seem to live by that one. Yet another proverb came to mind that they did adhere to, one that my mother repeated as we shuffled into the courtroom for our piracy trial. "Watch for guidance from above. Nothing happens by chance."

I slid the locket back behind my shirt. Satisfied that I was ready, I took a deep breath and marched toward the city with determined steps, my eyes focused straight ahead. Experience had taught me that showing confidence was the best way to avoid assault. Being a young girl in a foreign place by myself, I was already an obvious target. I didn't have to act like one.

Following a footpath next to the stream, I walked into the outskirts of the city where one-room shacks crowded the shore and each other, separated by narrow dirt roads arranged in a checkerboard pattern. This residential area might house employees of the factory, but the factory itself probably lay in a more centralized location deeper within the urban area.

When I passed the first shack, a silver-and-white bird about the size of an Alpha One blue jay alighted on my shoulder. Remembering the warning about friendly birds, I tried to stay calm, hoping to act like everything was normal.

The bird chirped, and the earpiece translated: "It is a fine day, is it not?"

"I guess so," I said in Humaniversal, hoping this bird would understand.

"For the time being, of course. The fineness of the day will soon change." The bird inhaled deeply. "We silver jays have a highly developed sense of smell. A storm is coming, and I love the scent of the air when one is approaching."

I kept my gaze straight ahead. The run-down residential area continued for another fifty paces or so. Beyond that, more modern buildings populated the area, some much bigger than the huts. "Okay. That's good to know. But why are you telling me all this?"

"A wise person always makes small talk before beginning a more serious conversation. It is an important negotiation skill, a way to gain trust."

I glanced at the bird out of the corner of my eye. "Does that mean I shouldn't trust you?"

"Not at all. I just want to make you feel at ease because I am a stranger to you."

"Well, you're not exactly doing that." I continued walking at a casual pace, wary of an ambush. This bird could have been sent as a scout or a distraction. "The more you talk, the more nervous I get."

"Very well. I will forego the small talk." The bird peeked around my neck and looked at my face. "Why are you here, human?"

Since the earpiece couldn't accurately translate tone, I had no idea if the question carried curiosity or suspicion. "I am here to purchase something."

"Ah. A customer for one of the merchants. Yet, you are young and unkempt. Are you a slave sent to make a purchase for your master?"

"I'll keep that to myself." Getting interrogated made me more nervous than ever. Since I was approaching the beginning of the inner city, it was time for me to ask the questions. "I'm looking for the ironworks factory. Do you know where it is?"

"Of course. The factory is the biggest employer in the city, which means that you are not a resident. Only a stranger would be unaware of its location."

I concealed a slight wince. I needed to be more careful about what I revealed. "What are you, a detective?"

The bird fluttered its wings. "I am not a detective by profession, but I am trying to deduce your purpose. Daylight is waning, and all visiting humans will be leaving for their ships soon. I assume, therefore, that you are purchasing an item that your ship needs before it departs. Am I right?"

"I have to admit, that's pretty close."

"I see. So you're a slave who has been entrusted to venture out alone to procure an essential item. Very rare for a child. Or perhaps a young teenager. I am uncertain of your age."

"You'll stay uncertain." I touched my collar. "And this will shock me if I try to escape. My master's not worried about me being out alone."

"Interesting. I have never heard of such a device. Who is your master? He or she is taking a great risk to leave you out in the open."

"Because the Alliance might catch my master?"

The bird let out a warble that sounded like laughter. "The Alliance has done nothing to stop child trading in a long time. The risk is that someone might steal you. Humans of your age and size are becoming more valuable all the time."

Now walking in the more modern area of the city, I scanned multi-story buildings that looked like apartments, schools, and houses of worship, complete with steeples and spires. Since the bird brought up the subject, it would be natural for me to probe for information that might reveal Oliver's location. "If someone stole me, where would he take me?"

"That depends on the purpose—that is, the work a slaver has in mind." The bird suddenly hissed in a way my ear device couldn't translate, then added, "If you are able to look to your left in a stealthy manner, then do so. I fear that your risk has increased substantially."

Without turning my head, I glanced that way. A trio of male Jaradians watched me from an apartment building portico to my left, their horselike eyes fixed on me as I passed.

I picked up my pace and slid my hand into my pocket, where the stun disk lay. "All right. Thanks for the tip about slavers, but it'll help even more if you tell me where the factory is so I can buy what I need and get out of here."

"It is near the city center. Proceed in the same direction and pass the Tauranta temple, the tall building ahead with the grassy play area for the Tauranta children. After the temple, you will reach the city center. Take a left turn, and the factory lies about two hundred human paces down that road on the right-hand side. It is impossible to miss it."

"Great. Thank you."

"But purchasing something at the factory is not your true purpose, is it?"

I frowned. Hiding anything from this detective bird seemed impossible. "What makes you say that?"

"Deduction. You are here alone with a slave collar well after the time most humans retreat to their ships, and you're going to the factory. Since some orphans are housed there, I suspect that you know one or more of them and hope to do something about their dire situation."

"Dire? How so?"

"They appear to be slaves. Although they are allowed outside without chains, they are always supervised to prevent them from escaping or being stolen. And I have seen them travel on a bus toward a work site. I am confident that they are forced to do so."

I nodded. This was a perfect opportunity. At the ironworks factory I could get the relay switch I needed and probe for information about Oliver at the same time.

Hearing footsteps, I glanced back. Five Taurantas followed me on the same path, the three Jaradians behind them as if using the Taurantas as a screen. The Taurantas appeared to be a family—two adults, one black and one royal blue, and three juveniles of various sizes, the larger two dark purple and the youngest sky blue.

I closed my hand around my stun disk and walked on.

"If you wish," the bird continued, "I can lead you on a shorter route to the factory."

"No, thanks." I kept up my brisk pace. Smaller Taurantas played on the temple's lawn to my left. Maybe no one would try to grab me if I stayed on the main thoroughfare. "I heard that some birds can't be trusted."

"I will ignore your attempt to insult me and wish you the best." The bird flew off my shoulder, orbited me in a tight circle, then landed on my shoulder again.

"Change your mind?" I asked.

"I got a better look at your face. You are in more danger than I realized."

"What? Why?"

"Not only does the city have slave traders, it also has kidnappers who might hold you for ransom, not to mention bounty hunters who would scoop you up like a dropped bread crumb."

I furrowed my brow. "Bounty hunters? There's no price on my head."

"Then you haven't seen the leaflets? You resemble a girl on leaflets that someone scattered around the city."

"What? How could I be on those?"

"I don't know, but I will find one and bring it to you."

"That would be helpful. Thank you. And sorry about the insult."

"All is forgiven. You are wise to be wary. And, by the way, my name is Perdantus. If you are in need, ask for me by name. All the birds know me, as do most members of other species."

"I'm Megan." The moment I said my name, I coughed, trying to cover it up at the last second. Maybe I should have kept my identity a secret. "Thank you, Perdantus. I will."

"You're welcome." He lifted from my shoulder and flew toward the center of the city.

Behind me, the five Taurantas turned away from the river and headed for the temple's massive front doorway, giving the Jaradians no more cover. They broke into a run toward me, their eyes locked on mine.

I pulled the stun disk out. Hoping to take the Jaradians by surprise, I ran straight at them. When one reached for me, I dropped to my back and aimed the disk at him, pressing the fire button in the same motion.

A short lightning bolt shot out and slammed into the Jaradian's face. As he squealed, he lumbered past me, but another grabbed me by the hair and lifted me off my feet.

My scalp burning with pain, I latched onto his wrist with my free hand and kicked him in the face with a heel, but he barely flinched. "This is the one," he said in a growling language as he continued holding me aloft. "There's no doubt."

"Why is so much being offered for her?" another Jaradian asked. "She's a scrawny thing."

The first Jaradian laughed. "Who cares how a human wants to spend money? As long as we get—" A fist slammed into his face. He released me and stumbled back. I landed on my feet, collapsed to my backside, and looked up.

A fourth Jaradian—purple and black—stood over me holding a

huge axe, ready to swing it. "Leave," he bellowed at the others. "This girl is mine."

The first Jaradian squinted. "When did you get back in the slave-trading game, Quixon? I heard you swore off it."

"Never you mind that." He reared back with the axe. "Do you want to keep your heads?"

The first Jaradian raised his hands and backed away with the other two. "We're going, but you'd better watch out. You won't always be the only one carrying an axe."

When they turned and hurried away, Quixon reached a hand toward me. "Come," he said. "Now."

Still sitting, I slid back. "Don't touch me."

"I'm not going to hurt you."

"Yeah. I'll bet." I aimed the stun disk at him. "You want to sell me as a slave."

"Ridiculous." He slapped the disk to the ground and stomped on it, crushing it to pieces. "Now get up and come with me."

I scowled. "Get lost."

He lunged. When I rolled to the side, something clicked. Just as he grabbed my wrist and lifted me, the collar sent a jolt into my neck. I screamed. My forearm and calf muscles knotted, paralyzing me.

Quixon roared and threw me down. My back slammed against the ground. The collar's jolt ebbed, and my cramps eased. I rolled into a backwards somersault and up to my feet, then limped—as quickly as my painful calves would allow—toward the Taurantas, who were now staring at me.

As I hurried along, I touched the collar's remote-control unit on my belt. When I rolled, something must have pressed the activation button. I would have to be more careful about that. Still, it turned out to be a good weapon. The electric shock in my body zapped Quixon as well. It hurt a lot, but at least it helped me escape.

The smallest Tauranta cried out in a series of gurgling roars. My earpiece translated. "Mother, look! That human is coming toward us!"

The female adult bared her teeth in what I hoped was a smile. "A young female human, if I am judging correctly."

"Correct," the adult male said. "And she made quite an escape from those Jaradian thugs. Unfortunately, I was too slow to help her."

"The result is a good ending." The female emitted a series of clicks. "She's a pretty little thing, isn't she?"

When I halted a few paces away, the older juvenile male stuck out his tongue. "Yuck. Ugly as a poop stick."

The younger male snorted. "Right. Skinny as a pole with brown stuff on top."

Not wanting to ask what a poop stick was, I stayed quiet as I glanced back at Quixon. He limped away, clutching his side.

"She's beautiful," the youngest said as she turned to the mother. "Can we keep her?"

The mother patted the little female's head. "No, dear. Humans are intelligent beings like us, which is why we have laws against using them as pets or slaves, though I have known a few to work for pay as household servants." She tilted her head and looked at me. "Did those ruffians hurt you?"

"Not much," I said, again speaking Humaniversal. "I think they wanted to sell me as a slave, but I'm safe now."

The male adult scanned the street. "I could never catch them, but I recognized one, and I know where to find him. When I do, I will see what he is willing to pay."

"Willing to pay?" I repeated. "What do you mean?"

The parents looked at each other as if confused, then the father bobbed his equine head in an exaggerated fashion, making him look more horselike than ever. "She doesn't understand our language well enough to know the idiom I used. She probably thinks I meant to sell something to the Jaradians. The idiom means to make them pay for their crimes."

"I see," the mother said. "Maybe you shouldn't use such colorful language."

"I understand. Good advice."

She set a hand on his arm. "I sense a storm brewing. I am already feeling its effects."

"As am I." He lumbered in the direction Quixon had gone. "I will return as soon as I can."

The mother turned toward me. "You should come with us. You'll be safe inside."

I shook my head. "I need to go to the iron—"

A loud crack sounded from above. The sky darkened, and a breeze ushered in much colder air. Light-blue snowflakes began falling, faster than they ever did at home.

The mother looked upward. "This is not good. Not good at all."

"What's wrong?" I asked.

"A battle storm. Only minutes away."

"A battle storm? What's that?"

"No time to explain." She grabbed my hand and pulled me toward the door of the temple. "Come, everyone. Hurry."

Although slight spasms still pinched my calf muscles, I had no problem keeping up with her slow pace. The older son ran ahead and pulled a thick rope dangling near a wooden double door. Something gonged inside. Seconds later, the two door panels divided with a low grinding noise, revealing a dim corridor. A row of flickering lanterns attached to each of the side walls provided the only light within.

The mother ushered her children inside and walked hand in hand with me, her growling voice whisper-soft. "Be silent. Just go along with what I say."

I nodded, though I wasn't sure I would obey her wishes. Now that my muscles seemed back to normal, I prepared myself to run at any moment.

As we walked together through the corridor, the children leading the way, the mother spoke with a louder voice. "Bannif, take your brother and sister to the sanctuary. Hurry on ahead. We'll meet you there."

"What about the sacrifice?" Bannif asked, pausing under one of the lanterns.

The light cast an undulating aura over the mother's scaly brow. "Tell the priest that the sacrifice has been provided."

"Yes, Mother." Bannif ran ahead.

I gulped. The sacrifice has been provided? Was *I* the sacrifice?

I jerked away from the Tauranta's grasp and ran toward the door, my heart hammering. The two panels slid closer together, groaning as the gap between them shrank. I leaped for the opening and thrust my arm through. The doors clamped down on it, pinning me there. Pain knifed from my wrist to my shoulder as the grinding shifted to a squeal.

I shouted, "It's crushing my arm!"

"I'm coming!" The mother Tauranta shuffled closer, faster than usual but still way too slow. When she arrived, she reached over my head with both hands and pried the doors a few centimeters farther apart.

The moment I pulled my arm out, she let go, and the doors thudded shut. She gave me a mother's penetrating glare, no translation needed.

"I . . ." I swallowed hard. "I don't want to be a sacrifice."

"Why wouldn't you want to be . . ." She shook her head. "Silly child. Your poor grasp of our language is causing too many problems."

I blinked at her. "So you don't want to kill me?"

"Of course not." She extended her hand again. "Come. I will show you."

I looked at her hand and shook my head this time. "I'm not a little girl."

"And yet you have so much to learn." The Tauranta lowered her hand. "Come along with me."

We walked abreast along the corridor, the lanterns casting their flickering light and painting the floor with competing shadows.

"What is your name?" she asked.

Still in stealth mode, I hesitated again, but at this point, what did it matter? My name meant nothing here. "Megan Willis."

"Two names. I hear many humans have three."

"Yes. On Alpha One, we have middle names. Mine is Ruth. But we don't use them much."

"I am Melda. My mate is Noldic. Our offspring are Bannif, Husk, and Dilippa. We have only one name each here, but there are few enough of us to allow for everyone to have a unique name."

I looked at Melda, her eyes glancing at me every few seconds. Why did she insist on watching me so closely? Maybe she thought I might get into more trouble or try to escape again. I let the thought go and shifted to another. "What's a battle storm?"

"You will learn soon."

"Are you worried about Noldic being out in it?"

She clucked in a laughing rhythm. "I appreciate your concern, but he is a responsible adult. If the storm becomes too severe, he knows where to find shelter."

We turned into another corridor on the right, a shorter one that ended at a massive cathedral-like chamber with rings of multilevel seats for the audience, and marble steps going down to a circular stage about ten paces across. An ornate, high-backed chair sat at the center of the stage with encircling spotlights on the floor aiming at it, though the beams were off at the moment.

I scanned the chamber for Melda's offspring. At the outer edge of the circular room, directly across from me, Bannif stood on a knee-high, ivory-colored pedestal. Husk stood on a similar pedestal to my left, separated from Bannif by ninety degrees, and Dilippa did the same to my right. A fourth pedestal sat directly in front of me, though no one stood atop it.

Melda pointed toward the stage. "Here is the altar of sacrifice. The sacrifice sits in that chair where everyone can look on. But have no fear. You will not be harmed."

I shook my head. "I still don't know what you mean by a sacrifice."

"We need a better word. Let me think." Melda touched her scaly lip. "A sacrifice, I suppose you could say, is a story. But it is more than a story: it is a pouring out of sorrows, grief, and pain, whatever is weighing us down or tormenting us. Sometimes we have questions we cannot answer, and such questions feel like . . . well . . . like those doors crushing you. We need relief. We need answers. Sometimes the answers themselves are painful, but they are also healing, like medicine on a wound."

I touched my chest. "So you want me to tell a story?"

"Of course. I believe that's why you were brought to us." Melda combed her scaly fingers through my hair. "I see pain in your eyes. You have suffered a great deal—loss, loneliness, heartache. Your story of suffering will be a magnificent sacrifice. By revealing the pain inside, you sacrifice the shield that we raise to guard our feelings, to protect the raw wounds from further injury. By lowering that shield, you show trust that all who are listening will sympathize or express pity, and you show faith that you will receive the answers you seek."

Her softly spoken words soaked in with a soothing sensation. "But how can you get answers just by telling a story?"

Melda smiled. "Not just by telling, dear. By emoting. By pouring out the grief in your soul. When we pour out, we need to be filled again with the answers we seek. And the cosmos holds all of the answers, because the stars have witnessed your story, and every word has been recorded. If the deity pities you, he will send to your mind what you need to know and provide the answers you desperately seek."

"Deity?"

She set a hand over her mouth. "I forgot. You have never been here. You know nothing about our deity."

"Right. Nothing." I looked up at the white ceiling, void of any icons or religious paintings. "Does he have a name?"

"We call him Draco. Others call him Stellar."

I squinted. "Draco? Isn't that a dragon? And stellar means stars, right?"

"Yes. Our deity is what some humans call the Astral Dragon."

"Oh. Then your deity is the same as mine."

She clicked her tongue, making a noise my earpiece failed to translate. "A deity can have differing names as long as it is the same person, and we know a person by his character. If a deity spawns evil followers, then you know they worship a false god, or at least they falsely worship a true god. There is very little difference."

A thud reverberated in the chamber, much like the sound of the entry door slamming closed.

"It's time for the sacrifice." Melda climbed onto the final pedestal and gestured toward the stage. "If you are willing. You are also free to walk away."

My throat tightened. Although I was no longer afraid of getting killed, something told me that being a sacrifice might be just as pain-ful. Yes, I needed to get out of this temple and find my mother, but I also needed allies, and doing this for the Taurantas might be the only way to get them on my side. I nodded. "I am willing."

"Go now. Sit at the center and wait for the lights. You will under-stand what to do next."

As I walked down the marble steps, cool on my bare feet, I studied the seats at each side. They really weren't seats at all. They were shorter pedestals set at intervals that allowed a tail to protrude behind it, the tail's end terminating in front of the pedestal two rows back.

I stepped past the circle of spotlights, sat in the chair, and looked toward Melda. More Taurantas began filing in and taking places on the surrounding pedestals. Every stare locked on me as the audience area filled with Taurantas of various shades of black, purple, and blue.

Their expressions sent mixed messages, smiles that seemed happy and bared teeth that looked ravenous.

My legs trembled. My head grew dizzy. In seconds, I might collapse. Then a soothing voice crooned to my left. From her pedestal at the perimeter, Melda sang a low note that washed into my senses like warm bathwater, relieving the tremors and settling the dizziness. Unlike her gruff, growling speaking voice, her singing was smooth, resonant, and entrancing.

Bannif joined in with a higher note from the pedestal directly in front of me, visible over the heads of dozens of Taurantas standing between him and me. Seconds later, Husk and Dilippa added their voices, both hitting even higher notes.

The notes blended into a mesmerizing chorus of joy. The emotions ignited a burning fuse threading through the audience that sizzled from one Tauranta to the next as they joined in, each hitting a different note. Maybe someone assigned notes to them, or maybe the notes were inborn, infused in their genetics. As if choreographed, the singers took breaths in turns, no two Taurantas inhaling at the same time, giving the song seemingly perfect consistency.

The ecstasy in their voices penetrated my heart. My own emotions swelled, ready to burst, but was I feeling joy? No. It was something else. Something negative. Sadness? Regret? Grief? All of those at once? It seemed that their joy had become a light that illuminated the depths of my soul, exposing a pit of gloom.

The surrounding lights turned on. The beams adjusted their angles until they aimed directly at my head—dark-blue auras, seemingly gathered from twilight, soft and soothing.

The songs softened as well, fading into the background, as if sung from another world. My eyes grew bleary. I tried to blink away the sensation, but each bat of my eyes sent me deeper and deeper into an alternate reality.

I stood alone in a dim expanse, surrounded by dark-blue light. A voice penetrated the dimness, strangely familiar. Was it my own? It seemed so, a softly humming choir joining it, supporting the words with background melody.

"I am an only child," the voice said in Humaniversal. "My parents are Julian and Anne Willis from Alpha One. We traveled together on a cruiser that transported small cargo shipments in our sector, though our ship could also travel through wormholes to distant parts of the galaxy."

An image surrounded me—the interior of the *Astral Dragon*. I stood on the bridge behind the dual console, my parents seated at the controls. The front viewing window showed a two-story building on the surface of a planet drawing near, as if we were planning to land soon. I stepped closer to my parents and tried to touch my father, but my hand passed through his shoulder.

Although startled, I felt no fear, only a peaceful assurance that I was here to watch, remember, and learn.

My voice continued, as if spoken from the ship's ceiling. "My parents' mission was to be a pain in the butt to the Alpha star system's government. They taxed us until just about everyone was as poor as a mop with three strings. They used our money to build a military empire that started expanding into other star systems. Although they were members of the intergalactic Alliance, the other star systems cast a wary eye on them, wondering if they might break away and become a threat to the fragile order that kept tyrants in check.

"My family and their allies, however, realized that the rise to tyranny had already begun, and we had to stop them. We raided their installations on some planets and hijacked a few of their ships, taking whatever we could to cripple them."

The *Astral Dragon* landed near a building. The boarding hatch dropped open, and my parents and their compatriots stormed out, shooting laser weapons. A nine-year-old version of myself ran with them, my frame shorter and my hair tied back for battle.

My view of the scene shifted with them and stopped at the open hatch. From there, I watched the action unfold. Our storm team killed several men guarding a fence around the building, wounded many more, broke the fence down, and set the building on fire. My nine-year-old self helped load the booty onto the ship and into the cargo holds as our gang ran out with their arms and backpacks full.

Like in my earlier memories when I killed a man, my heart sank. At the time, in the heat of battle, our crusade felt noble, righteous. These tyrants deserved to die. Now, from my new point of view as an observer, we looked like a pack of bandits looting and pillaging, more like greedy savages than freedom fighters.

"If we took money," my persona's voice continued, "we gave it to the poor. We kept the most useful weapons, destroyed the rest, and sold everything else, again giving the money to the people these monsters taxed into poverty, though we kept enough for ourselves to continue our raids."

I looked to the dark sky and shouted, "You're making excuses! Don't be so blind!" But the voice went on, as if not hearing my cries.

"Then one day the Alliance military set a trap and captured us." The image shifted to an all-too-familiar courtroom. With at least a hundred of our fellow citizens looking on from behind a well-guarded knee wall, my parents and I stood facing a judge's bench, our wrists and ankles shackled with chains fastened to a hook on the floor to keep us in place.

Now, instead of merely being an observer, I was the one in chains, stripped to my singlet and shorts. Smells penetrated my senses, burnt flesh and body odors. Blood dripped in front of my eyes, trickling from a stinging spot on one eyebrow. My parents, one to my left and one to my right, were gagged, their faces bloodied and dirty.

Judge Mason Statler, a sixty-something man wearing an ivory-colored robe and seated behind a lofty podium, glared at me from under a pale, sweaty brow. "Megan Willis, since you are not yet thirteen years old, you cannot be executed, but I can render a time-oriented judgment. You will be sent to a labor camp where you will work in the Alliance's iron mines. If you reveal your secrets, including where your parents have hidden their ill-gotten booty, your time there will be only five years because your confession will allow us to redistribute the goods to their rightful owners or their heirs, thereby lessening the damage you have caused.

"If, however, you fail to do so, the court cannot allow you to ever go free to regain the stolen goods, and we do not wish for taxpayers to supply you with a single morsel of bread past the necessary date. Therefore, assuming you refuse to repent of your crimes, you will be executed on the day you reach the age of thirteen."

My father gasped. My mother dropped to her knees and wept. I squared my shoulders and stood firm, though my lower lip quivered. I shouted, "I won't help you rebuild your military machine! I would rather die!"

As the crowd murmured and Judge Statler pounded a gavel, Captain Tillman walked in through a side doorway. At the time, I had no idea who he was. Our family had never encountered him during our missions. He approached the elevated seat and addressed the judge. "I can use Megan Willis on my next mission. Her experience as a cruiser mechanic is better used doing maintenance on my ship than digging through rocks in the quarries."

"I will allow it." Judge Statler nodded toward a guard. "Brand the girl as a pirate. Collar her. Imprint her limbs. We can't afford to let that foul creature escape."

I bit my lip hard. Those words had tormented my soul for far too long, and this time the fangs pierced more deeply than ever, their venom vile and stinging.

A guard unlocked my shackles and, with an iron grip on my upper arm, escorted me toward the door the captain had entered, not even giving me a moment to hug my parents. I twisted my neck and called out, "Mama! Papa! I love you!"

My mother's gag slipped down, and she cried, "I promise on the heart of the Astral Dragon, I will find you. Someday we'll be together again. Remember that promise."

I clutched my locket as the soldier hustled me from the courtroom. "I will, Mama. I will always remember."

We entered a new chamber—a small, windowless room with bare wooden benches lining three walls and sets of chains attached to iron floor hooks at the foot of the benches. The captain held the door and looked back into the courtroom. "I will return in a moment," he said, apparently to the judge. "Please wait for me."

When he closed the door and looked at me, I lunged for the knob, but he grabbed my wrist and handed me off to another man, who threw me onto a bench at the side wall. While two men held my arms and legs, an expressionless, hooknosed man with greasy dark hair stalked toward me, a branding iron in hand. The iron's fiery end, a bright-orange dragon, drew closer and closer to my upper arm.

I gasped shallow breaths. I had to stay strong. I couldn't let them hear me scream.

The brand pressed against my skin. My flesh sizzled. I screamed. The stench of burning flesh assaulted my senses.

As the hooknosed man pushed harder, I wailed, "Please! Oh, please stop!"

Captain Tillman grabbed the man's arm. "That's enough."

He lifted the brand, but the pain burned on with no relief. The two other men released my limbs, helped me sit up straight, and attached a shackle to my ankle, chaining me to one of the floor rings. Blinking through tears, I craned my neck and looked at my arm. The dragon brand pulsed like a red strobe, matched by torturous throbs that shot across my shoulders and into my skull.

A woman with gray hair tied back into a tight bun dragged a short stool close and produced a pen-like object. A long, thin tube ran from it to a wheeled, knee-high tank. "This stylus," she said in an even tone, "will fill the wound with ink to help ensure that the mark is permanent, and it will fight infection. It will hurt terribly but also provide healing in the long run. Do you understand?"

Biting my lip hard, I nodded.

She gestured toward the two guards. "Will I need them to hold you down?"

I glanced at them. The pair of beefy thugs stood motionless with arms crossed, looking oh so righteous as they glared at me with disdain. I refocused on the woman and shook my head.

"Good. Now hold still, and this will go faster." The pen flicked on, emitting a soft buzz. While she applied the ink, I steeled my body. Yes, it hurt like jabbing pitchforks, but not nearly as much as the branding iron.

In one corner of the room, a stooped woman with heavily

weathered skin held a mop with the wet end in a bucket. Wearing a maid's coif and a calf-length denim dress, she stared at me as if waiting to clean something, maybe my blood when the torture ended.

During the inking procedure, the hooknosed man set my prisoner's collar around my neck. After tapping on a computer tablet, he handed the remote unit to Captain Tillman. At the time, I had no idea what the collar meant, so I just stared at them, gritting my teeth as I tried to ignore the stylus's sting.

The collar snapped closed. I winced, then swallowed, feeling for the first time the collar's cruel compression.

As I sat in full view of all the Tauranta stares, new tears crept to my eyes. I tried to stifle them. I couldn't cry. I couldn't lose control.

But I did. I wept. I sobbed. Spasms rocked my body. I wanted to console myself, but I couldn't do anything but relive the horror as the vision played on.

Without a word, the captain attached the remote unit to his belt, still watching me as if studying my reaction to pain . . . or maybe enjoying it.

When the gray-haired woman finished the inking process, she twisted a sharp wedge onto the end of the stylus. "Now I have to draw conductive ink along certain nerves. This won't hurt as much, but the nerves are likely to make your muscles twitch, so I have to give you something to deaden them." From a pocket, she produced a finger-length glass vial filled with clear liquid. She removed the cork stopper and handed the vial to me. "Drink it all. It probably won't knock you out, but all of your senses will be deadened."

Still shaking with sobs, I took the vial and held it with a trembling hand. "Why . . . why couldn't I have this before they branded me?"

She gave me a mechanical smile. "That was punishment, dear. This is surgery."

I drank the bitter liquid and handed the vial back to her. After just a few seconds, numbing tingles crawled along my skin, and my spasms eased.

The woman looked at Captain Tillman. "I think she'll be cooperative. She's not going anywhere."

"Understood." He and the other men exited our chamber and entered the courtroom. When the door swung open, I caught a glimpse of my parents, my mother once again gagged as she and my father clasped each other's shackled hands.

When the door closed, the woman set the pen close to my neck. "You don't have to disrobe, but I will have to shift your clothing around to expose some sensitive areas. Again, if you cooperate, this will go faster."

"Okay." I swallowed, no longer feeling the collar. "Go ahead."

While she drew inked lines from my neck down to my arms and legs, my skin tingled. I tuned out the pen's buzz and listened to the proceedings. Previously, I had retained no memories of the rest of the ordeal, probably because of the deadening drug—but now in my vision, as if restored by the witnessing stars, the words returned to mind.

"Julian Willis," Judge Statler said, "you are sentenced to death for piracy. Take him away and empty the courtroom except for Anne Willis and Captain Tillman."

Footsteps and rattling chains followed. After a few moments, the noises silenced until the judge spoke again. "Remove her gag."

Although I couldn't see my mother, I imagined her glaring at Judge Statler and Captain Tillman, her jaw set and her fists clenched.

"Anne Willis," the judge continued, "I sentence you to death as well. Yet, I have granted an appeal by Captain Tillman that he will explain."

"Anne," the captain said, "you have the same choice Megan faces, except that your banishment will be to Beta Four."

"Beta Four?" Her voice sounded strained, like she was battling sobs of her own. "That's the same as a death sentence."

"Some have survived the cold. Knowing your grit and resolve, I expect you to be one of the few. In any case, your rules will be the same as Megan's. You will tell us where your booty is hidden by her thirteenth birthday or you will be executed. In addition, you will have to tell us who your allies are and their last known hideouts. If you meet both of these conditions, you will be released from Beta Four in five years."

"And Julian will still be executed," my mother said.

"Yes. Of course. There is no avoiding that. I'm sorry, but I couldn't extend my influence that far. He has killed many people."

"I don't believe a word you're saying. If you can free both Megan and me, you can find a way to free Julian."

"No, the Alliance must have a scapegoat, someone to blame. The story will be that Julian corrupted you and Megan and forced you both to join in his piracy. And he's the one who suggested the name of your ship, thereby insulting the Great Dragon. Although blasphemy isn't an official crime, the public hates it as much as piracy. If no one is punished for either offense, then it will foster a lack of trust in our system, not to mention encourage other pirates."

"You're the pirate, you cockroach. You would sacrifice my husband and use my daughter to blackmail me."

The captain let out an exasperated sigh. "I see that I have your answer. Yet, if Megan tells me what I need to know, then perhaps I can appeal for clemency for you, that is, if you haven't already died in the icy chill of Beta Four. Just remember, Megan's birthday arrives in less than a month. If she won't provide the booty information by that date, I am obligated to execute her."

The chains rattled once more. I imagined my mother lunging at him, restrained by the leg irons. "You monster! If you so much as touch a hair on Megan's head, I swear I will cut you into pieces."

"While you're on Beta Four? Not likely."

"I'll find a way. You will burn in hellfire."

"Your Honor," the captain said, "I'll send Gavin Foster to escort Anne to the Beta Four transporter."

The dragging of chains blended with muffled grunts. I imagined a guard gagging my mother again and hauling her away.

Tears trickled down my cheeks. My father would soon die, and my mother would be banished to Beta Four. Although I heard from Emerson that she had been imprisoned there, this reliving of my torture and hearing the pronouncement of her sentence felt like acid poured on an open wound.

When the gray-haired woman finished the inking, she looked

me in the eye. "You're falling asleep. Don't fight it. By the time you wake up, much of the pain will be gone. Why suffer more than you have to?"

I opened my mouth to answer, but my stomach churned. Nausea spiked. If I tried to say a word, I'd throw up for sure.

"I'll tell the captain that you're ready. Just sit quietly. You can't go anywhere."

When she left, I couldn't hold it back another second. I heaved my guts on the floor in front of me. The coiffed woman walked up, pushing a wheeled bucket and carrying a cup of water. "I was waiting for that."

Feeling a little better, I managed a whispered "Sorry."

"Sorry for what?" She handed me the cup and began mopping my mess. "You did good. Even the toughest men usually upchuck long before you did."

In my warped vision, she seemed fuzzy, wavering, as if she were swabbing a sea-tossed deck. I took a sip of water and washed down the acidic bile.

She glanced at me with wary eyes. "They have misjudged you, haven't they?"

I nodded.

"I knew it." She set her mop in the bucket and leaned closer. "You're wearing a life locket. Who gave it to you?"

Summoning my strength, I forced out, "My . . . my mother."

"Thought so. Most girls get 'em from their mama." She sat at my side. "Name's Doris. Don't tell me yours. Already heard it." She smiled, revealing gaps in her crooked teeth. "Do you know what the locket means?"

I shook my head.

"Then maybe your mama didn't know." Doris ran a withered hand through my hair, her sincere gray eyes sparkling. "Child, listen to me close. We don't have much time." She glanced both ways before continuing. "I saw how those monsters treated you. They like to yammer on and on about justice, and they dress in those fine robes, parading around like they're so pure. You'd think they pooped pearls." She wagged a finger. "But, no, their hearts are as black as a witch's cat. Here they are shackling a little girl with irons, torturing her with a burning brand, poking her with tattooing needles. All for what? Money. Power. A feeling of righteousness. They're hell's hypocrites."

She lowered her voice to a whisper. "Child, you're wearing a dragon's eye. I know, because while you suffered, your locket glowed, but the others were blind to it. The glow means that strength and courage are in you, locked in your soul and magnified by the Astral Dragon."

I moved my mouth, trying to ask why, but nothing came out.

She set a finger on my lips. "Don't try to talk. Just listen." She lifted my locket and set it in her palm. "You have a purpose, a goal. I don't know what it is, but you need to find it. Learn about love, real love, not the foolery that so many politicians and perverts wear like masks. Real love sacrifices. It shows mercy. It heals." She set the locket back on my chest. "Watch for signs. The Dragon will lead you to himself. When you find him, then you will learn what your purpose is."

I closed my eyes. Sleep carried me away. Fast-moving dreams took control, glimpses of the past five months that supported the new revelations—the captain delaying my execution, Gavin guiding me to put on the suit, my mother attacking the *Nebula Nine*, and even me hiding outside the ship and missing my rescue. Everything seemed orchestrated to put me in this place at this time so I could relive my horror and remember what I needed to know. I had something to do, a purpose to fulfill, though I had no idea what it might be.

A hush descended, quieting the background singing voices. I opened my eyes. I sat on the temple stage, surrounded by the worshipers who recently sang me into my sacrificial story. I rose from the chair on wobbly legs. From every direction, Taurantas stared at me, most of them with mouths agape. Their joy had fled, replaced by the pain that shredded my soul. Had they seen my visions? Heard my cries? Learned my secrets?

At the very least, they had watched me suffer. I felt stripped naked. Vulnerable. Empty.

I dropped to my knees, covered my face with my hands, and cried.

Soft growls drifted into my ears.

"What should we do?" Melda asked. "I didn't recognize her before."

Someone with a deeper voice replied. "Remember, this is a sanctuary. She is safe here."

"I trust you to do the right thing. You are wise and merciful."

"And you are kind. Yet, with the battle storm raging outside, I am not as certain as you are."

"I know what you mean. Goodbye, Essen." Melda shuffled away.

The words *sanctuary* and *safe* settled my nerves. As my crying ebbed, I stayed on my knees and tried to decide what to do next, but nothing came to my frazzled mind. After a few minutes of silence, a gentle hand touched my shoulder. "Child, your sacrifice was precious, indeed."

I lowered my hands and looked up. A short, wrinkled Tauranta stood in front of me, neither black nor blue, covered with gray skin and scales, probably a male if his deep voice meant anything. Besides him and me, the sanctuary was now vacant.

"Where did everyone go?" I asked in Humaniversal.

"They detected your grief and your need to weep alone."

"Could they see my story?"

He bobbed his head. "But most of our understanding came through your pain and sorrow. We tried to inject our joy but failed. It seems that your sacrifice was beyond our help."

"Why would you try to help me?"

"Transforming sorrow into joy pleases Draco." He extended a hand. "My name is Essen. I am the priest here."

I shook his hand but kept my name to myself, not that silence helped anything since Melda probably already spilled that information.

The priest pulled me to my feet. "Melda told me about the Jaradians who tried to capture you. Why were you walking alone?"

"Because I am alone here. A visitor."

"Are you unaware of the danger a young human faces in Bassolith, especially a female such as yourself?"

I brushed tears from my cheeks. "I know the danger. I mean, I know now. And I sort of knew before. I wasn't sure. But it didn't matter. I had to get a part to repair my ship and also to try to find someone. A boy. He needs to be rescued, and now I have an idea that he might be in the same place where I'll buy the ship's part. I thought while I was there I might have a look around for the boy."

"*Had* to? Do you mean you no longer have to?"

"I still need to get the part. But find the boy?" I looked away. "I'm not sure anymore."

"Did your experience here cause your uncertainty?"

I nodded. "This boy is the son of the Alliance captain you saw in my sacrifice story, the one who conspired to torture my family."

"Ah. I see. And now you no longer feel compelled to rescue the son of such a scoundrel."

I lowered my head. "Something like that."

Essen set a finger under my chin and lifted my head, forcing me to look at him. "Let me make sure I understand. You're not at all certain that this boy is here in Bassolith."

I shook my head. "The captain thought so, but there's no real proof. I think he might be at the ironworks factory—but that guess could be completely wrong."

"Interesting." Essen intertwined his fingers. "Would you like an escort? It's dangerous for you to be alone."

I nodded. "Just till I get to the factory. I might be there awhile."

"Very well. Follow me."

Essen lumbered through the sanctuary entrance. I caught up and walked in silence at his side. A cool breeze blew through the empty hallway, creating an eerie sensation. Why did everyone leave so quickly, including Melda and her family? They seemed so friendly earlier.

When we turned down another corridor, the exit came into view. The wind outside whistled and beat against the double doors, shaking them. "What about the battle storm?" I asked. "Are we going to walk in it?"

"It is the safest option for you. Fewer city dwellers will be out and about."

"Why do you call it that? A battle storm, I mean."

He touched his head. "It causes mental battles within, at least for us Taurantas. Normally we are a joyful people, but a battle storm can make the worst in us come to the surface—heartaches, worries, regrets—even when we are not directly in the elements. If we are not careful, we might even be tempted to hurt someone for selfish gain. You might say that the storm disables our moral compasses."

I laughed under my breath. "I guess I don't have to worry about the storm affecting me. I have negative thoughts no matter what the weather's like."

He smiled. "No, you have nothing to worry about, except for the bitter cold, of course."

I glanced at my bare feet. Although the soles were hard, they could still freeze, and any exposed flesh would get even colder, maybe frostbitten.

When we arrived at the exit, Essen opened a number pad on one of the doors and punched in a series of numbers. The doors parted, revealing a blur of icy flakes pummeling the air at a nearly horizontal angle.

Perdantus stood under the outer porch's overhang, shivering and holding a small, rolled-up sheet of paper in his beak. While Essen walked into the storm, Perdantus flew to my wrist and put the page in my hand. Then he hopped onto my shoulder and whispered into my ear. "I saw you enter the temple earlier and waited."

I nodded, not wanting Essen to eavesdrop on our conversation.

"The leaflet I gave you," Perdantus continued, "is one of many that were dropped from the sky not long before you arrived. Read it when you're alone." With a sharp flutter, he flew into the storm and out of sight.

"What are you waiting for?" Essen asked as ice began collecting on his head. "We must hurry."

"Coming." I stealthily pushed the leaflet into my pants pocket and stepped into the storm. As we walked in the direction I had come, bitterly cold wind knifed through my shirt and instantly chilled my skin. Needlelike ice stung my face, forcing me to close my eyes to slits. My fingers and toes had already numbed. At this rate, the journey to the factory would feel like never-ending torture, especially if I had to be escorted by this slow-as-a-glacier Tauranta.

Blinking at the sharp pellets, I looked around. No one was in sight. I was safe. I just needed to make a run for it. "Thanks for the company, Essen, but I'm freezing, so I'd better hurry on ahead."

He grabbed my arm. "You're staying with me."

"Let go!" I tried to jerk away, but he was too strong. "You're hurting me!"

"Then stop struggling."

He pulled me off the path toward a shack. I reached for the collar's remote on my belt and set a finger on the activate button. I could shock Essen, but the pain might paralyze me. I had to save that option as a last resort.

As we drew near, the shack's door opened. Noldic, Melda's mate, walked out with a Jaradian behind him. When they saw me, the Jaradian set several gold coins in Noldic's hand. "I don't have the thousand mesots yet," the Jaradian said. "I will pay you more when I get it."

After nodding to the Jaradian, Noldic gave Essen two of the coins and left, passing me without a glance.

I sucked in a chilling breath. They were all in on this kidnapping, every one of them. I pushed the remote's button. The collar shocked my neck. Electricity shot down my arm and into Essen. He let out a raging squeal and let me go.

I released the button and dropped to my hands and knees. My fingers numb and my muscles cramping, I scrabbled on the fallen ice, slipping and sliding. The Jaradian lunged, grabbed my ankle, and pulled me into his arms. I bit his hand as hard as I could and broke free.

As I limped away, his lumbering footsteps drew closer and closer behind me. I could almost feel his hot breaths on my neck.

A familiar voice rang out. "Megan, get down!"

I dropped to my stomach. A huge plume of flames blasted over me and into the Jaradian's face. The beast clawed at his eyes and staggered back toward Essen.

A hand grasped my wrist and pulled me up. "I've got you, Megan."

I blinked at the stranger, a tall man dressed in a parka and wearing a ski mask, a flamethrower resting at his hip. "How do you know my name?"

"Oh. Right." He pulled off the mask, revealing the familiar narrow face of First Mate Gavin Foster. "Let's go. Now."

I followed his lead toward the riverside path and slid my hands into my pants pockets. My frigid fingers touched the leaflet Perdantus gave me. I could look at it later. For now, I just wanted to keep my hands from getting frostbite.

When we reached the path, Gavin turned toward the city. Although it was a relief to walk with the wind at my back, traveling deeper into Bassolith felt colder all the same. "Where are we going?" I asked as I followed, my feet now numb to my ankles.

"To the *Astral Dragon*. We landed on a beach where this river empties into a bay."

"I thought maybe you found the *Nebula Nine*. Emerson's been sending low-power distress signals. I came to the city to get a part so I could fix the long-range transmitter."

"We didn't read any distress signals." He glanced back at me. "Where is the *Nine*?"

"Behind us. Back in the mountains."

"I think we're far enough away from those beasts now." He halted and knelt in front of me. "I found the rover. That's how I knew you had to be close by." He took his gloves off, pulled a sock and a shoe from each of his parka's pockets, and helped me put them on. "Why did you take them off?"

"It's a long story. I'll tell you and my mother everything when we get to the *Astral Dragon*."

"Sounds good." When he tied the second shoe, he put his gloves and ski mask back on and rose. "Stay close." He hurried toward the inner city again.

I jogged behind him, the heavy shoes slowing me down. Cold wind continued buffeting me, though the falling snow had ebbed. It seemed odd that Gavin was so concerned about my feet staying warm, yet he didn't offer me his parka, gloves, or ski mask. I could wear them, too big or not.

Once we entered the core of the city, several huge buildings with ice-covered spires loomed like frozen gods watching us with cold-blooded eyes. Gavin turned left onto a wide street where a dark dilapidated bus—an ancient, combustion-engine variety, big enough for about twenty passengers—sat parked at a curbside next to an expansive complex of buildings. Several fat smokestacks stabbed the gray sky and spewed black, ashy smoke into the clouds, further darkening the hazy blanket overhead.

As we passed the bus, several words on its side panel came into view, emblazoned in indecipherable yellow lettering. If someone spoke the words out loud, my earpiece could translate the message. Maybe Gavin had some idea what this place was all about.

"Do you know what these buildings are?" I asked.

Without slowing, Gavin scanned the complex. "Judging by the smokestacks, I'd say there are blast furnaces inside. Maybe some kind of metals foundry. Iron or steel or both."

I halted. This had to be the ironworks factory. The slaves probably traveled on that bus.

Gavin pivoted toward me. "Why did you stop?"

I shivered hard. "Just thinking."

"About the cold, no doubt." He pointed toward a door at the front of one of the ironworks buildings. "We'll let you warm up for a while at a furnace. We still have quite a ways to go. You'll freeze before we get there."

We hurried to the door. Gavin opened it without knocking and guided me inside. As we walked across an enormous dark room toward a blazing furnace, warning alarms rang in my mind. Pieces of a scattered puzzle started coming together. Gavin was too familiar with this place. He showed up just in time to rescue me from the Jaradians. He had my socks and shoes ready to put on. Everything was too convenient.

It was a trap.

I spun and tried to run, but my nearly frozen legs couldn't manage more than a hobble. Gavin rushed ahead and blocked the partially open door. "You're far too cold to go anywhere."

"Get out of my way." I tried to push past him, but he grabbed my hair, stopping me.

When he let go, he showed me a handful of ice crystals in his palm. "Look. You're freezing. You need to stay here for a while."

I shivered again, harder this time. "If you'd let me wear your parka and gloves, I'm sure I could make it to the ship."

"Then *I* would freeze." He set a hand on my shoulder and looked me in the eye. "Listen, Megan, I didn't come here to find you on my own account. I came for your mother's sake. But I'm no hero. I'm not going to freeze my butt off for you."

"All right. I can believe you're no hero. But why this place?"

"Like I told you, it has a furnace. A perfect place to get warm."

"Why did you walk right in without knocking?"

"What are you, a box of questions?" He huffed a short sigh. "Listen, when I was searching for you, I came here and asked the owner if he'd seen you. Good thing he spoke Humaniversal. Anyway, he said he hadn't seen you, but he's a friend of humans, and I was welcome anytime. I saw you were freezing, so I headed this way. Satisfied?"

I squinted at him. "Should I trust a guy who killed everyone on board the *Nebula Nine*? I know you planned the attack. I know you hid the air tanks. You wanted everyone dead."

"Everyone except you and Dirk. I made sure you both had your suits on before the attack. He's fine, by the way. He told us he thought you were still alive, which is why I was here searching for you."

"But you killed everyone else. Why?"

He looked away for a moment before locking his stare on me again. "You don't know the captain like I do. Or the other members of the crew. The captain handpicked them for a special mission you knew nothing about."

"I thought we were coming here to rescue his son."

Gavin nodded. "True, but that was only one of the reasons, and the other reasons don't matter anymore. It's over. He's dead. It's better that you never learn what he was up to."

"What about Oliver? Maybe he's still alive."

"Right. Maybe. But I can't work with maybes. I have to tell your mother that I found you so she can stop searching the countryside in this infernal storm." He gripped my shoulder with a firm hand. "You wait here while I go and tell her. Then we'll both come back for you. Deal?"

A cold gust blew in, refreshing the chill bumps on my arms. I couldn't face that storm again, not if I wanted to survive. "All right. I guess I don't have much choice."

"No. You don't." He slid a finger under the leather cord around my neck, drawing the locket out from under my shirt. "So this is the locket your mother mentioned."

I grasped the locket and stepped back, pulling the cord from his grasp. "What about it?"

"Give it to me. It'll prove that I found you."

"Yeah, right." I took another step back. "I'm keeping it."

"What?" He shook his head. "No, no, no. I just rescued you from slave traders. Without me, you'd be in chains, so I'm calling the shots here. And your mother already doesn't trust me. I'm not going back to her empty-handed."

"She *shouldn't* trust you," I growled. "You don't care about finding me. You just want the locket. You'll say you found it in a pile of ashes. Then you'll have what you want, and I won't be able to tell my mother that you murdered our crew. She probably has no idea that you hid the air tanks to make sure they wouldn't survive."

"What an idiotic thing to say. Of course she knew. She and Zoë and I planned the whole thing."

I scrunched my brow. There was that name again. "Who in blazes is Zoë?"

"Never mind." With a quick lunge, he grabbed me around the shoulders and held me while he drew the locket's cord over my head. His embrace pinned my arms to my sides. I couldn't even reach the remote.

He released me and stuffed the cord and locket into his parka's pocket. "Now wait here like I told you."

When he spun to leave, I grabbed his wrist and pressed the remote's button. "Give me my locket!" Again the collar shocked me. Cramps twisted my muscles into knots.

Gavin arched his back and yowled. He jerked away and turned to me with the flamethrower drawn. "You do that again, and you *will* be a pile of ashes!"

I crumpled to my knees and dropped the remote. As I gasped for breath and waited for my muscles to loosen, I slid back while giving him a hard stare. If he wanted me dead, he could have killed me already. He was going to a lot of trouble to keep me alive. "Go ahead and shoot."

He pulled the trigger. A stream of fire jetted from the nozzle and zipped over my shoulder, nicking my ear and catching my hair. I shrieked and batted the flames until they died.

My ear stinging, I glared at Gavin from my knees. "I don't know why you're working with my mother, but trust me, she'll see through your scheme soon enough."

"You're so blind. You have no idea what's really going on." He pointed at the remote on the floor. "You deserve another jolt, but I guess I'd better leave that with you. That collar will kill you otherwise. I don't know how to disable it."

I scooped it up and clipped it to my belt. "Like you care."

"I don't. But your mother does. We'll be back for you." He pivoted and walked out the door, closing it behind him with a loud thud.

I struggled to my feet, ran stiff-legged to the door, threw it open, and looked outside. To my left, Gavin jogged down the road toward the river, his frame veiled by the falling ice crystals. I limped after him. The frigid wind beat against my body, instantly chilling my exposed skin. But I couldn't give up. I promised to protect the locket with my life.

As I hobbled through the storm, something beeped. I halted and listened. It came from my collar. The alarm? Was the battery ready to die? If it did, the collar would kill me in less than five minutes.

I searched for a source of recharging light and saw only lamps on the tops of poles. I could never reach them. I hurried back to the factory, closed the door, and limped fitfully toward the furnace. Sitting as close to the fire as I dared, I listened to the rapid beeps. How painful would a fatal shock be? The crippling ones twisted my arms and legs into a knot, inflicting horrific pain. Maybe a death shock would be different—quick, more merciful, just a sudden jab and then nothingness.

The alarm quickened. I closed my eyes and whispered breathlessly, "Oh, please, please, battery, don't shut off. Collar, don't kill me. I'm not ready to die. I need to find my mother. I need to search for the Astral Dragon."

As I waited, gritting my teeth, Doris's words returned to mind. *Watch for signs. The Dragon will lead you to himself. When you find him, then you will learn what your purpose is.*

The beeping again grew louder and faster. The brand on my arm stung. Tingles ran along the conductive ink. At any moment, the shock was bound to strike me dead.

I opened my eyes and looked straight into the fire. The flames curled, fashioning a long neck, a spiny tail, and a draconic head.

I gasped. A dragon?

"Please," I said with a rasp, "don't let me die yet. I need your help. Right now. Please."

A whisper emanated, each word making the dragon shimmer. "Why do you wish to avoid death?"

I swallowed hard. Why would he ask that? "I . . . I have so much to do. Find my mother. Stop Gavin. Rescue Oliver and the slave children here."

"I see."

As the alarm continued its unrelenting clamor, the dragon's eyes appeared, red and pulsing. Had I given him the right answer? Was he waiting for more? I blurted out, "And to learn my purpose. Someone told me when I found the Astral Dragon, I would learn it."

The whisper sounded like a contented purr. "You already stated your purpose."

"I did? When?"

"A mere moment ago. Love of family. Zeal for justice. Compassion for the oppressed." The draconic image dwindled, its voice shrinking with it. "Pursue these treasures with all your heart. Sacrifice for them. And, if necessary, die for them." As if sighing, the fire blew a spray of ashes into my face, stinging my cheeks. When I brushed them away, the dragon was gone.

The alarm quieted. Seconds passed. No shock came from the collar. I let out a relieved sigh. "Thank you! Thank you! You won't regret helping me. And I'll fulfill my purpose. I promise."

09

My skin and lips drying out, I scooted back from the furnace and let my muscles relax. I was safe . . . for now.

I touched the collar, warm against my neck and even warmer on my fingertips. What just happened? Did the Astral Dragon stop the termination signal? Or did firelight recharge the battery? Had I witnessed a miracle or the results of science?

Either way, science couldn't explain the dragon itself—the shape, the voice, the message. He showed me my purpose. Not exactly marching orders. More like a way of thinking. A philosophy. *Love of family. Zeal for justice. Compassion for the oppressed.* I could pursue those, without a doubt. But die for them?

I breathed a long sigh. That remained to be seen.

The warmth on my skin still growing, I scooted back farther. Something crinkled in my pocket. I withdrew the leaflet Perdantus gave me and read it in the firelight. Not much bigger than my hand, the page showed a photo of me in the courtroom with manacles around my wrists and chains hanging to the floor. The caption said

in Humaniversal, "Reward of one thousand mesots for the live capture of this runaway pirate. If you apprehend her, bring her to the
ironworks factory foreman for your reward."

I touched the numerals on the page. Since so many were trying
to catch me, even a priest, that had to be a lot of money. And Gavin
must have created the leaflet. Only he had access to a photo from
the trial.

But why? Why did Gavin want to make me look like a criminal?
Why did he ask for my live capture? If he just wanted the locket, he
could have easily killed me to get it.

Then the truth hit me. My mother had a locket of her own with
a dragon's eye ruby inside. Its glow reflected my life force. She knew
I was alive. And Gavin realized if he killed me, my mother would
know right away. For some reason, he just wanted the locket, and he
probably wouldn't tell her about having it or finding me.

"Gavin's a snake!" I wadded the paper and threw it into the furnace. As it burned, I imagined Gavin roasting in the fire, hoping
the vision would cheer me up. But it didn't. Losing the locket was
like losing an eye. It was my only connection to my mother, and
not being able to tell if my mother was alive, I felt blind without it.
Somehow I had to get my mind off it or I'd start crying again.

I looked around at the room for a distraction. Only empty crates
and stacks of split logs lay in sight. With no finished metal products
lying around and no raw materials for smelting, this couldn't be a
functioning part of the factory. The furnace probably heated a resi-
dence or a work area or the foreman's office. Since the foreman was
apparently in charge of keeping me prisoner, I wanted to avoid him
at all costs. I had to leave. Now. Since my mother had already arrived
on the planet, getting the relay switch could wait.

Just as I flexed my legs to get up, something clicked at the door.
I turned that way. Nothing moved except shadows on the walls that
danced in time with the flickers of firelight.

I rose and padded to the door. I grasped the cold knob and
tried to turn it, but it wouldn't budge. I used both hands and tried
again. No luck. Someone outside must have locked it. And with no

locking mechanism on the inside, this wasn't just a furnace room. It was a prison.

My heart thumping, I walked around the room, looking for another exit—a second door, a window, anything. My gaze swept across a casement window near the ceiling, partially open, probably for ventilating heat from the furnace. Maybe if I stacked the crates and climbed on top, I could reach it, but once I squeezed outside, the jump down would probably be dangerous.

A bird flew in, perched on the windowsill, and shook itself hard, fluffing its feathers. Although the same size as Perdantus, it had more silver in its wings. It looked down at me and said in its chirping language, "Well, it looks like old Thorne has a new orphan to shelter. Where did you come from?"

Not wanting to trust this bird right away, I wrapped my arms around myself. "I just came in here to get warm, and someone locked the door."

The bird flitted down and landed on a shoulder-high stack of crates. "It's nothing to be concerned about. Thorne was probably passing by, noticed the unlocked door, and locked it without looking inside. Since he's here at home now, someone will be coming down soon to stoke the fire."

"How did this Thorne person get in without opening the door?"

The bird laughed. "Oh, you'll find out when you meet him. He often uses entry points that others are unable to access."

"Okay. But how do you know so much about what goes on here?"

The bird straightened. "I am Salsa, Thorne's personal assistant."

"Salsa. That's an interesting name. I met a bird who looks a lot like you. His name's Perdantus."

"Perdantus is my mate." Salsa flitted a few centimeters into the air and landed again. "A handsome fellow, isn't he?"

"Uh . . . yeah." I stared at her. It seemed so strange that a bird would have a job working for another species. "So you're an assistant to Thorne. Does Perdantus have a job?"

"Oh yes. He is a master negotiator. Members of every species hire him to negotiate contracts." She chirped a gleeful laugh. "One time, both sides of a contract tried to hire him. As you can imagine, that would never work."

"I suppose not."

Salsa hopped closer and peered at me for a few seconds before speaking again. "I know who you are. Megan Willis, the pirate."

I growled under my breath. "I'm not a pirate. Those leaflets tell lies."

"Oh, don't worry. I've seen it all before. The slave traders tell all sorts of lies to capture a wayward human child." She leaned toward me and whispered, "Your secret is safe with me."

Footsteps tromped above, approaching slowly. I searched for the source and found a wooden stairway at one end of the room. A girl descended, her shoulders slumped, her arms limp at her sides, and her scraggly blonde hair draped haphazardly over her shoulders. Wearing a filthy long-sleeved jersey and grimy gray pants, she looked like she had been working someplace dirty.

When she arrived at my level, I hid behind the stack of crates. She turned toward the furnace, staring blankly as if her thoughts had flown to another world.

As she drew nearer, the fire lit up her features. Pale and gaunt, she appeared to be no older than ten, though her face seemed older, worn and weary. Yet, her blue eyes sparkled as if fueled with vibrant energy from within.

She halted at a stack of firewood, hoisted the top log into her thin arms, and heaved it into the furnace. The fire roared and crackled. Moving like a mindless android, she repeated the process six times. When she finished, she brushed her hands on the front of her jersey.

Salsa whispered into my ear. "Well, if you won't introduce yourself, I will do it for you."

I hissed, "But the pirate part. She might get scared."

"Trust me. Nothing scares this girl." Salsa flew to the girl's shoulder and chirped loudly. "We have a new guest, Crystal."

"I don't care about the rats you make friends with," Crystal said in Humaniversal as she batted Salsa away. "Go count Thorne's money again."

Salsa flew a quick turnaround and landed on Crystal's other shoulder. "A human girl is here. Look behind the crates. And don't be so grumpy. She'll think you and I aren't friends."

Having no choice now, I stepped into the open and nodded. "Um . . . hi. I'm Megan."

Crystal turned toward me and stared with piercing eyes. "Beware," she said with an eerie voice. "I have magic powers."

I gave her a quizzical stare in return. "Magic powers? What are you talking about?"

With quick steps, Crystal closed the gap between us and looked up at me, the top of her head just a few centimeters lower than mine. When our eyes met, hers sparkled brightly, like diamonds glittering in sunlight.

Nearly blinded, I tried to blink, but my eyelids stayed open as if frozen in place. Yet, there was no pain. The light bathed my eyes in soothing warmth. As the sensation continued, the warmth spiked, getting hotter and hotter.

Finally, I stepped back and turned my head. I lost focus. Everything blurred. Where was I? What was causing the blast of warm air and the crackling noise? A fire?

Someone shook my shoulder. "Megan. Snap out of it."

I stared at a blonde-haired girl. She looked familiar. Where had I seen her before?

A bird sitting on her shoulder chirped, and computerized words translated in my ear. "Megan, I'm Salsa. And the girl is Crystal. Remember?"

I blinked several times. With each repetition, the girl and the bird clarified. Memories returned. Within seconds I remembered everything. "What happened?"

Crystal grinned. "I was just showing you one of my magic powers. I can make people forget what's going on. It lasts only a few seconds, but it's powerful, don't you think?"

I rubbed my eyes with my knuckles and looked at her again. She was perfectly clear now. "Yeah, but why? I didn't do anything to you."

Crystal crossed her arms in front. "Because you're bigger and older than me. If you're going to live here with us, I wanted you to know you can't boss me around."

"Live here? Boss you around? I came in to—"

"Crystal, will you ever shut up about your stupid magic powers?"

The new voice came from the stairway. A boy walked toward us, his arms loaded with split logs covered with ice. After setting them on top of the pile on the floor, he brushed crystals off his dark long sleeves and warmed his hands in front of the furnace while looking at me. "Who are you?"

"Megan." I took a step closer. He seemed so familiar. Wearing typical Alpha One denim pants and a polo shirt with an Alliance-logo-shaped discoloration above the pocket, could he be—

"I'm Oliver."

I managed to keep my body calm, though my words tangled as I uttered the usual response. "Nice to meets oo. I mean, meet you."

"Same." He nodded toward Crystal. "And never mind her. She's always showing off her magic powers to new kids. At least that's what she calls them. But they're not magic. She was just born that way."

"Oh. I've never seen a human with powers like hers."

"Have you ever been to Gamma Five?"

I shook my head. "Flew around it. My father landed in a pod there, but I had to stay on our ship."

He set a thumb on his chest. "I explored Gamma Five with my father. He learned that some children born there get special powers. When they're discovered, they're taken away by the government and kept in a lab, experimented on like rats. I guess Crystal slipped through the net."

"What?" I narrowed an eye. "That has to be a myth. Where you're born can't give you powers."

He shrugged. "Believe what you want. Crystal has powers. Come up with your own explanation."

"I will." His story gave me a natural lead-in for nailing down the final proof. I cleared my throat. "You mentioned that you explored with your father. Are you Oliver Tillman?"

His mouth dropped open. "Who told you my last name? Not even Crystal knows it."

"I know your father." I extended a hand. "Megan Willis. I'm here with the *Nebula Nine*."

"The *Nine* is here? On Delta Ninety-eight?" He looked at the door. "Where's my father?"

I shifted my weight from foot to foot as I drew my hand back. "Well . . . um . . . the captain is—"

"Crystal?" a man called from the top of the stairway. "Oliver? What's taking you so long? It's time to eat."

"I will delay him," Salsa said as she fluttered off Crystal's shoulder. She flew up the stairway and out of sight.

Crystal waved toward the stairs. "Salsa's our friend. She's always on our side. Not Thorne's."

"Does Thorne mistreat you?" I asked, glad to change the subject from Oliver's father.

"No whippings, if that's what you mean. I got plenty of whippings from the guy Thorne bought me from, so it's better here. And he gives us books. I love to read."

Oliver rolled his eyes. "Way too much, if you ask me. All those fantasy and romance stories going through your head. Puts your brain in outer space."

"Does not." Crystal refocused on me. "Thorne makes us work hard, though. And he calls us mean names sometimes. But that's better than starving or freezing to death."

Oliver nodded. "We have to work in Thorne's mine. Like Crystal said, it's hard, but at least he doesn't whip us. The slave traders around here like to use a braided whip. Hurts like hellfire."

I looked him over. In the photo, his cheeks were fuller and his skin more flushed with color. Now, like Crystal, he was gaunt and pale, as I had expected. "What do you do in the mine? Dig for iron ore?"

"Iron ore?" He huffed a laugh. "Do you think kids could dig enough for this factory?"

I frowned. "Don't laugh at me. I don't know what's going on here."

"Sorry. You're right." Oliver's tone softened. "It's not a normal mine. Thorne just calls it one 'cause it's in a deep cave. Bramble bees bring in sap from zoa trees and store it in holes in the cave walls. Then something happens to the sap that makes it glow. Maybe it's the minerals in the rocks, or the bees add something to it. I don't know."

I imagined the process. In my mind, a ball of sticky stuff emitted a golden aura. "The sap glows? That's weird."

"Pretty weird, I guess. Anyway, we call it glowsap. The name fits."

"What do the bramble bees do with it?"

"Lay their eggs in it. When the babies hatch, they eat the glowsap. Then they grow like crazy."

"How big do they get?"

He rolled his hand into a fist. "About like this. And their wings make them look even bigger."

"And don't forget the stingers," Crystal said, stabbing the air with her finger. "One sting, and you're dead. It's always fatal."

I cringed. "How do you protect yourselves?"

"Armored suits." Oliver thumped his chest with a fist. "We keep them just inside the cave. They're heavy, so we take turns. Four of us collect glowsap while the others go to the riverbank and make clay shells to put the sap in. The clay keeps the glowsap wet for the ride home. Thorne says if the sap dries, it's no good to him."

"What does he do with it?"

Oliver shrugged. "No clue, but whenever we have a good day finding the stuff, he gets excited about it. Sometimes we even get a sweet drink."

I pictured Thorne as a hulking Jaradian holding a clay egg in a meaty hand. What could someone like him do with glowing sap? Yet, if Oliver didn't know, I had no way of finding out. It was time to change the subject. If I could escape and get back to the *Nebula Nine*, I still needed that relay switch to call my mother. "Do you know where this factory's parts store is?"

"Sure." Oliver flicked his head. "Around the corner. It's not open now, though. Why do you ask?"

"I need a relay switch for the *Nine*. It's already purchased, reserved at the store in the captain's name." Not wanting him to ask about his father, I hurried to change the subject again. "How did you get here? To this planet and factory, I mean."

"It's a long story." He looked away for a moment, then back at me, his eyes misting. "You spill yours first. You're the stranger here."

"Yeah," Crystal said. "Like what's up with that bug-ugly collar? Looks like you pushed your head through a jar lid and got stuck."

I smiled, though I had no way to answer without revealing too many secrets. "I guess you could say it's a reminder."

"Like a charm bracelet?" Crystal whistled. "Weird place to put a charm bracelet, girl. A wrist or an ankle, I can see. But not your neck. If something caught in it, it might rip your head clean off."

"You'd better come," Salsa chirped as she flew down the stairway. She alighted on Crystal's head and looked at me. "I prepared Thorne for the idea that he has a new orphan in his family. He's expecting you to come with Crystal and Oliver. I also told him your first name because he asked."

"You call them a family," I said to Salsa. "Is Thorne adopting them?"

"Just come. All will be explained. Right now I have to collect something for Thorne." Salsa hopped from Crystal's head and flew out the window near the ceiling.

Oliver gestured with a hand. "Let's go. We'll talk more later."

Crystal led the way upstairs with Oliver behind me. While climbing the rickety wooden steps, I tripped on a loose board but kept my balance and continued. The air grew warmer. Sweat trickled down my cheeks, part from the heat and part from nervousness. In seconds I would meet Thorne, a person who sent orphans to work in a dangerous cave. Was he Jaradian? Tauranta? Human?

At the top of the stairs, Crystal opened a door and walked in. I followed, my head and shoulders slightly bowed, attempting a submissive posture. Inside, the air felt cooler, though warmer air followed in my wake until Oliver closed the door behind us.

Crystal strode ahead through the kitchen, staying to the left to avoid a work island at the center of the floor. Against the side wall, two dirty pots stood on a modern cookstove embedded in cabinetry. A wooden lockbox sat on the countertop near the stove, its lid closed, a sturdy padlock fastening the lid in place.

As I followed Crystal, a pleasant aroma of basil and garlic breezed by, promising something tasty. We walked single file into a spacious dining room with a long, dark table that carried myriad dents and scratches on its surface. At least a dozen high-backed wooden chairs surrounded the table, an empty one at the far end as well as the near end, and human children occupied most of the chairs at the sides. A bowl of soup sat in front of each child, vapor rising as they clutched spoons, all eyes trained on me.

I took a quick count—including Oliver and Crystal, there were six boys and six girls, all likely between the ages of six and twelve and all wearing dirty clothes, though their faces and hands were clean, and they appeared to be relatively healthy. Yet one girl, a black-haired wisp of a child, probably no older than six, seemed gaunt. She turned away from my stare and looked at her bowl.

"Cynda?" Crystal said as she walked toward the girl. "Are you all right?"

"I'm okay," Cynda said, barely audible. "Just tired."

Crystal patted the top of her head. "I'll do the sweeping tonight. Go straight to bed after we eat."

Cynda kept her stare on the bowl. "Thank you."

Oliver motioned for me to sit in a chair on one side next to the closer end. When I did, he sat adjacent to me while Crystal sat on the far end.

"Why do you two take those seats?" I asked.

"Oliver and I are the oldest," Crystal said. "We get the ends so we can watch the others."

I looked at the bowl of orange-tinged soup sitting in front of me. Apparently Thorne had placed it there after Salsa told him of my arrival. Yet, there was no empty chair for him. "Where will Thorne sit?"

Several children giggled, some covering their mouths.

I stiffened. "Did I say something wrong?"

When more giggles erupted, Oliver shushed them and looked at me. "Thorne doesn't sit. And he doesn't eat, at least not what humans eat. He's a Willow Wind."

I narrowed my eyes. "What's a Willow Wind?"

"You'll see in a minute." Oliver nodded at the other children. "Go ahead."

The children dipped their spoons into their bowls and slurped the soup. Oliver and Crystal did the same, though they glanced at the other children every few seconds as if watching for rule violations.

I looked around my bowl for a spoon but found nothing. Just as I took a breath to ask for one, a gust rode through the room. A spoon twirled slowly toward me and landed gently on the table near my hand.

"I apologize." The masculine voice emanated from the air. A swirl, tinted with silvery sparkles, tossed my hair and buffeted Oliver's shirt. "I had to find an extra one in a box. New arrivals are usually announced in advance, allowing me time to prepare."

The children paid no attention to the voice or the swirl as they continued eating.

"Are you Thorne?" I asked.

"Indeed I am." The swirl slowed and stood upright between Oliver and me, visible only because of the silvery glitter. His shape and consistency reminded me of the sparkling swirls I had seen in the forest, though their sparkles were white. "What brings you to my home, Megan?" As he spoke, the sparkles gathered around a gap where a man's mouth might normally be, and the hole emitted a stream of sparks with each word. "Lost? Runaway slave?"

I tried not to tremble, but a slight shake invaded my voice. "I . . . I suppose you could say the storm brought me. I was cold and needed a place to get warm."

"Well, that's not a complete answer, but I'm sure you're hungry. Eat the soup, and we'll talk later." In a burst of sparkles and a spinning gust, Thorne breezed out of the room.

Trying again not to be startled by the strangeness of Thorne's appearance, I focused on the soup. As I stirred it with the spoon, corn kernels welled up along with bits of dark-brown meat and unfamiliar orange vegetables sliced into irregular cubes. I slid a spoonful into my mouth, chewed the soft bits for a moment, and swallowed. The soup tickled my tongue with salt, a slight bite of bitterness, and a hint of something sweet. The warmth felt good going down. When I exhaled, the aroma of basil and garlic returned, a pleasant sensation.

I glanced at the children as they ate their portions. Although they all looked somewhat thin, they weren't malnourished, and the food tasted good. Since Thorne didn't whip them, maybe living here wasn't too bad.

When the children finished, Oliver nodded toward Crystal. "Your turn to supervise."

"I know. I know." She rose and clapped her hands. "Let's go. Do your evening chores, then wash your clothes and go to bed."

Most of the children collected their bowls and spoons and scampered from the room. One little boy clumped along in shoes that were much too large for his feet, forcing him to wear several pairs of socks to compensate. The shoes had short spikes on the soles, though they left no marks on the hardwood floor.

Cynda, however, stayed in her seat, staring straight ahead.

Crystal took Cynda's hand. "You look awful. I'll help you get ready for bed."

Cynda toppled from her chair and fell to the floor.

"Cynda!" Crystal knelt next to her. "What's wrong?"

Oliver leaped up and helped Crystal lift Cynda back to the chair. "Check her for stings."

While he held Cynda in place, Crystal peeled Cynda's shirt over her head, exposing her thin torso. Crystal ran a hand along Cynda's back and stopped near her waist. "Blazes! She got stung right here."

"Where the armored plates meet." Oliver set a palm over the wound. "Yep. It's hot. She must have bent over at the wrong time."

Crystal stomped her foot. "Claw of the Dragon! What are we going to do?"

"There's only one thing to do." Oliver hurried through the kitchen toward the door. "Hold her. I'll get the rope."

He jerked the door open and ran down the stairway toward the furnace room.

"Help me hold her." Crystal pinned one of Cynda's wrists to the chair arm. "I might not be able to do it alone."

"Um . . . sure." I rushed over and held the other wrist. "But she's a tiny little girl. Why do you need—"

Cynda stiffened. Her eyes opened wide. She jerked her head from side to side, snarling.

Crystal gritted her teeth. "Just hang on. And don't let her bite you."

"Why would she—" Cynda snapped at my nose. I dodged just in time. While I held her wrist in place, I leaned away from her mouth as far as I could. "What's going on?"

"Bramble bee poison. If we don't treat a sting right away, this happens."

Cynda glared at me with bloodshot eyes and barked like a vicious dog. Then she howled like a wolf.

"How long will she do this?"

Crystal grunted as she held on. "It depends. Sometimes minutes. Sometimes hours." She shouted toward the door. "Oliver! Where's that rope?"

"Here!" He dashed in carrying a coil of fibrous rope. "It wasn't in the usual place."

While Crystal and I held Cynda, Oliver bound her wrists to the chair arms and her ankles to the legs. When he finished, he stepped back and pulled me with him. Crystal backed away as well.

Cynda clenched her fists and fought against the rope. Again she snarled and barked, then spat at us, every moment jerking the chair and making the legs thud on the floor. "I hate you," she shouted. "I hate you all."

Crystal stepped closer and stroked Cynda's dark hair while staying out of reach of her snapping jaws. "Shush, dear girl. You don't mean that. We've been friends ever since you got here."

Cynda's face twisted. As her bare chest heaved, she spoke in a squeaky whine. "I know . . . It just . . . hurts so much."

"I'm so sorry, Cynda." Crystal's lips quivered. "Will you drink the tea if I make it?"

Cynda swallowed hard and nodded.

Oliver whispered, "The tea will knock her out, but we'll have to leave her tied up. She could start having fits again."

A lump swelled in my throat. "There's no way to save her?"

"Nothing that we know of. She'll get real bad chest pains and have a hard time breathing, but at least she'll be unconscious when that happens." Oliver grasped my wrist. "Let's go downstairs. You don't have to watch this. Crystal can handle it."

"All right." As Oliver led me to the door, I looked back. Poor Cynda stared at me, moaning, her eyes begging for relief, for escape, for a merciful end to her torment, but I couldn't do a thing to help her, and the thought crushed my heart.

After closing the door, I followed him down the steps toward the furnace room. Cynda's plaintive cries followed, as if lashing my back with a whip. But I couldn't let her pain make me suffer. None of this was my fault, and I was helpless to change it. I just had to concentrate on getting Oliver and me out of here.

When we reached the furnace level, we sat facing each other in front of the fire. He kicked off his spiked shoes and crossed his legs, his eager stare locked on me. "Okay. Thorne will be back soon, so we need to talk."

I glanced up the stairs. Cynda's cries had quieted. Maybe Crystal had already given her the tea. "It's kind of hard forgetting about Cynda."

"I know. That's why I'm trying to get our minds off her. Don't worry. Crystal's done this before."

"All right." I focused on him. "What do you want to talk about?"

His features tightened as he gave me a hard stare. "Where's my father, and why didn't he come with you?"

I spoke slowly, trying to tell the truth but dodging the whole truth. "We had an accident. And the ship needed a lot of repairs. I came into Bassolith to get the new relay switch, and I thought I'd look around for you at the same time. Then the storm hit, and I got stuck here."

Oliver nodded, an agreeable expression on his face. "What do you do on the ship? Cook? Galley cleaning?"

"A boy named Dirk does that. I'm a mechanic. A maintenance assistant."

Oliver blinked. "Someone as young as you?"

"I'm small, even for my age, so I can crawl through the shafts and do the dangerous stuff the droids normally do. Since I'm smarter than a droid, I'm better at it. And the crew members say I'm expendable. They don't care if I die or get hurt doing the job."

Oliver's face hardened. "Are you saying my father puts your life at risk because you're more expendable than a droid?"

"Yes . . . I mean, no. I mean, he isn't my boss. A lieutenant named Dionne told me—"

"Don't sweat it." Oliver waved a hand. "I'm just trying to figure everything out."

"Figure what out?"

"My father . . . he's not exactly . . ." Oliver shook his head. "I don't know how to say it."

"He's not thoughtful of other people?" I winced, hoping that wasn't too harsh.

"I guess so." Oliver pinched a splinter of wood from the floor and slung it into the furnace with more than the usual force. "After my mother died, he never said much to me. I guess I'm not surprised he doesn't care about what you do."

"He cared enough to keep me out of a labor camp."

His brow lifted. "A labor camp? Are you some kind of criminal?"

"The Alliance thinks so, but I'll save that story for later. Your father talked the judge into letting me come on the mission to find you. Maintenance work is more useful than digging through rocks."

"But you're a kid. Why did he think you could do maintenance?"

I averted my eyes for a moment before looking at him again. "I . . . um . . . did the same work on my parents' ship."

Oliver's eyes widened. "Really? What were they? Freight trans-porters?"

"Sort of. We did transport stuff. Small loads. Like weapons and money."

"So you did military transport. That's pretty exciting."

"Yeah. We transported military stuff, and I learned how to fix and run every part of the ship."

His brow scrunched. "Wait a minute. If you're a mechanic on the *Nine*, why didn't you stay to help with repairs?"

I cleared my throat, trying to buy time to invent a lie. "I'm an assistant. Dionne sent me here for the part I mentioned."

Oliver pointed at my belt. "What does that flashing light mean?"

I looked at the remote-control unit. A little bulb near the trigger button flashed red. The collar knew I was lying.

"Um . . ." Heat filtered into my cheeks. I had told hundreds of lies before, but telling one to Oliver felt different. He was my friend. I needed him to trust me. "I . . . I have something to tell you."

He smiled. "Your crime, right? I've been wondering what you did."

I nodded. "My crime and something else. The light means I lied to you. Get ready for the truth. You won't like it."

My story spilled out like a flood. I told him about my role as a so-called pirate from the time I was little, what happened to my parents, how I got collared and his father took me aboard the *Nine*, the attack from the *Astral Dragon*, the loss of most of the crew, and how I honored the dead with a ceremonial burning. The only secret I held back was the dragon's eye.

When I finished, he stared at me quietly, tears glistening in his eyes.

"Anyway . . ." I glanced at the remote. The light had stopped flashing. "I thought you deserved to know."

His chin quivered. The sadness in the air felt thick and heavy. Then he tilted his head a bit. "Wait a minute. So your mother attacked an Alliance ship and killed nearly everyone on board?"

I nodded, giving him a mournful expression. "I can't explain it. I guess she got into good-guy-versus-bad-guy mode. You know, whatever it took to rescue me."

"I get that, but who are the good guys, and who are the bad guys?"

I blinked. "What do you mean? The bad guys are . . ." I let the thought die. I knew where he was going, but my hesitation gave him an opening.

His tone sharpened. "Look, your parents used you. Whoever heard of a decent mother who'd let her kid do dangerous stuff like you do? And for what? Yeah, she'd say to stop tyrants, or free slaves, or something like that. Trust me, I know what it's like. I heard my dad make up excuses tons of times. No matter what he wanted to do, even if it sounded like the most awful thing in history, he managed to come up with an excuse to make it sound good."

I bit my lip hard. A chorus of defenses for my parents' behavior flew to mind, but they sounded lame. I had no answers.

Oliver pointed at my collar. "I'll bet my father even made excuses about torturing you with that thing."

I touched the collar and whispered, "Yeah. He did."

"It figures." Oliver raised a hand. "Listen, I don't mean to bad-mouth your parents. I'm just saying that maybe we shouldn't trust anyone. Besides ourselves, I mean. You and me."

I touched my chest. "Why do you trust me? I lied to you just a minute ago. And I'm a convicted criminal."

"Who risked her life to come and find me. I know getting the relay switch was your first reason to come to the city, but you were also planning to find me. Your lie detector stayed dark while you told that part. You didn't have to look for me at all."

"Yeah, well, I kinda *did* have to. I mean, since your father died, who else would? Right?"

"No one. That's my point. You did do it. That's why I trust you." Tears again glimmering, he blew a heavy sigh. "I don't know how else to explain it, all right? Let's just change the subject."

"That's fine." I tapped my chin with a finger. "What else do you want to know? Something about your father, maybe?"

"No. Not him." He forced a trembling smile. "How about Emerson? Is he still on the *Nine*? I tried getting that old chipster to break a rule a hundred times, but he never would."

"Yep. That's Emerson. Rules rule his world."

"I had so much fun on that ship. Well . . . a lot of the time." As Oliver looked at me, his smile slowly faded. More tears welled. He brushed one away and cleared his throat. "Okay. Um . . . now we need a plan to escape."

"Escape? So you really *are* prisoners here."

"Well, we're not allowed to leave unless we're on the bus to the mine. Thorne locks us in at night, so, yeah, we're pretty much prisoners."

"What about the other kids? What would we do with them?"

"Shhh." Oliver looked toward the steps. "Thorne's coming."

In a rush of swirling wind, silver sparkles cascaded down the stairway carrying a folded sheet of paper that landed on the floor next to me. When Thorne settled into a slowly spinning column at my side, a fresh stream of sparkles spewed from his mouth. "What is this all about?"

I picked up the paper and unfolded it while Oliver scooted close and looked over my shoulder. It was the leaflet with my photo.

Oliver read the note out loud. "Reward of one thousand mesots for the live capture of this runaway pirate. If you apprehend her, bring her to the ironworks factory foreman for your reward."

Edging out of Thorne's view, Oliver winked at me. "A pirate? Her? That's crazy. It's gotta be some kind of scam."

"A scam, you say?" Thorne's sparkles caressed my collar. "I noticed this device earlier and asked a factory worker about it. It's a prisoner collar, right?"

I pressed my lips together and nodded, hoping he wouldn't notice the remote clipped to my belt.

"So you're a pirate?"

"No." A lump swelled in my throat. I swallowed, the collar tightening for a moment. "Like Oliver said, it's crazy to think I'm a pirate."

A finger of swirling air pointed at the page. "Isn't that a photograph of you?"

I nodded again. "I was arrested for piracy, and they put a collar on me, but I'm not a pirate. I never was."

"Pirates never think of themselves as pirates." A sparkling hand snatched the page and wadded it into a tight ball. "It seems that someone dropped you off here for the night and hopes to come back for the reward when the foreman arrives in the morning. While we wait for that to happen, you will stay in the furnace room until I have a chance to speak to him. I will soon learn what is afoot here." His swirl tightened into a faster spin. "Oliver. Let's go."

When Oliver rose, Thorne's cyclonic air enveloped his arm and pulled him toward the stairway. Forced by the wind flow, he stumbled up the steps and disappeared above.

The door slammed. I ran up the stairs, but a lock clicked before I could get to the top.

"Salsa!" Thorne shouted from beyond the door. "Where are you? I need you to fly an errand for me."

Silence ensued. The rising heat drew new sweat, dampening my shirt. I walked down the stairs and tried the exit door again. It was locked, as expected.

I leaned against the wall next to the door and slid to the floor. What now? With no way to escape, what should be my next step? Would I have to stay in this furnace room all night?

My thoughts returned to Cynda and her terrible suffering. The poor little girl was probably going to die tonight, all because of Thorne's selfishness. I could deal with a little loneliness . . . a little pain . . . a little darkness. Not knowing what might be coming next seemed nothing compared to the certainty of a horrific death.

After a few minutes, my bladder prodded me. I rose and looked around, guided by firelight from the furnace. A small room housed a pitcher filled with water on a tiny table as well as a basin and towel. A chamber pot sat on the floor.

I used the pot and washed in the basin, then drank my fill from the pitcher. When I exited to the main room, Perdantus flew down from the window and landed on my shoulder. "Salsa told me about your plight. I spoke to Thorne on your behalf, telling him that you are the victim in this ordeal, not the perpetrator. He is no longer angry, but he is still suspicious and wants you to stay in this room until morning."

"Thanks, Perdantus." I looked at the window. "Where's Salsa?"

"Thorne sent her to summon the foreman. On her way to fulfill that summons, she told me of your predicament and asked me to discuss the matter with Thorne. I have more experience dealing with issues like this, that is, trying to persuade non-birds to act in a civilized manner."

"Salsa told me you're a negotiator. It's good to have you around." He bowed his head. "And it's my pleasure to help you."

"Well, thanks again." I scanned the room for something soft to sleep on, but only stacked crates and firewood lay in view. "I guess I'll just sack out on the floor and worry about everything later."

"Others have stayed here. Look behind the crates. You will find a mattress stuffed with straw and a blanket. Both are quite thin and have a number of holes, but I think you will find them more suitable than the bare floor." He looked up at the window. "The storm has finally ended, but the cold is just beginning. I suggest that you sleep close to the furnace, but not too close. Straw catches fire easily. I will check on your status later."

"Great. Thank you, Perdantus."

"You are quite welcome." He flew to the window and disappeared in the darkness.

After finding the mattress and blanket, I dragged them to the open floor in front of the furnace. I folded the blanket into a pillow, removed the collar's remote, and set it gently on the floor. I curled on my side and looked at the fire, resting my entire body for the first time since I awoke this morning.

So much had happened. I was too tired to mentally list everything. But one event again burst to the forefront of my mind. Back on the *Nebula Nine*, my mother said through the commlink, *Get on board now. We're going after her.*

Regardless of Gavin's motivations, my mother wanted to find me. Eventually she would see through his schemes and figure out where I was. Maybe she would get close enough to detect the *Nine*'s low-power distress call. Since Emerson had disabled Gavin's ability to control the ship, it would stay in place until I returned. Unless, of course, he already found it and somehow destroyed it.

Then another thought overwhelmed the others. My father was dead. And I missed him so much. When we all slept together on the ship, he would always be the last one to come to bed. I'll never forget the nightly soft kiss on my forehead before he settled down with a tired sigh. The forehead kiss, our family's tradition that sealed our oneness, always woke me up, but I didn't care. Knowing he lay nearby was worth it. We were together. Nothing else mattered.

Letting out a sigh of my own, I pushed the thoughts away and closed my eyes. I needed sleep. Only with a clear mind could I unravel all the mysteries and figure out how to escape this place, assuming Thorne and this unnamed foreman decided to keep me locked up.

Soon, exhaustion overwhelmed me, and everything fell into darkness, then into a lifelike dream. Dressed in coveralls that I sometimes wore while working on the *Astral Dragon*, I sat near the furnace where the real Astral Dragon appeared to me in the fire. In the dream, he crawled out of the furnace and sat next to me on his haunches. Completely white and sparkling in the fire's glow, he stared at me with piercing eyes, now blue instead of red. He said nothing. I said nothing. And that was okay. My parents always sang the praises of his goodness. Having him next to me was all I needed.

After what seemed like only a few minutes, a creaking noise penetrated my mind. I opened my eyes. Oliver walked down the last three stairway steps carrying Cynda in his arms, her limbs dangling limply and the rope dragging behind her, one end still tied to her wrist.

I sat up with a start. "Is she . . . ?" I couldn't finish. I already knew the answer.

He nodded. "No one's ever survived a bramble bee sting, at least no one I've ever heard about."

"I'm so sorry."

"Yeah. Me too. She was a good kid." He laid her on the floor, knelt at her feet, and began removing her oversized shoes.

I refastened the remote to my belt, scooted close, and knelt next to him. "What are you doing?"

"Getting her ready for the furnace. Her clothes can burn, but these shoes cost too much. Thorne always saves them."

My stomach knotted. "You just toss her in the fire? No funeral or anything?"

"Right." After setting the shoes aside, he coiled the rope on her stomach and looked at me. "Listen. It's bad in this place. We lose kids way too often, eight since I've been here. Cynda's the ninth, six to the bees and three to diseases. Thorne says to take it in stride. Death is part of life. No funerals. No tears. Just keep moving."

"That's . . ." An obscenity crept to mind, but I chased it away. "That's so cruel."

"Tell me about it." Oliver stared at Cynda, moving his lips as if praying. After a quiet moment, he brushed a tear from his cheek. "I think I'd rather be whipped than have to do this."

"Are you always the one to throw a dead kid into the furnace?"

"Always." He untied the rope from Cynda's wrist and laid the coil to the side. "Because I'm the oldest and biggest. It's easier for me to carry someone down here. Another reason is I never get sick, so if a kid dies from a disease, Thorne doesn't worry that I'll catch it. You know, from germs on the dead kid's skin or clothes."

"You never get sick?"

"Not since I can remember. My father told me I didn't get sick when I was little either." He slid his hands under Cynda's back. "You don't have to watch if you don't want to."

"Wait." I touched his arm. "Let me do it."

He shook his head. "Trust me. It's terrible."

"I know. I've burned bodies before. Remember?"

I waited for the light to come on in his eyes. Finally, he nodded. "All right."

"Good. Now go to bed. I'm sure you haven't gotten much sleep."

"I can't go to bed. I have to tell you something." He sat cross-legged between me and Cynda, his expression tight. "We've got trouble. Thorne talked to the foreman, a Jaradian named Axleback, and I sneaked close and listened. Looks like Axleback's been in on a plot for a long time. The Jaradians who kidnapped me put me here and told Axleback to keep watch. They're supposed to return when they get something done. One of them asked about a ransom, and another said there never was any ransom. That wasn't the reason they kidnapped me, but I couldn't get any more clues about that."

I sat in front of him. "No ransom, and they parked you here all this time. That doesn't make any sense. What do they want from you?"

"No idea. I'm just a kid. And almost too big to work for Thorne, but he wants me to stay. I'm like a supervisor."

"So you're trapped. This place really *is* a prison for you."

He pointed at me. "And for you. They need something from you. I think he called it a dragon's eye."

"A dragon's eye?" Although I thought I could trust Oliver, it would be better if he stayed in the dark about the locket. Then no one could force him to reveal that secret. I stealthily covered the remote's light with my hand. "What's a dragon's eye?"

Oliver shrugged. "I have no idea, but Axleback thinks you know."

"Why would he think that?" I shook my head. "Never mind. You don't know."

"One thing I do know is that you'd better escape tonight. Axleback said . . ." Oliver altered his voice to a deep growl. "She will tell me where it is in the morning or suffer like no human has ever suffered before."

I shuddered. "He speaks Humaniversal?"

"Yeah. Barely. You have to listen hard to understand."

"All right. So I have to escape. But how?" I rose and looked around for a panel that might open to a hidden passageway, but the walls seemed solid. No gaps anywhere. "Where's the best hiding place in this building?"

Oliver climbed to his feet and stood at my side. "You can't hide from Thorne. Since he's just a glittering wind, he can go anywhere. And this building's got only three floors—this one, the kitchen and eating area, and the dorms at the top."

I looked up, imagining the layout. "What if we could get to another building in the factory?"

"Lots of places to hide, but you can't get to them from in here." He nodded toward the window. "Unless you want to jump to your death."

I cringed. "Not especially."

"Then we'd better come up with another plan pretty soon. It won't be long till dawn."

"Ahem."

The sound came from the stairway. Crystal stood barefoot on the bottom step, her arms crossed, pressing her thin, ankle-length nightgown against her chest as she looked at Cynda's body. "I saw she wasn't in the chair. I hoped maybe she recovered, but I guess it was stupid to hope for a miracle."

Oliver lifted Cynda's hand and caressed her knuckles. "Miracles don't happen here."

"No. Never." Crystal walked toward us, her sparkling eyes fixed on Oliver. She stared at him for a long moment, then at me, then at him again. "You're hiding something. You know you can't lie to me, Oliver."

"I know. I know. Your magic powers." He gave me an apologetic look. "She knows when people are lying or keeping secrets. Not like she can read minds or anything. She just knows."

Crystal forked her fingers at us. "And you two are keeping a secret from me, aren't you?"

Oliver lowered his head, apparently afraid to look into Crystal's hypnotizing eyes. "We're planning to escape."

"Escape? You've been talking about that for months and nothing ever happens." Crystal shot a skeptical stare at me. "There's more. A lot more. Spill it, girl."

"All right. Here goes." I gave her a quick summary of what I told Oliver and explained our hope to sneak to the *Nebula Nine* and fly away. As with Oliver, I avoided telling her about the dragon's eye.

When I finished, she cocked her head, her stare still in place. "You're leaving out something important."

I nodded. "That's because there are things you don't need to know."

"Right, Crystal," Oliver said. "We all have secrets. I'll bet you wouldn't want Megan to know everything about you."

"No, I wouldn't." Crystal looked away. "And you'd better not tell her anything."

"All right. I'll keep your secrets if you'll keep ours. We're escaping today."

She crossed her arms again, more tightly this time. "I'll keep your secret. I'll even help you. But only if you take me with you."

"What?" Oliver shook his head. "We can't take every orphan in the factory. We'd get caught for sure."

"Who said anything about every orphan? Just me. After seeing what happened to Cynda, I don't want to be next. It's the worst possible way to die."

"But everyone would want to go," Oliver said. "What's so special about you?"

"I have magic powers that'll help us escape." Crystal jabbed a finger at him. "What's so special about *you*?"

"I was kidnapped, and the escape ship is my father's."

"Which one of us *wasn't* kidnapped? I was stolen from my mother when I was six. And who cares about whose ship it is? Does that make you better than the rest of us?"

Just as Oliver opened his mouth to shoot back, I held my hands up. "Wait. Stop arguing."

While they glared at each other, I took a breath and continued. "Crystal's right. Her powers can help us. And no one's more important than anyone else. The three of us can try to escape and then figure out how to rescue the others later."

"There." Crystal pointed at me. "That's good thinking. And Vonda can look after the girls after we leave. Bastian can watch the boys."

"I know," Oliver said, "but three escaping will be harder than two. We'll have to come up with a perfect plan."

I pointed at myself. "I've sneaked in and out of lots of places, and you two know more about this planet than I do. It's way better to have all three of us."

"Yeah." Crystal lifted her nose with a snobbish air. "And we're smart enough to outwit those stupid Jaradians. They're dumber than dingleberries." As she straightened her pose, her brow knitted. "Not Axleback, though. He's scary smart."

"Do any Jaradians know how to speak Alpha One?" I asked.

Crystal shook her head. "Some of them barely understand Humaniversal. Like I said, dumber than—"

"Dingleberries. I heard." I looked at Oliver. "I assume you know Alpha One."

He nodded. "I wasn't born there, but I lived there most of my life, at least whenever I wasn't on the ship with my parents."

"Oh? Where were you born?"

He smiled. "On the *Nine*. During an expedition. We were on our way to Gamma Five."

"Really? Then you're a space brat."

"Yeah. I heard that nickname way too many times. Even my father called me that sometimes."

I turned toward Crystal. "And do you know Alpha One?"

"Pretty well. I need help with some words."

"Good enough. We'll talk to each other in Alpha One. That'll help us keep secrets." I switched to that language and added, "Now let's put our heads together and come up with a plan."

Crystal laid an arm around each of us and pulled us closer until our heads touched. "Like this?"

I laughed. "Sure, but I'll have to be careful about using Alpha One idioms around you."

"Yeah, you're right about that." She blinked. "What's an idiom?"

11

After we settled on a plan and Oliver and Crystal went back upstairs, I gazed at Cynda's corpse, still lying on the concrete floor. Our trio had been talking for quite a while, trying to ignore the lurking shadow of death, and the sky was starting to pale. The children would be arriving soon for the day's work. Whether I had pushed my duty to the side intentionally or not, now it was time to face it head-on. I had to shove her little body into the flames.

I sat next to her and lifted her limp hand. As I imagined the process, tears crept in. How could I toss her away like a bundle of trash? She was a human being. Sacred. Obviously not to Thorne or other slavers, but she was a treasure to the Astral Dragon, someone he created for a purpose. And it seemed like that purpose had been left unfulfilled.

Now fully crying, I turned away. I couldn't do it. Not yet. I had to think about something else until I could muster the courage to suck it up and get the job done. Maybe thinking about our escape plan would occupy me for a while.

I looked at the window near the ceiling. Our plan called for me to gather crates, stack them next to the window, and lower myself out the window using rope we had tied Cynda with. At least I could get the process started by tying the rope in place. That would give me an excuse to avoid burning Cynda for a little while.

I climbed to my feet, stalked to a stack of empty crates, and gave it a hefty shove, toppling it. At this point, I didn't care about the noise. If Thorne investigated, I would tell him off. Maybe I was inviting that opportunity.

After knocking over two more stacks of crates, I lugged them one at a time to the window, restacking them into a staircase against the wall. When I finished, I picked up the rope, climbed to the window, and looked outside.

While the furnace's heat rode up my body, cold wind from the window buffeted my face. Light from the fire painted a quivering glow on another brick-and-mortar building about two body lengths in front of me. Below, darkness veiled the ground. How far might the drop be? Probably no farther than from the window to the floor inside.

I tied one end of the rope to the window's gear lever, dropped the other end outside, and listened for it to hit bottom. No sound returned. Since it was just a rope and not something heavier, the wind probably masked the impact.

Needing to find something bigger to test the drop, I climbed down to the floor and looked around. When my gaze met my makeshift staircase, I paused. Something was wrong. This way of escape was too easy, too obvious. Oliver said that they normally kept the rope in this room, and the crates seemed designed to be stacked this way, as if someone had created a puzzle and left the pieces lying around to be assembled.

But why?

I grabbed a small log, climbed the stack of crates, and poked my head outside. I dropped the log and listened again. After a couple of seconds, something crackled. The log burst into flames and burned in place, illuminating the area around it.

It lay on a long, narrow grating that extended into darkness to the left and to the right, some kind of burning channel with a powerful heating source beneath it, probably part of the metal-refining process.

At the thought of dropping to that channel myself, I cringed. Thorne wasn't worried about anyone escaping this way. In fact, he invited it. It seemed that if slaves were daring or stubborn enough to attempt it, he didn't want to keep them around. He needed compliant workers, not kids who would try to escape.

The idea cast a new shadow on Thorne's character. Even if he didn't whip his slaves, they were slaves nonetheless, children risking their lives to collect glowsap for a reason only he knew. If they got stung by a bramble bee, no big deal. They were expendable.

I sat on the top crate and scanned the room from my lofty perch. What now? For our plan to work, I had to get on the bus. If I stayed here instead of climbing out the window, my only hope was to create a distraction the moment they opened the door to let the orphans out.

Maybe I could make Thorne or Axleback think that I had tried to escape and died in the process, but would a dangling rope and a stack of crates be enough to convince them? Probably not.

As I looked around the room for another idea, my gaze fell on my feet. Since my magnetic shoes had so much metal inside, they would be a perfect decoy. Although going without shoes in the icy weather would risk frostbite again, no other workable plan came to mind.

I slipped the shoes off and dropped them out the window. The moment they thudded onto the grate, they ignited. Soon, the outer material burned away, exposing the metal lining. Seconds later, only shoe-shaped metal remained, glowing with intense heat.

I drew a mental image of myself burning in the fire, flames crawling across my clothes, but a hard shudder swept the thought away. How long would an entire body take to burn? The corpses of my shipmates burned for a long time, and the charred bones had to be crushed by the droid. If Thorne and Axleback couldn't find bones down there, they wouldn't believe the deception.

Yet, there was a way to take care of that problem.

Now with only socks on my feet, I climbed down to the floor again and hurried to Cynda's body. After gazing at her face for a moment, pallid and peaceful, I averted my eyes and pretended that she was a dead animal. I was lying to myself, of course, but this was the only way I could stomach my task.

I lifted her into my arms and carried her to the staircase. Grunting with the effort, I hauled her to the top and propped her on the windowsill in a slouched sitting position. The pose made the reality of what I was about to do come roaring back. She was a human being, not an animal, a toiling laborer for someone else's benefit. And now I was using her for my own benefit.

I gritted my teeth. What was I supposed to do? Take care of Cynda's body like she was still alive? Would that fulfill my purpose to have compassion for these child slaves? Not really. She was dead, and if I couldn't escape to help Oliver and Crystal, then other slaves would suffer. Cynda's suffering was over.

As new tears erupted, I set my lips next to her ear and whispered, "I'm so sorry, Cynda. I'm so, so sorry."

I rolled her out and looked down. She fell on top of my shoes and instantly burst into flames. Soon, nothing remained but her bones.

A sob crept up from my gut. I swallowed it down, drew my head back inside, and sat on the top crate. I bit my fist and wept quietly. Poor Cynda. She was so young, a lost child probably scared every day of getting stung, always wondering why she had to be in this awful place, so far from home, from her parents, if they were even alive.

And now Cynda was dead, killed by the hideous monster that haunted her. Could life be any worse than this?

I shook my head. No. This place was the worst of nightmares. Who could stand living in fear for so long?

A blaze rekindling in my mind, I rose and looked out the window again. A few embers allowed a glimpse of scorched bones and glowing shoes but little else. I whispered through tight lips, "I couldn't rescue you, Cynda, but I'm coming back to get your brothers and sisters. I won't abandon any of them. I promise."

With new energy flexing my muscles, I hopped down the crates to floor level and searched for a place to hide while waiting for the door to open. The stack of crates was too obvious, and the furnace was the only other object big enough to conceal me—way too hot for that.

My scan fell across the blanket next to the mattress. That might work. I dragged the blanket to the lowest crate, lifted the lid, and crawled inside, letting the lid drop over me. Now curled in the blanket and cramped by the crate's slats, I adjusted the remote at my hip to make sure nothing could bump against the trigger.

I peered through a hole in the material and a gap between two slats while I waited for the plan to proceed. Since Oliver and Crystal didn't know I hadn't climbed out the window, they would have to improvise along with me. They were smart. They would figure it out soon enough, especially since I was supposed to kick the crates over from the windowsill to hide my getaway scheme. When they noticed the stairway still standing, they would know that I had changed the plan.

After several minutes, the kids tromped down the stairs with Oliver in front of the line and Crystal at the rear, each carrying a small bag. Wearing coats and gloves, they gathered near the door. Thorne swirled down the stairs and joined them.

"I heard about Cynda," he said in a loud, echoing voice as the children watched him. "But have no fear. She was the first to die in many days. From what I was told, this tragedy could have been prevented. A bramble bee stung her between the plates of her armor.

"As I have told you a hundred times, you must never bend forward without watching for bees. Cynda ignored that warning. Her death was the result of her own carelessness. If you follow the safety precautions, the same will not happen to you." His silvery sparkles continued swirling as he paused for effect. "Do you understand?"

They all nodded, their expressions blank.

I suppressed a growl. Thorne didn't care a whit about Cynda or any of these kids. He cared only about getting glowsap. He was a monster, a windy, selfish monster.

Oliver's eyes narrowed as he looked past Thorne toward me. He stepped close to Crystal and whispered. She, too, looked my way. They had seen the crate staircase and maybe my crate moving slightly. I had to keep still and quiet.

The exit door unlocked and opened, letting dawn's light inside. A huge Jaradian walked in, dressed in body armor, including heavy boots and a metallic vest, probably Axleback. He spoke in a growl that my earpiece failed to translate. I mentally repeated the guttural sounds and came up with, "Where are Oliver Tillman and Megan Willis?" His Humaniversal was awful. I would have to work hard to get used to it.

Oliver raised a hand. "I'm here, but I have no idea where Megan went."

Thorne's sparkles spewed from his swirl. "What? How could she have gone anywhere? Every door is locked."

Oliver pointed toward the window near the ceiling. "That's not locked."

Everyone turned. Axleback stalked toward me and stepped on my crate, bending the lid and nearly cracking my back. The pressure lifted, and the crunching sounds above meant that he had climbed to the top of my staircase.

He roared, this time in a language my earpiece translated. "Tell the security guard to turn off the fires. We need to investigate the refining channel. Someone climbed down a rope and burned at the bottom. I see bones and metal shoes."

Crystal wailed, "Oh, Megan! Why did you try to escape?"

"Do you see the dragon's eye?" Thorne said to Axleback.

"No, but it might be covered by her remains."

"No need to stop the fires," Thorne said. "I can investigate without risk." He swirled out the door.

Above, tromping sounds followed. Axleback's weight again bent my crate's lid, this time cracking the thin wood. Pain roared across my ribs. A grunt tried to escape, but I held it in.

Axleback marched to Oliver and pointed a scaly finger at his face. "You stay here. Send the other children to the mine. I will deal with you when I return." He stormed out the door.

The moment he was gone, I burst out of the crate, set the lid back in place, and ran to Oliver and Crystal, making shushing noises to keep anyone from crying out.

Oliver waved a hand and hissed, "Everyone on the bus. Now."

When the kids began filing out the door, I blended into the line at the eighth position. Oliver hurried to my side and whispered, "When you get on the bus, go to the back. I'll be there in a minute. I have to get Cynda's shoes for you."

I looked down at my sock-covered feet. They might get soaked if I walked on anything icy. As I exited behind a dark-skinned boy of similar height, I reached down, peeled off my socks, and stuffed them into my pants pocket. I kept my head low. Since I was the only kid without a coat, I might be noticeable, but it couldn't be helped.

Outside, a stiff breeze chilled my skin, but after my frigid journey here with Gavin, it didn't seem too cold, especially since the furnace had warmed me to the core.

The black bus sat about fifty paces down the street, parked at the curb. The pavement appeared to be too icy to travel closer. As I walked toward it with the others, I looked around. Jaradians and Taurantas hustled along the walkways, many toward the factory, probably employees there. A few modern fusion-engine buses traveled the street, but no personal vehicles.

When we arrived at the bus, its side door opened, revealing two steps to climb to get in. A graying Jaradian sat in the driver's seat, a clipboard in hand. He called out in his language, "I don't care how cold it is today. You know the drill. State your name and worker number. We won't skip any steps."

I sucked in a frosty breath. Worker number? I didn't have one. I could pretend to be Cynda, but I had no idea what her number was.

When the first child in line climbed the steps and announced his name and number, Perdantus landed on one of my shoulders and Salsa on the other. Perdantus whispered in his chirping language, "Oliver sent us to you. Thorne and Axleback are arguing about whether or not you're dead. Thorne believes the bones outside the window belong to another girl, but Axleback thinks humans are not smart enough to devise such a brilliant plan. I advise you to butt in line before one of them comes out here. Since you're not dressed for the cold weather, and you're the only child wearing a collar, you are quite noticeable. I will distract the driver while Salsa tries to delay Thorne."

I unfastened the remote from my belt, slid it into my pocket, and whispered in return, "I need Cynda's worker number."

"I will try to get that for you," Salsa said.

"Good. I can't butt in line until I have it. I'll get to the bus too fast."

"I will hurry." Salsa took off toward the factory door, and Perdantus flew into the bus.

Ahead, three children had boarded, and the fourth, a redheaded girl, taller than the others, climbed the steps and spoke to the driver. "Vonda. Worker number eight, six, three, three."

After her, only three more children waited to report before my turn. If Salsa didn't arrive soon, I would be sunk.

Perdantus perched on the driver's shoulder. "Erdath, are you worried that the roads ahead might be treacherous for this ancient vehicle?"

Erdath grunted. "Not really. The storm was bad, but it should warm up quickly. And I have chains on the tires. I'll be fine."

The next child reported, a small boy with dark hair and big, protruding ears. "Norbert. Nine, one, zero, seven."

Erdath checked a box on his clipboard. "Next."

A little girl with ragged, shoulder-length light-brown hair climbed aboard. "Renalda. Nine, two, one, one."

"I checked your route ahead," Perdantus said. "I think you can make it through, though you will have to dodge some icy spots."

Erdath half closed an eye. "Since when do you fly scouting reports for me?"

Perdantus spread his wings. "This is my first time. What do you think of the service?"

"Suits me. As long as I don't have to pay for it." Erdath focused on the clipboard again. "Next."

The boy in front of me stepped up. I searched the sky. No sign of Salsa.

"Bastian," the boy said. "Eight, nine, five, eight."

I mentally ran through the list of numbers. They had a pattern based on child age and gender, but I didn't have enough data yet to be sure of Cynda's.

Salsa landed on my shoulder, breathing heavily. "Oliver doesn't know Cynda's number. Neither does Crystal. You're on your own. I have to return to distract Thorne and Axleback. They are examining the bones of the girl who died."

When Salsa flew away, Erdath called, "Next."

Perdantus chirped loudly in a rapid-fire cadence. "I know some birds are untrustworthy, but I hope to provide helpful service to other species whenever possible. I expect no payment, of course, but I hope for an occasional—"

"Shut up!" Erdath batted Perdantus off his shoulder.

While Perdantus fluttered around to find a new perch, I climbed the steps and said, "Cynda." Then I mumbled a guess based on the earlier numbers. "Eight, zero, six, six."

Erdath stared at his clipboard. "What?"

"Five, five," Perdantus said as he flew past my ear, then out the door.

I nodded. "Cynda. Eight, zero, five, five."

Erdath checked a box. "Next."

I hurried down the narrow aisle toward the back of the bus. Perdantus must have read my number off the clipboard sheet. He was proving to be a great ally.

As I passed the six rows of seats, the other children stared quietly. Oliver had probably warned them not to breathe a word about seeing me. When I reached the final row, I sat on the rear bench and hunkered down while peering over the back of the seat in front of me.

A few moments later, Crystal boarded, gave her name and number, and strode quickly to my row. When she sat next to me, she whispered, "Thorne convinced Axleback that those are Cynda's bones in the refining trench. We have to hide you."

Seconds later, Oliver reported his name and number and joined us, carrying the blanket I had taken with me into the crate. "Erdath didn't even notice," he said as he handed me a pair of shoes. "They're Cynda's. See if they fit."

I pulled the socks from my pocket and began putting them and the shoes on. "What's the blanket for?"

"To hide you."

I tied the first shoe. It was a bit tight, but not bad. "That blanket won't fool anyone."

"We have to try. It's all we've got." Oliver motioned with a hand. "Stand up."

I tied the second shoe and stood, watching the front as Erdath continued writing on the clipboard.

Oliver and Crystal sat on the bench. Oliver patted his thigh. "Now lay over our laps."

When I did, my head toward the aisle, they pulled the blanket over me. I could feel Oliver spreading one end over my feet and Crystal tucking the other around my head while I peered through a tiny hole in the blanket.

"Driver!" Axleback shouted in his own language. "Did any unauthorized human board this bus?"

"No, sir." Erdath showed him the clipboard. "Everyone is accounted for."

Axleback grabbed the clipboard and read it. After a moment, he threw it in Erdath's lap and roared, "Cynda is dead. She could not have boarded."

Perdantus flew in and landed on Erdath's shoulder. "I was here for the check-in procedure. I saw Erdath mark Cynda's name though she wasn't there. I'm sure I distracted him terribly. The mistake is my fault, and I apologize."

Axleback swatted Perdantus with the back of his hand, sending him crashing into the windshield. He slid down to the dashboard and stood there, wobbling as if in a daze.

His eyes fiery red, Axleback took a step toward the passengers, but his huge body wedged between the bench seats. He turned and walked sideways, his stare riveted on us. "What are you doing here, Oliver?" he roared in Humaniversal as he approached. "I told you to stay in the factory!"

I shuddered, and Oliver and Crystal shuddered with me. When Axleback stomped to us, he stopped, his thigh butting my blanket-covered head. A foul odor penetrated the material. I breathed through my mouth to keep from gagging.

Axleback spoke again in Humaniversal. "Where is Megan Willis?"

12

Oliver pointed toward the factory. "She told me she was going to escape through the furnace-room window. I heard you found a body. Wasn't it hers?"

Axleback shifted to his own language. "That was Cynda's body."

"Are you sure? Maybe—"

"Shut up." Something tugged the corner of the blanket. "Why do you have this?"

"It's the first cold morning of the season," Crystal said. "We wanted to keep our legs warm."

"Let me see under it."

Again something tugged on the blanket, but Crystal pressed it down on my ear. "Look at me," she said to Axleback. "Why are you on the bus?"

Axleback's voice came through in halting bursts. "To . . . to find someone . . . a girl, I think."

"Why are you searching here? This bus needs to leave right away."

Axleback blinked hard. "A bus? Why am I on a bus?"

"Just remember," Crystal said. "You found Megan's shoes with bones next to them. The body has to be Megan's. Humans are too dumb to fake a death like that."

"You're right." Axleback staggered toward the front of the bus, taking the stench with him. When he reached Erdath, he waved a hand. "Go. She's not on board." He stomped down the steps.

Erdath closed the door and drove away. Chains rattled underneath as they bit into the ice and propelled the bus forward.

Crystal patted the blanket. "Stay under," she whispered in Alpha One. "We have to get out of sight."

"I gotta admit," Oliver said, also in Alpha One, "your magic power worked perfectly."

"True, but when it wears off, he'll get his scales in a notch."

"Right. He'll come to the mine looking for Megan. And probably me."

"Only if he can find where the mine is. Thorne won't tell him. It's too big of a secret. Only Erdath knows."

"Thorne might tell. He wants that dragon's eye, and he thinks Megan has it. Since Thorne never comes to the forest anymore, he might send Axleback."

"And that would be trouble." Crystal pulled the blanket off me. "Rise and shine."

I crawled out and shifted to the bench across the aisle, blinking at the bright light. The ice-covered road reflected Yama-Yami's rays. The children looked back at us, their eyes wide but their mouths closed.

I exhaled heavily. "That was close," I said in Alpha One. "You guys did great figuring out my new plan."

"At first, I thought you got toasted." Crystal pointed at my feet. "You faked us all out with the shoes trick. Smart move."

"Yeah. Maybe. But I hated doing it." I lowered my head and whispered, "I dropped Cynda down there."

Oliver looked at Crystal. When she nodded, he faced me. "We guessed that. But you had to do it. Cynda would've wanted you to. Anything to help us escape."

"Us?" I glanced at the other kids. Some were still staring our way. "Who is *us*? *Us* three? Or *us* twelve?"

Oliver fidgeted. "We talked about this. The more we take with us, the harder it'll be to escape. Better for three of us to get out than none. You gotta admit that."

"I do." I heaved a sigh. "We'll stick with the plan, but if I can think of a safe way to get everyone out, I'm doing it."

"Fair enough."

Perdantus flew from the front of the bus and perched on my shoulder. "Unfortunately," he chirped softly, "I have become an unwilling stowaway on this journey. I was dazed by that beast's savage blow."

"Sorry about that." I nodded toward him as I spoke to Oliver and Crystal. "Perdantus was a great help. I couldn't have gotten on board without him."

Perdantus cocked his head. "Why are you speaking a different language?"

"It's Alpha One," I said in Humaniversal. "We're speaking it to keep things private."

"A smart move, and you should continue, but just be aware that I understand only a few words."

"Okay," I said to Oliver and Crystal in Alpha One, "when we want Perdantus to understand, we'll speak in Humaniversal. Otherwise, we'll stick to Alpha One." I looked at Perdantus. "I was saying that you helped a lot. I couldn't have gotten on the bus without you."

"It was a pleasure, Megan." Perdantus bowed, then toppled into my lap. When I helped him stand on my thigh, he shook his head. "It seems that I still need time to recover."

Oliver lowered his voice to a whisper in Humaniversal. "Time is something we don't have much of. One way or another, Axleback will find where the mine is, even if he has to torture someone."

"He can't torture Thorne," Crystal said. "Who else knows where the mine is besides Erdath?"

"Salsa knows." Perdantus fluffed his feathers, making his body look bigger. "And that worries me. She doesn't realize that she should stay away from him."

"Do you want to fly back and warn her?" I asked.

"I don't think I can fly at the moment, at least not that far. I will just have to hope Salsa's instincts protect her."

"We can all hope." I lifted a hand, wanting to stroke his feathers to calm him down, but that might be rude, even offensive. I folded my hands on my lap. "But maybe it's not so bad that you're a stowaway. You could be a lookout, like at the top of a tall tree."

"I will be glad to help. Even in my dazed state, I can make my way to the top of a tree."

Oliver nodded toward the window on his side, his expression somber as he spoke in Alpha One. "Time to get serious. Look around. Learn what it's like out there. We're way off the main road. The one we're on's not even paved. And we have to cross this stuff to get to the ship."

With Perdantus again on my shoulder, I studied the terrain, covered with ice and snow from the battle storm. Evergreen trees dotted the landscape, though none grew near the tops of the ridges. At times, birds flew here and there, some large, some small. Perdantus identified them for me, but I paid almost no attention. The species names filtered into my brain and leaked back out.

I blew a low whistle. "It'll be tough trudging through that ice."

"Not so bad with the spikes on our shoes," Oliver said. "The cold hit us like an avalanche this year. The river that runs through Bassolith is already frozen."

I looked outside again. The river lay to our right, a frozen sheet with just a few trickles giving evidence that the current still ran underneath, raising a memory of what Gavin had said about the location of the *Astral Dragon*. "Does this river lead to a bay?"

"Yep." Oliver pointed toward the front of the bus. "The mine is in one of the mountains that border the bay. Erdath will park on this side of the mountains, and we'll walk to the mine from there. The cave's not far. In fact, you can see it from the bus."

"How do you know about the bay?" I asked. "Have you been to it?"

"Just once. I sneaked there to see where the river went. It's not hard to get to."

"Perfect. I think that's where my mother landed her ship. We can go there when we escape. It's not nearly as far as the *Nine*."

"*If* we escape. It won't be easy. Axleback's bound to show up soon."

"Then we'll check the bay first. If the *Astral Dragon*'s not there, we'll stick with our original plan."

"All right," Oliver said. "The bay is primary now. The *Nine* is secondary. We'll work with that."

Moments later, the bus stopped at the end of the road about fifty meters from a line of trees. Erdath set the brake with a ratcheting grind and opened the door. "I'll be watching from the bus today," he called in the Jaradian language. "I have to take the chains off the tires when it gets warm enough. But don't get lazy. Your quota's still the same. We're not leaving till you make it."

As the children rose from their seats and fastened their coats, one of the girls whined. "But Cynda's dead," she said in Humaniversal. "Can't you lower the quota a little?"

"Not without Thorne's permission." He pointed toward the door. "Now go. Thirty filled shells. Don't try to fool me with partials."

The children trooped out, Oliver and Crystal trailing them, each carrying a lunch bag. I hunkered low in the back and peered over the seat again. As the kids climbed down the steps, Erdath used a pen to mark a page on his clipboard. When Crystal arrived at the front, she turned to Erdath and leaned close, pointing at her eye. "Do you see something in there?" she asked in Humaniversal. "Like maybe a little bug or a speck?"

He waved a hand and growled in the Jaradian language. "Get one of the brats to look."

"But they're already busy. You said we have to make quota without Cynda. And I know you don't want to stay later than we have to."

"It'll cost you." He eyed Crystal's bag. "Got anything good in there?"

"Oh, I don't know." She reached in and withdrew a meat pie. "Just this."

Erdath's eyes widened. "Where did you get that?"

"Thorne gave it to me 'cause Cynda was my friend."

"Softhearted old fool." Erdath licked his dark lips. "Tell you what. You give me that pie, and I'll see what I can do about the speck."

"Deal." Crystal set the pie on the dashboard and leaned close to Erdath again, pointing at her eye. "This one."

As Erdath leaned nearer, Crystal waved at me. I slid out to the aisle and tiptoed toward the front while Perdantus clung to my shoulder.

Erdath fell back to his seat, blinking. "What's going on? Where am I?"

I sneaked around Crystal and hopped to the ground. When my shoes hit a sheet of ice, the spikes dug in and kept me from slipping. Now nearing the trees, the other children tromped over the icy ground, Oliver looking back.

Crystal grabbed her pie, stuffed it into the bag, and joined me. Together we hurried toward the others.

Although the air was cold, rays from Yama-Yami brought relieving warmth. Water trickled over the ice and toward the river to our right, making long indentations in the slippery sheet. When we caught up with Oliver, he handed me a dark-brown muffin from his bag. "It's all I could get," he said as he and Crystal shifted to walking behind me, following our plan to shield me from Erdath's view. "Better eat it now. Food attracts the bees."

"Thanks." I stuffed it into my mouth and bit off half. As I chewed, I glanced back. Erdath stood next to the bus, staring at us, blinking as if trying to orient himself. He would probably recover soon, too soon for us to sneak off right away.

When we reached the tree line, Perdantus flew off my shoulder and landed on a low limb. "I am still too dazed to fly to the city, so I will stay here and work my way to the top of this tree. If I see someone coming, you should be able to hear my call."

"Thank you." I finished the muffin just as we stopped a few paces inside the tree line. Here, the river flowed more freely and wound through the forest in a serpentine course. To our left, a cliff loomed with a dark opening at the front, like a yawning mouth. A cleared path in the forest led to it, easily accessible from the road we had traveled. "Why doesn't Erdath drive closer?"

"He's scared of the bramble bees. They don't leave the forest, so he stays as far away as he can but still close enough to watch us. Taking the chains off the tires was an excuse. He always makes excuses."

"You said Thorne doesn't come to the mine. The bees can't hurt him, can they?"

Oliver shook his head. "He's afraid of other Willow Winds in the trees. They don't like that he left the forest for the city. It's kind of like being a traitor, I guess."

I hummed. "Interesting."

With Crystal and me at his side, Oliver lifted his voice, speaking in Humaniversal. "Okay, everyone, Crystal and I are going to teach Megan how to collect glowsap while the rest of you stay at the river and make shells. When we get back, we'll talk about who goes to the cave next."

Vonda took off her coat and hung it on a tree branch. "Won't you need a small kid for a fourth collector?"

"Not this time. We're just getting a little glowsap to train Megan. We'll be back soon."

"Good." Vonda pulled a bandana from a pocket and began fastening it over her hair. "The first freeze is always the hardest out here in the open. Takes a few days to get used to."

Just as Oliver opened his mouth to answer, a black-and-yellow insect the size of a human ear flew into the cave, its buzz as loud as a table saw. When it disappeared inside, I shuddered. "A bramble bee?" I said in Alpha One.

As the buzzing faded, Oliver answered in the same language. "Yep. A small one."

"Just as deadly?"

"Deadlier." Crystal shuddered. "The stingers are sharper when they're young."

"Think they can pierce Jaradian scales?" I asked.

She nodded. "Jaradians are scared to death of them. A sting kills them in minutes instead of hours. And the bees hate Jaradians. I think it's their odor."

"They're right. Jaradians reek." I looked at Oliver. "Do you have any rope here?"

"In the cave." He furrowed his brow. "What do you have in mind?"

"Insurance. The sharp, venomous kind."

"Are you thinking about lassoing—"

"Oliver?" Vonda set a fist on her hip. "What are you guys talking about? I can't understand a word of that gibberish."

Oliver waved a hand and reverted to Humaniversal. "Sorry. We're leaving now."

"Okay." Vonda walked toward the riverbank, clapping her hands. "Time to get to work. Since it's so cold, we'll start the fire first."

Oliver nodded toward the cave. "Let's go." As we walked among the trees, he watched a bee fly by. "You can try to catch one if you want, but it's crazy dangerous. Remember Cynda."

"Yeah. I remember." My heart sank along with my bravado, but catching a bee still might work. I needed to keep it in mind.

When we entered the cave, we stopped a few paces inside at a flat area illuminated by filtered sunlight. Oliver picked up one of four lanterns, struck a match on the side of a matchbox, and lit the wick. The lantern cast a flickering glow on the walls. Four sets of metal-plated clothes and matching helmets hung from spikes, two of the sets larger than the others.

Oliver collected the two larger sets and one of the smaller. "Which one of you is bigger?"

Crystal and I looked at each other from head to toe. "We're about the same," Crystal said. "I'm a little shorter, I guess."

"Which do you usually wear?" I asked.

She pointed. "The bigger one. Same for Oliver."

"Then I'll take the smaller one."

"Just hurry," Oliver said as he handed me the smaller set. "The bees will get aggressive soon."

Oliver and Crystal shed their coats and began putting their suits on over their clothes. Not wanting the remote's trigger to be pressed, I retrieved it from my pocket and set it on the ground before putting the suit on. It fit snugly but not uncomfortably, and the extra layer felt good in the cold cave, as did the plated gloves.

A pouch dangled from the outfit's belt, weighed down by something, but I didn't want to take off a glove to check it out. Oliver would probably tell me about it soon.

When I fastened the remote to my belt and put the helmet on, I lowered its glass visor over my face. "I think I'm ready."

Oliver tugged the plate on my back, sliding it down. "There's a slight gap here," he said, his helmet's glass shield still raised, making him easy to hear. "Don't bend forward when a bee's around, or one'll sting you where Cynda got stung."

Goose bumps ran along my skin. "I'll be careful."

Oliver lit two more lanterns and handed one to Crystal and one to me. "Something else to be careful about. Never let the fire touch the glowsap. It burns like crazy. Practically explodes."

I nodded. "Good to know."

As we walked deeper into the cave, the air cooled further and our spiked shoes crunched on the rocky floor of our narrow passageway. The three lights bounced across the walls in time with our uneven gaits.

"Megan," Oliver said, his voice echoing, "the pouch attached to your belt has an empty glass jar. That's what you'll use to collect the glowsap. It stays wet in glass long enough to get it into the clay shells. I already got the jar from the fourth suit."

I touched the pouch. "Got it."

A buzzing noise emanated from deeper in the cave, growing louder with each step we took. "I hear bees," Oliver said as he lowered his shield. "A bunch of them."

Soon, we came upon a wall with only a small, chest-high hole at the center. The barrier from the edge of the hole to the walls and ceiling seemed to be fibrous. "What is that stuff?" I asked.

Crystal touched the barrier. "Bee netting. Tough as stone. The bramble bees spin it and block the cave with it. They leave a hole big enough for them to fly through, but too high for anything that crawls and too small for anything bigger than they are."

Oliver tapped the net, making a clicking sound. "It's breakable with a sledgehammer, but if it gets broken, the bees stop making glowsap until they build it up again. That's why they send kids to do the collecting. The opening's too small for adults. Barely big enough for me."

I imagined myself wriggling through the hole. If Oliver had a hard time getting through, I probably would as well since we were nearly the same size. "And I guess no one can go alone. You need a boost to get through."

"Yeah, except the last kid through gets pulled from the other side. It's not easy." He intertwined his fingers and set his upturned hands near the floor. Crystal stepped on them and rode his lift. As she wormed her way through the hole, he continued pushing until she popped through.

After handing Crystal her lantern, Oliver boosted me in the same way. Crystal caught my wrists from the other side and pulled until I toppled out and rolled on the ground. She helped me up and checked my armor. "You're good to go."

Oliver reached the other two lanterns through the hole to Crystal and pushed his arms in. She and I worked together to draw him into our part of the cave.

When we had collected our lanterns, we marched on. After another minute, the corridor opened into an enormous chamber at least a hundred paces in all directions. Dozens and dozens of glowing spots shone all around, filling the wall with tiny beacons of light. The air smelled sweet, as if a field of flowers grew all around, though only stone surrounded us.

Somewhere out of sight, bramble bees let out a buzz that grew louder by the second. I shuddered hard. They were close. Too close.

Oliver whispered, "The bees are to our right, so we'll start over here." He set his lantern on the ground and walked to the left, following the curve of the wall as the glowsap provided plenty of light. Crystal and I set our lanterns next to his and followed.

He stopped at one of the little beacons in the wall and withdrew his jar. "There's a spoon inside. Just stick the spoon in the hole in the wall, scoop the glowsap out, and put it in the jar. You can use a finger to push it off the spoon, but whatever you do, don't lick your finger. That stuff will make you upchuck like you wouldn't believe."

I nodded. "Scoop the sap. Drop it in the jar. Don't lick it. Sounds simple enough."

"Simple but dangerous. The second you start scooping, the bees will attack."

I stiffened. "I'm not looking forward to that."

Crystal pointed at a glowing hole near Oliver. "I'll take that one. Megan, pick any hole that's close by."

I scanned the spacious chamber, too dim to see beyond a few steps away. "Where's the rope?"

Oliver pointed to his right. "Over there. You'll see it when you get closer."

"On my way." I walked in that direction until I came to a ladder. The rope looped over a pulley that extended from the ladder's top, one end dangling at eye level, a device likely used by the children to reach the higher holes in the wall. I pulled the rope down, wound it into a coil, and set it on the ground.

The buzzing noise erupted into a fury. Several bees zipped over to Oliver and Crystal as they scooped glowsap from their holes. The bees stabbed their backs with abdomen stingers again and again, but Oliver and Crystal paid no attention. Since the stingers struck the metal plates without getting damaged, they must have been made of something super tough.

I pulled the jar from my pouch, pried the lid off, and withdrew the spoon, all cumbersome tasks with my plated gloves. After taking a deep breath, I pushed the spoon into a radiant hole and scooped out a glob of glowsap.

One of the bees flew at me and rammed its stinger into the side of my helmet. The strike sounded like the pinging of a hammer against metal. As I continued scooping, I kept my back as straight as possible, frequently feeling the rear armor joint with a gloved hand to make sure the gap stayed closed.

By the time I emptied the hole, I had filled the jar halfway. I shifted to another hole and continued scooping. The buzzing grew louder. At least six bees attacked, one bigger than my fist.

I glanced at Oliver and Crystal. Even more bees buzzed around them, too many to count. As I continued working, I imagined the younger children scooping sap while these deadly bees attacked them. In my mind, Cynda stood at the top of the ladder while another child pulled the rope, lifting a new jar to her. When she bent to untie the jar, the armor joints on her back separated, and a bee jabbed her in the exposed area.

I grimaced as if feeling the sting myself. Nausea churned in my stomach. I felt like I might vomit even without tasting the sap. I shook my head, casting away the horrible thoughts. I had to concentrate on what I was doing.

Soon, Crystal called out, "Mine's full."

"Almost finished with my second one," Oliver replied. "How's it going for you, Megan?"

I used my finger to push a gob of sap into the jar. "Kind of slow. I think it's about two-thirds full."

"Good enough. Let's go."

I slid the spoon into the jar, snapped the lid back on, and pushed it all into the pouch. After grabbing the rope, I followed Oliver and Crystal toward the passage leading out, again careful to keep my back straight. Two bees continued pounding me, one attacking my helmet and the other my legs. The angry buzzing grew louder than ever.

We picked up our lanterns and entered the passage with a few bees following us. Once we pushed through the hole in the bee netting and settled ourselves and the lanterns on the other side, Oliver raised his helmet's shield. "Do you hear something?"

I stood perfectly still and raised my shield as well, but the buzzing racket made it impossible to hear anything else. "What does it sound like?"

"Perdantus!" Oliver leaped into a run. Crystal did the same. When I stretched a leg to try to match their speed, the undersized suit tightened, nearly making me trip.

I settled for walking at a fast pace. If Axleback had arrived, I couldn't reveal my presence, at least not yet. Maybe if I stayed back, I could surprise him somehow.

Several seconds later, light from the exit came into view. I blew out my lantern and hurried on, still carrying the coil of rope. With only one remaining bee buzzing nearby, Perdantus's loud chirps came through, though my ear device failed to translate his frantic call.

A deep voice pierced the cool stillness. "There you are, Oliver," Axleback growled in his own language. "You didn't stay at the factory as I ordered."

I halted, set the lantern down, and pressed myself against the side wall. Moving slowly, I peered around a rocky protrusion. Axleback stood a couple of paces outside the entrance, his hand behind his back.

"You were gone," Oliver said in Humaniversal, his helmet tucked under his arm, "and we still had to meet the same quota without Cynda, so I went with the bus."

Crystal set her jar of glowsap next to Oliver's in front of Axleback and took off her helmet. "That's why Oliver filled two jars. Now we have to put the glowsap in the shells before it dries out."

"What do I care?" Axleback kicked the jars, sending them flying against the wall. They shattered, some shards scattering on the ground and others sticking to the wall with the sap.

Oliver calmly hung his suit and helmet on a wall spike. "How did you find out where this place is?"

Axleback brought his hidden hand forward, his fingers wrapped around Salsa's throat. "As humans sometimes say, a little bird told me." He threw Salsa to the ground. She lay motionless, her body crushed.

Burning bile erupted into my throat. I swallowed it, but the scalding stuff sent tears into my eyes.

Axleback jabbed a finger at Oliver. "You and Megan Willis are coming with me."

Oliver stared straight at him. Although I could see only the back of his head, I imagined fierce eyes. "Why? What's she to you?"

"Money, a lot more than the measly thousand mesots on that leaflet."

"Who's paying it? Thorne?"

"Never mind that. Where is Megan?"

Oliver set a fist on his hip. "I don't know where she is."

"Liar!" Axleback punched Oliver in the face. He staggered back and fell hard. "Now tell me where she is or . . ." He snatched Crystal's hair and pulled her into a headlock. "Or I'll snap her neck."

Crystal gasped but stayed motionless, her eyes clenched shut.

"Wait," I called as I stepped into the open. "Don't hurt her. I'm here." With a hand wrapped around the rope, I planted my feet. "Now let her go."

"Remove your helmet. I want to make sure you're Megan."

I took the helmet off and dropped it. "Satisfied?"

Axleback threw Crystal to the side and took a hard step toward me. A bramble bee flew at his face. Axleback swatted it with the back of his hand, sending it crashing against the wall. It tumbled to the ground, flailed its wings, and wiggled until it sat upright, buzzing softly, obviously stunned.

"Come out of the cave," Axleback said as he retreated several steps. "Those beasts are deadly."

"That's true. Let's make sure this one won't bother us." I took my gloves off, tied the end of the rope in a slipknot, and lowered the loop toward the stunned bee. The moment the rope touched its body, it shot up and flew at me. I backpedaled and swatted at it, but it continued its assault, dodging my hands and stinging my armored chest again and again.

When it changed direction and flew toward my face, I grabbed its thorax. While it struggled and tried to stab my arm with its abdomen stinger, I pressed the remote's trigger button, holding it down for a split second. The collar delivered a short jolt. Pain roared down my spine. When the ink responded to the signal, electricity shot into the bee. It stiffened, stunned again for the moment.

My muscles cramping, I slipped the rope around the bee and tightened the loop. The bee sprang back to life and flew again at Axleback. Just as he readied a fist to swat it, I pulled the rope and held the bee in midair. It jerked and buzzed madly, like a ferocious flying dog straining at a leash.

Axleback waved an arm. "Get that thing away from me."

I nodded toward Oliver and Crystal. "Let them leave, or I'll release it. I wouldn't count on being able to swat it again."

"All right." His voice trembled along with his body. "They can go."

Oliver scrambled to his feet and helped Crystal up. He looked at me, worry lines etched in his face. "Are you sure?"

With the cramps easing, I gave him a firm nod. "Positive. Just go to the primary meeting place. I'll see you there."

They dashed past Axleback, giving him a wide berth, Crystal still wearing armor and carrying her helmet. When they had run out of sight in the woods, I pulled the bee back about a meter. "Now move to the side and let me go."

"Certainly." He sidestepped and waved an arm as if showing me the way out. "But as soon as you leave, I will snap the neck of every child at the river."

I blinked hard. "What?"

"You heard me."

I loosened my grip on the rope, letting it reel out until the bee was just out of Axleback's reach. "Leave now, or I'll let it go."

"It's a gamble, Megan. If my aim is true, and I hit that cursed bee again, I will catch you. If I don't, it might sting me. But you can't be sure. Either way, I will survive long enough to slaughter those children just as I did poor little Salsa, only with humans it will be much more pleasurable."

Perdantus flew at Axleback and flapped his wings in his face. I released the rope. The bee flew straight at Axleback again. He swatted at both the bird and the bramble bee, backpedaling as they attacked.

Axleback connected with a blow that sent Perdantus sailing. Before he could swing again, the bee stung him square on his horse-like nose. He knocked the bee away and held a hand over the wound.

"You fool!" Roaring, Axleback charged. I ducked under his arms, dropped to all fours, and crawled toward the cave's exit. He grabbed my ankle and dragged me toward him.

Trying to kick myself free, I looked back. A red welt had already swelled on his nose. His teeth bared, he jerked me into his grasp and wrapped a beefy arm around my neck. "You will die first. And if I have any strength, I will kill the others."

The bee flew into his face and stung him above the eye. He screamed and pawed at his face. The moment he relaxed his grip, I broke loose, tumbled forward, and blocked my fall with my hands.

When I rose and turned to run, something stung the back of my neck. I spun. The bee dropped to the ground as if exhausted. I stomped on its head with a spiked shoe.

I laid a hand on my sting wound and looked at the cave. A few paces inside, Axleback lay motionless, likely dead.

I panted, sweating. Before the night was over, I would be dead. Maybe I would bark and snarl like Cynda did, beg to be put out of my misery, but here in the forest there would be no tea to knock me out.

A sob erupted, but I swallowed it down, letting only a squeak break through. "Help me."

Within seconds, the Astral Dragon's words returned to mind, like a whisper riding on the breeze. *Sacrifice for them. And, if necessary, die for them.*

I inhaled deeply and tried to slow my breathing. If I had to die, I could help the others first. Hang the risk of stealing away with too many kids. Saving them all from Thorne was the only option. I would find the *Astral Dragon* or go to the *Nine*, and I would return to fly every one of them out of this festering pit.

And now it was time to focus on that goal without any distractions. My parents' training kicked in—take inventory, survey the surroundings, and use whatever assets you can acquire.

I took the jar of glowsap from the pouch, shed the protective suit, and shifted the collar's remote to my belt. Nearby, a two-person rover craft sat on the ground, its glass top open—likely the vehicle Axleback used to get here.

Movement at the river caught my attention. I hurried in that direction. Every step sent throbbing pain to my neck. When I arrived, Vonda and Bastian were supervising the children as they used spoons to dig clay from the riverbank and form it with their hands into oval shells the size of small melons. Two children stood apart and warmed themselves by a crackling fire.

Breathless, I set the jar on the ground. The kids stopped working and stared at me, their bodies dirty, wet, and shivering, though the air had warmed quite a bit. "Where are Oliver and Crystal?" Vonda asked.

Pain stabbed through my skull, making it hard to think, even harder to talk. I couldn't come up with anything to say except the truth. "They escaped to the bay. I'm going to find them."

Bastian stepped closer and studied me with his piercing brown eyes. "You look terrible. Are you all right?"

"She's not." Vonda set a hand on my cheek. "Your face is red, and you're breathing fast. Did you get stung?"

I nodded and lowered myself to my knees. "On the back of the neck."

"Let me see." Vonda lifted my hair, then let it slip from her fingers. "Norbert. Renalda. Get clay and magle weed. We need to make a poultice."

Norbert waded knee-deep into the river and began pulling water grass while Renalda scooped clay at the bank.

"A poultice?" I asked. "If the sting's fatal, what good will that do?"

"It will lessen your suffering. At least you probably won't bark and try to bite like I heard Cynda did. She didn't tell us she got stung, so we couldn't help her." Vonda whipped the bandana from her hair. "Renalda, mix the weeds and clay in this and get it warm."

Renalda grabbed the bandana and hurried with Norbert to the fire.

"Lie down," Vonda said as she gathered fallen leaves into a pillow.

When I did, Bastian dropped to one knee and lifted my legs over the other knee. "Comfortable?"

Although my head still pounded, my body pain eased. "Better than I was. Thank you."

Renalda ran to us, the bandana now wet and dirty. Vonda took it and slid it under my neck. The warmth felt wonderful, though the stinging sensation worsened. I grimaced tightly, looking at the children through narrow slits as they gathered around.

"When do you think she'll die?" Norbert asked.

A taller boy elbowed him. "Don't say that."

"Well, she *is* going to die."

"I know, but no use reminding her. She's already suffering enough."

Renalda knelt at my side and patted my hand. Tiny freckles covered her smallish nose and sunken cheeks, and cold blueness tinted her thin lips. In spite of her meager appearance, she looked pretty—beautiful, in fact, though the bee's poison might have been addling my brain. "I hope you don't die, Megan," she said. "I really like you."

I couldn't help but smile. "Thank you. I like you, too."

As I gazed at the children, images of them returning to Thorne without making their quota came to mind. They trooped to bed without supper, clutching their emaciated bellies. Cynda's corpse appeared as she lay near the fiery furnace, the scene narrated by Oliver's voice speaking Thorne's cruel, callous words: *Take it in stride. Death is part of life. No funerals. No tears.* To Thorne, these precious children were work animals, expendable, easily replaceable.

And less than an hour ago, I was planning to escape with Oliver and Crystal and leave them behind. I hadn't explained my new plan to rescue all of them, yet, they were still doing all they could to ease my suffering. They loved me no matter what. And now, I had to get up and love them back.

Summoning my remaining strength, I pulled my legs away from Bastian and struggled to my feet, one hand holding the poultice against my neck. Dizzy, I looked at Vonda and Bastian in turn. "Would you like to escape? Get on a spaceship and leave this planet forever?"

Vonda glanced at Bastian before looking at me again. "I would. I'm sure we all would."

"Then talk to the others. Get warm and dry at the fire. I'll be back as soon as I can. But first, I need a weapon." With stiff-legged steps, I staggered to the cave. After finding the dead bee, I stuffed the poultice into my pocket and picked up a sharp rock. Using its edge, I cut the bee's stinger off.

I tossed the stinger into Axleback's two-person rover and climbed behind the steering wheel. The inside smelled awful, like sweaty Jaradian and stale tobacco. I read the instruments on the control panel, written in Humaniversal. Simple enough.

I turned the engine on, grabbed the steering wheel, and pushed the dashboard's hand throttle. The rover lifted and scooted along the ground. I steered out of the forest and, not bothering to close the hatch, headed for the bus.

Erdath stood near the bus's open door, staring at me as I drew close, the tire chains lying on the ground at his feet. I stopped several paces away and, with stinger in hand, climbed out. Putting on a fierce expression and trying to look as strong as possible, I marched toward him, the stinger hidden behind me. With much of the snow and ice melted, the going was easy, though a bit muddy. When I stopped just out of reach, I set a fist on my hip. "Axleback is dead. I killed him."

"What?" Erdath edged closer to the door. "How could such a small human kill him?"

"With this." I whipped the stinger around and jabbed the air with it. "A bramble bee stinger."

Erdath gasped and scrambled into the bus. I dropped the stinger, lunged for the hood, and opened it. I jerked the spark plug wires loose and slammed the hood. As Erdath tried in vain to start the engine, I backed away.

When he emerged from the bus again, I picked up the stinger. "Start walking."

He gulped. "All the way to Bassolith?"

I nodded. "Now."

Erdath spun and took off at a jog, slipping and sliding on the wet ice.

When he was well down the road, I tossed the stinger into the rover, restored the spark plug wires in the bus motor, climbed in, and started it. I slid the seat forward, put the bus into gear, and stretched my leg until my foot pushed the gas pedal.

The bus rumbled ahead. I steered it into the woods along the path leading to the cave, drove into the mouth, and parked inside so that the exhaust pipe protruded into the open air. Leaving the engine and the heater running, I climbed out and, dodging a couple of bees, stumbled toward the river, calling, "Vonda! Bastian! Over here!"

Bastian's voice sounded within the woods. "We're coming!"

I halted about twenty paces from the cave, a safe distance from the bees. The pounding in my head returned with a vengeance. Calf muscles tightened in knotting cramps, and my lungs burned. Shots of adrenaline must have fueled my earlier actions, but now all energy seemed to be draining away.

When the children arrived and gathered around, I nodded toward the bus. "It's warm inside, and the bees can't get in. And I don't think any Jaradians will risk getting close. Rest there and wait for me to come back for you."

Vonda touched my cheek. "How are you staying so strong?"

Even her light touch burned, making me grimace. "I'm not strong. I hurt all over." I withdrew her bandana from my pocket, now cold. "I don't think this can help anymore."

"Probably not." She took the bandana and shook the clay out. "If you die before you can come back, what should we do?"

"I have Axleback's rover, so I'll at least make it to Oliver and Crystal. I'll tell them to come for you. I promise."

Her lips trembled as she replied. "Then go, my sister."

I raised my brow. "Sister?"

"Of course. You're family now." She slid her hand into mine. "And may the Astral Dragon speed your journey."

"And yours as well." I compressed her hand and smiled. "My sister."

Without another word, I strode toward the rover, my cramped muscles screaming in agony. I couldn't figure out which leg to favor, so I hobbled in an erratic path. Something lifted me on one side, then on the other. I looked each way. Vonda supported my left arm with her shoulder, and Bastian supported my right, both grunting as Bastian whispered, "We're here, Megan. We'll get you to the rover."

"Thank you," I said, my words barely audible.

When we arrived, Bastian and Vonda lifted me into the rover. After making sure I was settled inside, they closed the hatch and stepped back.

I started the engine, waved goodbye, and pushed the throttle. When the rover rose and glided forward, I steered it over the river and followed it downstream. As water sprayed to each side, Vonda's words returned to mind. *If you die before you can come back, what should we do?*

Reality returned and stabbed me in the gut. I was going to die. When and where, I didn't know, but my life would soon come to an end. And what had I accomplished in my few short years? I had robbed Alliance fortresses. I had helped my parents kill people. I had been a fugitive most of my life. In so many people's eyes, I was a pirate, a scoundrel, a murderer.

My parents had told me many times that life was sacred, but did they really live that way? Did I? Who was I to be judge and executioner of the men and women we killed and then later cry for Cynda? Weren't their lives sacred? Was I really that much of a hypocrite?

My questions fell unanswered except by the pounding in my head. I gripped the steering wheel more tightly and whispered into the air, "All I want to do is save my friends' lives. Please help me do that before I die."

14

After a couple of kilometers, I exited the forest and followed the river to a huge bay. Now over open water, I reversed course and jetted toward shore. Oliver and Crystal stood at the mouth of the river, Crystal no longer wearing her bee armor. They backed away across an expansive beach of yellowish sand and watched me land near the edge of the water.

I switched off the engine and got up, opening the hatch as I rose.

Crystal clapped her hands. "You made it!" she said in Humaniversal.

I replied in the same language. "Barely." I tried to climb out, but dizziness sent me tumbling to the sand.

Oliver rushed to my side and helped me up. "Are you all right?" He brushed sand from my cheek as he steadied me. "You look awful."

I almost blurted out the news of my fatal wound but decided to hold it back. What good would it do to tell them? "Thanks for the help." I scanned my surroundings—nothing but sand and water as well as trees that bordered the beach in a semicircle. No sign of the *Astral Dragon*.

"The ship has to be around somewhere." Forcing myself to stay balanced, I walked along the beach, Oliver and Crystal following. I came upon a deep depression in the sand near the water's edge, then another farther down. I turned ninety degrees and found two more depressions that made a line parallel to the first two.

I halted and pointed at one of the depressions. "A ship was here, a ship the size of the *Astral Dragon*."

Oliver looked up, shielding his eyes with a hand. "But where is she now?"

A weak voice came from the forest. "Megan?"

I looked that way. Where the beach ended, the terrain rose sharply through the woods to a high ridge. Thinking that anyone here who recognized me would know Alpha One, I responded in that language. "Yes, I'm here."

Oliver squinted in the same direction. "Who are you talking to?" he asked, also in Alpha One.

I continued scanning the area. "I heard someone call my name."

"I didn't hear anything."

"Me either," Crystal said. "We've been waiting on this beach quite a while. It's been quiet."

"I know I heard someone." With Oliver and Crystal following again, I walked toward the ridge, my heavy, spiked shoes digging deeply into the sand. When I reached the forest's edge, the going got easier on the hard, root-infested ground, though steeper as I ascended the slope.

Now in dense woods, I stopped and called, "It's Megan. Is someone here?" I listened, my head feeling like it was about to explode.

The voice returned, weaker than before. "Megan?"

I pivoted toward the sound. A few paces away, Dirk sat with his back against a tree, holding his knees close to his chest and shivering hard in spite of a thick sweater with sleeves that extended past his hands. He blinked at me with tired, bleary eyes. "Are you real?"

"Dirk!" I staggered to him, dropped to my knees, and pulled his shivering body close. His cheeks felt ice cold. "How long have you been out here?"

He spoke through chattering teeth. "I don't know."

"Who's this?" Oliver asked as he and Crystal joined me.

"Dirk, a friend from the *Nine*." I looked him over. "What happened to you?"

He spoke with an odd slur. "Gavin was looking for you. Came back to the ship and said he couldn't find you. But I saw him put this in his pocket." He pushed his fist out of the sleeve and opened his hand, revealing my locket and leather cord. "I picked his pocket. He lied about not finding you, so I went out looking for you myself."

"My locket!" I took the cord, draped it around my neck, and fastened it in the back. I ached to check the dragon's eye to see if it glowed, but I couldn't risk anyone watching. "Thank you, Dirk. This means a lot to me."

"I thought so. I knew you wouldn't just give it to him."

"Why did the *Dragon* take off without you?"

Dirk blinked several times. "When I got sucked out of the *Nine*, my suit tore. By the time the *Dragon* picked me up, I got . . . what did they call it?"

"Decompression sickness?"

"Yeah. Hurt like crazy." He grunted, wincing as he spoke, his words emerging with each gasp. "Your mom gave me pills . . . to sleep it off . . . I made my bed to look like . . . I was strapped in and asleep. . . . Then I left to look for you." After another tight grimace, he opened his eyes and looked at me. "I didn't get very far. I hurt my ankle, and I'm too dizzy."

"So you're drugged," Oliver said. "That's why you're dizzy."

"And it's getting worse."

I grabbed Dirk's wrist. "I'll take you to the rover."

As I began trying to lift him, Oliver pulled Dirk from me and set him back down. "You can't carry him. You look like you're about to keel over yourself."

"Then you and Crystal help me. The three of us together can do it."

Oliver grabbed my arm, pulled me to the side, and whispered,

"But like we talked about. There's no way we can escape with other kids slowing us down, especially someone who can't walk."

I glared at him, a growl vibrating through my clenched teeth. "I'm not leaving Dirk behind."

"Okay. Okay." He released my arm. "But maybe we can look at his ankle, somehow get him to walk on his own."

"Fine by me." I knelt at Dirk's side and touched his ankle. "Okay if I have a look?"

He nodded, his face tight.

I pushed his pant cuff up and slid his sock down. A walnut-sized purple lump protruded from the bone.

Crystal gasped. "That looks awful! Did you fall?"

"A couple of times." Dirk looked at me. "Think it's broken?"

I winced. "Yeah. Maybe."

Oliver knelt at Dirk's other side. "I did something like that to my ankle once." He glanced at Crystal and me in turn, as if nervous. "Let me show you what helped. It might hurt to try it."

Dirk nodded, biting his lip. "Go ahead."

Oliver set his hand over the lump and pressed down. Dirk lifted his head and yowled. After several seconds, Oliver let go and slowly lifted his hand. The lump had shrunk to almost nothing, and the color had faded from purple to pink.

As Oliver drew back, his entire body trembled along with his voice. "Um . . . that looks better."

Dirk exhaled heavily. "It is better, but I'm still dizzy."

I studied Oliver's strange reaction. He seemed surprised, even shocked. "How did you do that? The ankle thing, I mean?"

He glanced away for a moment before focusing on me. "It was just a lump, like a knot under his skin. I pushed it back into place."

I crossed my arms in front. "It doesn't work that way."

"Well . . ." After glancing at Crystal for a brief second, he lowered his voice. "Let's forget about it, all right? Not a word to anyone."

"If you say so."

Dirk moaned softly, then toppled to the side.

"Dirk!" I pulled him upright. "We can't wait. I'm taking him to the rover." I lifted him into my arms and held his limp body in place as I rose, his hot breaths warming my neck. "He'll probably stay asleep till the drug wears off."

Oliver scrambled to his feet. "No way. You can barely walk."

"I can make it to the rover. When we get to the bee cave, we can all ride in the bus to the *Nine*."

"The bus?" Crystal said. "Thorne's bus?"

"Right. It's parked in the cave, and the other kids are in it waiting for us. I'll tell you about it later." I took a step. My foot tripped on Dirk's leg, and we fell together and rolled on the ground.

When we stopped, Oliver pulled me to a sitting position. "You can't do this. It's impossible."

"I can, and I will." My heart thumped as I gasped for breath. Calling on my last energy reserves, I rose again, grasped Dirk's wrists, and hoisted him over my shoulder. "I'm not going to let my friend freeze out here. I'm going to try to save everyone, no matter what."

I trudged down the slope, my body bent, allowing me to see my locket as it swayed. For some reason, it glowed red, as if radiance from the dragon's eye seeped out. That hadn't happened since the day I got branded.

The glow seemed to pump a new surge of adrenaline through my limbs. But it probably wouldn't last long. I had to hurry and get Dirk into the rover before I collapsed.

"You don't have to do this," Oliver said as he walked at my side and held a hand on Dirk. "I'll help you carry him."

"Yeah," Crystal said from the other side. "Three of us will make it easy."

"He's already on my shoulder," I grunted, nearly out of breath. "Let's just get him to the rover."

When we arrived, Oliver and Crystal helped me put Dirk in the passenger's seat. Once we had him settled, I climbed to the driver's side. My energy rapidly melting, I looked at Oliver. "So what're you and Crystal going to do?"

"You'll get to the cave way before we do, so just go on from there with the bus. If you wait for us, you're more likely to get caught."

"He's right," Crystal said. "Tell us where your ship is. We'll meet you there."

I pointed toward the city, though it was far out of sight. "Follow the river upstream. When you get into the woods on the other side of Bassolith, look for my rover under some brush. I set a big stone at the river's edge to mark the spot."

"Wait." Oliver reached to the rover's floorboard and straightened with the bramble bee stinger in hand. "Why do you have this?"

"A weapon. I don't need it anymore." I pressed the control panel button and closed the hatch. When it clicked in place, I took off.

Again following the river, I drove through the forest, feeling like I might faint at any moment. I glanced at my locket. The gem's glow no longer seeped through to the outside, a mystery that I would probably never solve.

The muscle cramps worsened, making my head spin. To try to stay conscious, I talked to Dirk, launching into the story of what happened to me ever since he got sucked through the breach in the hull. Although he stayed quiet, his eyes twitched during the most exciting parts, making me think he could hear everything.

As I drove, the dizziness increased. My throat narrowed. Death was probably closing in. When we arrived at the cave, I landed the rover near the entrance and shut off the engine. Bees swarmed over Axleback's corpse, some biting into him with sharp teeth and pulling out stringy meat while others flew around as if waiting their turn. The flying bees blocked the entrance to the cave, making it impossible to enter on foot.

Something snapped. I looked toward the road leading to the city. Only a few steps away, six Jaradians stomped toward me, each carrying an axe.

I switched on the engine. Just as the lead Jaradian lunged, I pushed the throttle, sending the rover through the bees and into the cave, squeezing past the bus on my left. I spun a one-eighty in the rover and looked back through gaps in the flying bees.

The Jaradians huddled at a distance. One of them shouted,

"Surrender now, and we'll show mercy. You're just a child. What do you think you can do against six of us?"

A profane retort begged to spew from my mouth, but I held my tongue. We were safe for the time being. No need to enrage them. But who could tell how long the bees would swarm at that spot and protect us? And was it safe for me to open the hatch and try to get aboard the bus? With the smell of Jaradian permeating the rover's interior, probably not.

Something tapped on the hatch's glass. I searched for the source and found Perdantus pecking on the top. When I raised the hatch a bit, several bees zipped toward us. The second Perdantus flew inside, I refastened the hatch. The bees orbited the rover a few times before returning to the swarm.

Perdantus perched on my shoulder and chirped rapid-fire. "The children are safe in the bus. Before they boarded, they carried three of the armored suits in with them. We think Crystal wore the missing one when she escaped and probably shed it somewhere in the forest. Bastian is now putting one on and will bring the other two to you in a moment."

"Thank you, Perdantus." I let out a mournful sigh. "I'm so sorry about Salsa. You must feel terrible."

He lowered his head. "I am overwhelmed with grief, to be sure. She has been the most wonderful companion possible. I took her body to a lovely field of wildflowers and buried her before returning here. I think she would be pleased."

Again I ached to pet him, but I kept my hand in check. "When you attacked Axleback, you probably saved my life, and you were courageous to come to the rover unprotected. Thank you."

"Saving your life was an honor, but coming to the rover was nothing, really. Bramble bees don't find birds to be a threat. I had no fear of being attacked by them."

A moment later, a glove with metal-tipped fingers tapped on the hatch. I opened it slightly. Bees again flew to the rover, this time attacking Bastian as he pushed two sets of armor through the gap.

When I closed the hatch, Bastian retreated to the bus, and the bees left once more.

While Perdantus stood on the dashboard and gave advice, I slid a pair of armored pants and a vest onto Dirk, fastened them in place, and added the helmet. Every movement shot streams of pain through my limbs, but it was worth it. Dirk had to survive.

When I finished, I put the other helmet over my head and looked at Perdantus. "We're ready. Ask Bastian to help me carry Dirk. With the armor on, he'll be too heavy for me."

Perdantus cocked his head. "But you haven't put your suit on."

"It's too small to put on in this cramped space."

"Very well."

Again I lifted the hatch a bit, and again the bees attacked. Perdantus slipped out and flew to the bus. I closed the hatch and waited, watching bees dart here and there.

A few moments later, Bastian appeared and stood on the passenger side of the rover. I pressed the hatch button. Bees buzzed close yet again. The moment the gap grew wide enough, I squeezed out and joined him.

When we grabbed Dirk and began lifting him out, a huge bramble bee flew straight at me. It stung my glass shield and bounced back. A shout erupted somewhere. Oliver and Crystal burst through the curtain of bees, each carrying a tree branch, Crystal in an armored suit and Oliver unprotected, his shirt drenched with sweat.

Oliver smashed my attacking bee with his branch, then spun and hit another. Crystal swung her branch wildly, sometimes missing and sometimes striking bees. Bastian and I hauled Dirk from the rover and carried him toward the bus. "Close the hatch," I called. "The rover's attracting the bees."

While Oliver kept bashing bees, Crystal slammed the hatch closed. When Bastian and I neared the bus, the door swung open. Vonda sat in the driver's seat, a hand on the door controls. We hustled Dirk up the steps, propped him on a bench seat, and leaned him against a window.

Outside, while Crystal continued swinging her branch, Oliver ran toward the bus's open door. A bee landed on his back, but from where I sat looking out the window, I couldn't tell if it stung him or not.

Crystal slapped the bee away with her branch. Oliver leaped up the bus's stairs. No longer attracted by the rover, the remaining bees flew away and rejoined the others. Crystal threw her branch down and scampered up the bus's steps. The moment she boarded, Vonda closed the door.

Crystal jerked off her helmet and began shedding the suit. "Whew! That was close!"

"Yeah," Oliver said. "Good thing you found your suit again."

"And good thing you decided we should head for this cave instead of the ship."

"Easy choice. Megan looked half-dead. We had to help her." He walked down the aisle and stopped next to where I sat. "And now we have to get out of here. The Jaradians are setting up a big gun of some kind. It'll probably blast right through the bees and destroy the bus."

"Can you drive?" I asked.

"I . . ." Oliver's face paled. He clutched his stomach and bent double. "I feel sick."

I gasped. "Did you get stung?"

"I felt something." He reached for his back. "But it wasn't much."

Crystal lifted his shirt and touched a blemish near the middle of his back. "Blazes! You did get stung. But it looks different. Not as red."

"Yeah. It wasn't like what people say. I hardly felt it." Oliver sat on the bench across the aisle from mine. "But I feel it now, like a burn. And I'm sick to my stomach. I think I'm gonna pass out."

Crystal tossed her suit to an empty bench and slid next to him. "Here. Lean on me."

"I guess I'll have to drive." I rose and staggered to the front, where Vonda caught me and helped me sit in the driver's seat. "Everyone hold on. This might be a rough ride." I turned on the engine, shifted to reverse, and looked through the rear window. When I pushed the pedal down, the bus lurched backwards, burst through the wall of bees, and rolled over Axleback's corpse.

As the bus rattled on, the six Jaradians scattered from around a huge gun mounted on a four-legged bracket. Since turning quickly would take a lot of painful effort and probably cause a skid on the remaining ice, I kept the bus running in reverse on the path toward the city. We bounced and rocked. Creaking noises erupted everywhere, like the frame was about to fall apart. Perdantus fluttered from place to place while the children clung to their seats, most cringing or biting their lips as they watched me drive like a crazed drunk.

When we had driven well away from the Jaradians, I lifted my foot and let the bus slow to a stop. Now with more time, I shifted to forward, pushed the pedal again, and guided us into a slow turn until we faced the city. Ahead, only a few patches of ice endured the warming day. The bitter blast had departed as quickly as it had arrived.

With one hand on the steering wheel, I leaned back in the seat and laid my other hand on my throbbing head, but resting in that position meant that I could no longer reach the pedals. "Vonda, can you hold down the gas pedal?"

"I think so." She jumped from her seat and knelt next to mine, a fist on the pedal. "Ready."

"Push it about halfway down."

When she did, we rumbled forward. Barely able to keep my burning eyes open, I steadied the bus on the road. Fortunately, no one else traveled this narrow, unpaved path—no worries about dodging other vehicles. Yet, the Jaradians might soon chase us from behind. Although I saw no rovers near the cave besides the one I drove, the Jaradians got there somehow.

Still facing forward, I called out, "Someone watch behind us. Let me know if anyone's coming."

"I see rovers," Bastian said. "Pretty far back, but I think they're getting closer."

"Everyone hold on." I looked at Vonda. "Let's go. As hard as you can."

Using both hands, she slammed the pedal to the floor.

The engine clattered loudly, and the bus zoomed ahead, pushing me back in my seat. Children gasped. Some cried out. With the way ahead clear for the moment, I looked back. As the kids bounced, Crystal held Oliver with both arms wrapped around him while Norbert did the same to Dirk, Perdantus clinging tightly to Norbert's shoulder. Another boy held a clay shell close, probably filled with the glowsap I had collected, his other hand clutching his seat. Maybe he thought they would be punished if they went home empty-handed.

I turned to the front and focused on the city spires as we drew closer. "Give me updates, Bastian."

"I see four rovers, still closing in. Better go as fast as you can."

"This *is* as fast as I can." Again pain shot through my body. Even if I could get to my rover before the Jaradians caught up, I couldn't possibly ferry all the kids to the ship without some of us getting caught. My only hope was to make a turn somewhere and hide the bus before the Jaradians could figure out where we went.

And that goal seemed impossible, too. But I had to try.

15

I drove the bus into Bassolith. Soon, our path merged with a major road, cleared of all snow and ice. I careened onto it, barely missing an oncoming rover. Still driving alongside the river, I passed another rover, then an old steam-engine car, and rumbled on.

"One of the Jaradian rovers crashed," Bastian called. "Three are still following, farther back now."

"Good." My heart racing, I steered madly to get around the other vehicles. I bumped a blue two-person rover, sending it careening onto a side street. When a male Tauranta carrying a stack of boxes tried to cross the road from the right, I punched the horn. He threw the boxes and spun out of the way.

I whispered, "Sorry," then looked at Vonda. "Ease it back to halfway."

The bus slowed, allowing me to avoid three rovers and a line of little Taurantas marching in green school-like uniforms.

"They're gaining on us," Bastian said.

I looked ahead. To stay alongside the river and keep heading toward my hidden rover, I would have to turn off the main road and onto the narrower street I used to get into the city. At the moment, no one was walking alongside that street, but might that change farther down where it became a footpath leading into the forest? I had to risk it.

"Everyone hang on." I turned off the road and drove over the curb. We bounced wildly. When the bus settled, I glanced back. Several kids, including Oliver and Crystal, had tumbled into the aisle, though Dirk and Norbert managed to stay on their bench.

Oliver rose and helped Crystal and a couple of others get up. He lumbered to the front and stood behind me in the aisle. "I've been thinking. Since that bee stung Axleback's body so many times, maybe it didn't have much venom left when it stung me."

"They were eating him, not stinging him. The bee that stung you probably never stung him. There were hundreds of bees there."

"Maybe so, but I'm feeling better." He touched the back of my seat. "Want me to drive?"

"No. We're stopping in a minute." Ahead, the Taurantas' temple came into view. I pointed. "We're going to hide there. A little slower, Vonda." When the bus decelerated, I turned onto a gravel path that led around to the back of the temple. "Now let it go."

She released the pedal. I coasted into a parking space next to a larger bus that hid us from view on one side. When I shut off the engine, I called out, "Everyone duck down. Get out of sight."

"I couldn't tell if they saw us turn," Bastian said as he knelt on the floor.

"We can only hope and pray." I crawled from the driver's seat. Just as I was about to kneel, someone waved from the temple's rear door. I squinted at the female Tauranta and whispered, "Melda?"

"Who's Melda?" Oliver asked.

"A friend . . . maybe." When I opened the bus door, Melda hurried to it as fast as her hefty tail would allow. She stood on the gravel parking pad and spoke breathlessly. "I saw you coming. Follow me. I will hide you all."

"How can I trust you?" I asked. "Noldic betrayed me."

"You can trust me because there's no battle storm now." She waved a hand. "Hurry. We don't have much time to hide the children. Noldic wants to make up for what he did to you."

Holding a side rail, I walked down the steps. With the adrenaline rush ending, pain crashed in once again. When I touched down on the gravel, I toppled into Melda. She caught me and kept me from falling. "Dear girl! Are you sick?"

I nodded. "Very. I got stung by a bramble bee."

Melda gasped. "You poor child!"

"Megan!" Crystal leaped down and grabbed my wrist. "Why didn't you tell me?"

"I didn't want to—"

"Never mind. I can guess. You're being a hero." Crystal turned and helped Oliver navigate the steps. "This boy got stung by a bramble bee, too."

"Those stings are always fatal," Melda said.

"We know." I gestured toward the temple door. "Just hide them. Please."

"Them?" Melda repeated. "What about you?"

"I'm going to my ship." I turned to Oliver and set a hand on his shoulder. "I'll bring the *Nebula Nine* here. Emerson won't let anyone else pilot her. Just hide the best you can till I come. Since you're feeling better, you should take charge. And make sure someone helps Dirk."

He grasped my forearm with both hands. "I can't let you go without help."

"I will help her," Perdantus said as he flew from the bus and landed on my shoulder.

"But you can't pick her up if she collapses."

"Have no fear of that. This girl is the toughest human I have ever seen. Yet, she might need a lookout, and I can provide that service. We should continue following her plans. They haven't failed us thus far."

"All right. All right." Oliver waved a hand. "Go."

With Perdantus still on my shoulder, I walked away, heading around the temple on the far side, then toward the footpath. Since the Jaradians were searching for a bus or a group of kids, maybe I could slip past them unnoticed.

When I reached the footpath, I turned upstream, my head low as I walked alongside the river, careful not to look back as Perdantus updated me on what lay behind us. So far, no one followed.

Every step resounded with a pounding throb up my spine and into my head. How long had it been since the bee stung me? Two hours? Three? Cynda didn't survive much longer than that. I was running out of time.

Within a couple of minutes, I passed into the forest. I hid behind a tree and looked back. One of the pursuing rovers had parked in front of the temple, and two Jaradians stood at the door, apparently waiting to be let inside.

"The other rovers parked farther down the road," Perdantus said. "The Jaradians are likely searching as many places as they can. You have some time to rest."

"I can't. I have to keep going." I followed the stream to the stone, turned away from the water, and counted ten paces to the bush. There I dug out the bag holding the captain's computer tablet. I withdrew it and attached it to my belt.

Just beyond that spot, the rover sat unhidden, its hatch open, probably left that way by Gavin. Perdantus flew in and perched on the steering wheel. I tried to climb in with him but fell back and landed hard on my rear end.

"Are you all right?" he called.

"Give me a second." Sitting and staring at the rover, I heaved fast, shallow breaths. My heart beat erratically. My vision blurred. How could I possibly do this? With the Jaradians breathing down our necks, I had only minutes to get to the ship and return to save the kids.

Firming my lips, I whispered to myself, "I can do this. I *have* to do this." I struggled to my feet and crawled into the rover. When I settled in the seat, Perdantus fluttered to my shoulder. "Ignition," I said with authority. "And close the hatch."

The engine started, and the hatch lowered until it clicked shut. I pushed the throttle and zipped back to the river. Once over the water, I zoomed upstream, swerving with it as the course took me around trees and over rapids. Along the way, Perdantus talked about the trees around us and the Willow Winds who lived there, probably to get my mind off my agony, but the pain pounding in my head wouldn't let me process the information. I just kept driving forward.

The moment the *Nebula Nine* came into view, I slowed the rover. "Open the ship's cargo door." When the side door lowered, I flew the rover inside, parked it, and popped the hatch.

"Emerson," I called. "Prepare for takeoff." My own words pounded my skull.

"Preparing for takeoff, Captain Willis." As the cargo door closed, I climbed out of the rover, then up the ladder to the bridge, Perdantus still on my shoulder.

As I hobbled toward the captain's chair, the ship's engines started. "Emerson, do you have anything to report?"

"First Mate Gavin Foster boarded and demanded security clearance. I declined, of course. Then he—"

"Never mind. Tell me more later." I sat in the captain's chair, buckled in, and grasped the steering yoke while Perdantus flew to the back of the first mate's chair. "Shields up, Emerson, and full thruster engine power. We're in a hurry."

The engines revved. "Acknowledged, Captain. Shields are up. Thruster engine on maximum."

Holding the yoke with one hand, I pushed the takeoff thruster with the other. The *Nebula Nine* launched from the ground. I turned the yoke until Bassolith appeared in the front viewing window, then eased the rear thruster forward while pulling back on the takeoff thruster at the same time.

We rocketed ahead. I pressed the button to arm the ship's laser cannons and photon torpedoes. A target grid appeared on the window with a bull's-eye circle at the center. I soared over the forest, again using the river as a guide.

When the temple came into view, I pulled the rear thruster back to decelerate, though I kept the landing thruster running to stay elevated. At ground level, a rover sat in the temple's rear parking area, and two Jaradians stood with fat-barreled rifles pointing toward the temple door.

They jerked their heads toward the ship and aimed their weapons. Fireballs hurtled toward me. One glanced off the front window, while two others struck the ship with a sizzling thud somewhere out of view.

"Shields are holding firm, Captain."

"Good. Now to clear the way." As the Jaradians continued blasting fireballs, I grabbed the laser cannons' pointing wheel and turned it until the bull's-eye centered on the shooters. I pressed the trigger button and held it. Laser beams fired from their turrets and blasted into the slavers. The force slung their weapons away, and the two Jaradians crumpled to the ground.

I released the trigger and eased the ship closer to the temple, searching the area. Oliver ran from the rear door, grabbed one of the fallen rifles, and waved for me to land.

"Emerson, is that lot big enough to set the *Nine* down?"

"Negative, Captain. The closest potential landing area is one hundred sixty-seven meters away at an angle of sixteen degrees."

"Too far." I scanned the ground. At the front entrance of the temple, two Jaradians stalked toward the door, rifles and axes at the ready. They would be inside in seconds.

"We'll hover and collect the kids from the bottom hatch."

"You will have to lower the shields to do that."

"No choice. Lower them. Fly over the lot and hover close to the ground. I'm heading to the hatch."

"Acknowledged. But, remember, I cannot land the ship, even in an emergency. My programming will not allow it."

"Blasted stupid rules!"

"I am not the programmer, so I—"

"Never mind. Just get me as low as possible and give me laser cover."

"I can do that."

"Good. Do you know the difference between Jaradians and Taurantas?"

"Affirmative."

"Then aim for the Jaradians, not the Taurantas. If you get a clear shot, take it."

"Acknowledged."

I pushed up from my seat and staggered toward the ladder. Pain assaulted every muscle, every tendon, every joint. My head pounded, blurring my vision. There was no way I could do this. No way.

But I had to.

Gasping for breath, I clutched my locket and whispered, "Help me, Astral Dragon. I need strength."

I climbed down the ladder and descended to the lowest level, slowed by an air lock compartment that forced me to open and close two safety doors.

Once at the bottom, I stepped onto the floor where the two hatch panels joined. I grabbed the bottom rungs of an overhanging ladder and, after fighting off a bout of dizziness, called upward. "Emerson, I'm in position. Let's do it."

As the ladder descended, I set my feet on the lowest rung and grasped a higher one. The hatch panels split at the center and slid open. Air whooshed in and swirled all around, batting my hair and clothes and sending grit into my eyes. The landing thrusters had to continue running, forcing me to fight the wind and keep going, though my shirt flew in disarray and my hair whipped my face.

Perdantus flew down the ladder with a set of goggles in his beak. Battling the jets with beating wings, he landed on my shoulder and dropped the goggles into my hand. "Emerson said you would need these."

I slid them on, tucked my shirt in, and took a deep breath. "Thanks."

Below, the ground lay about five meters from my feet, gravel skittering with the thrusters' blast. Would the ladder descend that far? Not likely. I might have to improvise.

"I will alert the others." Perdantus flew off my shoulder and into the wind.

As the descent continued, the temple's rear entrance came into view. Perdantus fluttered around Oliver, probably shouting instructions, but the wind drowned all his chirps. The thrusters blasted the ground in a circular pattern, creating a wall of downward-rushing air around me. How Perdantus flew through that barrier, I could only guess.

Still holding a rifle, Oliver threw the door open and waved. Crystal hustled out, guiding Renalda and the other smaller girls toward me. Vonda and Bastian followed, supporting Dirk from either side as the other boys brought up the rear.

Oliver waved again. Noldic lumbered out with an axe in hand. Oliver stepped to the opening and fired the rifle into the temple, slowly backing away as he shot fireball after fireball.

Now under the ship, Crystal lowered her head, burst through the surrounding wall of wind, and stood directly under the ladder. She stretched her arms toward me, the constant swirl whipping her blonde hair into a frenzy. "Just a little more," she shouted, barely audible in the earsplitting din.

I looked at the *Nine*'s wing on the right. It nearly touched the temple's roof. We couldn't hover another centimeter lower. I had to hope the ladder would descend far enough to—

The ladder halted, still two or three meters from the ground. I bent my knees and stretched for Crystal's hand, but it was just out of reach. More children ran through the barrier wind and gathered around Crystal. At the temple entrance, a fireball shot out from inside, narrowly missing Oliver. The Jaradians were coming.

"Jump!" I shouted.

Crystal jumped. Her hand slapped mine and fell away. This would never work, especially for the little kids. With Jaradians closing in, I had to act now.

I curled my legs around the lowest rung, dangled upside down, and reached as far as I could. "Smallest first! Climb me like I'm part of the ladder. Let's go!"

"I'll guide from above," Perdantus called as he flew past me.

Crystal and Bastian hoisted Renalda into my arms. She climbed my body, ramming a knee into my stomach and banging a spiked shoe against my face. When she made it to the ladder, Perdantus shouted from the hatch, "Everyone take your shoes off! Tie them around your necks!"

While the kids obeyed, I looked toward the temple. Oliver faced the entrance from several meters away. Noldic hid at the side of the doorway holding an axe.

Crystal and Bastian lifted another girl to me. While she climbed, I continued watching the temple, trying to ignore her punishing knees and feet as she clambered over me.

Oliver dropped the rifle and raised his hands. When a Jaradian stepped out from the temple, Noldic swung his axe and bashed the Jaradian's head with the butt of the blade. The Jaradian crumpled and lay motionless.

The moment a third girl lifted into my arms, a blast of light slammed into Noldic. I glanced away, trying not to imagine the damage. When I looked back, he was gone—disintegrated, with only sparks remaining. Melda ran out, screaming. She knelt at the spot he had been standing and wept. I swallowed hard. Poor Melda. How awful!

I shook off a shudder and looked at Oliver. With a rifle again in hand, he ran toward the ship, shouting, "Hurry! We have to get out of here!"

When the girl scrambled up, Oliver burst through the wall of wind and halted below me. "Let me do that. You can't possibly lift them all."

My head pounded harder than ever. Darkness invaded my vision. Barely able to see Oliver's face, I shouted, "Just keep the kids coming!"

As another child rose into my arms and climbed, Oliver called out, "The last two Jaradians brought that big gun. They killed Noldic with it, and now they're taking it apart to bring it out." Oliver tossed the rifle to the ground. "I can't shoot a fireball through that wind. You should fly away. I'll hide the rest of the kids somewhere."

"Are you sure you can—" My locket dropped out from behind my shirt and dangled below me, visible as it swayed in the buffeting wind. It glowed brightly, pulsing red in time with my thumping heart. I licked my lips and shouted, "Never mind. Just go faster. Now."

As Crystal and Oliver lifted one kid after another, two Jaradians exited the temple, one carrying the bracket I had seen at the bee cave and the other a long-barreled gun as big as his body. They halted about twenty meters away and began spreading the bracket's legs on the ground.

Now only Oliver, Crystal, Bastian, Vonda, and Dirk remained below me. "Shields are down," I said, breathless and dizzy. "If that's a photon blaster they're mounting, it'll ground the *Nine*."

While Oliver and Crystal boosted Vonda, Bastian shouted, "Can't someone up there tell Emerson to raise the shields?"

A foot mashed my leg, making me grunt. "He won't obey anyone's voice but mine. And they have to stay down till we're finished."

With the ground bracket in place, the Jaradians began setting the gun on top. They would be ready to fire in mere moments.

Oliver and Crystal heaved Bastian into my arms. Although the heaviest kid yet, he crawled over me without inflicting pain. Maybe everything had turned numb.

A laser beam shot from the *Nine* and ripped a foot off one of the Jaradians. He collapsed and writhed on the ground. The other Jaradian ignored him and tightened fasteners on the gun's support. Only seconds remained.

"What are we going to do about Dirk?" I asked. "He can't possibly climb."

"Just hold him," Oliver said as he and Crystal lifted him. "We'll do the rest. Tell Emerson to retract the ladder."

The remaining Jaradian flipped a switch on the gun. Pulses of lights ran along the barrel, probably a sign of charging and getting ready to fire.

I hugged Dirk around the waist, his back against my face, but my arms felt weak and flaccid. I couldn't hold on for long. "Emerson! Bring us up! Hurry!"

Just as the ladder started to rise, Oliver leaped and grabbed the bottom rung, sandwiching me between his body and Dirk's. The ladder shook. Dirk slipped a notch. I latched onto his belt with my teeth and hung on.

"Crystal," Oliver shouted as he rose. "Grab me."

She leaped and wrapped her arms around his legs. Again the ladder shook. I clenched my jaws with all my might, sending peals of pain ripping through my head. No way was I going to lose Dirk. We had come too far.

A brilliant light appeared in the gun's barrel, the photon torpedo. Just as the Jaradian reached for the trigger, another laser beam shot from the *Nine* and blasted him in the chest. He staggered back and dropped, his body burning.

The other Jaradian, though missing a foot, crawled with his arms toward the gun. As low to the ground as he was, maybe Emerson couldn't lock on to him.

Oliver climbed rung after rung, grunting as he lifted Crystal with him. When he rose into the ship, Crystal swung to the side and dropped to the floor. Oliver leaped off the ladder and landed next to her near the edge of the hatch. The moment I rose high enough, several hands took Dirk from me, hauled me clear of the hatch, and laid me on the floor.

The sudden shift throttled my brain. Blackness washed across my vision like a flood. I could barely move, only enough to clutch my locket. At least it was still there.

"Emerson," Oliver yelled, "raise shields right now!"

I could barely whisper, "He won't. I have to tell him—"

The gun boomed. Something thudded. The ship rocked hard to the side, making my head smack the floor. The blackness swept my mind into its flood.

Many hands grabbed me, some holding my arms and some my legs and others pressing up against my back. Youthful whispers volleyed back and forth.

"Is she dead?"

"No. Real close, though."

"Are we gonna have to tie her up?"

"I don't think so. She got the poultice."

"She can't die. I love her."

"Me, too. She saved us all. She's the bravest person I ever met."

Cool air wafted across my chest as if someone had opened my shirt. Then something cold touched my skin in several places. A beeping noise began in a rhythmic pulse, close by and irritating.

I tried to open my eyes, but the lids refused to budge. Yet, I could feel that my hand clutched my locket. Maybe I never let it go.

Crystal's voice pierced the silence. "I think the electrodes are in the right place." My shirt closed, shutting off the coolness.

"Emerson," Oliver said, "what does your database say about bramble bee stings?"

"A normal injection of venom is always fatal for humans. Some have survived lesser doses."

"Like me. I think I hardly got any venom at all. Still hit me like a bus."

"Are there any treatments?" Crystal asked. "Anything that can raise her chances?"

"Only one that has been entered in the medical history," Emerson said. "There is an old saying among humans that it is sometimes helpful to be treated with the hair of the dog that bit you."

"So the bees themselves can treat her?"

"Not the bees. The sap they collect. When energized by the bees, the sap glows and becomes a powerful restoration agent. If the venom has not caused too much damage, the sap will regenerate her cells."

"That's powerful stuff," Oliver said. "I wonder why Thorne never tried to cure any of us with it—you know, the kids who got stung."

"Likely because of its value. Just a few milliliters costs more than most residents of Bassolith earn in a year. Yet, since it's so dangerous to collect, few are willing to risk their lives to do so."

"That's why Thorne wanted us to collect it," Crystal said. "He used us to get it because we're . . . what was that word?"

"Expendable," Oliver said. "But what good does it do to talk about it? We don't have any."

Gathering all of my strength, I whispered in a rasping voice, "Ask the kids."

"What?" Oliver's breath tickled my cheek. "Did you say something, Megan?"

I swallowed and tried again. "Ask . . . the kids. One of them . . ." I exhaled, unable to say another word.

"Check the kids!" Oliver shouted. "See if any of them brought some glowsap."

"On my way." Crystal's footfalls clattered, retreating in the distance.

Oliver's voice cracked with emotion. "Suppose we have some glowsap, Emerson. What do we do with it?"

"According to the medical notes, the sap is a powerful vomit inducer. So it cannot be taken orally. Yet, the medicinal elements—that is, the molecules that make it glow—can be absorbed by the skin. Once the sap's glow is gone, you will know that the medicine has been absorbed. Since the sap is sticky, however, it is a messy process."

"I don't mind getting messy. I can do it."

"In order to gain the greatest benefit, the sap should be applied on as much skin as possible. I suggest that one of your female companions apply it."

"That's fine. I'm sure Crystal will do it."

Sudden pain stabbed my chest. The beeping altered to a jumpy whine. Oliver shouted, "Megan!" Then everything fell silent.

I floated in nothingness, numb and cold, nothing to sit or stand on. From a backdrop of star-speckled blackness, a glowing white dragon flew toward me, his huge wings spread in a silent glide. He stopped in front of me, folded in his wings, and extended his long neck, bringing his glowing face close. Saying nothing, he cocked his head and stared with radiant blue eyes.

I stared back at him. His gaze felt soothing, similar to Crystal's, though it caused no confusion. "Are you . . ." Although I spoke, my voice failed to reach my ears. Maybe the dragon could hear me anyway. "Are you the Astral Dragon?"

The dragon neither moved nor spoke. A thought entered my mind, deep and resonant, obviously not my own. *I am.*

"Am I dead?"

Another thought penetrated. *In a manner of speaking. Your heart has stopped, and efforts are being made to revive you. Your life hangs by a thread. Whether or not the thread breaks is up to a gifted friend.*

"Gifted? Do you mean Crystal?"

The dragon's eyes pulsed like energized sapphires. *Crystal is gifted, to be sure, but her gifts will not avail you now. Another friend will need to use his gift if he wishes to save you. At this time, he is not even sure he is gifted, which is why I said your life hangs by a thread.*

"His gift? Do you mean Oliver?"

The dragon bobbed his head.

"Who can tell him?"

He needs to tell himself. Deep within, he knows. Yet, he is hesitant.

"Why? Doesn't he want to save me?"

With all his heart. His hesitation is not selfish in the slightest, but it is also a private matter. If he overcomes it and saves you, I am sure you will discern the reason for the hesitation. Otherwise, there is no need to know.

Something pressed down on my chest. Pain spiked. The weight lifted for a moment before returning with a heavy thud, repeating the cycle again and again, as if someone were jumping on my chest.

The dragon's eyes brightened further. *Your friend has prevailed over his scruples. He knows that life is a gift that must be protected. Our feelings are not a factor in that decision.* The dragon faded away, though the voice in my mind remained. *As you continue fulfilling your purpose, remember to watch for guidance from above. Nothing happens by chance.*

In the absence of the dragon's glow, everything around me returned to blackness. I continued floating. For how long, I don't know.

The beeping returned. Light came from somewhere, bright and irritating. I opened my eyes. A lamp stood over me, its long, segmented neck extending from a rod attached to the ceiling.

Soon, my surroundings came into focus. I lay on a bed in *Nebula Nine*'s sick bay. When I rose to a sitting position, my head throbbed, and electrodes attached to my chest pinched my skin. I pushed a finger past my open shirt and touched one of the electrodes. Something sticky coated my fingertip as well as my chest.

I looked at my hand, then my arm. They, too, were coated with something sticky. What was going on?

Memories flowed. This stuff had to be the glowsap. Since it was no longer glowing, I must have absorbed the medicine.

Something chirped. Perdantus perched on the rail at the foot of the bed. "Ah! You're awake. I will report your recovery." He hopped up and flew through the open doorway.

I peeled the electrodes off and closed my shirt the best I could. Fortunately, the material adhered to my sticky skin and stayed in place.

I slid off the bed, set my bare feet on the floor, and slowly transferred my weight until I stood upright without support. My legs tingled but not with pain, and my head ached though not nearly as badly as before.

Oliver and Crystal rushed in. When they saw me, Oliver smiled while Crystal shook a finger. "Claw of the Dragon! You'd better get back in bed, girl. You nearly died on us."

"Twice," Oliver said. "The second time was worse."

"Yeah." Crystal shook her fist. "At first, your heart started shaking like this." She looked at Oliver. "What did Emerson call it?"

He scratched his head. "Fibri . . . something."

"Fibrisomething? I don't think that's right."

"I'm not sure what it said. It happened while it was attaching the electrodes to her skin. I was standing in the hall because . . ." He shifted his weight. "You know."

Crystal smiled and added a wink. "Good thing you got over that."

"Yeah. Well. Let's hope it doesn't happen again." Oliver extended a hand. The remote lay on his open palm. "Anyway, Emerson told me to look for this and press the button. I found it on your belt. It shocked your heart and made it stop shaking."

I touched the metal ring. Now that I was aboard ship, it would recharge on its own. I was safe for the time being. "I guess this blasted collar's good for something."

"Yeah," Crystal said. "But that's not what saved you. Actually, the shock made your heart stop. Emerson said that had to happen first."

"Then how did I survive?"

Crystal nudged Oliver with an elbow. "Tell her."

He nudged back. "No, you tell her."

"You're the one who did it."

"All right. All right." Oliver's cheeks reddened. "I know CPR, so when your heart stopped, I came in from the hall and gave you chest compressions." He folded his hands behind his back and fidgeted. "I hope you're not mad at me."

I glanced at my shirt to make sure it was still covering my chest. Heat rose into my own cheeks. They were probably redder than his. "Um . . . no. I'm not mad. You saved my life."

Oliver blew out a long sigh, as if he had been holding his breath. "Good. Then you're not embarrassed."

"A little, but it's okay."

"You think *that's* embarrassing?" Crystal waved a hand. "That's nothing. If you knew all the places I rubbed that gook on you to suck the poison out, you would be so—"

"Hush, Crystal." Oliver's eyes narrowed. "Megan, did you notice if the bee that stung you stung anyone else first?"

I nodded. "Axleback. Twice."

"Then you didn't get a full dose." Oliver nudged Crystal. "Told ya. Now you owe me your dessert tonight."

She stomped a foot. "Blazes! I was hoping you'd be the first person ever to survive a full bramble bee sting."

I nodded toward Oliver. "I think his sting was a full dose. He just won't admit it."

He looked at his shoe as he dragged it along the floor. "Maybe. But we can't prove it."

"No. We can't." I smiled. My rescuer obviously didn't want to own up to his gift yet. And that was all right with me. "I'm just glad I survived a partial dose."

"Yeah. Me, too." Oliver's blush deepened. "I think we should change the subject."

"All right. No problem." A speaker embedded in the ceiling crackled. Emerson was listening. And that reminded me of a good question. "Speaking of surviving, what happened when I passed out? How did the ship survive that gun?"

Oliver grinned. "Emerson raised the shields just in time. We took a hard hit, but the shields held. It was scary and pretty amazing at the same time."

"But he doesn't know you. Did he break the rules?"

"Negative," Emerson said from the ceiling speaker. "Oliver has been listed in my database as an apprentice for several years. He was the only coherent crew member on board, so I obeyed his command. We are now in orbit."

Oliver saluted. "Any orders for me, Captain Willis?"

"Just one. Take over as captain. You're way more qualified."

He lowered his hand. "More qualified than you? You gotta be kidding me."

I touched my collar. "Oliver, I'm a pirate. A prisoner. I'm captain because no one else was left. You're the former captain's son. By rights, you should—"

"By rights?" Oliver shook his head hard. "It's not happening, Megan. You know way more about flying a ship than I do. So you're the captain, and that's final." He grasped my hand and pulled me gently away from the bed. "Shall we go to the bridge, Captain?"

I smiled. "If First Mate Oliver Tillman can spare me for a few minutes, I have to get cleaned up."

"Yeah." He drew his hand back, flexing it. "You're super sticky."

"Sorry."

"No problem. Anyway, I told Emerson we should run the gravity engine and fly in a wide orbit around Delta Ninety-eight until we decided on a better plan. Take your time."

"I'll help you clean up." Crystal crossed her arms and looked me over. "I mean, sorry and all that, but I know where I smeared the sap on your body. It'll be hard for you to reach some of it."

While Crystal helped me bathe in the ship's washtub, she brought me up to speed on what happened during my unconscious hours. Dirk recovered from the drug, but since he was still woozy, the other kids pitched in to help him prepare meals in the galley. Emerson assigned sleeping quarters, two to a room, but he left the captain's quarters open, not knowing if I would choose to sleep there or would want to stay in the old hovel where I was used to sleeping.

During the wash time, I caught Crystal glancing again and again at the dragon brand on my upper arm. After the fourth look, she finally blurted out in Humaniversal, "So what's up with the lizard thingy?"

I told her about my arrest, trial, and branding process. As I gave her the gory details, she flinched, then cried, but said nothing.

When we finished, I got dressed in cargo pants and a long-sleeved navy polo shirt that Crystal found in my room as well as a pair of off-white canvas shoes I usually wore when I wasn't working. She also gave me Captain Tillman's computer tablet, which they had taken from my belt when they carried me from the lower hatch.

After I fastened my belt, I reclipped the remote and tablet to it. Although we had all escaped, I was still a prisoner to the collar. Plenty of miracles had already happened, but this one had to wait awhile longer.

Something thumped overhead, probably kids in their new quarters directly above the washroom. For the first time since boarding, the reality of my situation struck home. I was in command of a powerful military space cruiser with a load of escaped children on board, and I had to figure out what to do next.

As I imagined the *Nebula Nine* orbiting the planet, a feeling of security enveloped me. We were alone, finally safe. Yet, were we? Might the *Astral Dragon* be looking for us? If Gavin was in some kind of conspiracy to capture me, he might know by now that I had escaped, and he also knew how to find me.

"Emerson," I called. "Are you still transmitting on the hailing frequencies?"

"Affirmative. That was your order."

"But it's the low-power signal, right?"

"Negative. Former First Mate Gavin Foster repaired the transmitter. I checked inventory at the factory's parts store, and it showed that the switch had been picked up. Perhaps he went there in search of you and identified himself, then the store clerk mentioned that he had a switch waiting for the captain."

I waved an arm. "Shut the signal down! Now!"

"Acknowledged."

"Crystal, follow me." We rushed together from the washroom, jogged to a ladder leading to the bridge, and began climbing. "Emerson, take us out of orbit."

"What is your new course, Captain?"

I leaped from the top rung and hurried toward the bridge, Crystal close behind me. "Just away from Delta Ninety-eight. Top speed."

"Shall I accelerate gradually?" Emerson asked. "No one is strapped in."

"Hold off. Send an alert in Humaniversal. Everyone should get in their beds and use the gravity straps to fasten themselves."

A horn sounded three times, followed by Emerson's voice, now speaking Humaniversal. "Proceed to your assigned beds and fasten the straps over you immediately."

I sat in the captain's chair and pointed at the physician's station. "Crystal," I said in Alpha One, "sit there and buckle the belt around your waist." I buckled my own belt and looked out the front window. The view showed nothing but bright specks on a black background with the targeting lines still in place. I focused on my console and checked the three-dimensional detection grid. A blip appeared near the edge of one quadrant. "Emerson, do you see that?"

"Affirmative, Captain. It appears to be a ship flying in the same direction we are. It will overtake us in three minutes, seven seconds."

Oliver ran in and slid into Gavin's seat at the control console an arm's length away. "What's going on?"

I pointed at the grid. "Someone's following us."

"What are we going to do?"

"Do you know how to navigate?"

"I think so. I watched the navigator enough to figure it out."

"Your console has maps. Find a sanctuary planet and plot a course."

"I'm on it." Oliver slid a finger along his console screen.

I refocused on the detection grid. "Emerson, is the ship hailing us?"

"Negative, Captain. It is running silent."

"Are its shields up?"

"Negative, Captain."

Dirk ran in, sat at the navigator's console, and buckled. "Everyone's secure, even Perdantus." He looked at the detection grid. "What's going on?"

"Shhh. Let me think." Memories of my parents handling a similar situation came to mind. We had executed a raid on a military installation a day earlier, and we were heading home to Alpha One when an unidentified, silent ship approached. "Emerson, maintain current speed. Make a turn, thirty degrees and negative twenty, two degrees per second. Tell me if the ship follows our new course."

"Turn commencing."

"Change the front window. Show me the direction the ship's coming from."

The viewing window flashed. The new angle showed an equally dark backdrop with different clusters of stars, the targeting grid still active.

I scanned the darkness. Nothing seemed unusual. "Emerson, highlight the approaching ship."

A tiny red circle pulsed over an even smaller white dot near the edge of the bull's-eye. As the seconds passed, it drifted closer to the center, reached it, and stayed there.

"The pursuing ship performed the same turn," Emerson said.

"I can see that." Sweat dampened my brow as I studied the ship. Still no sign of anything unusual. "Is she in hailing range?"

"Affirmative, Captain."

"Hail the ship. Use Captain Tillman's voice print and send the standard request for identification in Humaniversal. Put everything on the speakers."

"Acknowledged."

As I set a hand on the rear thruster, ready to accelerate, Captain Tillman's voice emanated from the ceiling speakers. "This is Captain Tillman of the *Nebula Nine*, commissioned by the Galaxy Regulatory Alliance, home base Alpha One. We have detected that your ship is following ours. Identify yourself and your purpose."

Silence ensued. I stared again at the viewing window, imagining

Oliver, Crystal, and Dirk doing the same or maybe staring at me instead, wondering what my next decision might be.

"Captain Tillman," a man with a sharp, authoritative voice said from the speakers. "This is Admiral Fairbanks of the *Nebula One*. Why are you in this system? According to my records, you're supposed to be policing Beta Four."

"Emerson?" I hissed. "What's going on?"

"Captain Tillman kept his mission off-the-record. He needed complete secrecy."

I narrowed my eyes. "Even from the admiral? Why?"

"Captain Tillman did not inform me of his reasoning."

"Okay. Switch outgoing transmission to my console's microphone. Transmit my words in Captain Tillman's voice." I pushed the rear thruster a tiny fraction, increasing our speed slightly. When my microphone's light turned on, I cleared my throat. "Admiral, with all due respect, I am not authorized to answer your question." My words came through the speakers in Captain Tillman's voice.

The other ship responded. "Not authorized? Captain, I am the one who authorizes the entire fleet's missions. I demand an explanation."

My mind raced. More memories of my parents' tactics flooded in. "Admiral, until I can verify your identity, I will maintain silence protocol regarding Alliance missions."

"Then we will exchange ship identity codes. Transmission commencing."

I turned off the microphone. "Emerson?"

"Every Alliance ship has an identification code that can be transmitted in an encrypted format. Only another Alliance ship can decrypt it."

"Did you receive theirs?"

"Affirmative. That ship is, indeed, the *Nebula One*."

"Send them ours."

"Commencing. For your information, the *Nebula One* will overtake us in one minute, fifty seconds."

I increased the rear thruster another notch and looked at Oliver. "Did you find a sanctuary planet?"

He looked up from his console. "The closest one is three days from here at top speed. We can get to Delta Ninety-five in about four hours. It's uninhabited, but the air is breathable. I can't tell why no one lives there. And there's also a wormhole an hour away. It leads to—"

"The Beta system. I know. That's the one we came through. It'd take weeks to get to the other end."

The admiral's voice returned to the speakers. "Captain Tillman, we verified your ship's identity. I assume you have identified ours. Now tell me why you are in the Delta system."

I switched the microphone on again. "We are on a rescue mission, Admiral Fairbanks."

"A rescue mission? Whom are you trying to rescue?"

"My son, Oliver. He was kidnapped by Jaradians. I'm sure you heard about it."

Anger spiced his tone. "You secretly used an Alliance ship for a personal mission? Captain, you of all people should know that this is a protocol violation of the highest order."

I reached deep in my memory to try to mimic the captain's way of speaking. "I do know, Admiral, but I had to keep our plans confidential. We couldn't afford a leak, and I had no access to another long-range ship."

"One moment, Captain." The admiral's transmission terminated.

I whispered to Oliver, "Any other places to go?"

He leaned close, keeping his own voice low. "Nothing else, unless you want to go back to Delta Ninety-eight."

The transmission restarted. "Captain Tillman, we are receiving a distress signal from your ship."

I switched the microphone off again. "Emerson?"

"His statement is true. A distress signal began exactly twenty seconds ago. It is coming from the cargo hold."

"Who's been in the cargo hold besides me?"

"Former First Mate Gavin Foster. As I mentioned earlier, he boarded and demanded security clearance. You did not allow me to continue the report."

"Then continue it. Hurry."

"After repairing the transmitter, he proceeded to the cargo hold and tried to start the other rovers docked within, but they, of course, did not recognize his voice. I suspected that he might be trying to sabotage the ship, so I deployed tear gas. He departed quickly and did not return."

I clenched a fist. "He wasn't trying to sabotage the ship. He was planting a transmitter so he could find us later. He fixed the transmitter to make sure the distress signal worked."

"That is a logical conclusion, Captain Willis."

"Captain Tillman," Admiral Fairbanks said. "I am awaiting your explanation."

I turned the microphone on. "The distress signal is a mystery, Admiral. We are investigating the source."

"Yes, you do that. And we will help you. Decelerate in standard fixed increments and prepare for rendezvous and docking. I will be on board shortly."

As I stared at the viewing window, my fingers trembled on the rear thruster knob. My gut wanted me to shift it to max and zoom away. My brain said that would be stupid. The bigger, faster ship would catch us easily.

Maybe it would be best to let him board. After all, we were just kids without any idea what we were doing. The orphans would be taken to a sanctuary planet, and Oliver could find whatever family members he had left. And me? I would probably be executed before the day ended or maybe sent to the labor camp. Terrible, yes, but at least the kids would be safe. That was sacrifice, fulfilling my purpose. I guess I could die at peace with myself.

I breathed a silent sigh. "Proceeding as commanded, Admiral." I switched off the microphone and turned the thruster down a notch. "Emerson, continue our deceleration, program a rendezvous with the *Nebula One*, and prepare for docking."

"Acknowledged, Captain. Program commencing."

I turned on the internal announcement system and spoke into the microphone. "Listen, everyone. An Alliance ship is going to dock with us, and they'll find out we're just a bunch of kids, so we're—"

"Captain Willis," Emerson said. "The *Nebula One* has raised its shields. Another ship has entered the detection zone and is closing in at high speed."

My heart thumped. "Raise our shields."

"Raising shields."

"Cancel docking maneuvers. Arm all weapons." I shouted at Oliver, "Plot a course for Delta Ninety-five."

"You got it." He tapped on his console. "I'll have it in a minute."

"Emerson can do it faster."

"Yeah. He's helping me. Just a few seconds."

"Captain Tillman," the admiral called through the speakers. "The approaching vessel has been identified as a pirate ship. I see that you are preparing for battle, I assume for the same reason. We will coordinate our defense according to battle protocol three. Acknowledge immediately."

I turned the transmission microphone on, my entire body trembling. "Acknowledged." I switched it back off. "Emerson, can you do what he's talking about?"

"I can program our movements to follow the designated battle protocol, Captain, but only through initial positioning. The remaining decisions rest on the captain's discretion."

"Then move us into position and give me a front view."

"Commencing, Captain." The scene on the front window flickered, and the star clusters swept from right to left. When the movement stopped, the *Nebula One* appeared in the lower right-hand portion of the viewing window. It slowly shifted toward the center, then downward as if we were going to park directly over it.

Oliver leaned close to me. "I have the course to Delta Ninety-five plotted. It's on your console. You can switch to it whenever you're ready."

"Captain," Emerson said, "I have an urgent alert. The approaching ship is similar in characteristics to the one that attacked the *Nebula Nine*."

I sucked in a breath. "The *Astral Dragon*?"

"I do not know its name. I know only that it is the same class. It is premature to assume that it is the same ship. I can confirm that its shields are raised and its weapons armed."

"Are we in the protocol position?"

"Affirmative, Captain."

I pointed toward the front. "Put the approaching ship on screen. If the admiral hails it, route the transmissions to our speakers."

"Acknowledged."

The window flashed again and transformed into a view of darkness with a million stars in the background, no ship in sight. Since most pirate ships were black, that wasn't a surprise.

"Emerson, outline the approaching ship."

The screen drew white lines along the edges of the ship. Its sleek form and short wings, withdrawn for space flight, were unmistakable.

I whispered, "The *Astral Dragon*."

Oliver leaned close again. "I wonder who's flying. Your mother or Gavin."

"I don't know." I looked at the ceiling. "Emerson, can you send a message to the *Astral Dragon* without the admiral knowing about it?"

"Negative, Captain. You could encrypt a message so that the admiral could not understand it, but he would know you sent one."

The *Astral Dragon* drew within a kilometer and halted. All three ships now floated in nothingness, shields up and weapons armed. We were at an impasse. If only I could send a signal.

I looked up, imagining the lights on the top of the ship. They might work. I searched my console. "I have control of our top lights, don't I?" I spotted the dial. "Never mind. I found it."

I turned the roof light on and off, trying to send the letters "MW-U?" in Intergalactic Morse Code—my initials followed by a request for identification. My mother would understand, though Gavin probably wouldn't.

The admiral's voice returned to our speakers. "Captain Tillman, lock your photon torpedoes on the pirate ship's port turret. That ship's class has a vulnerability at that point. If we both hit it at the same time, we should breach the hull. I have some more powerful torpedoes on board, but they haven't been fully tested. They will have to wait for another time."

I finished the coded message and turned on my microphone. "Doesn't protocol instruct us to offer terms of surrender?"

The admiral laughed. "Are you instructing me about protocol? A ship's captain who ignored protocol to embark on a secret mission for personal gain?"

"Are you saying I should ignore protocol now, Admiral?"

A light on the *Astral Dragon*'s roof blinked. As the short and long flashes continued, I began typing the message on my console.

"Captain, are you being . . . Wait. What is the pirate ship signaling?"

I finished decoding the message and looked at my screen. It said "AW-FL2D95"

I whispered, "Mother."

"What?" the admiral asked. "Did you say *mother*?"

I bit my lip. I forgot that the microphone was on. I switched it off and stared at the message. AW meant Anne Willis, but what did FL2D95 mean?

"Captain Tillman," the admiral barked. "Send me your personal identifier."

I looked up. "Emerson?"

"That is a unique code for the ship's captain. It is not on any computer or database. Only the captain himself knows it."

A tremor rattled my voice. "Then we're sunk?"

"In a manner of speaking, yes."

"Captain Tillman," the admiral said, "you have five seconds to transmit your personal code. If you don't, I will lower your shields and destroy your ship."

"Emerson, can he do that?"

"As admiral of the fleet, he has access to a command he can send to our ship to lower the shields. I cannot override it."

With Oliver looking on, I whispered my mother's message out loud, "FL two D nine five." Then I spoke louder. "Fly to Delta Ninety-five. My mother wants us to go there."

"Captain Willis," Emerson said, "our shields are going down. The *Nebula One*'s photon torpedoes have locked on our ship. What is your command?"

"We're getting out of here." I touched the screen on Oliver's course icon, ready to activate it. "Everyone check your buckles."

"We cannot get out of the *Nebula One*'s firing range before it can hit us," Emerson said.

Something flashed on the screen. A photon torpedo shot from the *Astral Dragon*, its trajectory toward our ship but too low to strike it.

"She's attacking the *Nebula One*. This is our chance." I grabbed the yoke and shoved the throttle. I flew over the *Astral Dragon*, then pushed our ship into a Z-axis dive behind it, using my mother's protected ship as a shield.

"Emerson, give me a rear view and set magnify to full." The viewing window flashed and showed the *Astral Dragon* between us and the *Nebula One*, darting this way and that to block one torpedo after another. Both ships shrank in our view as we zoomed away. As each torpedo struck the *Astral Dragon*'s hull, the ship jerked, then fired back. The scene looked like two impenetrable brick walls shooting glowing rocks at each other.

Soon, the battle dwindled to flashing pinpoints, much too far away to tell what was going on. Still, I knew the flashes meant that my mother was battling furiously to keep me safe. But would *she* be safe? Years of experience taught me that she knew what she was doing. She would want me to focus on my own safety.

I exhaled loudly and looked at Oliver. "Can we still use that Delta Ninety-five course now?"

Oliver nodded, a hand over his stomach. "Go ahead. I'm trying not to barf."

"There's a bag under your console." I tapped the course icon and released the yoke. While maintaining speed, our ship turned slowly, barely enough to notice. When our course straightened, the ship accelerated. I looked again at the viewing window. Now stars were the only lights. The admiral could no longer see us with the naked eye, and my mother was sure to keep him occupied until we were out of scanner range.

"Emerson, give me the front view."

"I will do so, but for your future convenience, you might want to note that you can access any view from your own console."

"Let me try it." I looked at the icons and found one for the viewing window. When I tapped it, the console screen displayed twelve cameras, each providing a different view from around the ship. I tapped the one for the front view. "Got it, Emerson."

Still at the physician's station, Crystal looked out the viewing window. "So, four hours to the next planet?"

I glanced at my console. "Three hours and fifty-seven minutes, to be exact."

"Anything we should do while we wait?"

Her question jolted a memory. "The distress signal. We have to shut it off. I'm sure my mother used it to find us, but Admiral Fairbanks knows about it, too."

"I pinpointed the source," Emerson said. "If you will go to the cargo hold, I will lead you to it."

"All right." I unbuckled and rose. My legs trembled, and my entire body felt drained. "I'm on my way."

Oliver touched my arm. "I'll go. I know my way around. And Dirk can help me." He looked at Dirk. "Right?"

Dirk unfastened himself from the seat. "Yeah. Sure."

"Great." I smiled at both of them. "Thank you."

When Oliver and Dirk left, Crystal walked to me, leaned her head against my shoulder, and yawned. "How do you tell when it's bedtime in outer space?"

"Now's a good time, if you ask me." I nodded toward the sleeping quarters. "Everyone can snooze if they're ready."

"Yep. They washed while you were unconscious." Crystal walked toward the sleeping quarters. "They're already strapped in bed. I'll tell them the danger's over. Perdantus was with them the whole time, so he probably kept them calm."

I settled back in the captain's chair and let out a long sigh. Things were looking up again. We escaped from Thorne, the bees, the Jaradians, and even a suspicious admiral. And now we would soon land on an uninhabited planet—no slave traders to hassle us. Then my mother would come, assuming she escaped the *Nebula One*, which was likely since she was well armed and shielded. We would fly together to a sanctuary planet, find good homes for the kids, and then I would take off on the *Astral Dragon* with her.

Questions about the admiral's presence so far from the Alpha system pricked at my mind, but I yawned them away. The hours I had been unconscious hadn't provided nearly enough rest. Yet, I couldn't sleep. Not yet. I still had to pilot the ship to Delta Ninety-five and land her safely.

Dirk walked in with a can of vitamin water. Smiling, he extended it to me. "You look like you could use a drink."

"Thanks." I took the can and popped the tab. "Did you find the transmitter?"

"Yep. It has a timer. Whoever put it in there wanted it to go off exactly when it did."

I took a drink and set the can on the console. "Where's Oliver?"

"Helping get the kids to sleep. He and Crystal know them better than we do, so they can settle them down."

"True. We're practically strangers to them."

Dirk nodded toward my can. "Want anything else? I mean, since you're the captain now, it's my job, you know."

"Yeah." I gestured with my finger for him to come closer. When he did, I whispered, "Are there still sugar cookies in the pantry?"

He copied my quiet tone. "Yeah. Why?"

"Get 'em. Then tell Oliver and Crystal to come to the captain's quarters, and we'll eat every last one of them."

Dirk grinned. "Sure, but why are we whispering?"

"Because Emerson records everything while we're out here. We wouldn't want him to record our sneaky business on the ship's official log, would we?"

"Nope. See you there soon." He spun and hurried toward the ladder.

"Captain Willis," Emerson said, "you are the captain of the ship. You need not be sneaky. If you want cookies, they are yours for the taking. No one will question the acquisition."

I winced. "So you heard us, huh?"

"Yes. My audio input sensors are highly sensitive. You will find it difficult to be surreptitious in most areas on this ship."

"Surreptitious? What does that mean?"

"Sneaky."

"All right. All right. I get it." I rose and hustled to the captain's quarters. After using the toilet, I kicked off my shoes, shed my belt along with the computer tablet and collar remote, and jumped into the middle of the captain's soft double bed. I propped my head up with a pillow and leaned back on the headboard, looking out the open door to the corridor, waiting for my friends to show up.

At my side, the captain's night table caught my notice. A book with the title *Castaway Survival Guide* sat fastened in a bracket. I plucked it out and read the table of contents. It was filled with all sorts of useful information—probably an interesting read, but definitely not for tonight. After scanning some of it quickly, I set it back in the bracket.

When Oliver, Crystal, and Dirk arrived, we ate cookies, drank vitamin water, and told stories, laughing, rolling, and tickling each other until exhaustion took hold. When we couldn't fight it any longer, we fell asleep, the four of us lying in a row. The close contact felt like home. It was wonderful.

After what seemed like only a few minutes, Emerson called, "Captain Willis, you should come to the bridge."

I shot to a sitting position. "What's wrong?"

"There is no immediate danger, but I am detecting a problem with our destination."

"On my way." I rocked up to my knees and climbed over the foot of the bed. "You guys can sleep if you want, I have to go."

"I'm coming," Oliver said in a sleepy voice. "I'll meet you there."

I grabbed my belt, scooped my shoes off the floor, and ran sock-footed to the bridge. When I arrived, I looked out the viewing window. A planet loomed in the distance, tiny, though as bright as a star and fiery orange.

"Emerson, is that Delta Ninety-five?"

"Affirmative."

I slipped on one of my shoes. "Why is it that color?"

"Seismic and volcanic activity are extremely high. According to the ship's database, this occurs approximately every one hundred years, which is why the planet is uninhabited. Any colony would be forced to evacuate soon after becoming established. I estimate that this episode began only a few Alpha One days ago."

I crouched and began tying my shoes. "Does that mean we can't land on it?"

"Only an exploratory flyby can determine that, but the atmosphere will probably contain high levels of sulfur dioxide and hydrogen sulfide. Whether or not you can breathe it depends on the concentration levels. In any case, the air will be fetid."

I finished tying and straightened. "Fetid?"

"Stink."

I slipped my belt on and buckled it. "Gotcha."

When I took my seat at the console, Oliver, Crystal, and Dirk walked in, Crystal rubbing an eye with a knuckle.

"I heard the problem," Oliver said.

I pointed at the viewing window. "See for yourself. Looks like the planet's on fire."

Crystal stared. "Blazes! Literally!"

"Yeah. We'll have to get closer to see if there's a place to land."

Oliver sat at the first mate's station. "If we do find a safe spot to land, it'll be better than going somewhere else. No one will think we'd be stupid enough to hide on a planet that's on fire."

"True. But when my mother finds out about this volcanic stuff going on, she'll probably think the same thing. If we do land, we need to let her know."

Dirk walked close to the front window, staring at the scene. "How will she find you?"

"When she gets close enough, she'll probably send a hailing signal, and I'll answer with ours. I don't want to broadcast ours too soon in case the admiral's listening. But I'm worried that when she sees the planet like this, she might just fly away, thinking we went back to Delta Ninety-eight."

Oliver nodded. "Makes sense. Maybe we *should* go back."

"No, she said Delta Ninety-five, so that's where we're going. If it's possible, I mean."

Emerson broke in. "Seven minutes until the course program adjusts speed for gravitational effect, Captain."

"Got it. Call the sleeping quarters and tell the kids to stay strapped in." I reached over to Oliver and touched his arm. "Want some flying lessons?"

"Uh . . . sure."

"All right. When the time comes, I'll let you take over, but I'll keep my hands on my yoke just in case."

"Okay." He touched the yoke on his console. "If you're sure."

I grinned. "Not sure at all. You have to prove yourself."

"Thanks for piling on the pressure."

"Captain," Emerson said, "considering the rigors of atmospheric entry, may I suggest that someone occupy the engine room? Your chosen person can follow our instructions should the need of a manual adjustment arise."

"I'll do it," Dirk said as he hustled toward the bridge's exit. "I've been down there plenty of times."

"Great. Thanks." When Dirk left, I looked at Crystal. "This could be a rough ride. If you'd rather get in bed with the others, I won't think you're a coward."

She huffed. "What's a little danger? I'm . . . whatever the Alpha One word is for being in danger a lot without being scared."

"Experienced?" I offered.

"Well, yeah. With bees. Not with flying straight into the jaws of hell. But they're pretty much the same. If your armor splits, you're dead."

Emerson spoke up. "I think the word you're looking for is *unflappable*."

"You mean, not like a chicken?" Crystal nodded. "Yep. I'm unflappable."

I laughed. "All right, Miss Unflappable non-chicken person. Get buckled."

"Yes, Captain." Crystal sat in the physician's seat and fastened the belt. "Ready."

I turned toward the viewing window. Delta Ninety-five's details had clarified. Fiery orange covered the land mass, glowing through a gray haze, while spots here and there appeared to be somewhat green. Two oceans covered about a third of the planet. Haze also shrouded the water's bluish hue.

"Emerson, I'm switching to manual operation." On the screen, I slid the control icon from the computer's console to mine and Oliver's. "Monitor the engines for any problems, and open the communication channel to Dirk."

"Acknowledged. The channel is now open."

I looked at Oliver. "Hold your yoke, and get ready to feel the *Nebula Nine* as we adjust to the gravitational pull. You kind of extend your mind and make your body part of the ship."

Oliver grasped his yoke. "All right. I'll try."

"Dirk," I called, "everything all right down there?"

"So far. The screen says the fusion engines are running fine. Everything else is humming along."

"Good. Report anything unusual." I looked at Oliver again. "Time to adjust. Right now all thrusters are off, and inertia kept us moving at the same speed for quite a while, but Delta Ninety-five's gravity is making us accelerate. We have to slow down or we'll slam into it."

For the next couple of minutes, I guided him through the basics of maneuvering. As I shifted the yoke and adjusted the thrusters, Oliver felt his yoke, watching me and glancing at the viewing window. When we had decelerated and settled the ship into an orbit close enough to scan the ground, I set the window to show the planet as we zipped around it.

Our distance allowed a view of nearly the entire sphere as we passed over a hazy ocean, then a landmass dotted with erupting volcanoes that sent fire and smoke upward, feeding the haze. The land around the volcanoes burned red, fading to ashen black with more distance from the lava. Farther still, greenery took over in places lava hadn't yet reached, but we were too far to tell if the green represented grass or trees and if the greenery covered flat areas or mountainous ones.

"We need a landing spot as far as possible from any volcano, something flat." I glanced behind me at Emerson's screen. "Emerson, scan for a landing place in a green zone. If you find a good one, we'll shoot for it on the next orbit."

"Acknowledged."

"Hey, Megan," Dirk said through the speakers. "Since we're in orbit now, I guess it's all right to mention something. It might be nothing, but I noticed that a floor panel was loose when I got here. No one in engineering would've left it that way."

"What?" I wrinkled my brow. "No. That can't be. I was working on the thruster wiring network under the floor. I know I put all the panels back and snapped them tight."

"Well, one wasn't. I put it back, but I thought I should tell you."

A mental warning flag popped up. I couldn't just drop the issue. "Take the panel off and move it to the side so Emerson can see what's below."

"All right. Just a second."

"Emerson, when he gets the panel open, send a video feed of the subfloor wires to my screen."

"Acknowledged."

I released the yoke and looked at Oliver. "Keep us steady while I check this out. You probably won't have to do anything."

Oliver licked his lips. "Sure. Doing nothing works for me."

My console monitor shifted to a view of the engine room from the ceiling's perspective. Dirk sat on a chair in front of the head engineer's console, drumming his fingers. Behind him, a floor section lay open, exposing a network of wires below.

I slid my fingers on the screen, magnifying the view, then moved it around to get a good look at everything. My splices seemed intact, but something dark lay under the wires, an unfamiliar box of some kind.

"Dirk, go to the open floor. I need you to shift some wires to the side for me."

"No problem." A second later, Dirk appeared in the view as he knelt at the edge of the opening. "Which ones?"

"The set closest to you. The green, black, and white group that are tied together."

When he pushed them aside, I magnified the view even more, centering on the box. Whatever that thing was, it wasn't there when I worked on the wires. "Dirk, see that dark box? It's about the size of your palm."

"Yeah. What is it?"

"That's my question. It's kind of fuzzy on the camera. Can you read any lettering on it?"

He pressed close and peered at it. "Nope."

"Can you tell if it's fastened, maybe bolted in or stuck with glue or tape? Don't try to move it. Just tell me what you see."

As Dirk looked even more closely, his head blocked my view. "I see some dried glue around it, so it's probably stuck."

"Then I didn't accidentally drop anything down there."

Dirk drew back. "Let's just hope it's not a bomb."

"If Gavin had a bomb and wanted to blow up the ship, he could've done it when he was here. And it looks too small to do much damage."

"Can you send the view to me?" Crystal asked.

"Sure." On my screen, I slid the icon to her console.

She squinted at her display. "It looks like a buzz biter," she said in Humaniversal. "When you said it's a box, it made me wonder."

I shifted to the same language. "What's a buzz biter?"

"When the cave got too many bramble bees in it, we sometimes set a little box in the middle of the floor. It makes a sound that attracts the bees, and they surround it. Then, like a bomb, another noise explodes from the box and kills them." She snapped her fingers. "Just like that. A bunch of dead bees."

I imagined the scene. Dozens of bees hovered around a small black box. "How does the buzz biter know when to send out the killing noise?"

"Before we put it down, we set a timer for about a minute. That gives the bees plenty of time to fly to it."

I spoke toward Emerson's console in Alpha One. "Emerson, do you detect any signal from that box? Check every frequency."

"Signal scan commencing."

I turned toward Oliver. "Any problems flying?"

"Nope." He cracked a nervous smile. "I've been practicing, you know, shifting around a little to get a feel without messing up the orbit. I think I'm getting it."

"Great. Want to land her?"

"Land her?" He trembled. "Are you kidding? I couldn't—"

"Yeah, I was kidding. Don't have a moose."

"Captain Willis," Emerson said, "I am detecting a signal from the device. The frequency is higher than all communications channels. As Crystal guessed, it is in the range of certain insect categories."

Crystal fluttered her eyelids. "I knew it all along."

"Don't be so smug. Emerson, could an explosion of noise at a frequency that high cause any damage to the ship?"

"A high-frequency noise impulse could affect almost any circuits and computer equipment, similar to what would happen with an electromagnetic pulse."

"So anything electric could get fried."

"Affirmative."

I looked at Crystal. "What about the timer? How long could you set it for?"

"We always set it for a minute." She fingered the air. "It has a dial on one side. I think it went all the way to several hours in case you wanted to leave it somewhere overnight, you know, to kill an entire colony, but Thorne never let us use it more than once in a while. If you kill bees, you don't get as much glowsap. So every few weeks we had to do a count so he could estimate how big the colony was. If it got big enough, he let us use a buzz biter, but we always had to bring the dead bees home."

"He told me he did experiments on them," Oliver said. "He never said why."

I nodded. "Maybe we should pry the box loose and send it through the jettison chute."

Oliver frowned in a skeptical way. "What if moving it makes it go off?"

"Good point." Still staring at my console screen, I focused on the box. "If it goes off while we're in flight, we'll probably die. If we land first, we'll be safe. We can move it then. Emerson, have you found a good landing spot?"

"There are no ideal locations, but I found a few that pose no immediate risk of fatal consequences."

Crystal cocked her head. "What does *consequences* mean?"

"Stuff that happens." I changed the main window to show a front view. "Emerson, plot a course to the safest spot. I'll manually follow it. Oliver, together on the yokes. Time for more practice."

"I will plot a course for a certain flat meadow within walking distance of a river," Emerson said. "A water source will be essential. Captain Tillman planned to replenish our water supply on Delta Ninety-eight, so our inventory is getting quite low, not only for drinking but also for the fusion engines. Remember to test the water to make sure it's potable."

Crystal narrowed her eyes. "What's *pot*—"

"Drinkable," Oliver and I said at the same time.

"Oh."

The landing route appeared on my console screen. I extended our wings and guided the ship toward Delta Ninety-five. Soon, tiny bumps let us know that we had entered the upper atmosphere, bumps that would probably worsen as the air thickened.

A frightening thought jabbed my mind. If moving the buzz biter could make it go off, might this jostling do the same thing? I wasn't conscious when we left Delta Ninety-eight, so I had no idea how much turbulence we experienced then, but the atmosphere here was probably much more volatile.

Of course, I could abort the landing, but if the buzz biter was on a timer, it would go off while we were in space. We would be stranded in a vacuum. And, like I said before, that would be deadlier than being stranded on a planet. Our best choice was to get rid of the thing now but as carefully as possible.

I gripped the yoke with both hands. "Dirk, let's get that thing into the ejection chute. Move it like you're carrying a fragile egg."

"Are you sure?" Dirk asked.

I glanced at Oliver and Crystal. Both looked at me with the same question in their eyes. "No. I'm not sure. It's just a hunch."

"I'm not going to ask what a hunch is," Crystal said, "but I trust you. All the way."

Oliver nodded firmly. "Dirk, you heard the captain. Get rid of that thing."

"Gotta get something to pry it loose with."

A hard bounce shook the ship, then another. The volcanic eruptions had probably stirred the air into a bubbling cauldron. According to the chart, we would land in six minutes. Maybe I could shorten that time and cut down on some of the bouncing.

"Dirk?" I called. "Do you have it yet?"

"I just popped it loose. It feels strange, like something's alive inside, moving around."

"It's ready to blow!" Crystal said.

"Hang on, everyone!" I retracted our wings and pushed the *Nebula Nine* into a deeper dive.

"Whoa!" Dirk shouted. "What're you doing?"

"Trying to land. Throw it in the chute!"

He grunted. "It's uphill!"

"Just a second." I reextended the wings and leveled the angle, flying at about five kilometers above the ground. "Can you do it now?"

"Yep." He grunted again. "It's in the chute. Gotta send it through the air lock."

"Hurry!" I flew over a volcano. The hot air shot us upward. The force jerked my body toward the ceiling, tearing my hands away from the yoke, but the lap belt kept me from flying off my seat. Oliver and Crystal yelped as they bounced hard.

I grabbed the yoke again. "Dirk? Did you do it?"

"No! What is this, a bronco ride? I hit the ceiling, and now I'm on the floor."

"Emerson! Send that thing out!"

"Activating chute air lock," Emerson said. "Five seconds until jettison."

"Dirk, grab something and hang on." I turned on the landing thrusters. The ship bounced harder and harder. I could barely hold the yoke at all.

From the sleeping quarters, children screamed, but I couldn't do anything about it. They would just have to hang on with the rest of us.

"Air lock activated. Sending device through."

Sharp clicks sounded all around. The lights flickered, then blacked out. The viewing window's grid disappeared, and my console darkened. I held my breath. The buzz biter must've activated before Emerson could eject it!

Ahead, a green expanse drew closer and closer. I jerked on the yoke, but nothing happened. In seconds, we would crash.

Another updraft kicked the ship from below, slowing our descent and leveling our flight. The scene in the viewing window shifted left to right at a dizzying speed. I threw my arms over the console, grabbed the edge, and shouted, "Brace for impact!"

PART

02

MAROONED

✦

The ship slammed into the ground and skidded. I peeked at the front window. Dirt flew in every direction. We bounced, slid a while, bounced again, and slid some more.

Rocking with the ship, I gritted my teeth and held on. At the speed we were flying, our momentum might last for multiple kilometers. I prayed we wouldn't hit a boulder, or worse, a hot lava field.

After several more seconds, the ship stopped. I lifted myself from the console and looked out the window again, now showing the actual view in front of the ship instead of a camera feed. Dirt covered the bottom half, while light filtered in from the top half, providing a view of the hazy sky.

I looked at Oliver. His torso sprawled over the console the same way mine had, his eyes closed. Crystal sat at her station, staring at me, her hair in disarray. "Is Oliver all right?" she asked.

"I'll check on him and Dirk. You check on everyone else." We both unbuckled. While she hurried to the sleeping quarters, I set a pair of fingers on Oliver's throat and detected a strong pulse. Breathing a sigh of relief, I patted his cheek. "Oliver, can you hear me?"

He lifted his head, blinking. "What happened? I thought we were done for."

"We crash-landed—more like skidded, really."

He rubbed a bump on his forehead. "How much damage?"

"No idea." I spoke into the air. "Emerson? Are you still with us?" No one answered.

"Blazes! I guess he got fried. I'll have to check everything manually." Oliver's eyes widened. "Megan. Your collar."

"What about it?" I touched the collar. It seemed loose. Very loose. I ran my fingers along it until they came across a gap. It was open. I pulled it free and held it in front of my eyes. "The buzz biter must've knocked it out. Emerson told me it would open if it lost power."

"Well, at least something good happened."

"Yeah." I unfastened the remote and put it and the collar on my console. As I stared at it, I massaged my throat. It felt so good to finally be free from that blasted thing. Yet, a sense of loss blended in. The ability to deliver an electrical shock with my hands helped me a few times, especially while capturing the bramble bee. Without it, I probably couldn't have overcome Axleback.

Oliver snapped his fingers. "Megan. You zoned out. We need to get to work."

"Right. I have to check on Dirk." I hustled toward the corridor leading to the engine room ladder. I slid down and found Dirk sitting on the floor, his back against a console cabinet. When he saw me, he grinned, though a grimace tightened his face. "Great landing, Captain."

"Oh, shut up." I crouched in front of him. "Are you hurt?"

"Yep." He touched his knee. "I banged it against a console when I fell from the ceiling. Hurts like crazy. I think I busted it."

I winced. "Not a monkey anymore, huh?"

"Sure. Blame me. I can take it."

"Let's get you to sick bay. We'll see if Oliver can do something to help you."

"Why Oliver?"

"Because . . ." I grabbed his wrist, helped him rise, and supported him as he hopped toward the ladder, not sure if I should give away Oliver's secret. "Because he helped you the last time you got hurt."

"I don't remember. Everything's hazy."

"You were drugged then."

As he hopped on one foot to the top, I climbed behind him. When we arrived at sick bay, I helped him get in bed. With each motion, he grimaced and squelched a moan. Once he settled, I tried to push his pant leg up to his knee, but the swelling and his pain wouldn't allow it.

After finding a scalpel, I sliced his pants at the knee and exposed the joint—puffy and deep purple. No wonder he was in so much pain. I found some pills that would knock him out and gave him a full dose. Since he couldn't help us, he might as well sleep. That would also give Oliver a chance to use his gift without being seen if he still wanted to keep it a secret.

When I returned to Oliver on the bridge, Crystal joined us. After I gave them a quick update on Dirk, she nodded toward the sleeping quarters. "The other kids are all right. Just some strap marks and lots of jitters. I told them to stay put until we figure out what we're going to do."

"Everything's fried," I said, "so we can't transmit a distress signal. Since we're going to be here quite a while, we'd better invoke survival protocol."

"We'd better do what?" Crystal sighed. "Can we please stop speaking Alpha One? We're not making secret plans anymore."

"All right." I switched to Humaniversal. "This is an Alliance ship, so we have a series of things to do if we get stuck somewhere. It's all in a book I saw in the captain's quarters."

"What's first on the list?"

"I just read the first few pages, but water first, then food. We'll look for the river Emerson mentioned and test the water. If it's not drinkable, we have ways to purify it."

"And food?" Oliver asked.

"We brought enough to last the crew several weeks, and we have vegetable seeds in case we're stranded somewhere past that. There's a section in the book about testing soil, fertilizing it, all sorts of stuff."

"Let's hope we don't have to stay that long." Oliver rose from his seat. "Can we go outside?"

"Probably, but we'd better do it the safe way. I'll put on a pressure suit and go through the roof air lock with an air-check meter. While I'm gone, get the survival book from the captain's bedside table. It has a list of stuff we need and where it's stowed. You and Crystal bring as much as you can to the bridge. Then if the air's okay and there's nothing dangerous around, we'll go to the river together."

When Oliver and Crystal turned to carry out my plans, I called, "Oliver. Wait."

He and Crystal stopped and pivoted. "Something else?" he asked.

I waved for Crystal to go on. She gave me a quizzical look before hurrying from the bridge.

I stepped close to Oliver, fumbling with my fingers as I tried to figure out how open to be about what I knew. "Before you help Crystal get the stuff we need, why don't you go to sick bay and check on Dirk?"

"Didn't you say he's sleeping?"

"Yeah. He's sleeping. But maybe you can . . . I don't know . . . do that thing you did with his ankle last time? Since he's out cold, it won't hurt him, and . . ." I averted my gaze but kept watching him out of the corner of my eye. "And no one will see you."

Oliver pushed a hand into his pocket. "You figured it out."

I refocused on him. Better to let him say it than for me to guess wrong. "Figured what out?"

"That maybe I have a magic power, too." He shrugged. "Well, sort of."

I compressed his shoulder. "Oliver, just spill it. We'll figure it out together."

"Not yet. Let's wait till I see Dirk again, and then I'll talk to you and Crystal about it at the same time. She deserves to know."

"Fair enough." After Oliver left, I collected my pressure suit, helmet, and gloves from the various places I had left them earlier and put them on. Since my air tank was empty, I searched for another one in Gavin's former quarters. As expected, the crews' missing tanks were fastened by tie lines under his bunk, stowed there by the treacherous first mate. My ears heated, but I quickly doused my anger, retrieved one of the tanks, and strapped it in place on my back.

After finding the air-check meter and attaching it to my belt, I pressurized the suit and climbed the ladder from the bridge toward the top hatch. When I reached the air lock, I pushed the release button. Nothing happened. At the side of the hatch, I turned the manual control wheel and forced the hatch open. I climbed through and closed it behind me, darkening the air lock chamber.

Now standing, I reached up, felt for the next wheel, and slowly turned it. As the hatch slid to the side, light poured in. Above, a hazy, reddish sky blanketed everything.

I climbed out and stood on the *Nebula Nine*'s roof. As I turned in place, I took in the scene. Grass, ferns, and other ground vegetation surrounded the ship in all directions, making a skirt of green that extended at least several kilometers, ending in forested hills and valleys. In one direction, a steaming volcano loomed, maybe twenty kilometers away. Lava streamed down its slopes in forking rivulets, though the direction it flowed at the base lay out of view behind a forest.

In the midst of the trees, smoke rose here and there in pockets, probably from fires sparked by molten rock. I unfastened the air-check device from my belt and turned it on. Since it was portable and battery-powered and not connected to anything on the ship, it survived the buzz biter.

The device's thermometer displayed 35 degrees Celsius—pretty hot, but tolerable. Meters on the top indicated 24 percent oxygen, 68 percent nitrogen, 5 percent carbon dioxide, and small percentages of inert gases. The sulfur dioxide content stood at 0.3 parts per million and 45 parts per million for hydrogen sulfide, both of which were in the meter's orange caution zone but not in the deadly red zone, meaning that we could breathe the air safely, but not for more than eight hours. It would be better if we wore filter masks while outside.

I walked along the roof and looked down at the ship's frame, now half-buried in the turf at the end of a long skid mark. The ship had unearthed roots and stones and tossed them about, clearing much of the frame, but dirt completely covered the hangar door for the rovers, and a half-buried boulder blocked any hope of digging them out. We would have to travel everywhere on foot.

Fortunately, the transmitting antenna was undamaged, though half of one wing had been torn off, probably now lying somewhere behind the ship in the piles of dirt and debris we had dredged.

Dents and gouges marred the hull's surface from bow to stern, some probably punching through to the inner cavity. If this had been an airless planet, the vacuum would have sucked every molecule of air from our ship, and we would all be dead. Patching holes was a high priority, maybe even higher than finding water. Otherwise, the sulfur gases would leak in and make the ship's air dangerous for long-term breathing.

I refastened the air-check meter and returned to the bridge, making sure to close the hatches tightly on the way down. After shedding the suit, I walked or crawled to every chamber in the ship that bordered the exterior wall, using the meter to search for any sign of sulfur. In the span of an hour, I found three holes in the hull and applied temporary plastic patches, making a note to bolt or weld metal ones in place later.

When I finished, I returned to the bridge. Oliver, Crystal, Vonda, and Bastian stood in front of Emerson's console, Perdantus on Oliver's shoulder.

Oliver used his foot to nudge a box on the floor. "We found one water test kit and one bottle of water purifier tablets. Let's hope the river water doesn't need this stuff. At least we have lots of air filter masks and seeds. In about eight weeks, we'll be able to feed an army."

I stooped next to the box and picked up a seed packet. "We'd better plant them right away and ration the food we have in storage.

It'll take weeks or months to repair the ship, if it's even possible. We lost half a wing, and I don't know where it is."

"We'll find it," Perdantus said. "I will conduct an aerial search. A wing section that large should not be hard to locate from above."

I tossed the packet back to the box. Fortunately, my ear translator wasn't zapped by the sonic bomb. I could still understand his chirping language. "While you're up there, you'll see that the ship already did the plowing for us. And the soil looks good. We just have to smooth it out. We don't have any gardening tools, but we should be able to find something to work with."

Bastian raised a hand. "I'll organize that. We had almost a full night's sleep. We'll be fine."

"We'll be fine after breakfast," Vonda said. "Since Dirk's hurt, I'll get everyone something to eat."

"Perfect. Thanks." When Vonda and Bastian exited, I looked at Oliver. "Did you check on Dirk?"

"Um . . . yeah. He was still asleep, but the knee looks pretty good. Not much swelling at all now."

"Now?" I asked with a prompting inflection.

He glanced at Crystal and me for a moment, then twisted his neck to get a look at Perdantus.

He flew from Oliver's shoulder, calling, "I will see if Bastian needs help."

When Perdantus disappeared, Oliver slid both hands into his pockets. "Yeah. Dirk's knee was bad when I went in. Most likely a broken kneecap. But I set my hand on it like I did to his ankle, and . . . well . . . it healed."

Crystal let out a whoop. "I knew it! You have magic powers, too! You healed Megan, you healed Dirk twice, and the big, bad bramble bees can't kill you! You're a healer."

Oliver scowled. "Hush up, Crystal. I'm not a healer."

"What do you mean?" I asked.

"If I was a healer . . ." Tears gleamed in his eyes as his voice cracked. "Then Cynda wouldn't be dead. Or any of the other kids that died. I tried putting my hands on all of them, but it didn't work." He drew in a deep breath, settling himself. "I've been won-dering for a long time if I had some kind of power, but it never worked on anyone except me. But I kept trying. Dirk was the first person I could help."

I nodded slowly. "Maybe the power's growing. It needed some kind of spark to get started."

"Maybe."

Crystal opened her mouth to say something but thought better of it. She ran a hand up and down his arm and stayed quiet.

Guessing it was time to change the subject, I infused a bit of excitement into my tone. "Want to go with me to find the river?"

"Sure," Oliver said. "It'll be fun exploring a new planet."

"Fun?" Crystal crossed her arms. "Um . . . what about danger? You know, animals with sharp teeth and claws."

"You've got a point," I said. "Animals are bound to come to places like this to get away from the lava."

Oliver cringed. "Ouch. You're right."

"Double ouch, because the door to the rovers is blocked. And Gavin took all of our weapons. I have a welding torch and some wrenches, and we can find branches, but that's about it."

"Then we'll need air support." Oliver whistled. "Perdantus! Come back to the bridge, please."

While we waited, Crystal shifted from foot to foot. "Okay. I'll go, but I'm taking some food with me, like the mincemeat muffins I saw in the galley. Maybe I can talk whatever beasts they have here into eating them instead of me."

Perdantus flew in and landed again on Oliver's shoulder. "How may I be of service?"

When we filled him in on our plans, he flitted his wings. "I will be glad to go with you. I should be able to locate the river from the sky and guide your way."

Once again I wanted to stroke his lovely feathers, and once again I refrained. "That'll help a lot, but won't you need a mask? We don't have one that'll fit you."

"Not to worry. We silver jays are a hearty lot. Not long ago I negotiated a contract for a coal-mining company. I spent several hours—"

"It's all right," I said, waving a hand. "I'll trust your judgment."

Oliver, Crystal, and I collected what we needed, placed everything in backpacks, and put on the masks. We exited to the roof and climbed down to the ground while Perdantus took to the sky, calling, "I will return soon with a report."

Oliver blinked. "The air burns my eyes."

"It stinks, too," Crystal said. "Like rotten eggs."

I slid my backpack off. "Yeah, it's stronger now. Maybe the wind changed." I fished the air meter from the pack and checked the readings. "Yep. Not in the deadly range, but it's pretty bad. Maybe it'll be better in the forest."

After a couple of minutes, Perdantus landed on Oliver's shoulder and extended a wing. "That direction. Perhaps five kilometers. Follow the slope downward. I will guide you from the treetops."

"Five kilometers?" I whistled. "That's a long way to go to get water, especially if we have to haul it back uphill."

"We could set up camp near the river," Oliver said. "Then only you and I would have to hike to the ship to work on it. Better just two of us trudging up the hill than everyone."

"Good point. We'll see what the air quality is like when we get there."

"Shall we go?" Perdantus asked.

I nodded. "Lead the way."

He flew downslope at a fast pace toward a tree line that stood about half a kilometer away. When we entered the forest, the stench decreased. I checked the meter. The level had dropped well into the safe zone.

We took off our masks, stowed them in our packs, and walked on, following Perdantus's chirps of "This way" and "Over here" and "Follow that gulley."

The turns took us downward through rainwater trenches as we weaved around densely packed trees and trudged through underbrush, all the while listening for running water.

Yet, the only sound besides our own rustling and Perdantus's instructions was a faraway rumble, like a dull background noise—maybe volcanoes erupting, rocks falling, or even thunder from a distant storm. Who could tell what all this volcanic activity might do to the weather? The green grass and trenches proved that it rained at least once in a while. But did it come in gentle drizzles or torrential downpours? The latter could be dangerous. We would have to be watchful.

Although the odor of rotten eggs dogged us, other smells countered it—blossoms on bushes as well as aromatic leaves crunching under our feet. As we plunged deeper into the forest, the air cooled. I peeked at the thermometer—27 degrees Celsius, quite a drop, but still far from chilly.

After we had walked about four kilometers, Crystal halted. "Wait. I hear water."

"Which direction?" I asked.

She pointed in the direction we had come, but we had seen no water along the way.

Darkness loomed in the sky. Thunder rumbled, much closer than before. And now we stood in the middle of a trench, the worst place possible.

From a treetop, Perdantus shouted, "Run to high ground!"

We scrambled toward the edge of the trench. Just as we leaped clear, water surged down the slope and flooded the trench in a foaming frenzy.

My heart racing, I stared at the flow for a moment before exhaling heavily. "That was close."

Crystal shouted toward the treetops. "Thanks, Perdantus."

"You are quite welcome," he called from a high branch.

"Let's check the water here," I said. "It'll be fresh from the clouds." I took off my pack and withdrew the test kit, a handheld, battery-operated computer with a screen. After filling a glass tube with water, I inserted the tube in the device and turned it on. A few seconds later, readings filled the screen. "The pH is pretty low, in the orange zone. Lots of minerals. No bacteria to speak of."

"Then it's drinkable?" Oliver asked.

"It's a little acidic." I poured out the residual water. "Not enough to hurt anything."

Perdantus landed on my shoulder. "This rainwater cascades into the river less than a kilometer away."

Oliver looked downstream. "Then what's our next move? Find a place to set up camp at the river?"

A loud thunderclap shook the ground. I spun and scanned the darkening sky in the direction of the ship. Getting caught in a storm while in a valley would be a terrible idea. "We'd better hustle back. We can try again later."

Perdantus hopped from my shoulder and took wing. "Listen for my calls."

We ran upslope. Huge droplets penetrated the canopy and fell on us, soaking our shirts within seconds. Perdantus's chirps led us onward, but soon the rattle of rain on the leaves and the roar of rampaging water in the nearby trench drowned his voice. No matter. Finding our way back was simple, just follow the trench for two or three kilometers, then angle right until we exited into the meadow.

Yet, rain blinded us, and bending trees made everything seem unfamiliar. Flashes of lightning and peals of thunder assaulted our senses as the cacophony grew.

We stopped and looked around. The trench was no longer in sight. "Which way?" Oliver shouted as water dripped from his nose and chin.

Rain continued pounding, making it hard to think. We needed to head up the hill, but two directions led to higher elevations. The wrong one might get us lost. I searched the trees. Perdantus was nowhere in sight.

I shook my head. "I don't know. We'll have to try one and see—"

Something growled. I spun toward the sound. A huge cat prowled down one of the paths. I pointed toward the other one. "That way! Hurry!"

Crystal threw a muffin toward the cat, and we ran together without looking back. We slipped and slid, sometimes having to claw with our hands to scramble up the incline.

Soon, Perdantus chirped from a tree branch to our right. "This way! This way!" As we followed in a mad dash, he flew to tree after tree, making the same call. After a few moments, we broke into a small glade with a log cabin in the middle. We ran to its front porch and stood in the shelter of its overhanging roof, breathing heavily.

I scanned the forest for the big cat. Rain dripped from the roof and blew through the myriad trees, partially veiling the view. No cat prowled anywhere in sight.

"I thought no one lived on this planet," Oliver said.

"Maybe not anymore. Obviously someone used to." I pushed the front door. It opened on noisy hinges, revealing a dim room with a dining table that extended from near one side wall to the other. A pair of unlit lanterns sat on top of the table near the center, and ten wooden chairs stood neatly all around. A fireplace and stack of wood adorned the back wall, and an open door on each side of the fireplace led to other rooms.

Perdantus flew in and perched on the back of one of the chairs. He shook out his wet feathers. "This looked like a suitable shelter, and the ship is still a good three hundred meters away. Better to get dry here than to risk being eaten by that feline monster." He shuddered. "Oh, how I despise cats."

"Thank you, Perdantus." As I stepped inside with Oliver and Crystal following, a wooden floorboard creaked, and rain pattered on the metal roof, though no water dripped from the ceiling. A desk sat to our right against the front wall, a lantern on its warped surface.

I flicked the lantern's switch, but it stayed dark. I pulled the top drawer open. A spiral notebook lay inside along with a box of batteries. I withdrew both, laid the notebook on the desk, and inserted a battery into the lantern. "Probably solar with a battery backup."

When I flicked the switch, a tiny bulb under the glass flashed to life. I opened the notebook and read the first page, loudly enough to overcome the noise.

A record of the Asher family: Winthrop, Phyllis, and the eight children they brought to sanctuary on Delta Ninety-five, beginning on ASD forty-one-sixty-two-point-seventy-three.

I looked at Oliver and Crystal. "ASD is Alliance Standard Date. So that's just two years ago based on Alpha One years."

"Skip to the end," Crystal said. "Find out what happened to them."

I riffled through the pages until I came to the last entry and again read out loud.

When Phyllis became ill, tending to these children turned into a burden that I could no longer bear. They are obedient and willing to work, but since I had to care for my wife in so many ways, I could not find the energy to direct them in their chores, and they are too young to manage the duties themselves. Children of their ages also seem to get sick and injured often, and, unlike Phyllis, I have no medical training. One of the children also possesses unique abilities that I don't understand, nor do I know how to deal with these odd talents. This girl surprises herself as she learns her gifts, and the revelations sometimes scare her. They frighten me, as well. It seems that the folk tales about Gamma Five might be true after all.

In any case, I admit that I am the weak link. This immense responsibility requires a better man than I. Whenever Phyllis was strong, we could move mountains together. Whenever she was weak, I could barely rise from bed. And my inability to rise continues to this day.

Since the ground tremors are increasing, and the volcanoes are spewing ash, I fear that the season of fire is upon us. I plan to hail our allies tonight, and the ship should arrive within a week to take us away. I don't know what we will do with the children. The official sanctuary planets are no longer safe for them, more like a shopping center for traffickers than a haven for orphans. Perhaps the admiral will have some ideas. Goodbye, and may the one who finds this journal have a better outcome living on this planet than we did.

Winthrop Asher

"The admiral?" I turned to the previous page and scanned for the admiral's name. "Do you think he means Fairbanks?"

Oliver shrugged. "No clue. The Alliance has more than one admiral. Maybe nine or ten, and I have no idea how long Fairbanks has been one."

"Since Fairbanks is in this star system now, I'm betting it was him. No telling what he did with those kids."

"And one of them has a Gamma Five gift," Crystal said. "I wonder if it's a magic power like mine or Oliver's."

Oliver pushed wet hair from his forehead. "I wasn't born on Gamma Five. Maybe the gifts have nothing to do with the planet."

I closed the notebook. "Maybe we'll find more clues when we read the whole thing. At least we might learn something about living here."

Perdantus flew to my shoulder. "There are more buildings behind this cabin. One looked like a kitchen and another like a toolshed. I also noticed cisterns for collecting rainwater, which are now overflowing. This might be an excellent place for everyone to live while you're repairing the ship."

"If the air's okay." I unfastened the air-quality meter and checked the readings. "Yep. In the green zone. I guess the trees are like filters."

"Perfect," Oliver said. "We can plant a garden where the ship plowed and live here. They're not that far apart. And if we find tools, it'll make everything easier."

"Let's check the place for beds," I said. "We have more people than they did. It might be a tight squeeze."

With the lantern in hand and Perdantus still on my shoulder, we walked toward the back of the cabin and entered the doorway on the left. It led to a small room with four single beds, two on each side, all furnished with a pillow and blanket. An alcove served as a closet with handmade wooden shelves and a hanging rod, though no clothes had been left behind. When we entered the other door, we found an identical arrangement. Apparently these two bedrooms housed the eight children.

I scanned the area. No other beds in sight. "I wonder where the adults slept. Maybe on a mat that's not here anymore?"

Oliver stood next to a narrow gap between two beds. "Not much room for a mat. Maybe they slept in another building."

"Either way, there won't be room for all of us." I touched my chest. "Since I'll be working all hours on the ship, I'll sleep there."

"Same for me," Oliver said. "And Dirk probably won't be able to walk very well for a couple of days, so he'll want to stay on the ship, too."

Crystal crossed her arms. "I want to stay with you guys, but I don't have an excuse like you do. I don't have a bum knee, and I can barely put a jigsaw puzzle together. I won't be any help fixing a spaceship."

"But we'll need someone to run and get things for us," I said. "And besides, I need another girl on board. Dirk's fun, and Oliver's smart and everything, but you know what males are like."

She wrinkled her nose. "They smell bad and make terrible jokes."

"Exactly."

"All right, you clowns," Oliver said, "four of us will sleep in the ship. The rest will squeeze in here, and we'll put Bastian and Vonda in charge."

I nodded. "Good. We'll head to the ship as soon as it stops raining."

Crystal shivered. "What about the cat?"

"Perdantus will watch for it." I twisted my neck and looked at him on my shoulder. "Right?"

He fluffed his feathers. "I will do what I can, but I would be a mere warning signal, not a means of escape. Perhaps we should search the other buildings for a weapon."

Oliver pointed at him. "Now *that's* the way males think. We might smell bad, but we're ready for action."

"I beg your pardon," Perdantus said with a huffing chirp. "I most certainly do not smell bad."

"All right. Whatever." Oliver patted his shoulder. "Want to search the other buildings with me? The rain is letting up."

"Certainly, but I will fly instead of riding on your shoulder."

"Why?"

"Because, Oliver, you *do* smell bad."

Crystal and I laughed. Oliver stuck out his tongue but grinned as he left. While he and Perdantus were gone, Crystal and I started a fire in the fireplace and stood in its drying warmth while I read more of the journal out loud. The early pages gave details about gardening, hunting wildlife, digging cisterns, and the like.

Near the end, I came to a part that revealed what happened to Phyllis. She and Winthrop were picking angel berries in a trench when a sudden storm sent a rush of water that swept Phyllis toward the river. Winthrop escaped the surge, ran down to the valley, and rescued her from the river. The air was cold, and she took a chill. She later developed pneumonia and passed away. Another week elapsed before he wrote his final entry.

I closed the journal and held it against my chest. "That's so sad."

Crystal nodded, her eyes red. "The same thing nearly happened to us. This place is dangerous."

Tears welled, but this was no time to cry. "We need to change the subject." I laid the journal on the dining table. "The rain stopped. Let's see what the guys found."

Just as we turned toward the door, Perdantus flew into the room, and Oliver walked in behind him, carrying a long gun. Smiling broadly, he laid it and a small box on the table. "It's an old-fashioned shotgun and lots of shells, perfect for hunting in the woods. No worries about that big cat as long as we have this."

I ran a finger along the dark metal barrel. "Do you know how to use it?"

"Sure. My father taught me how to . . ." He looked away for a moment, then cleared his throat and continued in a more somber tone. "He taught me how to use lots of guns."

"Then let's take it to the *Nine*. We need to get things started. The ship's not going to fix itself."

We exited, closing the door behind us. With Perdantus chirping instructions, we made our way toward the meadow. As I walked,

I counted the steps and identified landmarks such as oddly bent trees and mossy boulders. If I were to come to the cabin alone, especially in the dark, I needed to make sure I could get there without a bird as a guide.

When we reached the ship, we climbed onto the broken wing and walked to the roof with Perdantus circling above. While Oliver turned the wheel to open the top hatch, I slid my pack off and looked back at our path—a 437-step course, not bad at all.

To the ship's rear, the plowed ground bore several newly made furrows, though one of them ended abruptly. The storm probably chased the kids back into the ship before they could finish.

When Oliver opened the hatch, I climbed into the air lock chamber, opened the next hatch, and made my way down the ladder, followed by Crystal, Oliver, and Perdantus. All of the kids except Dirk sat in a circle on the floor in front of Emerson's console, four with flashlights in hand.

"What are you doing?" I asked.

Vonda rose, her smile thin. "Um . . . a guessing game."

"Oh? What were you guessing?"

Her cheeks reddened. "Don't get mad. It was Renalda's turn to decide what to guess, and she wanted to guess who would be the first to die here."

I stared at Vonda, anger simmering. Why would they play such a morbid game? Had they seen so much death that they had become calloused to it? Or had death become a way of escape from their misery? Either way, it wasn't their fault. The slave traders had filled their lives with toil and sorrow. I had to remember that.

After taking a deep breath, I looked at Renalda while trying to keep my feelings in check. "Why did you want to guess that?"

Renalda smiled, though her lips trembled. "It's just a game. We say whoever's right will be the first to go home."

I half closed an eye. "Where is home for you?"

"I don't have a home. When my parents died, I got put in an orphanage."

"Then you knew you couldn't win the prize."

She shrugged. "But it's fun. And it probably won't take long to find out who wins." She pointed at the roof. "When that storm came, we nearly got hit by lightning."

Vonda nodded. "It was real close. We all got scared."

"I see." My anger faded completely. How could I be mad at scared kids? I clapped my hands and injected energy into my voice. "Well, I have good news for everyone." I told them about the cabin and that children just like them lived there a couple of years ago, though I skipped the parts about Phyllis dying and our escape from the cat. When I mentioned that the air was clean and that everyone could play outside without masks, they cheered.

When the cheers faded, I asked Vonda and Bastian if they wanted to be in charge of survival plans while Oliver, Crystal, and I repaired the ship. They readily agreed.

After packing some food and extra blankets and pillows, Vonda and Bastian herded the other kids out of the ship and toward the cabin, Perdantus leading the way and Oliver going along with the shotgun. Crystal went as well so Oliver would have some company on the way back to the ship. Since they had plenty of daylight remaining and lanterns at the cabin, they left the flashlights behind.

While they were gone, I grabbed a flashlight and checked on Dirk. He sat in the sick bay's chair, a flashlight of his own in hand and his sliced pant leg rolled up. When he saw me, he set the beam in my eyes. "About time you got back, Miss Pirate."

I dodged the light. "Oh, really? Did you miss me, Mr. Pickpocket?"

"I missed the danger. I mean, look, how often do I get to be shot out into space without a lifeline? How often do I get to crash on a volcanic planet? When you're not around, life's kind of boring."

I huffed. "How long did you practice that speech?"

"Ever since you left. Nothing else to do." He lifted his brow. "So what's going on in the outside world?"

I recited the same summary I gave the others, including our decision to keep him on the *Nebula Nine*, and I added the news about the big cat. When I finished, he extended a hand. "Help me up. My knee feels a lot better. I'm gonna try to walk."

I concealed a smile, not wanting to give away Oliver's secret. That was up to him. "Are you sure?"

"Don't worry. When I woke up, the swelling was gone. Just a bruise. But thanks for the excuse to stay on the ship. I want to help you get it running again."

"Great. I have just the job for you." I hoisted him up and helped him climb to bridge level. Once there, I set him on the chair at Emerson's console. "Emerson once told me that you're a computer technician. Think you can get him running?"

"No harm trying, I guess." Using a pocketknife, he pried a front panel off the console and peered inside with the flashlight. "What a mess. And it smells like burnt rubber."

While he worked, I hurried to my old hovel and found the ship's maintenance manual. When I brought it back to the bridge, I sat in the captain's chair and started reading the long troubleshooting checklist, listening to Dirk grumble as he crawled within Emerson's innards.

After about an hour, Oliver and Crystal returned, both with shoulders sloped.

"Is something wrong?" I asked.

"Yeah," Oliver said. "A lot."

I cocked my head. "What?"

He leaned the shotgun against the wall. "After we dropped everyone off and got them settled in, I thought I heard the cat out back, so Crystal and I went looking for it, me with the gun and her with a heavy rake we found in a toolshed. Anyway, we didn't find the cat, but we did find a grave."

"A grave?"

Oliver nodded. "Pretty deep in the woods. All we saw was a skeleton arm sticking out of the ground. I guess rain washed the dirt away. We raked more dirt and uncovered the whole skeleton." He let out a sigh. "It was Phyllis Asher."

"What? How do you know?"

He touched his wrist. "She had a pink bracelet with her name and Winthrop's name. Other bones were scattered around, and I found a third arm. So another person must have been buried there or close by. It looked adult sized, so maybe Winthrop."

"Then what happened to the kids?"

"No clue."

"I have a clue." Crystal set a hand on her head. "When I touched Phyllis's skull, I felt her crying out to me."

Oliver rolled his eyes. "A new magic power?"

"No newer than yours, Mr. Healer. Anyway, it was like a ghostly voice saying, 'Find our children. Save them.'"

Goose bumps crawled along my skin. "That's way too creepy."

"I know, and I can't shake it. We have to find out what happened to them."

Oliver raised his hands. "Listen, believe what you want. Right now Yama-Yami is setting, and I'm tired. Let's go to bed and get an early start tomorrow."

I nodded. "Sure. Sounds good."

After the four of us shared a quiet meal in the galley, we went to our quarters, Oliver in the first mate's room, Dirk in the navigator's, and Crystal and me together in the captain's suite.

I let Crystal borrow a pair of shorts and a T-shirt while I chose my clothes for bed, sweatpants and a V-neck jersey. I unbuckled my belt and set it on the night table. The computer tablet, flashlight, and remote were still attached. Seeing the remote raised a smile. It no longer had control over me. Keeping it close didn't make sense anymore, but it still felt good all the same.

When we crawled into bed and settled down, all was quiet until Crystal slid closer and whispered, "I'm glad we can be together."

"Yeah, me, too. I was almost always alone before."

"You're my best friend now. I mean, Cynda was my best friend, but I think you would be now even if she was still alive." Crystal nestled in her pillow and slid her hand into mine. "You're like the sister I never had. I feel like I finally have a home."

I compressed her hand. "Then wherever you and I are together, that'll be our home. You and me."

After a minute or so of silence, Crystal began breathing steadily.

She was asleep, at peace and content—but I couldn't sleep yet. I stared at the ceiling and mentally replayed the recent space battle in the field of darkness—three ships at an impasse.

Questions again flooded my mind. Why was Admiral Fairbanks in this star system? What was his relationship with Winthrop Asher? Who killed Winthrop and Phyllis? Or did she really die of pneumonia while he died for another reason? If so, did the kids bury them? Or maybe this admiral showed up and buried them. And my biggest question: Where was the *Astral Dragon*? My mother told us to come to Delta Ninety-five, but she hadn't shown up yet.

Since my mother sent us to this planet, she probably didn't know that it had entered its season of fire, as Winthrop called it, but it didn't make sense that a few volcanoes would stop her from at least looking for us here. Our ship was out in the open, easily found by any ship with fully equipped scanners.

I took a quick look inside my locket. The dragon's eye glowed. My mother was still alive. Whatever the reason for her absence, we had to repair the *Nebula Nine* and search for the *Astral Dragon*. Nothing was more important.

When my questions ran out, I finally fell asleep, though peace and contentment seemed far away.

How long I slept, I don't know. In the midst of a dream about finding buried skeletons, something clanked. I opened my eyes to darkness. I grabbed the flashlight from the belt on the night table, flicked it on, and scanned the room. Crystal still slept at my side. Nothing seemed unusual.

I rolled out of bed, put on my clothes from the day before, including my canvas shoes, and walked to the bridge. Dirk lay curled on the floor, snoring lightly. Emerson's front panel stood open, and tiny lights emanated from inside. Had Dirk gotten up early and fixed the circuits?

I looked at the console monitor, easy to see with daylight coming through the front window. "Emerson? Are you working?"

The monitor turned on. Words ran along the screen. *I am functioning with all inputs but only text output. Dirk has worked wonders to get me this far.*

"That's great." I turned the flashlight off and looked upward. "I heard a noise outside, like something hit the roof. What do your sensors tell you?"

New words appeared. *Something did, indeed, hit the roof. If it made a dent, it is inconsequential.*

"I guess I'll check it out anyway." I set the flashlight down on Emerson's console. "What time is it here?"

Early morning. Half an Alpha One hour after sunrise.

"Good. I didn't sleep too late." I climbed to the roof, opening the air lock hatches along the way. When I emerged outside, I stood at the top and inhaled. The recent rain had washed away much of the sulfur and freshened the air. I looked around. All of the other kids, including Oliver, were hauling the detached section of the wing toward the ship, some pulling from the front and some pushing at the back, still about a hundred meters to go.

I shouted, "Need help?"

Oliver halted and signaled for the others to rest. He looked at me and grinned. "Yeah. I threw a big rock on the roof to wake you up."

"From way over there?"

"No, genius. I came close and threw one."

I gave him a fake frown. "You put a dent in the roof."

"So now there are a hundred dents instead of ninety-nine." He waved. "Get down here. This thing weighs a million kilos."

I climbed down to the partial wing and jumped to the ground, slipping for a moment on the damp soil. When I joined them, I grabbed a protruding metal rod at the front and set my feet, Oliver to my left and Renalda to my right, our backs to the ship.

"All together," Oliver said. "Now!"

As we pulled, grunts erupted all around. We dragged the wing section for several minutes. Jagged pieces of metal gouged the ground underneath, making the going a lot harder.

When we came within a few meters of the ship, Renalda slipped under the front portion of the wing. She yelped, then fell silent.

I shouted, "Stop!" When everyone halted, I called under the wing while still lifting, "Renalda, are you all right?"

She didn't answer, though I could hear rapid breathing.

"Everyone keep lifting! I'll check on her." I released my grip and crawled under the wing. About a meter away, Renalda lay faceup, her eyes closed.

I trembled but managed to speak in a soothing tone as I crawled closer, though my back rubbed against the bottom of the wing as it lowered slightly. "Renalda, I'm coming. I'll pull you out."

Her eyes opened, and her voice squeaked. "I . . . I don't want to die, Megan."

"Just stay calm. You're not going to die." I kept my voice steady for her sake, not sure of my own words. I pushed myself farther in and grabbed her wrist. "I've got you. Now try to stay still while I pull you."

"Okay."

"Megan," Oliver called, "you'd better hurry. Our hands are slipping."

"Then lift and push it back! Now! Give me everything you've got!"

The wing rose. I let go of Renalda, shifted to my haunches, and set my hands on the wing's underside. Adrenaline surged. I pushed with all my might, rising as the wing retreated on its path. When it cleared Renalda, I lunged to her as the wing dropped a hair's breadth away.

Kneeling, I touched a bloody spot on her torn shirt. Something had stabbed her in the chest, maybe a protruding piece of metal.

"No! No! No!" I felt for a pulse at her neck. Her heart was still beating. I shouted, "Someone get a stretcher from sick bay!"

"I will." Bastian took off in a sprint.

"Oliver, get over here! Now!"

He rushed to Renalda's side and laid a palm over her wound, heaving fast breaths. He looked at me, his forehead deeply etched, obviously worried.

As I bent close to Renalda, my locket dangled from the cord, pulsing red. I had no time to think about what that might mean, so I shoved it behind my shirt and whispered, "We're getting something to carry you with."

"Okay." Her eyes fluttered open. "Want to know who I guessed would be next to die?"

"No." Sobs shattered my voice. "No. I . . . I don't want to know."

She swallowed hard. "It doesn't matter. I got it wrong. I guess 'cause I don't have a home to go to."

Her swallowing motion drew my eyes toward her throat. A locket similar to mine lay on the ground attached to a thin chain that looped around her neck. I slid my hand under the locket and pinched it open. A dragon's eye lay within—dull, no hint of a glow. "Where did you get this?"

She swallowed again. "From my mother."

"Did the gem glow before she died?"

She gave a weak nod. "My . . . my . . . mother . . ." She closed her eyes and stopped breathing.

"Renalda?" I let the locket go and gave her a gentle shake. "Breathe, Renalda! Breathe!"

She gurgled but showed no signs of life.

"Oliver?" I stared at him, ready to sob. "Why isn't it working?"

Already crying, he shook his head. "I don't know, Megan. I don't know. Something doesn't feel right."

"Oh, Renalda! I'm sorry! I'm so, so sorry!"

While I wept on my knees, Oliver lifted his bloodstained hand and looked at the others. "Everyone go to the cabin. Bastian, leave the stretcher here. We'll take care of Renalda."

"What about the big cat you told us about?"

"Perdantus is watching for it. And the shotgun's leaning against a tree over there."

"But I don't know how to shoot—"

"Just point it and pull the trigger!"

"All right. All right."

"Let's go, Bastian," Vonda said. "Oliver's just upset."

"Aren't we all? If we would've stayed with Thorne, Renalda would—"

"Hush!"

Whispers followed, then the shuffling of shoes. Soon, all was quiet.

Oliver grasped my hand. "She's gone. We can't help her."

"Wait." I drew Renalda's chain over her head and draped it over my own. The locket lay against my chest, smearing blood on my shirt.

I rose and looked at Oliver through a blur of tears, my vision shaking as spasms wrenched my gut. His own tears trickled down his cheeks. He slid his hands deep into his pockets. "What're we going to do, Megan?"

"Do?" The word squeaked, barely audible as I spoke through a sob. "What do you mean?"

"This." He waved an arm toward the broken wing. "This whole survival thing is way too big for us. We're just kids."

"I know." I brushed tears with my knuckles, still battling the spasms. "But . . . but what else *can* we do? Give up?"

"Maybe." He averted his eyes. "Dying fast is better than dying slow."

I inhaled deeply, settling my gut. "We're not going to die. We're going to fix the ship and—"

"Really?" He gestured toward Renalda. "Did trying to fix the ship keep her from dying?"

"Don't say that. It's not fair. It wasn't my idea to drag the wing over here."

"No, it wasn't." Oliver's face twisted as his voice pitched higher. "Don't you get it, Megan?" He pointed at himself with a thumb. "It was *my* idea. Renalda's dying was my fault. When Perdantus and I found the wing this morning, I talked everyone into dragging it here. I wanted to surprise you. Because . . . because . . ." He closed his eyes and sobbed.

I slid my arms around him and held him close. We cried together, cheek to cheek. He was right. We were just kids trying our best to be adults. We used big words, flew a spaceship, burned dead bodies, and escaped from a slaver, but where did all that get us? Stranded on a planet that felt like it might explode at any minute.

And now Renalda was dead. How many more might die while I repaired the ship? Could I even do it at all? Now my job seemed like the most impossible task in all the universe.

As our crying eased, I patted Oliver on the back and bent away enough to see his face, my arms still around him. "Why did you want to surprise me?"

He gave me a weak smile, looking away and back again as he fidgeted. "Well, I guess I just wanted to do something to impress you." He nodded toward Renalda. "But see what I did? I messed up. I cost Renalda her life. And I couldn't heal her. I don't know why."

I set my palms on his cheeks and looked him in the eye the way my mother did when I really needed to hear something. "Listen, Oliver. It wasn't your fault. It wasn't anyone's fault. And you don't need to impress me. You literally saved my life from those blasted bees. And you restarted my heart when I was dead. To me, you're a hero."

We hugged once more and cried for a little while longer, saying nothing. When we drew apart, he pushed his hands into his pockets again. "I guess we'd better bury her. I can get a shovel from the toolshed."

I wiped my eyes on my sleeve. "Not burn her?"

"You mean like Cynda?" He shook his head. "We burned dead kids because we had to, not because we wanted to."

"I get that, but Renalda doesn't have a home, and this planet shouldn't be where she stays." I looked into the hazy sky. "Let's send her to the Astral Dragon, and we'll take her ashes on the ship when we leave."

"All right. If that's what you want." Oliver gestured toward the forest. "We have plenty of dry wood at the cabin."

"I'll tell Crystal. She'll want to say goodbye."

"And I'll ask the other kids if they want to come, but don't be surprised if no one wants to, including Crystal."

The following hours flew by in a blur. After I retrieved the accelerant from the ship and Oliver and I built a small pyre on a bare patch in the meadow, Crystal reluctantly joined us. As Oliver guessed, none of the other kids wanted to come. While Renalda's body burned, I said a few words about sending her to the Astral Dragon, but they were clumsy and sounded stupid, though Oliver and Crystal didn't seem to think so.

When I finished, I set the two life lockets side by side over my shirt. Mine no longer glowed. The dragon's eye itself was probably still glowing, just not brightly enough to show on the outside. Why would it pulse that way sometimes and not others? It always seemed to do it when someone was sick or close to dying—first Dirk, then me, and then Renalda. Was it like a warning beacon? Why give me a warning about Renalda when there was nothing I could do to save her? Or maybe it pulsed for a different reason that I hadn't figured out yet.

I looked again into the sky. As some of Renalda's ashes swept upward in the smoke, grief drew new tears. One trickled over my lip and into my mouth, salty on my tongue and bitter in my mind. The Astral Dragon had appeared to me three times—once in the furnace, once during a dream, and once while I lay without a heartbeat. Each time, he brought comfort and assurance, making me believe that I could do the impossible. At every step, I pursued my goals with all my heart. I sacrificed. I even died. I believed in him.

And for what? Now I was marooned on a planet that was ready to explode, and a little girl lay burning on a pyre—a child with no home and no family to kiss her goodbye.

The bitterness swelled until it erupted from my gut. I shouted, "Where are you now, Astral Dragon? You kept me alive to help these kids. Now one of the smallest is gone. She needed the most help, but she got stabbed in the heart. It didn't have to happen, but you let it happen." I clenched my fists and screamed, "What in blazes are you doing?"

I lowered my head and wept. Oliver reached for me, but I spun away. "Just . . ." I sniffed in a halting breath. "Just leave me alone."

"Sure. I understand. Let's go, Crystal."

After they left for the ship, I stayed near the fire and cried for a long time, feeling sorry for Renalda and for myself. When I finally settled, I collected her ashes and bone fragments in a jar, took them to the ship, and stowed them in a cabinet under Emerson's console with those of the crew members, hoping I might be able to find Renalda's relatives someday. Maybe they would remember her and want a keepsake, morbid as it might be.

I gazed at the jars, imagining the people each one represented, seeing them walk around the bridge like phantoms. They all had lives. They cherished loved ones. They each had a purpose, prematurely crushed in untimely death. Those purposes would never be realized.

As new tears welled, I blinked away the phantoms. I couldn't let grief thrash me again. I had to focus on the main goal—to help everyone else survive. My other goals—to find my mother and stop the slave trading—would have to drop in priority. And grief had to wait for another day.

That night, Crystal and I lay in bed, both staring at the darkness. Crystal whispered, "You asleep?"

"Nope."

"Still thinking about Renalda?"

"Trying not to."

"Same. But if we don't sleep, we'll be exhausted tomorrow. We should do something that'll take our minds off her."

I turned toward Crystal. "You already have an idea. Spill it."

She turned toward me as well, her face barely visible in the dim lavatory light we always left on. "Remember Captain Tillman's log? On his tablet? We could watch that."

"But we could never guess the password. We stopped trying."

"*You* stopped trying. Oliver and I figured it out. We didn't tell you because you've been so busy."

I waited through a few seconds of silence. "Okay, Miss Dramatic Pause. What's the password?"

She grinned. "Space brat."

I laughed. "That's perfect."

"I know. But Oliver didn't think so." She lifted the computer tablet from the night table, turned it on, and set it on my chest. "You're the captain. You should start it. Oliver and I exited the program as soon as we got the password right."

"All right. Here goes." I started the log and entered the password. A calendar popped up with highlighted dates, probably the days the captain entered something. I scrolled back to the month Oliver was kidnapped and tapped the highlighted date.

A video started. Captain Tillman's face filled the screen, redness in his eyes and stubble across his cheeks and chin. "ASD forty-one-sixty-two-point-seven-five. My son, Oliver, was kidnapped today." He sniffed and wiped his nose before continuing. "I requested leave from my usual duties to pursue the kidnappers wherever the search may lead. I hoped to gain command of the *Nebula Two*, one of the larger Alliance vessels and certainly one of the fastest. Such a ship would provide plenty of stores and allow us to take longer voyages if needed.

"Unfortunately, Admiral Fairbanks denied my request, saying that setting aside valuable assets for a mission that is doomed to fail would be foolhardy. No one has been able to put a dent in the child trafficking business. The traders are smart and know how to hide. Finding a single child on a single ship somewhere in the cosmos is impossible, a waste of time.

"Although I argued as forcefully as my rank would allow, he did not relent. In fact, with regard to the traffickers' excuses for their trade, the admiral played the devil's advocate far too well. I wanted to punch him in the nose. But, of course, I didn't. I merely gave him a polite nod and left, knowing that my only chance to rescue Oliver was to play along."

He glanced around, as if worried about an eavesdropper. "Although this ship, the *Nebula Nine*, is not as big as the *Nebula Two*, she is fast enough, and maybe a smaller vessel will be better for a stealth operation. In any case, it won't be too hard to sneak away from my Beta-system patrol mission and search for my boy. I just have to be ready to answer the questions that are sure to arise."

After another sigh, he nodded. "Because of shifting priorities, I will not be recording regular log entries, but I will provide an update at the appropriate time." The video ended, and the screen turned dark.

"Wow," Crystal whispered. "That's intense. And every word was true."

I turned toward her. "Your powers work on recordings?"

"Yeah. Sure. It's all about the voice and facial expressions. Stuff like that."

"Okay. Let's see what else is here." I scanned the calendar until I found the next entry, twenty Alpha One days later. When I tapped on the date, a new video began, again showing the captain's face, clean-shaven this time. He stood next to Emerson's console near an old-fashioned radio unit that sat on the console's desktop, the casing off with a few parts scattered about. After reciting the date, he picked up one of the parts and inserted it into the unit. "My suspicions have been confirmed. The conspiracy to traffic children is wider and deeper than I imagined earlier. You see, I had often questioned why these traders wanted human children. I thought it was because they're more easily controlled than adults, and they don't eat as much."

He picked up another part along with a screwdriver and began screwing the part in place. "Now I have a new theory. Although children aren't able to carry heavy loads, they are small enough to enter places adults can't go. What if this epidemic of child snatching has nothing to do with the ease of control or the cost of feeding, but everything to do with size? What kind of slave labor requires entering a small space or squeezing through a narrow access point?"

I whispered, "Right, Captain. Only kids can get through the bramble bee netting."

"Whatever the reason . . ." He snapped a third piece into the unit. "The problem is spreading. Many children have gone missing, too many for a single slave operation, and the snatchings have not come from a small, concentrated area. They are occurring through-out the galaxy. It is risky and time-consuming to transport children long distances, which means the snatchings are likely for local slave markets or labor camps that are multiplying. The purpose has to be highly profitable.

"Then I wondered why a trafficker would kidnap my son. There are plenty of orphans, homeless waifs, and runaways to choose from. With such a sea of easy opportunity, why take an immense risk by stealing the son of an Alliance officer? It made no sense."

The captain slid a case over the radio unit. "That's when a new idea occurred to me. It sounded insane at first, but since I was already grasping at straws, I followed up on the idea. There's an old fable that some children born on Gamma Five have special gifts. Some even call it magic."

Crystal gasped. "He's talking about kids like me!"

I set a finger to my lips. "Hush and listen."

"In any case," the captain continued as he fastened the unit's cover on with a screwdriver, "I discovered that the number of missing Gamma Five children per capita is almost ten times higher than any other planet. Those kids are targeted."

The captain set the screwdriver down and glanced around again. "I am about to reveal something that I now find embarrassing. When my wife was pregnant with Oliver, we went on an expedition to Gamma Five so that he could be born there. Young and foolish, we thought it would be fun to give him the opportunity to claim a magical birthplace, though we never really believed in it. I can only guess that someone found the birth record at the hospital and searched for him." A tear slipped down his cheek. "What was meant to be a fun lark might have turned into a death sentence for our boy."

As more tears trickled, Captain Tillman touched the top of the radio unit. "This was to be a gift for Oliver. I started building it the day before he was kidnapped, and I summoned the strength to finish it today. It will be ready for him when I finally bring him home." He swallowed hard, his eyes reddening. "That's enough for today." The video ended, and the calendar reappeared.

Crystal gasped. "Holy tuna fish! Oliver was born on Gamma Five. That's how he got his healing powers."

"I heard." Although the captain had vanished, the image of his tearful face stayed in my mind. For so long, I didn't think of him as anything but a self-serving monster, but his love for Oliver was real. I couldn't deny it.

Crystal hissed. "What're you waiting for, Megan? Pull up the next one."

I rolled my eyes. "So watching the log will help us sleep, huh?"

"Stuff the snark and stop pretending you're not dying to keep going."

"Okay. Okay." I searched for the next entry, but the dates were blank for a long time. When I finally found one, I looked at the month. It was during our flight through the wormhole. I tapped the date.

Captain Tillman appeared, again neatly groomed. "Today is crucial for my infiltration plan. I am taking a step that is disturbing on many levels, but, as I mentioned before, I will do whatever it takes to get Oliver back." He cleared his throat and continued. "I learned that the head of one of the trafficking factions is a husband-and-wife team that hopes to create an army of superior soldiers they call the SS Squad and use them to murder anyone who stands in the way of their hope of intergalactic dominance. They keep their identities secret from all parties within the organization. I have code names but no real ones. There are strong rumors that the man is an Alliance military officer, which gives him a lot of freedom to traffic without interference. I hope to expose him, but I need to infiltrate the trafficking network.

"And now an opportunity has arisen. We captured a notorious pirate couple, Julian and Anne Willis. The court sentenced them to death or exile, and I took their daughter, Megan, into custody. Better for her to be of service to me than to waste her considerable talents at the juvenile labor camp."

Crystal poked my ribs. "He's talking about you."

"I know. Shhh."

"Megan is," the captain continued, "even at her tender age, an experienced mechanic, which gave me the pretext to request her. Yet, I had a more important reason. According to my sources, she has a gem called a dragon's eye. The same lore that produced the Gamma Five legend also says that a bearer of the dragon's eye will greatly enhance the powers of any magical child. In essence, the dragon child makes the gifted one into a superpowered dynamo, a perfect candidate for the SS Squad."

Crystal grabbed my arm. "You did that to Oliver! You're the reason he's a healing dynamo!"

"I'm not stupid, Crystal. Now hush."

The captain lifted an eyebrow. "After weeks of research, I now believe the lore is true. With the dragon's eye in my possession, I can arrive on Delta Ninety-eight with a lure to fish for clues to Oliver's whereabouts and learn how to counter the goals of the SS Squad conspiracy. And now that I have had the opportunity to interrogate Megan with the help of a lie detector, I am sure she hid the dragon's eye somewhere on the ship. But I can't quite extract the precise location, no matter how I pressure her to tell me, even with a painful torture device."

I ran a hand along my throat, now free of the collar. It seemed odd that he would tell the log about torturing me. That would make him look bad if anyone but him ever accessed it.

"Yet, there is another way I can use Megan, even if she never gives me the dragon's eye. I can take her to the slave market on Delta Ninety-eight and put her up for bid. If I claim that she has a dragon's eye, she is sure to draw a lot of attention.

"Also, if Oliver is alive, maybe the same person who is holding him will make himself known. You see, my research revealed that a slaver on Delta Ninety-eight is buying Gamma Five children who haven't yet exhibited special powers. They are cheaper than gifted children, and he considers them to be an investment, hoping for the powers to eventually arise, which would make them far more valuable to the SS Squad buyers, especially if they could combine their powers with those of a dragon's eye child.

"When I learned of this slaver, I sought my first mate's advice about how to leave our patrol without alerting the Alliance. He advised me to bide my time for a few months and continue patrolling the Beta system and interrogating Megan while he arranged everything. At the time, I trusted him to do so, and the plan seemed to work. Yet now, for reasons that I am not ready to divulge, I am wondering about his loyalty. Perhaps I will explain more in a future log entry. For now, I must concentrate every effort on my goals."

Captain Tillman clenched a fist. "If my suspicions are correct and the SS Squad is real, the mass-murder plot must be squashed. Except for finding my son, there is nothing more important."

I tapped the screen, stopping the video. "I've heard the rest."

"Okay. If you say so."

"I say so." My heart thumped. A cold sweat emerged. Everything was clear. I had long wondered what the captain's alternative plans were. Now I knew. I was going to be bait. Slave bait. And the dragon's eye power was real. Like Crystal said, Oliver never could heal anyone till I came around. And he couldn't heal Cynda because I didn't have the dragon's eye then. Gavin had taken it from me. Yet, why couldn't he heal Renalda? My dragon's eye was pulsing at the time. And what about Crystal's powers? Were hers enhanced?

"Crystal, have you noticed—"

"Yeah. Like right now I already knew what you were going to ask. And hearing Phyllis's voice? Never happened before. That means you don't even have to be with me. I heard it while you were at the ship."

I whispered, "I made you a dynamo."

"More than once. When I climbed into the *Nine* while you were hanging from the ladder, I got stronger then, too. I don't know about Oliver, but there's no way I could've done that with my puny arms."

"And I had more strength, too." I touched my locket. "I had the dragon's eye then, and it was pulsing light. And when Oliver healed Dirk, Dirk had just given it back to me."

"So you make yourself a dynamo, too." Crystal pulled the bedsheet up over her head. "I'm sleeping with some kind of spooky witch."

"Get serious." I grabbed the sheet and pulled it back down, revealing her grinning face. "Listen. We should call Oliver in here. He needs to hear what his father said. And Dirk, too."

"Why Dirk?"

"Because he knew Captain Tillman. It's only fair to let him in on it."

"You're right. I'll get them." Crystal slid out of bed and exited the captain's suite while I set the log back to the first entry and made it ready to play.

When the boys arrived with Crystal, I patted the mattress. "Sit. I have something to show you."

Wearing a loose T-shirt and baggy sweatpants, Dirk yawned as he crawled up onto the bed and sat cross-legged. "I hope it's important. I was dreaming about blueberry pie."

Dressed almost identically, Oliver joined him. "Not me. I couldn't sleep."

"Renalda?" I asked as Crystal and I sat across from them.

Oliver nodded. "So what's this all about?"

"Here. Check this out." I set the tablet on the bed so Oliver and Dirk could see it, then played the first entry and watched Oliver's expression. He stared at the screen, motionless. Tears gleamed in his eyes, but he said nothing.

I played the other entries without comment. Although Dirk's face changed expressions several times, Oliver remained relatively stoic.

When the log finished, I tapped on the tablet. "This changes everything."

Oliver looked at me and brushed away a tear. "What do you mean?"

"Up till now I've been all about helping everyone survive so I could get off this planet and find my mother. Now we know that the slave trading is a whole lot bigger than we thought. And it reaches to the highest levels."

"And my father was trying to stop it," Oliver said.

I pointed at him. "Exactly. And trying to find you at the same time. Maybe he didn't go about it the way I think he should've, but he was trying to do something super important to help kids. We gotta give him credit for that."

Oliver nodded, a new tear emerging. "That helps a lot."

"Yep. Like I said, this changes everything. We've got a huge job to do."

"And that is?"

I clenched a fist. "Finish what your father started. We'll still be in survival mode, but our goal now is to rocket out of here so we can figure out who's behind the SS Squad and shut them and all the slave traders down for good."

Crystal clapped her hands. "Yeah! I love it when you're so fired up."

"Hush." I elbowed her, but I couldn't suppress my smile. "All the dynamos here need to be fired up."

"Dynamos?" Dirk asked, yawning again. "I don't feel like a dynamo."

"Well," Crystal said, eyeing him, "maybe you can be an honorary dynamo." She quickly related our conversation about dynamos and the fact that she and Oliver had unusual powers because of their birth on Gamma Five while I got mine somehow from the dragon's eye. When she finished, she added, "And you can be a spying dynamo, Dirk. You're super sneaky."

Dirk's face lit up with a wide smile. "A spy. I like it."

"Then it's settled. Together, we're a perfect team." Crystal laid her palm on the mattress at the center of our circle. "Is everyone in?"

I blinked at her. "What do you mean?"

"I read an old novel a couple of months ago. When this team of kids got ready to do something exciting and dangerous, they put their hands together in a stack to get motivated."

Dirk set his hand on top of Crystal's. "Like this?"

"Perfect." She nodded toward Oliver. "And you?"

Oliver set his hand on Dirk's. "All the way."

Crystal faced me. "One more."

"Well . . ." I moved my hand over theirs, not quite touching. "On one condition."

"And that is?" she asked.

I furrowed my brow, hoping to communicate the seriousness of the moment. "When we say we're a team, we have to really mean it.

We trust each other with everything. No secrets. Blowing up the slave trading's going to be dangerous. We might get hurt or even killed. We have to know we've got each other's backs. No matter what."

Everyone stayed quiet for a moment as if absorbing my words. Finally, Crystal offered a firm nod. "Yeah. Good reminder. And I'm still in."

Oliver and Dirk added their own nods. "Our hands are still there," Dirk said as he looked at me.

"Then mine is, too." I added my hand to the top. "We've got a long way to go, but starting tomorrow, we'll know what we're working for and why. We can do this. Together."

"Kaboom!" Crystal thrust her hand upward, separating the others. "That's the way to get us motivated, Megan!"

After we hugged each other and said good night, Crystal and I crawled under the bedcovers again. Although Renalda returned to mind, I was able to chase the sadness away with thoughts of our new goals and my passion to fulfill them. We really could do this if we worked together. Soon, exhaustion flooded my body. In spite of the new excitement, I could barely keep my eyes open. "We'd better catch some sleep, Crystal." I nestled into my pillow. "That's an order."

"Yeah. Right. You make me into a supercharged dynamo and charge me up with your speech, and I'm supposed to sleep. Wish me luck with that."

"Good luck, Crystal." I yawned. "Maybe go to the bridge and read one of the manuals Dirk's using to repair Emerson. That'll knock you out." I closed my eyes and immediately dropped into a dreamless sleep.

The next day, while Dirk continued working on Emerson and the other kids planted the garden, Oliver and I took a panel off the broken wing section, hammered out its dents and bent portions, welded the rips, and reattached it to the ship. That process alone took four hours. Then we analyzed the components inside the broken wing that the panel once covered and made a list of everything that appeared to be damaged so we could find those parts in our inventory.

Evening arrived sooner than we expected, whether because we were so consumed by work or because Delta Ninety-five rotated faster than we were used to, we weren't sure. Either way, Oliver and I completed only a tiny fraction of the wing. It became clear that the wing reconstruction alone would take weeks, and repairing the entire ship would take months.

The next morning, thanks to Dirk, Emerson's voice returned. He was able to scan the ship for damages we couldn't see, which was great, though the scans revealed that we had a lot more work to do than we realized before. At least the long-range transmitter still functioned. Yet, since the admiral would be monitoring the area for a signal, I couldn't risk sending one. My mother would have to find me without it.

Emerson also kept track of the Alliance Standard Date for us. A day on Delta Ninety-five lasted 19.7 Alpha One hours, compared to Delta Ninety-eight's 23.5, which threw off our body clocks. It took more than a week to adjust.

As we worked, days stretched into weeks and weeks into months. Our food stores began running out, but fortunately, the garden grew quickly in the rich soil and bore fruit and vegetables, including green beans, tomatoes, squash, carrots, corn, eggplant, way too much okra, and a vegetable I had never seen before, a weird cross between cabbage and cauliflower that tasted like a potato.

Of course, before eating the produce, we tested it in an analysis scope attached to Emerson. He was able to search every molecule for problems the sulfur-infused soil might have caused. Our extra care turned out to be unnecessary. Everything passed the tests.

During the many days on the planet, we all grew. I rummaged through the closets of the *Nebula Nine*'s crew and found more clothes than I expected. Bastian, who had amazing sewing skills, altered the clothes to fit us, including two shirts for me, one with short sleeves and one with long.

Oliver and Vonda took turns hunting small game, mostly tailless rodents that ranged from rat to raccoon in size. Perdantus proved to be a great help as he perched in treetops and spotted our targets. Although we saw quite a number of ground birds that resembled quail, for Perdantus's sake, we never hunted them. Vonda shot a hoofed creature as big as an elk. It tasted like venison, though it was as tough as shoe leather. Still, it filled our bellies for quite a while.

We never saw the big cat again. Maybe the gunshots scared it away. In any case, our early encounter with it turned out for the best. If it had not stalked us, we might have hurried straight to the ship and never found the cabin. When I pondered this one day, my own words to the Astral Dragon returned to mind. *What in blazes are you doing?*

I clutched my locket and Renalda's together. Maybe he was doing far more than I realized.

Long days of work meant lots of sweat and plenty of dirt. Three times a week, I bathed in the river with the girls. I'm not sure how often the boys took a turn, but based on Oliver's varying odors, probably about once a week.

Early on, Oliver turned thirteen years old. Crystal turned twelve, and Dirk eleven. Since we called ourselves a team, the four of us stayed together nearly all the time. We became like brothers and sisters, including heated squabbles that stung for a few hours but vanished like fog at the next sunrise. Over time, even the spats diminished as we worked together, sweated together, bled together. We grew to truly love each other.

I also became good friends with Perdantus. I took the first step to boost our relationship by putting away the translation device and working hard to learn his chirping language. Since Oliver and Crystal already knew it, they helped me figure it out. Dirk picked it up without help. The little monkey seemed to be able to talk to anything, including the droids.

Because of our growing friendship, I actively sought Perdantus's company. During our first several weeks on Delta Ninety-five, he stayed distant most of the time, perched on treetops, singing songs of lament about his dear Salsa. He also kept watch for the cat and other dangers, though his size prevented him from helping in other ways, much to his annoyance.

As I listened to his treetop songs, I realized the depth of his heart, how much he cared for his mate, how much he missed her and hoped for the day when he could see her again in the home of the Astral Dragon. Before meeting him, I thought of birds as flighty and shallow, even lacking a real mind or soul. His songs taught me better.

Once each week, in the evening after work, I followed his song to whichever tree he had chosen that day. When I called to him, he flew down and perched on my shoulder for a leisurely walk, though I always kept the shotgun in hand in case the cat showed its whiskered face.

We talked about everything, my life as a so-called pirate, my grief over losing my family, and my hopes for the future. He added tidbits about his life as a negotiator and the reason for Salsa's decision to work for Thorne. Although she hated the children's slavery, she hoped to make life better for them by bringing extra food and chirping a warning when Thorne became angry.

Whenever we talked about Salsa, Perdantus's mood turned gloomy. I sometimes probed more deeply and asked about his grief and his own hopes for the future, but he always changed the subject, which made me wonder if he didn't trust me yet with his deepest thoughts and feelings.

One day that changed. Oliver and I had just transferred a heavy panel from the broken portion of the wing and welded it back onto the ship. It took all day to straighten it, pound out the indentations, and reattach it. We were both hot, sweaty, and exhausted.

When Oliver left to cool off in the river, I stayed at the ship and sat cross-legged in the shadow of the wing, sipping from a can of vitamin water, too tired to make the river journey.

Perdantus landed on my pants-covered knee and looked up at the ever-growing wing. "Your repair project is coming along quite well."

"Thank you." I set the can down and sighed. "We have a long, long way to go."

"One day at a time, Megan. One day at a time."

"I know." I looked out at the broken portion, still massive, much of it bent, dented, and twisted. "I guess when I get this tired, I can't see the light at the end of the tunnel."

"I understand. Darkness and exhaustion are blinding veils. Yet, the light is ahead. It has to be. Otherwise, it's not really a tunnel at all. Every tunnel has an end."

"Good point. But it's hard to see that when you're in the dark part."

"Which is precisely why you must keep going. You will never find the light if you despair in the darkness."

Salsa came to mind, Perdantus's own dark tunnel. Not wanting to question his counsel, I hesitated to mention her, but maybe my question would help him work through it. "Are you despairing about Salsa's death?"

"Ah. A fair question." He spoke with a formal chirping cadence, as if reciting from memory. "Grief is not the same as despair. I hurt, but I have hope. I will see Salsa again, and that hope is far greater than my hurt." He breathed a sigh. "I say that to myself whenever I feel despair trying to break through. It helps, because it's true. I have to choose to believe it."

He stared at me as if waiting for a response, but I had no idea what to say. Yet, I did get his main point. Believe the truth, especially while struggling through the darkness.

He peered at me with one eye. "I hope that this tunnel you are traversing ends soon without more of the traumatic suffering you have already endured. But even if your pain must continue, remember this proverb. 'For the generous heart, suffering yields the solace of sympathy.'"

"Solace. That means comfort, right?"

"Yes. And we offer solace to others through our sympathy— comforting words, commiserating tears, and deeds of kindness."

"And touches of affection?"

Perdantus tilted his head. "Yes, those are important as well."

"Okay, then." I reached a hand toward him and gently ran a finger over his chest.

He backed away. "What are you doing?"

"Giving you a touch of affection." I withdrew my hand. "Are you offended?"

"Not at all. I am surprised but not offended."

"Surprised? Why?"

"A touch of affection is reserved for someone you love. I see us as allies, comrades in pursuit of a great purpose. Isn't that so?"

"Definitely. But I also see you as family." I inched my hand toward him. "And I love everyone in my family. Including you, Perdantus."

"Oh . . . I see." He shuffled his clawlike feet along my pants, bringing him closer. "In that case, by all means."

I again rubbed his chest with my finger. He closed his eyes and sang a few warbling notes, happy notes, the first I had heard from him in a long time.

After half a minute or so, I set my hand in my lap. "Thanks for the talk."

"You are quite welcome, Megan. And thank you for accepting me as a family member." Without another word, he flew away.

After that conversation, our friendship grew even more quickly, and he began teaching me negotiating skills, including a confident stance, the courage to walk away from a bad deal if necessary, and most important of all, the fact that a good negotiator always goes for the heart to close a deal. For most people, an appeal to the emotions is far more powerful than a position of logic. Yet, it has to be genuine. A false appeal uncovered is the kiss of death.

Part of my negotiation lessons included vocabulary drills. Perdantus insisted that using big or unusual words would help me overwhelm a verbal opponent, especially when the opponent had to ask what a word means. Psychologically speaking, providing a definition was like adding something extra to a deal, thereby giving me an advantage overall. It made sense, so I studied hard.

The others studied as well. Oliver, Crystal, and Dirk learned as much as they could about the *Nebula Nine*, the cabin kids borrowed and read my textbooks, and Vonda and Bastian combed the Ashers' journal for survival skills. They learned about the land, where to find fish in the river, how to dig new cisterns, and how much of the harvest to save in the Ashers' underground storage cave, dug by Winthrop shortly after he arrived on the planet.

Vonda compiled a list of the Ashers' children's names on a new page, gathering them from various entries, though the journal made no mention of which child had unique abilities, as Winthrop had called them. I tore the page of names from the journal and scanned it quickly. One name stood out—Zoë, the name I had heard twice before. A coincidence? Maybe. But I would keep it in mind. I stowed the page on the ship, vowing that I would search for all the kids when we could finally leave this planet.

According to the journal, this region never turned cold enough to kill the crops, so all we had to do was follow Winthrop's schedule for rotating them. If we always kept some plants in their fruiting stage, we wouldn't have to keep much food in storage.

We also learned the seismic cycles. Feeling slight tremors allowed us to predict earthquakes and nearby eruptions. Although the volcanoes spewed lava, steam, and smoke, polluting the air and veiling the sky, a breeze kicked up every evening, sometimes hailing a refreshing thunder-shower and nearly always clearing the air enough to see the stars at night.

During those hours of clear darkness, I reserved a few minutes of alone time. Well, not exactly alone. The stars kept me company. I sat on top of the *Nebula Nine*, looked into the black sky, and searched the brilliant clusters, praying that one of the points of light would move, revealing itself as a light from a spaceship, hoping that the *Astral Dragon* had come to rescue us. But the bright dots just twinkled, unable to answer my prayers.

Each night I opened the locket and looked at the glowing ruby, and I whispered the same words into the sky. "Mama, I'm here. Come and find me. But if you can't, I'll come and find you. Someday."

And I always cried. Why? Lots of reasons, but one gnawed relentlessly at my soul. Sitting in darkness on the roof of a broken spaceship reminded me of the awfulness of my situation. I was small . . . so small. The vastness of space said so. And my problems were way too big. How could a girl—still a child, really—repair a ship like this? And what about the slave traders? Apparently, their evil business had spread throughout the galaxy. How could someone so small fight something so big?

The cosmos answered with a cold, empty voice. *You can't. It's impossible.*

That's when the tears flowed. I listened to the voice. And I believed it, at least during those darkest hours. That's when Perdantus's advice returned to mind. To battle the darkness, I ended every crying session by praying to the Astral Dragon, asking for help, for light, and especially for my mother to find me. In spite of all the tragedy, I had to believe. I had no other anchor.

Early on during our days on the planet, I began a new project. I set the prisoner collar and the remote-control unit on a worktable and dismantled them. Using their design schematics provided by Emerson, I began a mission to figure out how the shock system worked, including how the collar sent signals to the ink on my arms and legs, making my muscles cramp. My goal? To make the collar a useful tool instead of a torture device.

Night after night, I worked on the collar, cutting it into sections and taking out its circuits. I found the spare collar and remote unit Gavin mentioned and included them in the process. After several weeks I had fashioned two bracelets that fit my wrists. Pressing a remote's button still triggered a shock, and the bracelets sent the same signals to the ink. My muscles responded with cramps, as usual, and electricity again pulsed from my hands. So far, so good.

Then I moved to step two, and for that, I needed help. Earlier, our team members vowed to keep no secrets from each other, so, because I needed a girl's help, I told Crystal first. If we could get my project to work, we could spring the surprise on Oliver and Dirk later.

Crystal and I hunted through the supplies and found a cache with a stylus and conductive ink. A little booklet gave instructions on how to use them, apparently provided to reink a prisoner if the initial application stopped working properly.

Learning quickly, Crystal rerouted the bracelets' signals by drawing new conductive ink lines that bypassed my forearm muscles and concentrated the electrical impulse in my hands and fingers. Then when I pressed the button, electricity crackled in arcs along my palm and between my fingers. Although the sensation stung and drew a shudder, I quickly got used to it, and my hands could deliver an electrical pulse anywhere I touched with only a little pain to myself.

On my calf muscles, Crystal rerouted the ink to bypass pain receptors, causing the muscles to flex with power instead of crippling spasms. A press of the button enabled me to jump 50 percent higher than before and run about 30 percent faster, at least in a short spurt.

Since using the remote units proved to be cumbersome, Crystal implanted their signal-generating circuitry in my upper arms, a painful and clumsy process that took much longer than we expected. But when we finished, I was able to use muscle flexes to activate the circuits, one kind of flex to send electricity to my hands and another to send an impulse to strengthen my calf muscles. We also installed an on-off switch on the bracelets, a safeguard to make sure I didn't accidentally activate them. After days of practice, I trained myself to use both features easily, my left biceps controlling my left hand and calf and my right biceps controlling the right side.

Night after night, we worked to the point of exhaustion, but when we finished, the time and toil felt completely worth it. We invented scenarios to give me practice—zapping imaginary villains and leaping over obstacles. We had a blast.

During the day, we continued working on the ship, never taking a day off, though bad weather sometimes cut our hours short. After eight months, I stood next to the almost-completed wing. One panel flap lay open underneath, exposing a set of movement-control wires. Only one broken strand remained. I reeled a few centimeters of wire from a spool and called to Perdantus, who stood on the wing. "Just one more cut."

He flew to my arm and clipped the wire with his beak.

"Perfect. Thanks."

"A pleasure to be of service." He returned to the wing and continued watching. "This is an extraordinary day, Megan. You should be proud of this accomplishment."

"I am." I set the spool on the ground. "But I couldn't have done it without everyone's help." When I spliced the new wire with black tape and a plastic sleeve, I closed the panel and walked out from under the wing. "Finished. Let's see if it'll retract."

"Excellent. I will tell Oliver." Perdantus flew into the ship.

I set a hand on my hip and smiled. Could it be that we had done the impossible? The engines and thrusters had passed their tests. Pressurizing the cabin proved that we had sealed all the leaks. Every electrical component, some newly replaced and some repaired, worked perfectly, including Emerson.

Now the time had come to test the biggest repair job, the end result of countless hours of work and the spilling of gallons of sweat and blood. Of course, we didn't need the wing in outer space, but we could never fly through the atmosphere without it. We would be stuck on this planet forever. After so many tear-filled nights, I finally believed that maybe, just maybe, we had a chance to leave this unstable rock. The light at the end of the tunnel had come into view.

Seconds later, the wing began pulling into its sleeve. The metal skin scraped over the rough spots, but the motion never slowed. When the wing clicked in place, I let out a loud whoop.

Oliver climbed out of the hatch. Leaving the cover lid open, he stood with his fists on his hips and gave me a smile. "Congratulations, Captain Willis."

I leaped onto the wing, scrambled to the roof, and wrapped him in my arms. I squealed, "We did it! We really did it!"

He stepped back and poked my forehead. "You did it. I was just one of the grunt-work guys."

Crystal and Dirk jumped out of the hatch and joined us, both brimming with smiles. Perdantus flew up as well. He perched on my shoulder and chirped, "Your accomplishment is truly extraordinary."

I rubbed his chest with a finger. "Thank you, Perdantus, but I didn't fix everything. I couldn't fabricate some specialized valves we need."

"Ah. The internal air locks. But I assume you're not going to let that stop you. They're not critical systems, if I am not mistaken."

"If we spring an air leak somewhere, they're more than critical. They're lifesavers. But, no, we'll leave without repairing them. Otherwise we'll be stuck here forever. Oliver and Crystal practiced putting on pressurized suits, so they're good to go. I'll make sure to drill any other kids who go with us."

"So when's the test flight?" Dirk asked.

Pressing my lips together, I looked at Yama-Yami as it neared the horizon. We had maybe an hour of daylight left. "In the morning. If the flight passes all the tests, we can pack and leave by midday."

"What's left to pack?" Oliver asked. "We already loaded all the food and water we can handle."

"Just the kids who want to come with us, I guess."

Oliver looked at Crystal. "What's the latest count? Who wants to go, and who wants to stay?"

She raised a pair of fingers. "Only two want to go, and they're not real sure. Everyone else wants to stay. They say they've never had it so good."

"I can't blame them." Oliver turned toward the forest. "We'll have a meeting at the cabin tonight and explain everything. I don't know about you guys, but I think we should try to talk them all into staying.

This planet is probably better than any sanctuary we could find, especially after what Winthrop wrote in his journal about those places."

"I'm with Oliver," Crystal said. "The four of us should leave, 'cause we practically rebuilt this ship by ourselves. It's our home, and now we're like family, but the others are pretty tight with each other, like there's two different families here. I mean, we're friends with them and all, but it's not the same."

"If I may intrude," Perdantus said, "I wish to go with you on the *Nebula Nine*. The birds I have introduced to the children will be of sufficient help for them, and I assume that I will be able to aid you at your next destination. Besides that, the climate here does not agree with me. I prefer colder weather."

I rubbed his chest again. "Of course. You're family now."

During the early evening hours, we held our meeting. Crystal pushed pretty hard for the cabin dwellers to stay. I offered the counterpoints that we couldn't predict the future, that one of the volcanoes might explode and hurl boulders at the cabin and cover the forest with rivers of lava, but since seismic activity had lessened over the weeks, my warning seemed to fall on deaf ears.

In the end, all of the cabin kids opted to stay on Delta Ninety-five. We decided that if the test flight went well, we wouldn't come back. No use risking an extra landing and takeoff. So, once we departed in the morning, we might never again see those we left behind.

After a tearful goodbye, the four of us hiked back to the ship and settled on the bridge. Dirk leaned back in the captain's chair with Perdantus on his shoulder while Oliver, Crystal, and I settled on the floor in front of Emerson, the room illuminated by the lights on his console.

I folded my hands in my lap. "So we're leaving tomorrow. I think we should head straight to Delta Ninety-eight and see what Thorne's up to now. Any thoughts on that?"

Oliver shrugged. "I guess you're right. Thorne's our only way to learn more about the slave trading. It's a good place to start."

"And maybe we can find my mother to give us help." I pulled my locket out and opened the back. The dragon's eye still glowed. "All I know is that she's alive. Not much to go on."

Oliver intertwined his fingers. "They're kind of linked, aren't they? I mean, whatever happened to your mother is probably connected to the slave market."

"You're right. Then we'll go to Delta Ninety-eight. But I don't know how long it'll take us to get there."

"Just a second." Crystal jumped to her feet and sat at the navigator's console. She flipped a switch and slid her finger around on the screen. After a few moments, she winced. "Not good. Delta Ninety-eight's orbit is way out of whack from ours. Compared to us, it's zooming around Yama-Yami super quick. Anyway, it's about a seventy-six hour trip if we left right now. Probably another hour by the time we leave tomorrow."

I whistled. "That's a long haul compared to how long it took to get here from there."

"Yeah," Oliver said. "Anything we can do during the flight to look for your mother?"

"Maybe." I focused on the ceiling, imagining radio waves flying through space. "Emerson, have you been scanning for signals?"

His console lights blinked faster. "Affirmative, but I have received only space static. Yet, that is inconclusive. Our position on the ground is not ideal for listening, and the volatile atmosphere hampers all transmissions. When we leave, we will open the reception angles. We will also be able to send signals to more areas and try to hail the *Astral Dragon*."

"Won't that be dangerous?" I asked. "Admiral Fairbanks might still be scanning for a signal from us."

"You are correct, but there are ways to disguise a call."

"What ways? The admiral can catch any frequency we use."

"A coded transmission. Is there a language your mother knows that the admiral is unlikely to understand?"

"Maybe. She has an ear translator, just like mine." I looked at each face, searching for an answer, but how could they help? Surely the admiral knew both Alpha One and Humaniversal. When my gaze fell on Perdantus, I smiled. Maybe he held the answer. "How about the call of a silver jay?"

PART
03
DEPARTURE

The next morning, we rose early and took our places, me in the captain's chair, Oliver at the first mate's console, Crystal at the navigator station, and Dirk in the engine room with Perdantus. A low hum emanated from below, a good sign.

I opened the communications links throughout the ship. "Dirk, how are the engines?"

"Purring like kittens. Everything's at a hundred percent."

I looked at Oliver. "Report?"

"I dug us out the best I could and cut the roots. I think we're good to go."

"All right, then." My heart pounding, I curled my fingers over the landing thruster throttle. "Let's do it."

Crystal waved a hand. "Wait."

I spun toward her. "What?"

"I couldn't sleep last night, so I went out to the bridge, and asked Emerson to read the general log from your trip to Delta Ninety-eight.

When he got to the part about you being thirteen, I asked him when your birthday is."

"So?"

She smiled and bounced in her seat. "It's today."

"Today?" I narrowed my eyes. "Are you sure?"

Crystal nodded. "We've been so busy, we stopped keeping track of the Alpha One calendar a couple of months ago. According to Emerson, today is your fourteenth birthday."

Warmth spread through my cheeks. A whole year had passed since the day I was supposed to be executed. And that was great, except that Crystal probably wanted to celebrate, maybe sing a song, but I couldn't. Not yet.

"We'll celebrate it soon." While looking out the viewing window, I pushed the throttle forward. The ship lifted a few centimeters, then stalled and shimmied as it tried to shake free from the remaining dirt that had partially buried it.

"We need more power," Oliver said. "We probably still have roots around us."

"You said you cut them."

"I must have missed some. I couldn't get under the ship."

"Hang on." I pushed the throttle, grabbed the yoke, and turned it back and forth again and again, making the ship wiggle.

Popping noises sounded all around. Dirt flew into the air and spilled down the viewing glass. Finally, the ship broke free. I opened the rear thruster, making us zoom forward as well as upward as we angled toward space and sank in our seats. The sudden g-force spike pinched for a moment, but the escape sensation felt amazing.

Within seconds, the volatile atmosphere made the ship tremble as if we were driving that old bus on a bumpy road back on Delta Ninety-eight. I called out, "Dirk, do you have a reading on that wing? Is it doing all right?"

"Good so far. The air's bumping it pretty hard, though. Can you get into space quicker?"

"Only if you want g-forces to push your stomach into places it's never been before."

"Yeah. Right. Carry on, Captain. I'll let you know if the wing has a problem."

I looked at Oliver and Crystal in turn. "I'm not sure what's worse for the wing, g-forces or rough air."

They both shrugged. "You're the captain," Oliver said. "Your call."

"Just a hunch, but I think we need to bust out of this soupy air. Get ready for a squeeze."

"How do I get ready?" Crystal asked.

"Just . . . I don't know. Just know it's coming. And don't barf your guts out." I boosted both thrusters. As we shot ahead faster and faster, it seemed like someone dropped an elephant in my lap. My face pressed against my skull, and my eyes ached. The ship bucked and bounced, making the pressure even worse. I could barely breathe, much less shout, but I managed two loud words. "Dirk! Report!"

"It's . . . rattling . . . but . . . holding."

Soon, the bouncing eased. As I brought both throttles back, my body began lifting from my seat, halted by the seat belt.

"Gravity on?" Oliver asked, his fingers on a dial.

I nodded. "In increments. Turn that dial to the programmed setting. It'll do the increments for you."

"Got it." Oliver adjusted the dial.

As my body sank back to its seat, I switched the front window to the rear camera's view. On the screen, Delta Ninety-five slowly shrank in the inky blackness.

"Everything all right, Dirk?" I asked.

"The wing's fine, but my guts are all over the floor."

"Yeah, well, clean them up. You know where the mop is."

I toggled the switch to retract the wings. They drew in halfway, then stopped. A red light flashed on my console. "The repaired wing is stuck. It won't retract all the way. I'll have to extend both again."

"Extended wings won't hurt anything out here in space," Oliver said.

"True, unless we go into battle. More area to get hit by something." I set the switch back to the original position. Within seconds, the wings extended to their full lengths. "Done."

Crystal called from her seat. "I got the course set, Captain. Can I switch it over?"

"In a minute." I released my yoke and looked at Oliver. "The *Nebula Nine* is yours. Take us in a wide orbit around Ninety-five before we chase Ninety-eight."

"All right!" Oliver grabbed his yoke and smiled. "Here we go!"

As the ship changed course, I spun my chair toward Emerson's console. "Are you picking up any transmissions?"

"Affirmative. Now that we are away from the interference caused by the planet, I am receiving a variety of communications coming from and going to Delta Ninety-eight. Most of them are in the product-merchandise category, instructions for delivery, docking, and the like, though, as expected, nothing involving slave trafficking. A few are encrypted with a military-grade complexity, but the usual keys fail to unlock them. Since Admiral Fairbanks knows that our ship is no longer in his control, I assume he altered the keys throughout the fleet."

"To keep us from listening. At least we know he's still close by."

"Close is a relative term, and we do not know if the transmission is from the *Nebula One*. We can conclude, however, that at least one military ship is within communication range."

"Let's see who's listening for us." I unfastened my strap and walked toward Emerson's console. "Perdantus, would you please join us on the bridge? It's time to send a message."

Seconds later, the flutter of wings emanated from the speakers. Perdantus flew in and landed on my shoulder. "I am ready," he said, bowing his head.

"Good." I flipped on the long-range transmitter. "Emerson, do you have a suggested frequency?"

"Since Perdantus is native to Delta Ninety-eight, I suggest that we use the channel the traders of the planet use to communicate with passing ships. If the admiral picks up the transmission, perhaps he will believe that it is actually coming from the planet."

I nodded. "With the silver jay call as background noise."

"Then we should chatter a bit," Crystal said. "You know, we'll fake the transmission. You and I will talk, and he'll chirp in the background."

I gave her a skeptical look. "Two human kids talking between the planet and a ship? Who's going to believe that?"

"Emerson can change our voices, right? If two people here on our ship talk, I'm sure he can make it sound like they're talking from different places."

I looked at the console. "Emerson?"

"In short, the answer is yes. If you want the details, I can explain."

"No. Just tell us what to do." I turned toward Crystal. "What's your plan?"

"Just follow my lead." She touched the console. "Emerson, I need a voice print of a man and a woman. Adults. Someone the admiral wouldn't recognize. And they have to be pretty young. You know, young enough for romance."

"Romance?" I rolled my eyes. "What are you up to?"

"Hush a minute. Let Emerson think."

"I have chosen a man," Emerson said, "a twenty-year-old apprentice aboard the *Nebula Five*. He should be relatively obscure. Only a few women match your criteria. I suggest a navigator from a deep-space scout ship. She is twenty-one years old."

"Perfect. When I talk, change my voice to the woman's. When Megan talks, change hers to the man's. She'll be Steve on Delta Ninety-eight. I'll be Linda in a distant cargo ship. Got it?"

"Affirmative, but it will help if you are in separate rooms. That way I can pick up your voices on different microphones."

I nodded. "So Perdantus will go with me and send the real message."

"And what is the message?" Perdantus asked.

I looked upward. What would work even if Admiral Fairbanks translated the silver jay language? "How about this? 'Oh, Astral Dragon, I love the beauty of your planet, the one the humans call Delta Ninety-eight, though we silver jays call it the Protected Pearl.'"

"No, we don't," Perdantus said.

"It's code. Megan means 'pearl,' and Willis means 'protector.' My mother is obsessed with the meaning of names."

"I see. Please continue."

I bit my lip as I formulated more words. Then, speaking slowly, I said, "We need you now, Astral Dragon. Come and visit your child, your daughter. All of us here await you." When I finished, I looked at Perdantus. "Should I repeat it?"

"No need." He lifted his head and sang my message with a lovely melody. Although he altered the words a little, the most important ones stayed the same.

"That's great. We'll go to my old hovel. It's quieter there. Maybe it'll sound more like a planet outpost."

"And we have a lot of ship noises up here on the bridge," Crystal said. "It'll be perfect."

I stepped closer to Oliver. "How's it going?"

"Great." He swiveled my way, a hint of disappointment in his expression. "Is it time to set the course?"

"Yep. Don't worry. You'll get another chance to fly solo."

Crystal skipped over to her station and sat in the chair. "Setting the course, Captain." She grinned. "I've been waiting all morning to say that."

"All right, you clown. Just give me a signal when you want to start the conversation."

With Perdantus on my shoulder, I walked from the bridge and climbed down the ladder to my hovel. When I sat on my old cot, I looked up at the ceiling. "Can you hear me all right, Emerson?"

"Affirmative. Crystal is also in place. I assume she will begin. You will hear her words in the voice of the chosen surrogate."

"A surrogate? That's a replacement, right?"

"Correct."

I leaned my head toward Perdantus. "Perch somewhere across the room so you're in the background. We'll do this until you repeat the message three times." When he flew to a bracket on the far wall, I cleared my throat. "We're ready."

The sound of a woman emanated from the speakers. "Oh, Steve, darling, I miss you so much. When will you leave that horrid planet?"

The moment Perdantus began singing, I spoke toward the ceiling.

"Linda, how I long to be with you, but I have to stay for a while. I still have a lot of work to do."

"But it's so cold on Delta Ninety-eight." Her voice turned sultry. "And I am so warm."

I cringed. She was overdoing it. "I know. I know. But my ship won't return for weeks. I'm stuck here."

"No, Steve. I am on a cargo ship on the way to Delta Ninety-eight. We're landing in . . ." She paused for way too long. "In ten minutes. I will steal you away, my darling, and we can be together once again."

"Yes. Meet me at the ironworks factory in Bassolith. I have some business to attend to there. Then I will sneak away with you."

"I will look forward to that moment, dearest Steve."

I shook my head. This conversation sounded like a bad romance novel. Since Perdantus was nearly finished with the third run-through, I needed to wrap it up. I rose from my cot and walked to the room's privacy dial on the wall. "Linda, that moment cannot come too soon. I will see you there." I turned the dial, shutting the microphone off.

Perdantus exhaled. "How did I do?"

"Fantastic. What did you think about our performance?"

He flew to my shoulder. "To be frank, it was terrible, but it might have worked. Humans do tend toward dreadful sappiness at times."

"True. Let's hope for the best."

I climbed the ladder and walked back to the bridge. When I arrived, Crystal grinned. "That was great, wasn't it?"

I attempted a convincing smile. "We did what we could. Let's hope my mother hears it."

"If she is near Delta Ninety-eight," Emerson said, "the transmission will reach her in a few minutes."

"Then if she gets it and figures it out, she'll show up at Delta Ninety-eight long before we do."

"Correct, unless our assumption is invalid. She might not be close to the planet or even in this star system. If that is the case, you might arrive long before she does. And if she is too distant, she might not receive the transmission at all."

Crystal rolled her eyes. "Thanks for the boost, Emerson."

"Either way," I said, "we need to get there as soon as possible. I don't want her to show up and not find us."

"We are able to get there sooner than the navigation program's estimate of seventy-six hours," Emerson said. "That time of arrival is based on average cruising speed. We can accelerate to a much higher speed and arrive in approximately half the calculated time—that is, thirty-eight hours. We just have to be careful to accelerate and decelerate gradually in order to avoid putting harmful g-force stress on your bodies."

"Then let's do it. Everyone brace yourself again. That includes you, Perdantus."

"I found an excellent refuge earlier." He flew from the bridge and into the sleeping quarters.

Crystal sat at her station and held the sides of her seat. As the ship accelerated, my body bent toward the rear. I set my feet and straightened. Although the g-force continued pulling me, it wasn't nearly as bad as what we experienced during our quick takeoff.

After we grew accustomed to the force, Dirk joined us on the bridge, and we sat cross-legged in a circle in front of Emerson's console, Dirk to my left, Oliver to my right, and Crystal across from me.

When Perdantus rejoined us and perched on my shoulder, Oliver looked around the circle. "So what do we do now?"

"We eat something," Dirk said, patting his stomach. "I'm starved."

I blinked at him. "Already? We just ate an hour ago."

"I puked my breakfast. But don't worry. I cleaned it up." He rubbed his hands together. "I found pizza ingredients in the last of the original stores."

"Pizza?" Crystal tilted her head. "What's that?"

I squinted. "You mean you never read about pizza in your novels?" She shook her head.

I patted Dirk on the back. "Go for it."

"All right!" He leaped up and scurried toward the galley, calling, "Does anyone like okra on pizza?"

"Ewww," I said. "No okra. It's so soft and slimy."

"Suit yourself. I'm putting some on my slices."

When Dirk's voice faded, Oliver looked at me. "Any new thoughts about what we should do when we get to Delta Ninety-eight?"

"Not yet, except that we need to go to Bassolith. If my mother heard the transmission . . ." I smiled and rubbed Perdantus's chest with a finger. "That's where she'll look for me. Since Thorne's glowsap collecting probably ended when we took his slaves, he had to get new ones, and maybe he needs more. We just need someone to pose as a trafficker who'll take us to the market."

"Why?" Crystal asked. "You don't want Thorne to buy us, do you?"

I lowered my hand from Perdantus and pointed at Crystal. "That's exactly what I want."

"But he'll recognize us," Oliver said. "By now he knows we're the ones who messed up his bee business."

I shrugged. "So? He probably needs us. You two are experienced, no training necessary. He'll just post a better guard to keep us from escaping."

"Okay, but why? What do you have in mind?"

"Getting information. Thorne has to be the one who's buying Gamma Five children as an investment. He's the key to learning everything." I glanced from Oliver to Crystal and back again. "I saw a lockbox in his kitchen. Do either of you know what's in it?"

They both shook their heads. "It's important, though," Crystal said. "Once I asked him about it, but he brushed me off. I can tell he's hiding something important in that box, but I never tried to look in it."

"It has to be important," I said. "Maybe a link to the bigger picture. I'm guessing his glowsap collecting business was a pilot, you know, a test to see if they can expand to other planets."

Oliver's eyes took on a faraway look. "Since those planets would need bees . . ."

"What?" Crystal and I said at the same time.

He refocused on us. "Remember Thorne always told us to bring any dead bees to him. I'll bet some had eggs, and he collected them to send them to other planets."

"To start their operations," I said. "Since the newbies have no experience with bramble bees, they have to go to Delta Ninety-eight to learn. Maybe that's why Admiral Fairbanks came. He brought someone to study Thorne's system, but Thorne didn't have any collectors to show them."

Crystal nodded. "It takes weeks to get good at collecting, even if you have someone teaching you, and Thorne didn't have a teacher. We took them all."

I pointed at her. "Exactly, which is why he'll want to buy us. Even if he's trained new kids, he can always use more who already know what to do."

Oliver tensed. "And maybe he'll want to buy us to get revenge. He never whipped us, but some punishments are worse than whippings, like no food for days."

"Have you ever had a whipping?" Crystal asked him. "I mean, from a slaver?"

"No, but it can't be worse than starving."

"Yes, it can." Crystal lifted her shirt in back. Raised welts crisscrossed her skin, too many to count. She lowered her shirt. "I'd rather starve to death than get whipped again."

Oliver cringed. "Sorry, I shouldn't have said that."

"How long ago did it happen?" I asked.

"I got whipped three times. The last one just before Thorne bought me from a human slaver at a gem quarry in the Epsilon system."

I leaned closer. "If you don't mind my asking, why did he whip you?"

"I do mind." Crystal's eyes sparkled with tears. Her lips trembling, she whimpered, "Can we change the subject?"

"Okay. Sure. So . . . um . . . so we need a way into the slave market. Someone to make sure Thorne buys us. We can't just surrender to him or he'll know we're up to something."

Perdantus chirped, "I know a fellow who might help, a Jaradian named Quixon. He has experience in slave trading."

I tapped my chin. "Quixon. I met him when I first went into

Bassolith. He saved me from some other Jaradians, but I wasn't sure if he did it to help me or if he wanted me for himself."

"I assure you," Perdantus said, "that he wanted to help. He once viewed humans as you view dumb beasts on Alpha One. In the past, he whipped children to keep them in line and even hot-iron branded them with a symbol of his ownership. He thought nothing of forcing them to work in his crop fields with inadequate clothing. They burned in the warm season, froze in the cold, and suffered from nettle stings, insect bites, and various gashes from stones and the like. In short, Quixon was a fool, blind to many human frailties."

I blinked at him. "How do you know so much about humans?"

"I have read many of Crystal's books. They are quite enlightening."

I huffed. "Well, don't believe everything you read in them. They're novels. Fiction."

"I understand. Much of the romance seemed far-fetched. Now, to continue my tale, one day Quixon was preparing to whip a newcomer on his bare back. The little boy was unaware of all the rules, and Quixon intended to teach him with the schoolmaster of pain."

Crystal winced but said nothing.

Perdantus lifted a wing. "Now mark this important detail. Quixon always administered the whippings late in the evening when he had drunk his fill of nettle beer, and drunkenness and darkness addled his vision. On this particular evening, however, he had run out of beer and was quite sober. Just as he raised the whip, an older slave boy pushed the newcomer out of the way and took his place at the whipping post. Quixon bellowed, 'What are you doing here?'

"The older boy, now noticing Quixon's sober state, folded his hands in a begging posture. 'Please, sir,' he cried. 'Whip me instead of him.'

"Surprised by the plea, Quixon lowered the whip, stared at the older boy, and said, 'Why would you take his whipping?'

"The older boy showed Quixon his striped back, covered with bleeding red welts. With tears running down his cheeks, he took the smaller boy's hand and said, 'I've been doing it for everyone, and you were always too drunk to notice. Please don't stop me from taking this poor little fellow's place.'"

Perdantus paused and looked at each of us in turn. Then in a warbling, mournful series of chirps, he continued. "This beautiful portrait of sacrifice taught Quixon the lesson he needed to learn. These children were not dumb brutes. They had feelings. Hopes. Dreams of a better life. And they most certainly had love, that precious giving spirit that Quixon knew nothing about until he witnessed it lived out in a bleeding boy's heartfelt plea."

A familiar lump swelled in my throat. Tears coursed down Crystal's cheeks, while Oliver sniffed, his eyes red.

Perdantus took in a deep breath. "Ah, what an emotional whipping Quixon suffered. And a well-deserved one. As you might have guessed by now, he disavowed slavery, properly fed and clothed the children, and financed their journey to a sanctuary planet. Ever since that day, he has hired paid laborers for his farm. Yet, for reasons I do not know, he has not been a publicly vocal opponent of slavery, which leads me to believe that perhaps he would be a good choice as your slave trader. Because he frequented the market in those days, some traders won't recognize him as being antislavery, though I imagine that Jaradians close to him likely know of his recent change."

"And he'll want to help us stop the slave trading," I said as I brushed away a tear. "He sounds perfect."

"Except for two issues," Perdantus said. "One, he is still fond of nettle beer. We'll have to find him in a sober state. Midmorning is our best opportunity, after his hangover headache eases and before he starts drinking again. And two, at heart, he is still a money-hungry soul. Since we have no financial resources, it might take some innovative persuasion to convince him to help us. Let's hope the plight of suffering children will be enough."

Crystal blinked her tear-filled eyes. "All right. We have a plan to get into Thorne's home, but once we see what's in the lockbox, how do we get out? It was hard enough last time."

I shrugged. "Impossible to plan until we know what Thorne will do to keep us from escaping. We'll have to wing it. I can't make a plan till I see what I'm up against."

Oliver sighed. "I guess that makes sense, but it doesn't make me feel any safer."

"Me either, but safe or not, we've got to do something to help the kids he must have bought by now, and all other slave kids."

"Right." Crystal punched the air. "We gotta bust this thing wide open. If we don't, who will?"

"Pizza's ready," Dirk called over the speakers. "Come and get it."

We joined Dirk in the galley, sat at one end of the eight-person dining table, and shared a cheese-pepperoni-macaroni pizza with a birthday candle standing at the center. After Crystal led the singing of "Happy Birthday," I blew out the candle, and we dug in. I had never tried macaroni on a pizza before, but it tasted really good. As promised, Dirk put boiled okra on his slices. He got a big kick out of dramatically slurping the wilting, slimy stuff and watching us cringe. Although we gave Perdantus a full slice, he chose to eat only the crust as well as a couple of other crusts we discarded.

After eating and playing a lengthy jungle-safari role-playing game moderated by Emerson, we went to bed, Crystal and me again in the captain's quarters, Oliver in the first mate's, and Dirk in the navigator's. According to our body clocks, bedtime still lay a few hours in the future, but Emerson advised that we adjust to Bassolith's day-night cycle in time for our arrival.

As Crystal and I lay in bed, I looked at the darkness, unable to fall asleep right away. After a few minutes, I whispered, "Are you awake?"

"Yeah." Her voice quivered. "I'm thinking about Renalda."

"Okay . . ." I stretched the word, hoping to prompt her to explain.

"It's weird. She was maybe seven years old. Eight at the most. But she never acted like a little kid. It was like she was always old, always watching, always thinking. Hardly ever smiling."

"Why were you thinking about her?"

"I was wondering why Thorne bought her. She wasn't born on Gamma Five, so it must have been because she probably didn't cost much."

"And she was compliant."

"Compliant?" Crystal repeated. "What does that mean?"

"Obedient. Submissive. Easy to bend."

"Yes, she was." Tremors invaded her words. "And . . . and I'm glad. If she wasn't compliant, she might've been sold to . . . to someone who would whip her. And I don't think I could stand thinking about poor little Renalda getting whipped." Crystal's voice pitched higher. "It . . . it hurts so much."

My own sob threatening to erupt, I slid my hand into hers and caressed her knuckles with my thumb. Maybe just being here brought her some comfort, but I had to do more. I had to kick the slave-trading monster in the teeth and never let it devour a child, or anyone, ever again.

I curled my free hand into a fist. We would start the moment we landed on Delta Ninety-eight. We would find Quixon and infiltrate the slave market, this time with our eyes wide open. How long might it take? That didn't matter. Even if the slave market swallowed us whole, we would find a way to blow it apart from inside the monster's belly.

Exhaling slowly, I let my rage cool. Soon, exhaustion took over. During the months I spent on Delta Ninety-five, I rarely slept more than five hours at night, partly because I was so busy trying to repair the ship and make myself an electric android, and partly because the days and nights were so short. Whatever the reason, the cycle of constant work throughout the day and short rest periods at night had worn me to a bare thread.

I fell asleep. Dreams came and went, most of them about me in the bee cave holding Thorne's lockbox. I tried putting glowsap inside, but it kept draining out the bottom, as if holes had been drilled there.

During that dream's third cycle, Emerson's voice knifed in. "Captain Willis, your presence is needed on the bridge immediately."

I snapped my eyes open. The door stood ajar, and light from the bridge filtered in. Crystal was gone. How long had I slept?

I threw off the bedcovers. "Emerson, what's going on?"

"We have an emergency. We will enter an asteroid field in five minutes, seven seconds."

I rolled out of bed and lurched forward. The inertial force had reversed. We were decelerating rapidly.

Feeling like my bladder was about to burst, I stumbled toward the vacuum toilet in an alcove. "All right. Shields up. Continue emergency deceleration. I'll be there in a second."

I relieved myself, threw on long work pants and a T-shirt, and dashed toward the bridge, zipping my pants on the run as the g-forces pushed me along.

When I arrived, I found Oliver sitting in the first mate's chair and Crystal at the navigator's station, both with tight lines in their foreheads. Dirk stood close to the front viewing window, staring at the stars with Perdantus perched on his shoulder.

Oliver pointed at the viewing window. "You can't see it yet, but the asteroid field's straight ahead."

"It's too big to go around," Crystal added as she looked at her console screen. "And we can't stop in time."

I looked at Emerson's console. "How did we miss something that big?"

"It is not on any map, and it appeared only moments ago. I fired the front thrusters immediately, but our current deceleration rate will not be enough to avoid the field. A rate that rapid would create fatal g-forces."

I pivoted toward the front again. "How long till impact now?"

"Two minutes, fifty-six seconds. Shields are up, as commanded."

I bit my lip hard. This was bad, really bad. I hurried to the window and stood next to Dirk. Only stars were visible on a dark backdrop. "Magnify with light enhancement. Let me see the field."

The window flashed and changed to a view of a black cloud with a ragged dark-blue border. The cloud moved like a swarm of gnats, each particle tiny but discernible. "How big are the asteroids?"

"Now that we are getting closer, I detect that the field is actually an enormous cluster of meteoroids and micrometeoroids, ranging in size from dust particles to palm-sized stones. Even so, at high speed, they could tear holes in the hull if the shields break down. And that many impacts could easily cause such shield degradation."

"Which way are they moving?"

"In the same direction we are but not as quickly. We are overtaking them."

I imagined the impact—hundreds of meteoroids ripping the *Nine* apart. We couldn't avoid the field, but maybe we could avoid a disaster. I strode toward my console. "Everyone strap in, turn your chairs toward the rear, and lock them in place. Dirk, take the doctor's seat. Perdantus, find a tight spot and squeeze in."

We dashed to our seats while Perdantus flew from the bridge. When we had all buckled in, faced the rear, and locked our seats in place, I called, "Emerson, decelerate as fast as you can without killing us, and turn on forward lights to maximum. Arm the laser cannons. I'll tell you when to start shooting."

"Affirmative. Increasing front thrusters now. You will have to alert me if the pain is too great or if you feel that you are close to passing out."

As Emerson put on the brakes, my body pressed against the back of my chair. My ribs squeezed my lungs harder and harder, forcing me to gasp. Dizziness washed through my brain, and dark spots invaded my vision. "Emerson . . . ease off . . . just a little."

The pressure faded, allowing me to breathe, but the dizziness continued. I could stand the pain, but I couldn't afford to pass out. I glanced at Oliver and Crystal. Both drooped in their seats, maybe unconscious. "A little more, Emerson."

Seconds later, my mind cleared, though pain persisted. "Oliver! Crystal! Are you still with me?"

Oliver lifted his head and blinked hard. "Yeah. Yeah. I'm good." Crystal just moaned, her head low and her hair covering her face. Dirk sat at his station with wide eyes and a wobbling head.

"Emerson," I said, "give me a countdown to impact in seconds. Increments of five."

"Thirty seconds . . . twenty-five . . ."

I fought for breath after breath, pushing my chest muscles to expand my rib cage. Excruciating pain ripped through my torso from side to side.

"Twenty . . . fifteen . . ."

I grimaced at each torturous pang. We had to survive this, but how? Would it be better to let Emerson blast away at the meteoroids and hope for the best? Sit on my hands like a scared rabbit and trust a computer?

"Ten . . ."

I shook my head. No, I had to take this battle on myself.

"Five . . ."

"Emerson, give me weapons control!" I unlocked my chair and spun toward the front, trying to ignore the g-force pressure. Our lights shone on a mass of gray debris hurtling toward us. I grabbed the laser-control joystick protruding from my console, my finger on the trigger. I set a targeting grid on the front window, shifted the red bull's-eye circle over a large stone, and fired.

A shimmering laser beam blasted the stone into dust. The particles splashed against our windshield without harm. Then a massive dust cloud swarmed over the armored window, while larger stones flew by to each side. As they struck the hull and bounced off the shields, vibrations ran through the floor and into my chair.

"Oliver, take your laser stick and help me shoot."

He spun his chair and grabbed the joystick. "How does it work?"

I reached over and set his targeting grid on the front window. "Yours is blue. Mine is red. Just point at the big ones and pull the trigger."

"Got it."

"Dirk, monitor the shields. Give me updates." While Oliver and I blasted away at the larger stones, I called out, "Crystal! Are you awake?"

She shook her head and turned toward me, blinking. "Yeah. I mean, I think so. Kind of spaced out."

"Snap out of it. I need you. Emerson should have mapped the field by now. Chart a course through the thinnest parts and show the vectors on the front window."

"I'll try."

Emerson spoke up. "I put a three-dimensional map on Crystal's screen, but there are too many projectile trajectories. It is impossible to calculate a single best path. She will have to use subjective analysis."

"What does all that mean?" Crystal asked.

As I blasted a huge stone, I shouted, "Just guess!"

"All right! All right!"

After a few seconds, a yellow arrow appeared on the screen, starting at the center and extending toward the upper right—Crystal's vector arrow. With one hand on the laser trigger and the other on the steering yoke, I turned the ship in that direction until the arrow disappeared.

"Shields are at seventy percent overall," Dirk said, his voice shaky. "The weakest point is at thirty."

I gulped. "Thirty? Where?"

"The repaired wing. At the extension joint."

"Blazes! I *knew* I should've doubled that panel's shielding."

"Too late now. It's still dropping. Now it's twenty-eight."

"Emerson, stop the deceleration. Hold our speed steady. Dirk, get our pressure suits and air tanks and bring them here."

"I'm on it." The moment the g-forces eased, Dirk leaped from his seat and ran from the bridge.

While Oliver and I blasted stone after stone, I steered into Crystal's updated navigation vectors. Pings and thuds rang from all over the ship. Constant tremors shook us, and the lights flickered. With each turn, the fragment sizes decreased, and the veil of dust thinned, but it seemed like the field's violent assault would never end.

As we flew on, we zipped by a ship that appeared to be moving at the same speed the particles were, but I got only a passing glance. "Emerson, did you see that ship?"

"Affirmative. I saved a short video clip of it. I assume you will wait to view it later."

I blasted another big stone. "You assumed right."

"Got the suits." Dirk ran in and dropped an armload of suits on the floor. He looked at the physician's console screen and slid a finger on it. "Shields are at fifty percent overall and . . ." He gasped. "Minimum is five percent. That wing panel is about to fail. I still need to get the helmets and air tanks. It'll take two more trips." He dashed out again.

"What happens if that shield hits zero?" Crystal asked, a whimper invading her voice.

I fired at a stone, pulverizing it. "Maybe a hull breach. We never repaired the automatic air locks that lead to the hull space, so if we get a breach, all the air will get sucked out. We'd die without the suits."

Crystal's face paled. "Maybe I should help Dirk. We're almost through the field. Just keep flying straight."

"Go."

Crystal ran out, calling, "Dirk, wait for me."

While Oliver and I continued pounding the stones with laser blasts, we glanced at each other every few seconds. At one point, he smiled but said nothing. He was enjoying this. Pretty crazy way to have fun.

Soon, Dirk and Crystal returned with the rest of the gear and set a suit, helmet, and tank next to each of our seats. When they took their places again, Dirk looked at his console screen. "Megan," he said, breathless. "That wing panel is at zero. The shield is down. The panel next to it is at twelve percent."

My heart sank. "We won't last long. One more hit on that panel, and we're done for." I looked out the front window. A few tiny meteoroids pelted the surface, then only dust lay in view. I pumped a fist. "We're through!"

When we finally broke into the clear, I leaned back and blew a long sigh. "That was way too close."

"Perdantus," Dirk called, "the emergency is over. Come back to the bridge."

Seconds later, Perdantus flew in, landed on Emerson's console, and fluffed his feathers. "If this happens again, I will not choose the laundry chute. You definitely need to add air freshener in there."

An alarm blared.

"Hull breach, Captain," Emerson said. "Scanning for location and severity."

"I see it." Dirk pointed at his screen. "It's that wing panel."

Emerson's console monitor displayed a schematic of the entire ship with a red X flashing near the fracture point of the repaired wing.

"How bad is it leaking?" I asked.

A number appeared above the X: 21.2. "It is a slow leak," Emerson said. "Depending on the metabolism of the crew, the ship has about twenty-two point seven hours of air remaining. It will reach a level that is a danger to human life in twenty-one point two hours."

"That's not good." As the alarm continued blaring, I looked out the front window. "How long till we get to Delta Ninety-eight?"

"If we maintain our current speed, it will take much longer than our air supply will last, including the air in your tanks. I suggest returning to our previous acceleration/deceleration algorithm. If we do, we will arrive in twenty point one hours."

I scratched my head, barely able to think. "Will you please shut off that noise?"

The breach alarm fell silent.

"Okay. About twenty hours." I stared at the wing on the schematic. The number above it dropped to 21.1. "So we have about an hour of extra time. And we have our space suits. We should be all right."

"Affirmative, but there are many unknown factors. Leaks of this nature can grow rapidly, even catastrophically. The most likely cause, of course, is a meteoroid impact. Once we begin accelerating again, g-forces might cause an expansion in the breach."

"But if we don't accelerate, we'll definitely die."

"Affirmative, Captain."

"Then we'll accelerate, but we'll get the suits on now just in case and leave the air tanks off until we need them."

Dirk spun toward me. "Wear those clunky things for twenty hours? They'll be huge on us."

"Yeah, but if that hole gets bigger, we might not have time to put them on."

Dirk pointed at Perdantus. "What about him? We don't have a bird suit."

"Like you said, the suit'll be huge on you. Make sure he stays close, and if we lose a lot of air, put him in the suit with you."

Perdantus chirped, "I do enjoy my friend's company, but I hope to avoid your proposed arrangement. I don't mean to be rude, but his odor is typical of young human males. It is similar to the soiled undergarments I encountered in the laundry chute. As I said before, we need some air freshener."

Crystal snorted. "I think we have a can in the galley. It's called anti–boy smell."

"All right, you two. Knock it off. This is serious." I looked at Emerson's screen again. "When we hit the atmosphere, the wing's gonna get smacked by a lot of pressure. We need to know how much damage there is."

"Impossible to determine without a close inspection," Emerson said.

"A space walk is dangerous." I looked at the schematic again. "I could send a camera drone to check it out. If the damage doesn't look bad, I won't have to go out there."

After finding a camera drone in the maintenance supply cabinet, I set it in the exit air lock, released the air, and, using a remote-control joystick box, guided the drone's thrusters while watching the images on Emerson's screen.

When the camera focused on the wing's leak point, I raised the magnification until a tiny rock clarified at the center of an indentation. It seemed to glow with a silvery light.

I squinted. "What kind of meteoroid is that?"

"I can conduct an analysis," Emerson said. "I suggest that the drone take a small sample. Be careful to leave the meteoroid in place. It is partially plugging the leak."

I toggled the box to control the drone's pincers. After snipping off a small piece, I put it in the drone's collection compartment. "Time to bring you in."

When the drone arrived, I went through the air lock routine, retrieved the sample bag, and set the tiny fragment onto a glass plate under Emerson's analysis scope. A brilliant laser shot from the scope and bathed the fragment in multicolored light. After several seconds, the beam shut off.

"It is metasilver," Emerson said. "A rare metal of extremely high value."

Crystal's eyes widened. "I've heard of it. In one of my novels a wizard used it to make a potion. If you drink it, it makes you a powerful warrior."

Oliver stared at the tiny fragment. "I thought metasilver was a myth."

"It is not a myth," Emerson said, "though its properties are often exaggerated, and storybook tales have caused its value to increase. In theory, it can be used as a superior electrical conductor. In practice, it is too rare to do so. Those who believe in the exaggerations keep whatever samples they find or purchase, believing they can create this wizard's potion."

Perdantus flew from Dirk's shoulder and landed next to the scope. "Perhaps being hit by this meteoroid was fortuitous. Quixon is highly superstitious. He fancies himself an alchemist and makes various potions. I'm sure he is aware of metasilver's value even if not its mythical characteristics."

I pointed at him. "So we offer it to Quixon in exchange for his help."

"Precisely my point. It seems that we have received a timely gift in spite of the danger. As humans sometimes say, this is the cloud's silver lining, quite literally. A dust cloud brought us metasilver."

"If it's so valuable," I said, mumbling my thoughts out loud, "that might explain the ship I saw in the field." I looked at the computer console. "Emerson, show me the video clip in slow motion."

On Emerson's monitor, a spherical ship appeared, a hatch open with a suited man floating at the end of a tether. In seconds, it zipped by from left to right. "Can you identify the ship?"

"It is an Alliance deep-space exploratory pod, a small vessel used to collect samples of atmosphere, soil, and organic matter from unexplored systems."

I whispered, "The Alliance is collecting metasilver."

"That is a reasonable conclusion to draw."

"And I'll bet Admiral Fairbanks is mixed up in this."

Crystal shook her head. "It's like all of this is one big . . . um . . ."

"Conspiracy?" I offered.

"Yeah. Conspiracy. But let's think about it later. We've got air problems to worry about."

"Right. Emerson, calculate an updated acceleration-deceleration plan. Let's hustle to Delta Ninety-eight."

For the remaining hours, we ate more pizza, played more games, and slept according to the schedule Emerson provided. Since the breach remained stable and our air supply diminished no faster than expected, we decided not to wear the suits constantly, though we kept them nearby.

When we got out of bed for the last time during this flight, the air seemed thin, as if we had awakened on a high mountaintop. We all dressed for cold weather and ate a light breakfast, staying quiet for the most part, not only because of worry; we also hoped to use as little oxygen as possible.

Later that morning, Oliver, Crystal, and I sat at our usual stations, while Dirk monitored the engine room with Perdantus. Delta Ninety-eight came into view in the front window, a bright yellowish dot at the center. "What time is it in Bassolith?" I asked.

"Yama-Yami has recently risen," Emerson said. "You will enter the city during the midmorning hours, as planned."

I took a deep breath, but my lungs begged for more. "What's our air status?"

"Although you are already showing symptoms of oxygen deprivation, you have approximately forty-seven minutes before you begin feeling serious effects that might hamper your ability to operate the ship."

"And time to landing?"

"Twenty-six minutes."

"So twenty-one minutes extra." I nodded. "We can make it."

"Slightly more. We will enter the atmosphere in nineteen minutes, at which time we can open the vents."

"Right. I remember. Let's hope it's not so bad this time." I set my hands on the console yoke. "Let's get this bird on the ground. Keep a watch on the damaged wing."

"Acknowledged, Captain. Final deceleration commencing in three seconds."

When the three seconds expired, g-forces hit hard, making me lean forward against my seat belt. Delta Ninety-eight grew larger and larger through the viewing window and on my console screen. We would be there soon.

After nearly a minute, the forces eased, and I settled back in my chair.

"The flight-course program has completed," Emerson said, "and the ship is cruising at approach speed. Captain Willis, you are now in control for the landing sequence."

As I reached for the throttle, dizziness swam through my head. I glanced at the pressure suit and air tank on the floor next to me. If we could get into the atmosphere without putting them on, landing would be a lot easier. "Emerson, are you sure about our oxygen supply? I can hardly breathe."

"The most recent deceleration shifted the remaining air. You are sitting in a thin zone. I suggest that you put on your suit while you still have time."

"Oliver," I said, pointing at his suit. "Put yours on."

He shook his head. "You first. I can hold us steady."

Anger rose from my gut. "Are you disobeying an order?"

He scowled. "Shut up with the order stuff. I'm not putting on my suit until you put on yours."

I clenched a fist. "This isn't a ladies-first ship, Oliver. You have to obey me."

Crystal called from her seat. "What's wrong with you two? You've never argued like this before."

"They are suffering from oxygen deprivation," Emerson said. "It can mimic a form of dementia. Crystal, I suggest that you put on your suit and help the captain and first mate with theirs."

Gasping for breath, I blinked at Crystal. She seemed to be moving in slow motion as she put on her suit while Emerson gave her instructions, his voice warped. If I were really suffering from oxygen deprivation, why didn't this sensation happen last time? Could it be because oxygen loss happened so fast then but slower now?

Oliver set his forehead against his console and moaned. "I think I'm gonna puke."

His call sparked my energy. I rose from my seat on wobbly legs and picked up my air tank, my brain swimming in a sea of fog. "Crystal, you can help Oliver with his . . . um . . . whatever. I'll get mine on myself."

"Okay." Her helmet muffled her voice as she lumbered toward Oliver. While she helped him, I pushed a foot toward one of the suit's pant legs but missed. I lost my balance and toppled toward the floor. My head banged on something, and everything turned black.

When I opened my eyes, green grass surrounded me, and Yama-Yami peeked over a distant mountain. Perdantus, perching on my leg, chirped, "We have been in a similar situation before, Megan."

"Yeah. Seems familiar." I looked past him. The *Nebula Nine* sat on the ground, one of its wings propped against a knoll, the other extending down the slope. Although the cockeyed position looked odd, the ship appeared to be undamaged. "Who landed us?"

"Why, the first mate, of course. Commanding the ship when the captain is disabled is his responsibility."

"Oliver landed it?" I sat up and looked around. My head throbbed, and my vision shifted in and out of focus. A stream ran near a forest in the midst of some mountains. We were close to the same spot I landed the ship the last time. "Where are the others?"

Perdantus hopped to the ground. "They went out to test the rovers, leaving me to stand guard over you. We assumed you would be fine after getting enough fresh air."

"Yeah, but I've been knocked out a bunch of times. I feel like the weak link."

"Nonsense. You merely expended the most energy. Exhaustion and oxygen deprivation play no favorites. In fact, I passed out before you did."

"Thanks for being so nice." I climbed to my feet and walked toward the ship, my legs feeling like Dirk's boiled okra.

As I drew near, a buzzing noise rose behind me. I spun that way. Three rovers zipped out of the forest, hovering over the river in single file, the lead one driven by Oliver. They settled to the ground side by side within a few paces of me. Oliver opened his hatch and stepped out. When Crystal and Dirk climbed out of their rovers, Oliver grinned at them. "Wasn't that great?"

Crystal nodded, her face pale. "Mostly great. After I got over being sick."

When they looked at me, I smiled in a sheepish fashion. "Looks like you three are ready to ride."

Oliver hurried to me and gave me a hug. "I wish you could've seen it. I actually landed the *Nebula Nine*."

I glanced at the tilted ship. "I see that."

He dug a hand into his pocket. "Yeah. Well, I almost got it perfect. Not bad for my first time, though."

"You did great. Really great. And thanks for taking care of me." With my legs feeling stronger, I walked to the down-sloping wing and found the chunk of metasilver firmly embedded in a small hole. I withdrew my pocketknife, pried the thumb-sized chunk out, and held it in a pinch where everyone could see it. Its slick, silvery surface glowed, casting a faint white sphere around it.

Oliver touched it with a fingertip. "So this is metasilver. A little rock that nearly killed us."

"Yep. I'll have to fix the hole later." I slid the chunk into my pocket. "Okay, let's get roughed up. We're going to a slave market."

"I will leave now," Perdantus said. "When I find Quixon, I will return and guide you to him." He took off and flew over the forest toward the city.

For the next few minutes, we smeared dirt on our arms and faces, mussed our hair, and tore our pant cuffs. While we prepared, Dirk kept his head low and said nothing.

I shifted close to him and whispered, "What's wrong?"

He gave a light shrug, his head still low. "I'd rather not talk about it."

"Hey . . ." I set a finger under his chin and forced eye contact. "It's me. Megan. You can tell me anything. You know that."

He glanced at the others before whispering in return. "All this talk about collecting glowsap. And those bees." He shuddered. "I'm scared to death of bees."

"You are?" I brushed a clump of mud from his ear. "That *is* a problem. These bees are enormous. I'll have to think about it."

"Yeah. You do that. I don't want to be the only coward here."

"You're not a coward." I grabbed his wrist and pulled him close. "Get some food, and we'll stuff ourselves before we leave. We have no idea when we'll eat again. Then we'll all brainstorm. I won't tell anyone you're scared of bees."

"Thanks." Dirk dashed into the ship. I entered the ship as well, found a small patch in the maintenance room, and welded it over the wing's hole. By the time I finished, Dirk returned carrying a tray covered with mincemeat muffins.

Sitting in a circle on the grass, the four of us ate muffins while reminding each other of our goals—get Quixon to help sell us to Thorne, find Thorne's contacts to learn who runs the slave-trading industry, destroy the glowsap-collecting system, and rescue whatever kids Thorne had working for him.

As before, we couldn't strategize about details, except to decide that we would speak to each other in Alpha One to keep our conversations secret. After months of listening to us talk to Emerson and joining in the conversations, Crystal became fluent in the language, and Perdantus learned to understand it as well.

I also had some other ideas, including a new one that might solve Dirk's bee-phobia problem.

"Everyone wait here a minute." I ran into the ship, found the things I needed, put them in a duffle bag, and hustled back out. When I took my place in the circle, I set the bag in front of me. "We know Admiral Fairbanks has been monitoring transmissions. I thought of a way to lure him into the city."

"How?" Crystal asked.

"Using the radio Captain Tillman repaired." I looked at Oliver. "I grabbed it from your quarters. I hope you don't mind."

He waved a hand. "No problem, but I haven't had a chance to test it yet."

"I think we can figure it out." I reached into the bag, withdrew the old transmitter, and set it on the ground. "This is a base unit. And this—" I pulled out a smaller device and set it next to the base—"is a walkie-talkie. I can talk to the base unit with it and listen to what's going on wherever we put the base."

"A spy tool," Oliver said. "How do you plan to use it?"

I touched the base unit. "First, we have to find a place where Admiral Fairbanks would hear about a message we'll send. Then we'll put this unit near that place, somewhere no one will see it, like maybe a locked room, and turn up the volume. Then I'll go somewhere else and talk to it with the walkie-talkie, and my voice will broadcast through its speaker. Maybe say something that'll get Admiral Fairbanks to do what we want."

"Like what?" Crystal asked.

I shrugged. "I don't know exactly what yet, but something that'll make him go to his ship. Then one of us will follow him, sneak on board, and see what we can learn about his operation."

Dirk whistled. "You're one crazy girl, you know that?"

"Yep." I pointed at him. "And you're one crazy guy, the perfect choice."

He stared at my finger, then at me as he shook his head hard. "Uh-uh. No way. I'm not sneaking onto an admiral's ship. It's suicide."

"Not for a sneaky guy like you." I touched my locket. "You snatched this right out from under Gavin's nose. You're a spying dynamo, remember?"

A smile began to emerge, but he forced it back. "Yeah. I know. But . . ."

"Think about it, Dirk. This way you'll stay out of the slave market." I mouthed, "No bees."

He glanced at Oliver and Crystal before heaving a sigh. "All right. I'll do it, but the admiral might be a lot more trouble than you think."

"Not likely. I think he'll be loads of trouble." I reached into the bag and withdrew commlinks for everyone. "We'll also need a way to communicate with each other, since we'll be splitting up." I lifted one for them to see. "It sticks to the inside of the flap that's over your ear canal, like this." I pressed the adhesive side in place in my ear. "They transmit to the *Nine*, and the signal gets boosted and echoed to everyone else's link. The sender has to be within about five kilometers of the *Nine*, but the receivers can be a lot farther. That means if the sender is in the city, sending a message should be no problem, but the outskirts and beyond could be trouble. Also, I set the encryption with a nonmilitary key, so the admiral's nosy spies can't listen to us."

While the others inserted their commlinks, I continued. "The microphone is super sensitive, so you can't leave them on all the time. Otherwise, we'll be hearing everything everyone's doing. You give it a slight squeeze to activate it." I demonstrated by pinching my commlink.

Oliver set a finger at his ear. "I feel it tingling."

"Right. That's a signal that I want to talk. Now pinch yours." When he did, I spoke again. "Can you hear me through the link?"

He nodded. "Yeah. It's weird, though. Kind of like you're a bug in there with a tiny voice."

"It takes some getting used to. Anyway, just pinch it again to turn it off."

After everyone tested the links, I slid my translator piece into my ear next to the commlink. I would need it to talk to Quixon.

One more thing remained undone. I took a deep breath, nervous about keeping this secret in spite of our vows. "I have something else to show Oliver and Dirk." I withdrew the two bracelets. When I slid them over my wrists, snapped them in place, and switched them on, I flexed my biceps to activate the signal. Arcs of electricity covered my palms and fingers.

"This is what Crystal and I worked on at nights after you two went to bed." I flexed again and cut the signal, then touched the switches on the bracelets to manually turn them off. "I made them from prisoner collars. What do you think?"

"Amazing!" Dirk said. "Now you're a lethal weapon."

Oliver cocked his head. "Why didn't you tell us about this before? Keeping secrets?"

"No, I just wanted to surprise you. If I was keeping secrets, I wouldn't be telling you now." I ran one of the bracelets up and down my arm as far as its looseness would allow. "I made these so I could help us get out of any trouble we might run into."

Oliver gave me an approving nod. "Gotta admit, they're really great."

"Anything else in the bag?" Dirk asked.

"Just a way to disguise myself for the slave market. You'll see it when I put it on."

Soon, Perdantus returned and landed on the front of the middle rover. "I found Quixon. He is sober and free of pain. We should go at once. I will meet you where the stream exits the forest." He leaped and flew toward the city.

"Let's get moving." I shoved the two radio units into the duffle bag and handed it to Oliver. "Take these and drive lead over the stream. There's no space for me inside, so I'll ride on top of your rover. I won't get splashed as much that way."

The three drivers stepped into their rovers and closed the hatches. I climbed on top of Oliver's hatch and squeezed it with my legs. As he accelerated, I hunched over and laid my palms on the glass at each side. Seconds later, we plunged into the forest and flew over the stream.

Water from the rover's jets blasting the river sent a fine spray into my face, making me turn my head. Behind me, the jet sent a deluge over Crystal's rover and forced her to back off. Soon, Oliver's increased speed sent the spray to each side, keeping it out of my eyes and allowing me to look around. From this vantage point, the forest seemed different—closer, more vivid, more alive.

Above, something swirled in the canopy. A cyclone of white sparkling light twirled down toward me like a tornado funnel dropping from a cloud. I instinctively ducked, but I couldn't escape, not without a potentially fatal jump.

The sparkles encircled me, tickling my face and arms. A masculine whisper emanated from the spin, close enough to overcome the rover's noise. "Who are you, and where are you going?" he asked in Humaniversal.

I concealed a tight swallow. This creature looked like Thorne, except with white sparks instead of silvery gray, most likely a Willow Wind. "I'm a visitor from Alpha One, and I . . . I mean, *we* are going to Bassolith." I gathered my courage and added, "Why are you asking?"

"I saw a sheet of paper with your face on it. Although I can speak and understand verbal Humaniversal, I cannot read or write it, so I did not understand the reason for the paper." The sparks brightened. "I assume you are an important person."

"Um . . . not really. Someone was trying to find me."

"Were you lost?"

"Not exactly. I knew where I was. The person looking for me didn't, though."

"Interesting." The spin slowed. "What is your name?"

"Megan Willis."

"Megan?" His sparks brightened along with his voice. "I have met the person who was looking for you."

"You have? What did he say to you?" I mopped wetness from my brow.

"He?"

"Yes, he. Why?"

"The person I met was a woman."

My heart thudded. "A woman? Was her name Anne?"

"I never learned her name. I found her wandering not far from here, her and a young girl."

"How long ago?"

"In your time increments, perhaps several months. I am not certain."

I ducked under a stream of water. "What happened to them? Where did they go?"

"She told me that she landed her crippled ship in a place that is hidden from the city. Then she hiked into my forest, hoping to reach the city to search for you, but she seemed anxious about getting caught by someone she did not name."

"So she must still be here. In the city, I mean."

"I assume so. We Willow Winds made sure she and the girl stayed safe until they exited the forest, though we never saw anyone who might accost them. Even if we had seen an assailant, we would not have physically harmed him. We could certainly frighten him or block him with a mighty wind."

I mopped my brow again. "Wait a minute. You won't harm someone?"

"No. Willow Winds do not inflict physical harm. We are able to cause others to suffer indirectly by withholding an item necessary for survival, or we might hurt someone without intent to do so, but we do not intentionally inflict pain."

I whispered, "Just like Thorne. He won't whip his slaves."

"Like who?"

I cleared my throat. "Thorne. He's a Willow Wind I know in Bassolith."

The swirl tightened around me, and the sparks flashed with a dazzling brightness. "How do you know him?"

"He kept me a prisoner in his factory. I helped the children escape. His slaves, I mean."

The sparks dimmed, and the swirl slowly expanded. During his silence, the buzz from the rovers and splashes from the stream continued, background noise as I waited for his next response. Finally, he said, "You speak the truth."

"Are you a friend of Thorne?"

"No. Thorne is a traitor to our kind. We keep to the forests.

To ourselves. Though we offer help to other species when needed. Slavery is abhorrent to us."

"Then why does he enslave children? Why did he leave the forest?"

"Those are mysteries I have not been able to unravel. I know only that he was unsatisfied as a Willow Wind. He craved substance. Physical presence. He cares not that these things lead to mortality."

I pondered his strange words. Thorne was trying to become physical? And that would lead to mortality? What kind of creatures were these Willow Winds anyway? "Are you immortal?"

"As long as there is air and energy, yes. Our essence consists of both."

"Well, I hope to stop the slave trade in Bassolith. If you have any advice about how to weaken Thorne, that would help a lot."

"The only advice I have is based on what I have already told you. Thorne needs air and energy. If you remove one or both from his environment, he will perish."

I nodded. Now we were getting somewhere. A way to stop Thorne. "How can I find a place without air or energy? I can't take him into outer space."

"Going into outer space is not the only way to remove air from an environment, but I prefer not to give you ideas." The Willow Wind laughed. "Telling others how to kill me is not good for my health."

I chuckled to be polite, though his joke didn't seem funny. "Any idea how he plans to get substance and what he'd do with it?"

"I cannot fathom his purpose. Substance binds the unbound and limits the limitless. Why anyone would choose a self-imposed prison is beyond my comprehension."

"Is it possible for you to come to Bassolith with us? We could use all the help we can get."

"That is impossible. A storm looms, what the citizens of the city call a battle storm. We prefer to stay in the forest during such violence. The trees block the wind, and lightning hits their tops instead of us. Although we are immortal, we try to avoid pain."

I nodded. "That's reasonable."

"We are nearing the edge of the forest. It is time for me to leave.

I wish you well on your journey." The sparkling swirl expanded and lifted over my head. Seconds later, he was gone.

I exhaled. So much new information! The *Astral Dragon* had landed in a crippled state, and my mother was on Delta Ninety-eight, maybe even in the city. The girl she was with might be the mystery girl, Zoë. Maybe damage from the battle with the admiral forced them to land, and that's why she never looked for me on Delta Ninety-five.

When the edge of the forest came into view, I slapped the glass to signal Oliver. He slowed, veered away from the stream, and stopped in the dense underbrush. Behind us, Crystal and Dirk did the same.

Water beading at the edges of my hair, I climbed down and lifted Oliver's hatch. "Boy, do I have a lot to tell you," I said in Alpha One.

He narrowed his eyes. "Besides how wet your face is?"

"Shut up and listen." When Crystal and Dirk joined us, I gave them a detailed account of what the Willow Wind said. When I finished, I spread my hands. "So my mother is probably close by, but since we don't know how to find her, we should stick with the plan."

"You're right." Oliver reached into his rover, grabbed the duffle bag with the radio units, and handed the walkie-talkie to me and the base to Dirk. "Finding your mother might be impossible."

Although it was my idea to press on, his agreement darkened my mood. With my mother so close, I ached to search for her. I took the duffle bag from Oliver and slid the walkie-talkie inside. "Anyone seen Perdantus?"

"I know how to find him." Oliver whistled a warbling call three times. "If he's close, he'll be here soon."

A moment after we hid the rovers in the bushes, Perdantus flew down and landed on Oliver's shoulder. "I apologize for being late, but I had trouble encouraging Quixon to hurry. Come to the river's edge. He should be there at any moment."

I trudged through the underbrush with the others. When we arrived at the river, I looked downstream. The black-and-purple Jaradian walked toward us, his dark boots splashing in the water near the bank.

He stopped about five paces away and crossed his beefy arms over his barrel chest. "You know, Perdantus," he said in his language, translated by my earpiece, "no one at the market would offer the scum from a slop bucket for these children. They look too weak to even breathe."

"You would know best, Quixon. You are the expert." Perdantus flew to my shoulder and whispered, "He has not yet agreed to help and has assumed a negotiation stance. Use your skills well."

Quixon focused on me. "We've met before."

I set the duffle bag down and crossed my arms, hoping to match his confident pose. "We have," I said in Humaniversal.

"You never thanked me for rescuing you from those slavers."

"What did you expect? You were carrying an axe, and you never said you were rescuing me."

"Did you think a rescuer would come without a weapon?" He grunted. "Clearly we had a communication problem. Let's hope for better today."

"Agreed."

He scanned me from head to toe. "I assume you're the leader of this ragtag group, but it looks like you don't even know how to stay out of the river."

I nodded toward his feet. "It seems that I'm not the only one."

Quixon looked down, then at me with a smile. "You have a quick wit, young lady, but your quip is ill-informed. First, my boots are waterproof. My clothing is always prepared for any elements I might encounter. Second, I walked in the water to hide my tracks. You never know when someone might be following you."

"My mistake. I didn't realize that you're paranoid and self-important enough to think someone would want to follow you."

Oliver hissed, "Megan!"

I hissed back, "Quiet!"

Perdantus flew from my shoulder to Oliver's and began whispering into his ear. I hoped he was explaining my negotiation methods.

Quixon looked at Oliver, then at me again. "Let's get down to business. I understand that you want me to take you to the slave market and sell you, preferably to Thorne."

I nodded. "Except the *preferably* part. If Thorne doesn't buy us, we have to change our plans. We don't want to be sold to anyone else."

"Well, that presents a problem. The market is a public auction. It is loud, dirty, smelly, and filled with scoundrels who want to get in and out as fast as possible. The slaves go to the highest bidders, no exceptions. And I don't know if Thorne will even be there."

"He'll be there if you spread the word that you have the girl who was on the leaflet several months ago."

"Oh?" He squinted. "Ah. I remember that now. Very interesting."

"So it won't be hard to get him to come. That'll make your job easier."

"Not quite. Once that word gets out, we might have more people bidding for you. Obviously you are very important to someone. Your ransom potential is high."

I tightened my crossed arms. Quixon was right. The only way I could solve every problem would be to make us look as valuable as possible to Thorne without anyone else knowing my identity. What did Thorne want more than anything? Substance, yes, but what else?

I glanced down at my locket, exposed as it dangled over my damp shirt. That might work.

"Okay, we'll do it this way. We'll leak word to Thorne that you have Oliver and Crystal. He'll want them for their experience. I'll just be part of the package. I can disguise myself so no one will think I have any value, and I have a way to make sure Thorne is the highest bidder."

Quixon lifted his brow. "You do? What is it?"

"I'll keep that to myself."

He took a step closer and straightened to his full height, a well-known intimidation move. "If you don't tell me, my role in this will be more difficult."

I stood my ground, my stare locked on him. "Perhaps so, but that is the deal."

"The deal. Yes. That brings us to the most important part of our meeting." He stepped out of the water and walked within reach, his horselike face close enough to give me a whiff of his stale breath and fetid body odor. "What's in it for me?"

Again I stood my ground, refusing to budge or even cringe at the smell. "Your reward is the knowledge that you're helping us smash the slave-trading market here."

Quixon laughed. "That's a good joke. You want me to stroll into the auction to sell children as slaves, even though I have worked my butt off for three years to scrape the filth of the very same market off my hands. And most of the others know it. They'll think I'm a setup, someone who's infiltrating the market to find out who the buyers are." He lowered his voice to a conspiratorial whisper. "It could be dangerous. Very dangerous. Thorne might pay more than usual for you, but the price won't be worth it to me. Not even close."

"Oh, it's worse than that," I said, trying to keep a flat expression. "When he pays you, I want you to give the money to me."

Quixon's eyes flared. "What? Are you completely out of your mind? You think I'd do this for no payment at all?"

Once more I kept a straight face, though my lips begged to burst into a smile. I had set the trap by igniting his emotions. Time for the final bait. "No, but . . ." I pushed a hand into my pocket, withdrew the chunk of metasilver, and displayed it on my palm. The glow shone even more brightly on my moist skin. "I thought maybe you'd do it for this."

He stared for a moment, then leaned close. "Is that . . ." He touched it with a fingertip and whispered, "Metasilver."

"Yes. This much metasilver is worth—"

"—a king's ransom," he said with a trembling voice.

"Then you'll do it?"

"Yes. Yes. Of course." He extended his hand. "Payment up front."

"How do I know I can trust you?"

"What?" Quixon drew his head back. "You insult me!"

"Take it however you like, but you know you'd demand collateral if it was the other way around."

"That's true, but I don't have collateral worth nearly as much as the metasilver."

"Oh, I think you do." I set the chunk on his palm.

He stared at it, his mouth dropping open.

I leaned close and spoke with all the passion I could muster. "Just like the slave boy who took the beatings for the other children, I'm risking beatings, and I'm willing to risk death to help the poor kids escape from their torture." I closed his scaly fingers around the metasilver. "And now I am trusting you with this payment, because I believe in your compassion for those who suffer under the stinging whips of their cruel masters." I looked straight into his eyes. "Quixon, will you help me?"

"But . . . but what about collateral?"

"Your word is your collateral. That's all I need."

Quixon fixed his gaze on me for a moment before nodding. "I'll do it. Everything you asked."

"Thank you, Quixon."

Thunder rumbled. Thick clouds rolled over the tree canopy, dimming the forest.

He looked at the sky, then at me. "Come. Hurry. We don't have a moment to lose."

26

Quixon turned and jogged downstream at the edge of the river. I picked up the duffle bag containing the walkie-talkie and ran behind him, the others following.

"Where are we going?" I asked, panting as I caught up with Quixon.

"The Tauranta temple, if you must know." A growl spiced his voice. "They have a bus there we can use."

When we broke out of the forest, bluish sleet pelted our heads and shoulders. Wind swept across the footpath and blew us sideways, but we kept our balance and followed Quixon to the Tauranta temple's rear parking lot. He hustled to the temple's bus, slid its door open, and waved us inside.

Oliver, Crystal, and I tromped in and found seats while Dirk sneaked into the temple's back door, Perdantus on his shoulder.

Sitting on the front bench on the right side of the bus, I pinched my commlink and whispered in Alpha One, "Dirk. What are you doing?"

His voice came through my earpiece. "I figured now was as good a time as any to separate."

I glanced at Oliver and Crystal on the bench across the aisle, Crystal sitting closer to me. They both pinched their links as well. "That's fine," I said, "but stay away from all Taurantas. They'll stab you in the back during a battle storm."

"Gotcha. I'll keep out of sight until the storm's over and then look for a place to hide the base unit. I'll call you to test it when I'm ready."

"Sounds good." I turned off my commlink.

As wind buffeted the bus, making it sway, Quixon closed the door, settled into the driver's seat, and looked at us in the wind-shield's rearview mirror. "I see you lost a couple of friends. Too bad. That bird is probably smarter than all of you combined."

"You can quit the negotiation games," I said in Humaniversal as ice pellets hit the bus and raised a noisy racket. "Our deal is done."

"Quite true. Quite true." He spoke toward the bus's dashboard. "Give me control." A second later, he pushed a button, starting the engine.

I eyed the dashboard. Apparently it understood Jaradian com-mands. I leaned toward Quixon. "Why do you have access to the temple's bus?"

"Anyone can control it." He pushed the throttle and eased the bus toward the road. "The temple has terrible security, which is why your friends were able to enter the building without knocking."

"So you're stealing their bus?"

"No, of course not." He laughed as he drove on the deserted street toward Bassolith's center. "Don't worry. They know me. I've borrowed it before."

After a moment of silence, Crystal's whisper came through my commlink. "He's lying." I turned toward her. She set a hand to the side of her mouth as she continued. "He *is* stealing this bus."

Oliver added a whisper of his own. "Let's see what else we can find out." He raised his voice. "Where are we going, Quixon?"

"To the ironworks factory to tell Thorne about you. Since the next market is in three hours, he needs to know right away so he can prepare."

"But you're just going to tell him about Crystal and me, right? Megan stays a secret for now."

"Of course. That's the plan. Though Thorne wouldn't tell anyone about Megan, I'm sure. He doesn't want competing bidders."

"He *is* going to tell Thorne about Megan," Crystal said, continuing at a stealthy level. "Why would he do that?"

I whispered in return. "If a battle storm affects Jaradians like it does Taurantas, he might be planning to betray us. And there's not a whole lot we can do about it. Unless . . ."

I leaned forward, again speaking in Humaniversal. "Quixon, it's a good thing you're on our side. If you weren't, you could tell Thorne about me and ask for money to make sure the secret doesn't get out. That information's worth a lot. Like you said, Thorne doesn't want competing bidders."

Quixon coughed. "Yes, you're right. It's a good thing. But even if he found out, there would be no harm done. Like I said before, he'll want to prepare for new slaves."

"You're right. No harm. Just remember that any money you get from him you have to give to me."

He waved a hand. "Oh, no, no. That wasn't part of the deal. You get the money for the sale. Nothing else."

"But there *is* nothing else, right? Since you're not going to tell Thorne about me, he won't give you any money on the side."

Quixon made a harrumph sound before continuing. "Did Perdantus teach you to argue so well?"

"He did teach me a lot." I sweetened my tone. "Quixon, we all know you're smart. That's why you're thinking about how to get more money out of this deal. But if you tell Thorne about me, chances are he'll try to steal me before the market ever begins. Then neither of us will get anything. So here's my new offer. The reward money for my capture was a thousand mesots. Whatever Thorne pays at the market, you get to keep half of the amount above a thousand mesots. I guarantee you that he will pay a lot more if he doesn't know about me ahead of time. As a shrewd negotiator yourself, you know the value of an emotional punch in the gut, and I know how to deliver it. But I need the element of surprise."

Quixon sighed. "Fair enough. You win. I'll tell Thorne about the other two and not you. But getting more than a thousand for a sparrow like you is impossible, unless you somehow lay diamond eggs."

"Is there anything you can do to manipulate the bidding? Like auctioning us off yourself?"

"It's not a common practice, but I stepped in as auctioneer for my own slaves on two occasions when the normal auctioneer lost his voice."

"Can you do it for us this time, even without him losing his voice?"

"Perhaps. In this weather, he might gladly allow me to step in."

"Good. Let's do that."

Crystal whispered to me in Alpha One, "He's telling the truth now."

I nodded. "Let's hope it lasts."

Soon, Quixon parked the bus at the ironworks factory directly in front of the door leading to the furnace room. He shut off the engine with a command, opened the bus's door, and descended the steps. "Close door."

The door closed on its own. When the precipitation veiled Quixon's retreating form, I pinched my commlink. "Dirk, give me an update. What's your status?"

"I found the perfect spot for the base unit," he said, his voice small and distant in my earpiece. "A human military guy got in a rover, so Perdantus and I hitched a ride on the back without him seeing me. He went into a tall building, a black one with . . . um . . . what do you call those tall pointed things?"

"Spires?"

"Yeah. Spires. And at the bottom of the spires, it has ugly statues of those Tauranta things all around. Anyway, since the storm's so bad, this guy never heard me sneaking behind him into the building. Now I'm in kind of like a radio room. It's got a fancy microphone and a soundboard with lots of channels. One's labeled emergency. I figure I can switch the board to that channel, and you can talk, pretending to send an emergency call. When the admiral hears your voice, he'll get here in a hurry."

"Perfect, except that you might get caught. As soon as you start broadcasting, someone's bound to show up there."

"Not if we make it fast. Say something short, and we'll scram. Perdantus is keeping watch in the hall, so we should be safe."

"All right." I withdrew the walkie-talkie unit from the duffle bag and drew it close to my lips. "Set it up."

"Already done. Start talking."

I pressed a button on the unit's side and spoke breathlessly. "Calling Anne Willis on the *Astral Dragon*. This is Megan. I'm in Bassolith on Delta Ninety-eight. I can't tell you exactly where or they'll catch me. Come and find me. Hurry!"

I released the button. "All right, Dirk. Get out of there."

"Disconnecting the unit. I'll be on my way in a second."

"Good. If you can sneak around and learn where the admiral might be, do that, and let's set up another broadcast to keep them guessing."

"Got it," Dirk said. "I'll let you know what I find out."

I pinched my commlink, shutting it off. When I returned the walkie-talkie to the duffle, Oliver rose from his seat. "I'm going into the building to see if I can hear them talking. I don't trust Quixon."

I nodded. "Just be careful."

He opened the bus's door and hustled out. I tried to watch him, but with blue sleet and snow pelting every window, I couldn't even see the building, much less Oliver.

About half a minute later, Quixon boarded the bus. Standing at the front, he brushed blue ice crystals from his head and clothing. "Where's the boy?"

I put on an innocent expression. "He went out for a second. There's a chamber pot just past that door."

"I know. I used it myself. I didn't see him around."

I shrugged. "Maybe he saw you and went somewhere else."

"Well, he'd better stay out of sight. When I told Thorne about him and Crystal, it was like he turned into a tornado. Black sparks flew everywhere. I've never seen him so furious."

"Black sparks? Not silver?"

Quixon shook his head. "I know what you mean. When I first met him, he had white glitter, then the next few times they were gray, or silver like you said. Now they're black. And he's more . . . solid, I guess you might say. More glitter. Less wind. Smells a lot worse, too. But he still has plenty of bluster. He claimed ownership of all his escaped slaves."

Oliver leaped up the steps and brushed ice from his hair. "Thorne's right behind me. Let's get out of here."

I hunkered low. Quixon shut the door, started the engine with a verbal command, and pushed the throttle. The bus slid for a second before roaring away.

I risked a peek over the bottom of a window. A swirl of blackness spun madly behind us. Dark sparkles spewed from the mouth area. Whatever Thorne was shouting, the words couldn't break through the storm's fury.

When we drove out of sight, I straightened in my seat, and Oliver sat on the bench across the aisle. "Thorne tried to catch me. He's as mad as a mama bramble bee. You can bet he'll be at the market."

Quixon glowered as he focused straight ahead. "He'll claim that he shouldn't have to buy you. The market has some unwritten rules. One is that owners don't have to buy their own escaped slaves. They just have to pay a finder's fee."

Oliver huffed. "He can talk about rules all he wants, but he never officially bought me. He didn't want my name on any record. And he never bought Megan, either. Crystal's the only one he can claim."

"Good to know. We can use that information." Quixon stopped the bus close to a circular building attached to what looked like a small outdoor coliseum. "We're here. Let's hope the storm stops soon."

I looked through a window at the sheets of falling blue ice. "If it doesn't stop, will they cancel the market?"

"No, but we won't have as many buyers and maybe no human buyers at all. That means lower prices, so some of the sellers might wait for a better day." Quixon withdrew a gray flask from his pocket, untwisted its cap, and took a swig. After putting the flask away, he smacked his lips. "If the weather stays bad, the only slaves will be the ones the sellers want to get rid of the most. It will be a buyer's market."

I pulled my locket up by its leather cord and let it dangle in front while keeping Renalda's locket hidden behind my shirt. "Don't worry. Thorne will pay plenty. I'm holding out for at least five thousand mesots."

"Five thousand! That's outrageous! Not even entire families have ever sold for that much. And what if there are no other bidders? He won't bid more than the standard minimum for children, one hundred mesots each for you and the boy and a ten-mesot finder's fee for the girl."

"Don't worry. He'll pay a lot more."

"But what if he doesn't?" He pointed a dark finger at me. "You talk a lot about negotiation tactics. One is that you have to be ready for all possibilities."

"If he doesn't, we walk away. That's a smart tactic, being willing to walk away from a bad deal. Then we'll work on another plan."

"But you *want* him to buy you. What's so important about getting that much money?"

"You never know when I might get in trouble, and maybe we can buy freedom for other slaves. I don't have any metasilver left, and I know from Jaradians like you that I have to pay a lot to get help."

"All right. All right. You made your point." Quixon's shoulders sagged. "I suppose I'll be a laughingstock for holding out for that much money, but at least I have the metasilver."

I withdrew the walkie-talkie from the duffle bag again. "While we're waiting for the storm to let up . . ." I pinched my commlink and spoke in Alpha One. "Dirk, are you listening?"

"Yeah," he whispered though my commlink. "But I have to be quiet. I followed the admiral to Thorne's home. I'm in that furnace room you told me about. Thorne and the admiral are upstairs talking, and the door up there is open. At least I think he's the admiral. He's a gray-haired military guy with two other soldiers following him like little dogs ready to lick his boots."

"So he was already on the planet, but my emergency call probably lured him to Thorne. We'll go to the second step, get him to lead you to his ship. Can you hear what they're saying?"

"Not from here. Maybe if I stood at the top of the stairs, but that's too risky. Nowhere to hide."

"Right." I turned toward Oliver and Crystal. "We need a place to put the radio base unit where the admiral can hear it but not see it. Any ideas?"

Oliver nodded. "There's a loose board in the stairway floor over a cubbyhole at the top landing. I used to hide stuff like shiny stones I found at the cave that I thought I could use later."

"Is your stuff still there?"

"Unless someone moved it, but there's room for the radio in the hole."

"Okay, Dirk," I said, still speaking Alpha One, "find the cubbyhole at the top landing, put the radio in there, and hide."

"But the door's open. I'll be in plain sight."

Crystal set a hand near the bus floor, as if Dirk could see her gesture. "Not if you stay low. Thorne meets with people in the dining room, and there's a work island in the kitchen that'll block their view."

After a silent pause, Dirk replied. "All right. Better than bees, I guess."

I flashed a thumbs-up at Crystal. "Right, and when the admiral leaves, follow him. After what I say, he'll probably lead you straight to his ship."

"Got it."

"Let me know when you're ready." I held the walkie-talkie close to my lips with a finger on the talk button.

Quixon growled. "What's all that gibberish going on back there? And what's that odd little box you have?"

I gave him a disarming smile and replied in Humaniversal. "Just speaking my home language and testing something from my ship."

"Well, it sounds like nonsense. It means you don't trust me."

"Nope. Not even a tiny bit. Unless you're getting paid."

Quixon laughed. "All right. Score one for the smart-mouth. But I'll earn your trust. You'll see."

"Ready for transmission," Dirk said.

I cleared my throat, pressed the walkie-talkie button, and spoke loudly in Alpha One. "We can't stay here. Now that we know where the *Nebula One* is, maybe we can sabotage it. Let's go!" I released the button. "All right, Dirk, get ready to follow. Let us know what you find out."

"You got it."

We continued listening. A man shouted in the distance, and another noise sounded like pounding footsteps even farther away. After a few moments, Dirk's breaths came through, quick and shallow, as if he were running. I ached to ask him for updates, but he probably had to stay quiet. I pinched my commlink and put the walkie-talkie back in the bag. "All right. Dirk's on the move. The plan's working so far."

Quixon pointed at the windshield. "The storm's letting up. We need to get ready before anyone else comes. We'll find your chains and clothing inside."

I lifted my brow. "Clothing?"

"Market clothes. Standard practice. They're designed to show what buyers want to see—muscle tone for ability to work, bruises to see if you're clumsy, stripes on your back to see if you're obstinate. That sort of thing."

"We'd have to be practically naked to show all that."

"Yes, the process is degrading for the slaves, but buyers see it as a practical necessity. I realize Thorne won't care about these things, but if you come to market as you are, buyers will be suspicious."

"I've been through it," Crystal said. "It'll be colder than an ice bath out there, especially for Oliver. Boys have to go shirtless. Girls get to wear shirts, but they're sleeveless, and they're cut low in the back, like Quixon said, to show whip scars like mine."

I rose with the duffle bag in hand, shivering. "That's cruel."

Crystal scowled. "Yeah. They call it practical. I call it disgusting, rat-faced mongrels peeking at kids' bodies. They make me want to puke."

"The human buyers, right? I mean, to the Jaradians we're just animals."

Crystal nodded. "The Jaradians just whip you. Humans can do worse things. Lots worse."

"Let's hope we don't have to worry about that."

Quixon led us off the bus, glanced around as if nervous about someone seeing him, and hustled us through a narrow doorway. A sign over the lintel bore a word written in a local language, unreadable to me. Inside, we entered an area with plain wooden benches, rows of metal lockers embedded in the concrete walls, and curtained chamber-pot stalls, dark and dirty. Yet, the place smelled better than it looked. The air carried a hint of a cleaning agent, maybe ammonia.

Quixon used a key to open a locker and withdrew a burlap bag filled with clothes. "I have several sets left over from my days as a slaver. You can look through them to find something that fits. Since ice is on the ground outside, you can keep your shoes on." He dropped the bag onto a bench and pulled chains and manacles from the locker. "Hurry. Others will be here soon. I'm going out to the arena to ask to conduct your sale myself."

When Quixon left, Crystal dug through the bag and passed around clothing, actually more like moth-eaten rags. Leaving my duffle on the bench, I took a shirt and a pair of shorts in my size, entered a chamber-pot stall, and closed the curtain. After using the pot and putting the clothes on, I looked myself over.

A gap between the bottom hem of my shirt and the waistband of the shorts exposed my torso from just below my rib cage to my navel. The tight shorts covered my bottom but not much more, exposing my thighs and calves, including the conductive ink. Also, the sleeveless shirt left the dragon brand out in the open for all to see.

Even with my planned disguise, buyers might recognize me as the pirate girl on the flyer from months ago, which could make the bidding chaotic. Yet, maybe my conductive bracelets would keep their eyes on my wrists and not my arms. They were odd enough to be a distraction.

Carrying my other clothes and feeling more self-conscious than ever, I pushed the curtain to the side and stepped out. Oliver and Crystal were already dressed and sitting on the bench waiting for me.

Crystal rose and compressed my biceps. "Wait'll the buyers get a look at these guns."

"Guns?"

"Yeah, that's what they call bulging biceps in my novels."

"I suppose that'll help the bidding go higher." I looked at my waist, taut and rippled with muscle. "No soft spots. I guess that helps me look like a slave. Maybe all that work moving wing panels paid off."

Crystal poked one of my ribs. "More like you've been skipping too many meals. You're always too busy to eat."

Oliver stood and joined us. His muscles bulged all over, the strongest physique I had ever seen on a boy so young. "Ready for your disguise?" he asked.

"I guess so. I'm not sure how much good it'll do with my brand showing."

Oliver examined my arm. "Yeah. No one's going to miss that dragon. I can't believe I never noticed it before."

"I always kept it covered." I pushed my clothes into the duffle, withdrew a grease pencil I used to mark ship equipment, and handed it to Crystal. "This one's red. Use it to paint my face with cuts. I have another one in the bag that's black. That'll be for bruises. By the time you're done, I won't look like the girl in the picture."

"I can try to cover your brand with a huge bruise," Crystal said. "Or at least make the dragon look like something else."

Quixon bustled in. "It's set. I will be your auctioneer." He blinked at us. "What? Aren't your chains on yet?"

"No." I peeked around him. "Is someone coming?"

"Yes, yes. Another seller. You can't be seen without the chains. Take them to a chamber-pot stall and put them on. Now."

Oliver grabbed a set of chains and hurried to one stall while Crystal took the other sets of chains. The two of us squeezed into a second stall and drew the curtain. While she painted my face, back, and upper arms with cuts and bruises, the rattle of chains drifted in along with shuffling noises. I couldn't tell how many other slaves might be out there—maybe one, maybe ten. Fortunately, there were plenty of other chamber-pot stalls. Crystal and I could stay in this one for a while.

When she finished, she set her hands on her hips and looked at me. "Not perfect, but the buyers won't be close enough to know it's all fake."

"But do I look like me? That's what's important."

Crystal smiled. "Girl, you're a total mess. Even your own mother wouldn't recognize you."

"Good."

We helped each other put wrist and ankle shackles on. A thick chain ran between my ankles, another between my wrists, and a third joined them vertically. Since the lengths were short, we had to shuffle our feet just to walk. No chance of running away.

Crystal whispered, "It's slave time. Head low. No eye contact with anyone. And no talking." She pushed the curtain to the side and shuffled out, her shoulders slumped and her stare at the floor. I slid both lockets behind my shirt and followed, mimicking her slouch. Quixon met us at our bench, one fist clutching a ring of keys, his other hand holding my duffle bag. He glanced at me and grimaced, then led us toward an exit on the opposite side of the room.

As we followed, I sneaked a peek at the only other slave, a girl with a thin frame and ebony skin and hair. Her somber expression reminded me of Renalda, though this girl was older, maybe twelve or thirteen. Dressed in market clothes similar to ours, she appeared to be waiting for someone, her ankle chains padlocked to an iron ring embedded in the floor.

Resisting the urge to try to make eye contact, I continued our slow march into a wide hall that led to a closed door about twenty paces ahead. A cold draft funneled through, evidence that the door probably led directly outside.

"The buyers have gathered," Quixon said. "Thorne is out there along with two others, one Jaradian and one human." He stopped next to the door, and we halted with him. "You three will be sold after the girl you saw. We'll wait here. Her seller is talking to the auctioneer."

Soon, a huge Jaradian walked from the preparation room, leading the other girl by a long rope that led to her wrist chains. When he shoved the door open, cold air burst in, instantly chilling my bare skin. I shivered hard. This ordeal might be worse than I imagined.

As the girl passed me, her worn-out shoes sliding along the floor, she whispered in Humaniversal, "Don't worry. Everything's going to be all right." Then she lowered her head and shuffled on.

I blinked. Why would she say that? Being so young and all alone, how could she be so confident?

Crystal leaned close to me. "There's something different about that girl."

"I noticed. But what is it?"

"I don't know yet. Just . . . different. I'll work on it."

Outside, ice covered a grassy field. Twenty paces away, the Jaradian slaver led the girl up three steps to a wooden platform about ten meters long and three meters wide. A second Jaradian stood near the center holding a clipboard, probably the auctioneer.

The slaver turned the girl to face the stadium-like seats that rose in levels, much like in the Tauranta temple. He hurried off the stage, calling, "I will collect the purchase price when the sale is over. It's too cold to wait out here."

In front of the seats, Thorne hovered in place at ground level. He looked so different. He swirled, as always, but now he had vague appendages similar to arms, legs, and a head, black sparks spinning within them. Two other potential buyers stood beyond him, a Jaradian and a human.

Quixon took another quick drink from his flask. "Come. We are to stand next to the stage and wait for our turn."

As he led us outside, cold wind knifed into me and flapped my ragged clothes, making the chill even worse. I shivered harder than ever. My teeth chattered. When we halted, Crystal and I huddled close. Oliver stepped in front of us, partially blocking the wind.

"You don't have to do that," I said, my clacking teeth breaking up my words. "You have less clothes on than we do."

"I know." He steeled his body, though he was unable to keep his arms from trembling. "Maybe it won't take long."

I looked at the two other potential buyers standing below us. The Jaradian was the same one who tried to buy me from Essen, the priest. Since the storm assailed us at full force at the time, maybe he didn't get a good look at me then and wouldn't recognize me now.

The human buyer wore a black ski mask and a gray parka that looked exactly like Gavin's. A thick mustache protruded from the mask. Gavin had no facial hair the last time I saw him, and I got the impression that his boyish face probably couldn't grow anything more than peach fuzz. If he really was Gavin, I would have to keep my own face hidden. He was far more likely to recognize me than the other two were.

On stage, the auctioneer looked at his clipboard and called out, "This human girl is named Andrea. As you can see, she is not malnourished, has no bruises or whip marks, and is old enough to work hard at almost any task. The minimum is market standard, but she is worth considerably more. Please bid quickly so we can get this over with and go home."

Thorne waved one of his new appendages. "She will soon be too big to work in my mine, but I can use her for a while and resell her later. Two hundred mesots."

"Two hundred ten," the Jaradian buyer called.

Thorne laughed. "Who will train her, Castol? Will a Jaradian with a bee phobia try to teach a frightened human child how to dodge bramble bees? I would pay money to see that."

"I have to start somewhere." Castol nodded toward the three of us. "Expert trainers are next on the docket."

"The yellow-haired girl is mine," Thorne said. "I am paying the finder's fee for her."

"You can have her. I want the boy."

"We'll see about that, but you'd better save your money. Look how strong he is. He won't go cheap."

The auctioneer waved a hand. "Gentlemen, if you're finished arguing, we'll continue."

Thorne's voice seemed to thunder. "Two hundred fifty."

Castol glared at Thorne but said nothing. The auctioneer looked at the human buyer. "Are you here to bid or are you merely watching?"

"I am waiting to bid on the next group," the man said in Humaniversal, his voice deep and coarse. "I am not interested in this girl."

I bent my brow. He didn't sound like Gavin. Besides, did Gavin even know Humaniversal? Maybe he did by now, but how could he understand Jaradian without a translator? Had he learned that, too?

"Very well," the auctioneer said. "If we have no other bids, then the girl will go to Thorne for two hundred fifty mesots."

"Get down here, girl," Thorne bellowed. "Now that we're done with the floor sweepings, let's get to the valuable goods. I'll pay when we're finished."

Crystal whispered, "Thorne's changed. He reeks. I can smell him from here. Maybe because his sparkles turned black. And he's meaner than he used to be."

"Or maybe he's mad at you and Oliver," I whispered in return.

Crystal crossed her arms and shivered. "We'll see."

The auctioneer pushed Andrea toward the edge of the stage. "You heard your new master. Get along, now."

As she shuffled down the steps, her chains clinking, I watched her carefully. She had said everything would be all right. Was getting sold to Thorne her definition of "all right"?

When she reached ground level and passed us, my locket rose from behind my shirt and slipped down in front, as if the wind had picked it up and dropped it again. I grabbed it and put it back in place. Andrea looked straight at me, then quickly faced ahead. She half walked and half slid the rest of the way to Thorne and crouched just out of his reach, shivering hard.

The human buyer took off his parka, wrapped it around Andrea, and stood with hands on hips. I eyed him closely. No way did Gavin have even a drop of that kind of compassion. And now with the parka off, revealing a long-sleeved military uniform, he seemed smaller than before, certainly shorter than Gavin and bigger in the chest. Since he wore a sidearm at his hip that looked like a laser pistol, maybe he was one of the admiral's soldiers.

Quixon led our group up the stage steps and set the duffle bag down with the key ring on top of it. When we faced the front, I stared at the three buyers. The human and the Jaradian gawked, scanning us as if we were cuts of meat.

Reality hit me hard. We were up for sale. Half-dressed to display our fitness, we really were nothing more than frozen offerings from a butcher shop. I hugged myself, unable to fend off the bitter wind or the sick feeling inside. I had never felt so naked in all my life.

27

Thorne drew closer, spinning madly. One of his arms protruded, as if pointing at Oliver. "You ruined my operation. It took me months to get it running again."

Oliver crossed his arms, again steeling himself to stop his shivers. When he looked at me, I read his expression. He wanted so badly to tell Thorne off, but that might make things worse.

Shivering hard with my own arms crossed, I gave him a quick shake of the head.

He faced Thorne and spoke in an apologetic tone. "You're right. I did. And it was stupid. I wanted to be a hero for the girls, you know, be a man." He looked down at his feet. "I guess it didn't work out."

Thorne's spin slowed a bit. "And I assume the others were caught up by your leadership. You alone claim responsibility."

Crystal's teeth chattered. "It wasn't his fault. I begged him to help us escape."

"This I can believe." Thorne shifted closer to me. "And who is this half-dead girl? I don't recognize her. She was never one of mine, was she?"

I kept my mouth tightly closed, glaring at him as I played the role of a feisty, disobedient slave.

"She's Kylie," Quixon said. "If you're finished interrogating them, can we start the bidding?"

Thorne drifted back. "The boy's too big now, so he's not worth much. Five hundred for the lot of them, including the finder's fee for Crystal."

I studied Thorne for any sign of hidden motivation, but lacking a readable face, he gave away nothing. He suspected Oliver was gifted, far more valuable than a lowly laborer, but he wanted to bluff his way to winning Oliver at a lower price.

"Six hundred," Castol said. "Just for the boy and the wounded girl—Kylie, or whatever her name is. Let Thorne have Crystal, as the rules state."

Quixon waved a hand. "Since we are agreed that Thorne will win Crystal for the standard finder's fee, then the bidding will continue for the other two. We have a bid of six hundred mesots for the pair."

"One thousand," Thorne said. "That's far more than they're worth."

Castol laughed. "If so, then you wouldn't bid that much. I know your operation needs the boy. It's not nearly as productive as before. It's time for a bit of competition." He thrust a hand toward Quixon. "Twelve hundred. But just for the boy. I don't care about Kylie."

"She's food for the vultures," Thorne said. "Let's leave her out of this."

Quixon started swiveling his head toward me, then quickly turned back. Obviously he couldn't be seen getting instructions from one of his slaves. "Yes, that is acceptable."

I cringed. No. That was exactly the wrong answer. The way I looked, no one would buy me. Now the only way to fix the problem was to reveal my secret earlier than I had intended.

"Good," Thorne said, the black sparkles coming from his mouth spewing with less force. "Fifteen hundred for the boy."

While everyone stared at Quixon and Oliver, I retrieved my locket and opened the back, exposing the glowing dragon's eye. I angled it toward Thorne. Although he had no discernible eyes, he didn't seem to be looking at me. Castol also failed to look toward me as he and Thorne continued upping the bid in increments of a hundred mesots.

The human buyer, however, walked closer to me, his eyes narrowed. Then he spun toward Quixon, raised a hand, and called out, "Auctioneer!"

Quixon focused on him. "Yes?"

"It's too cold to stand here and wait for this bidding war to end." He gestured toward me. "I would like to buy Kylie and leave."

"What is your bid for her?"

"Considering the condition she is in, I will pay the standard minimum. One hundred mesots."

Quixon looked straight at me, confusion in his eyes. Obviously our plans had been blown to pieces.

Thorne shifted my way. His spin whirled faster than ever. He had to have seen the dragon's eye. "Two hundred for Kylie."

I snapped the locket closed and covered it with my hand. Maybe this would work out after all.

"Five hundred," the man said.

Thorne growled. "For a broken-down whipping post? Are you mad?"

"Never you mind. If you want to pay more, then bid more. Otherwise, leave Kylie to me."

"I see that you're one of the deviants. Wanting to buy a girl who cannot defend herself. I won't allow you to take advantage of her. Seven hundred fifty."

The man glowered at Thorne. "One thousand."

"Wait," Castol shouted. "What about the boy?"

Thorne's arm protruded again and waved. "You can have him for whatever your final bid was. I have Crystal to train my workers. Twelve hundred for Kylie."

"You're up to something devious, Thorne. A moment ago, Kylie was vulture bait. Now she's a priceless treasure. You know something I don't." Castol raised a hand. "Thirteen hundred for Kylie."

The man laughed. "Are you two blind? She's half-dead. Cuts and bruises from head to toe."

"Then drop out of the bidding," Thorne said. "Fifteen hundred."

Castol growled. "Sixteen hundred."

The man raised his hands. "You two are out of your minds. Let's end this now. Two thousand mesots. Now go home with your coveted prizes, one with the boy, the other with Crystal. I will take this ugly little hobgoblin of a girl."

I winced. Even though my ugliness was just a disguise, the words stung.

"You go home," Thorne said. "Four thousand."

Castol gasped. "You truly are mad."

Thorne's sparkles shot out in a violent eruption. "Mad? If you think I am mad, then leave me in my madness and drop out. Take the boy and leave."

"I will." Castol withdrew a bag from his coat pocket, counted out a stack of gold coins, and set them on the stage. "Where are his clothes?"

Quixon nodded toward the duffle bag near his feet, the key ring still on top.

Castol grabbed the ring, unlocked Oliver's chains, and opened the bag. "Get dressed, boy. You're mine now."

When Oliver obeyed, Castol reattached the chains, left the key ring on the stage, and pulled him to the ground. As they left, Oliver looked back at me, apparently trying to communicate with his eyes. Being chained, he couldn't easily reach his ear to activate the commlink. I tried to read his expression—confident, determined, as if saying, *Just follow the plan. I'll escape somehow and find you.*

I nodded, my shivers shaking me harder than ever. Could things get any worse?

The human buyer crossed his arms. "Back to business. The previous bid was four thousand mesots. I bid five thousand."

"Six thousand," Thorne said with a confident tone. "Don't try to compete with me. You will lose."

"Is that so?" The man stared straight at Thorne. "Ten thousand mesots."

More sparkles erupted. "What? Ten thousand?"

"You heard me. Will you bid higher?"

Thorne's sparkles blazed like black fire. "Who are you?"

"A man who hates to lose."

"We'll see about that. You had to register to bid here. I will learn who you are and report you to the authorities as a deviant predator."

"Do your worst, windbag." The man walked to Andrea and lifted a hefty leatherlike pouch from his parka's inner pocket. He set the pouch on the stage, opened its flap, and began counting out gold coins. "Get your clothes on, Kylie. Quixon, take off her chains so she can dress here and now. If she tries to run, I will catch her."

"Unchain Crystal and Andrea as well," Thorne grumbled as he floated onto the stage with us. "Crystal, get dressed. We're leaving immediately."

Still standing on ground level, the man continued counting the money and laying coins on the stage. Quixon removed the shackles from my wrists and ankles as well as Crystal's and Andrea's. Crystal and I gathered our clothes from the duffle bag and put them on over the market clothes. By the time we finished, the man counted the final coins and slid them back into the pouch. "Exactly ten thousand mesots. Good thing Thorne decided not to bid higher." He closed the flap, leaped up to the stage, and extended the pouch toward Quixon. "Will you trust my count?"

"Yes, of course." Quixon took the pouch and looked at me with a tight-faced expression, maybe to ask how he could give me the money with the man and Thorne watching.

Since I had no idea, I shook my head and whispered, "Not yet."

In a sudden gust, the lower half of Thorne's swirl enveloped Crystal while the upper half spun around me. Bitter cold and a foul stench assaulted my senses. My hair and clothes flew in disarray as he dragged me toward the edge of the stage.

"Oh no, you don't," the man yelled as he grabbed my arm and held on. "I bought her. She's mine."

Something snapped. My lockets flew away and joined the black sparks in a violent twirl. Thorne lifted off the stage, taking Crystal to ground level with him. She screamed, "Let go of me, you twisted fart!" Like a rampaging tornado, they zipped through a doorway between seating sections and disappeared.

I stared at their exit path, my shivering hand over the bare spot where my lockets used to be. Once again I felt naked, exposed, vulnerable. Thorne had stripped me of my most valuable treasure, violated me with his putrid wind, destroyed my hopes. All four of us were now separated. Together, we had a chance. Alone, all was lost.

"Well," the man said as he released me, "Thorne made quite an exit. He even left the other girl behind."

I looked at Andrea. Still half-buried within the man's parka, she, too, stared at the doorway.

The man nudged my shoulder. "Here. I think this is yours."

I turned toward him. He held a leather cord with a locket dangling from it. "I saw it drop when that windbag tried to steal you."

"My locket!" I took it from him, tied the cord at the back of my neck, and opened the clasp a tiny crack. The dragon's eye still glowed. When I closed it, I looked at the exit again. Thorne must have taken Renalda's locket. Soon he would discover that the dragon's eye inside had lost its glow. What might he do then?

The man set a hand on my shoulder. "Let's go, Megan."

When he pushed, I resisted. "How did you know my name?"

"I saw your face on a leaflet." He withdrew a handkerchief from a pocket and wiped it across my face. "Did you think you could hide behind a mask?"

He folded the handkerchief and reached to wipe again. I back-pedaled and took a defiant stance. "Who are you?"

"A man not to be trifled with." He tossed the handkerchief at me. "Get cleaned up. We have to go."

I caught the handkerchief. Maybe showing a sign of surrender might help me get information. I began wiping my face. "Do you report to Admiral Fairbanks?"

He glanced at Quixon and the auctioneer as they whispered together a few paces away. Quixon took a couple of coins from the pouch and gave them to the auctioneer, most likely a commission. My buyer grasped my shoulder firmly and spoke in a low tone. "It's best not to answer your questions where others might hear us. You will soon learn all you need to know."

I looked at his gloved hand. Maybe I could shock him and make a run for it, but then I wouldn't get any answers about the admiral. Better to gain some information first and escape later.

When I had wiped as much of the grease off my face as I could, I gave him the soiled handkerchief. "I'm ready."

With his hand still on my shoulder, we walked down the steps together. The man pointed at Andrea. "What are you going to do with this girl?"

"Thorne left without paying for her," the auctioneer said. "Do you want her? With the price you paid, no one will question you getting both."

"What would happen to her if I don't take her?"

"The law says she goes to the orphan colony, though I would probably offer her to Thorne again for the minimum. Once he cools off, I think he'll take her."

"I suppose I can find some use for her." He patted Andrea on the back. "Let's go. You can keep my coat on."

The three of us walked out together, the man with a hand on each of us. Yama-Yami slid close to the horizon, signaling evening's onset. Although the wind stayed cold and blustery, having my own clothes on felt warm compared to the skimpy outfit. I could handle it.

As we walked alongside an icy road, I glanced at my buyer every few seconds. He opened his mouth a couple of times as if ready to say something, but when a Jaradian or a Tauranta or a bird passed nearby, he clammed up, apparently not wanting anyone to hear what he had to say.

I scanned the surrounding buildings. Most of them were tall with black spires and gargoyle-like statues perched at the tops of dark stone walls. This area seemed similar to the one Dirk described. Maybe one of the buildings served as a military office for the Alliance. If so, that might be where our buyer was taking us.

Not far away, the smokestacks from the ironworks factory loomed in the midst of the spires. Since evening approached, Crystal was probably there with Thorne and whatever other slaves he now had. I would have to escape tonight and join her before the morning bus ride.

As we walked, a vibration tickled my ear. I pretended to scratch it and activated my commlink. Dirk's voice came through. "I'm on the *Nebula One*. Can't talk now. Just thought I'd let you know. I'll call everyone later."

I waited for a moment to see if either Oliver or Crystal would reply, but no other voices emanated from the link. They, too, were probably in situations that demanded silence. I pinched my comm-link again and switched it off.

The buyer guided us into an alley that separated two of the spired buildings. He stopped at a door near the back of the alley, unlocked it with a key, and opened it a few centimeters. Setting his ear next to the gap, he listened for a moment before opening the door fully and ushering us through.

Once inside, he closed the door, struck a match, and lit an oil lantern. The wick's tall flame cast flickering light throughout a square room about three meters across and only two meters high. A bare mattress abutted the far wall, and a desk stood next to a wood-paneled wall on the left side, a radio system with several antennas on its surface.

The man set the lantern on the desk and gestured toward the mat-tress. "Sit. We have a lot to talk about when I come back. I'll be just a minute. I have to scan the perimeter for sound detection devices." He walked out and closed the door behind him. The lock clicked. I couldn't escape, at least not yet. Since he wanted to make sure no one could listen in to what he was about to do next, the situation seemed more dangerous than ever.

Andrea shed the parka and gave it to me. "Just rest, and we'll talk."

"Um . . . sure." I sat on the mattress, my back against the wall, and spread the parka over my legs.

She slid out a desk drawer, withdrew a small canvas bag, and opened it, looking at me with a sad sort of smile. Her bright brown eyes shone, easy to see with her tight curls pulled back and tied with an elastic band. Since her bag was already here, she was familiar with this room. "Do you have any questions?" she asked.

"Yeah, you said everything would be all right. What did you mean?"

"Well . . ." She pulled a pair of pants, a long-sleeved shirt, and a thick sweater from the bag. "I was trying to comfort you. I didn't realize who you were until that moment."

"You mean, you know me?"

She slid the pants on over her market shorts and zipped them. "I'm an agent sent to spy on the slave trading. Andrea's my under-cover name. My real name is Zoë."

I gasped. "Zoë? Were you ever with my mother on the *Astral Dragon*?"

Zoë smiled in a coy manner. "I'll let our buyer answer that question. Be patient."

I let the new information tumble through my brain. Since the buyer probably knew my mother, maybe I would be all right. "Okay, then, how about this one? Were you ever with the Ashers? Winthrop and Phyllis?"

She sucked in a sharp breath, then quickly recovered, her expression calm, though her voice quivered. "Um . . . I can't talk about my past. You know, being an undercover agent."

"Then you *were* on Delta Ninety-five. I read about you in the Ashers' journal."

"Maybe you did." She pushed her arms through the shirtsleeves and slid her head through the hole. "And I know a lot more about you than you could possibly guess." After pulling the sweater's hem down to her waist, she untied the elastic band in her hair, releasing dark curls that poofed out as if triggered by a spring. "You've been separated from your parents for a long time, haven't you, Megan Willis?"

"So you know my last name. What else do you know?"

"A lot, but I'm not allowed to tell you how yet."

"All right. Whatever." I slid my hands under the parka. "At least we're warm and dry in here."

"Yes, but I'm not supposed to be here. We wanted Thorne to buy me so I could spy on him. We'll have to work on a new plan."

"We? Who is we? You and our buyer, or you and my mother?"

Her coy smile reappeared. "I can't tell you that either."

The lock clicked again. The door opened, and our buyer bustled in. When he closed the door, he took off his gloves. "No eavesdropping devices that I could see, and no one followed us. Now I can finally do this." He jerked off his ski mask, releasing auburn hair that dropped to his shoulders. He then stripped off the mustache and looked at me, smiling. "I'm sorry for being so secretive, Megan. I couldn't afford to let anyone know."

I stared. My buyer was a woman. A familiar woman. My brain scrambled, unable to register. Then her lovely face clarified. And that voice. No longer low and gruff, it was music—sweet, impossibly beautiful music. Could it really be true?

Tears welling, I whispered, "Mama?"

"Yes, Megan." She spread her arms. "We're finally together again, just like I promised."

I leaped up and ran into her embrace. "Mama! It's you! It's really you!"

"Oh, Megan." She hugged me close and kissed my forehead. "I missed you so much."

"I missed you, too." I drew back and looked at her face, the face I had seen in my dreams for so many nights, though torn away at every waking dawn. "What about Papa? Have you heard anything?"

"Only what the computer records say, that they executed him just a few minutes after I last saw him."

I caressed her cold cheek. "But you don't believe it, right?"

"I'm not sure what to believe. I can't see why they would kill him right away. He had information about the members of our cause. I thought they would torture him to get it."

I ran a hand through her hair. "So maybe there's hope. Maybe he's on a prison planet like Beta Four."

She clasped my hand and kissed my knuckles. "It's good to have hope, but we have to be realistic. It's better to assume that he's dead." She lifted a thin chain around her neck, raising a locket from behind her shirt. "I wish I had one of these for him. It gave me hope for you every day. As long as the dragon's eye glowed, my search would never stop."

I gazed at her locket. Now that I had some theories about its power, I wanted to blurt them out, but it might be better to ask questions. "Why does the gem glow? Besides saying that I'm still alive, I mean. Captain Tillman wanted my dragon's eye. Thorne wants it. Gavin stole it until someone got it back from him. And what about Gavin? Why were you working with him, and where is he now?"

"So many questions!" She smiled in the glowing way I had ached for for so long. "How about if I start with how I found you?"

I returned the smile. "Yeah. I got ahead of myself."

"Let's sit." She guided me back to the mattress, and the three of us sat cross-legged in a circle. "First, when I was sentenced to death, Gavin joined our cause because he knew our trial was unjust. He piloted the transport to Beta Four, registered me there as a prisoner, and helped me escape without the prison keepers ever knowing about it. You see, there are no boundaries on Beta Four. It's a small, cold, barren planet, and the prisoners live underground. Troublemakers get banished outside, where they either find a new cave or freeze to death. As you might guess, the keepers rarely check on prisoners who can't possibly escape.

"Gavin returned later with the corpse of a woman my age, branded it with a pirate symbol, and deposited it on one of the planet's coldest mountains. I assume they found the corpse and thought she was me, reported me as dead, and that was the end of Anne Willis. I was free to do what I wanted, to find you."

"Why did it take so long?" I asked.

"I had so many unavoidable detours. First, I met Zoë—she can tell you her story later—and when I learned how horrible the slave trade is, I knew I had to do more than just pity the poor kids who were trapped in it. Then I learned that your imprisonment might be tied in with the trade, but I wasn't sure how. I had to do a lot of digging to learn what Tillman was doing with you."

"Yeah, it was really twisted. I guess it makes sense that it took a while."

"It did." She pointed at me. "Since you had the dragon's eye, though, I wasn't worried about you hearing I was dead, so I never risked sending you a message. I just worked with Gavin to set up an attack on the *Nebula Nine* to rescue you."

The image of my fellow crew members came to mind as I set each one ablaze. Although I kept my expression the same, grief welled up inside. I had to ask the question. "Everyone on board died. I know Captain Tillman deserved it, but what about Dr. Cole? He was always on my side. He was just obeying orders."

Her expression hardened. "Dr. Cole was still part of the crew that was escorting you to your doom. And *just obeying orders* has been a lame excuse for committing atrocities across the galaxy."

I stared at her fiery eyes. I had heard that speech so many times when my parents rationalized killing soldiers who defended against our ship's raids. At the time, I always nodded in agreement. Those faceless soldiers meant nothing to me. Now I knew the names of the dead, the names of some of their spouses and kids. And I was the one who had to burn their corpses and watch a droid collect their bones and ashes. They meant something to somebody.

"Megan . . ." She caressed my cheek. "You've been through so much. I'm sure it's all confusing to you. But you have to understand that we're in a war, a war against tyrants, against slave traffickers, against predators. They don't care who they kill. Men. Women. Children. Whatever it takes to get what they want. If we're so careful that we never have any unintended casualties, then we can't possibly win. And that would mean more innocent lives lost in the long run."

She drew her hand back and clenched a fist. "We have to fight fire with fire. Yes, maybe we'll kill a few dozen innocent people. Maybe even more than a hundred. But if we don't come at those monsters with guns blazing, they'll kill thousands. Tens of thousands. And they'll keep enslaving innocent children in every star system."

Her words sounded so much like Captain Tillman's when he demanded the dragon's eye. Were they really that similar? The thought stirred nausea in my stomach. "Are you saying it's a trade-off? Lose a few people to save a lot?"

"Yes, that's exactly what I'm saying. In a war, innocent people die. There's no way to avoid collateral damage."

Although intimidated by her passion, I managed a whispered "Maybe we just haven't tried hard enough."

She poked my knee with a finger. "Then you tell me, Megan. How could I have rescued you without a surprise attack? How could Gavin have taken you off the ship without killing the captain? And how could we have killed the captain without killing the rest of the crew?"

I infused a bit more courage into my voice. "The same way you did it without killing Dirk and me. Make sure everyone had suits on. Except the captain, I mean."

She laughed under her breath. "How could we have done that? If everyone had put their suits on, do you think I could have just spirited you off the *Nebula Nine* without confronting the crew? A battle aboard ship could've killed everyone, including you and me. I planned your escape for weeks. It was the only way."

I wanted to say, "And it didn't work," but that would've been too harsh. The rescue would have worked if I had let Gavin know where I was. "I . . . um . . . I'll think about it."

"Of course you will. I know it's a difficult subject, and we all have to be comfortable with where our conscience leads us." Her smile returned. "Back to Gavin. After we battled Admiral Fairbanks long enough for you to escape, we took off, hoping he would follow us. When he did, our shields started going down unexpectedly. I couldn't outrun him, and I certainly couldn't turn and fight, so we ditched the ship on Delta Ninety-eight. At least we would have air to breathe and a fighting chance to survive."

"So was the ship completely disabled? Is that why you didn't come looking for me on Delta Ninety-five?"

She nodded. "We sustained damage during the landing. We couldn't even take off."

"Then how did you get away from Admiral Fairbanks?"

She raised a finger. "Exactly my question. Since he didn't chase us into the planet's atmosphere, I got suspicious, so I looked into the reason the shields failed."

Zoë grinned. "We asked Sonya."

I smiled in return. Sonya was the *Astral Dragon*'s version of Emerson, just as smart, but far more snarky. She took some getting used to. "What did Sonya tell you?"

My mother's features tensed. "That the shields and engines went down because of a virus in the operations part of the system. Gavin denied installing the virus, of course, but I didn't believe him, and I forced him to leave. The moment he was gone, I told Sonya to strip all security clearance from him. I never saw him again, but since he took a flamethrower, I had to be careful wherever I went."

"Yeah. That flamethrower is dangerous. I know from experience, but I'll tell you about that later."

"Fair enough." She touched my knee. "Anyway, my guess is that he had been communicating with Admiral Fairbanks all along. He was playing both sides to see who would eventually get your dragon's eye, the admiral or me. They knew the ruby would die if they killed me, so the admiral didn't finish me off when he had the chance. He just wanted to ground me."

"Okay," I said, "but why was Gavin trying to kill me? He put a noise-pulse bomb in the *Nine*. Everyone on board could've died."

"No, no. He wasn't trying to kill you. He hoped to disable the *Nebula Nine* while it was on the ground, because we didn't want you to leave the planet without us finding you. He set a timer and kept coming back to try to overcome Emerson's security blocks. You escaped with the ship before the timer went off. But he told me he put a beacon on the *Nine* so we could find you."

"Okay, then why did you leave with the *Astral Dragon* before the timer on the *Nine* expired? I saw that you had landed on the beach by the bay."

"Because Gavin said the admiral had pinpointed our landing site. So we took off, planning to return when we could."

"He lied." I lifted my locket on its cord and showed it to her. "He stole my locket and was in a hurry to get away. He didn't want you to find me in the city."

She stared at me for a long moment. "That means the tracking beacon Gavin planted on the *Nebula Nine* wasn't so I could find you. It was a trap to lure me into a battle with Admiral Fairbanks, to bring us all together at the same time."

"Right." I dropped the locket back to its place. "Good thing Dirk stole the locket back for me."

"Dirk did that?" She clapped her hands. "That's perfect. Poetic justice. When we left the beach, I didn't know he wasn't on board until it was too late. That little rascal would make an excellent pirate."

"Yeah. I guess so. Anyway, that story's all straight in my mind, but there's still a lot I don't know." I half-closed an eye. "Like why were you at the slave market today?"

"To make sure Zoë's sale went through. Like I said, I'll let her tell you her story. For my part, once I had secured the ship, I left with Zoë. At the time, we weren't sure if Gavin was still around, so we went off the path and into the forest. We got lost for a while, but a kind Willow Wind helped us find our way. Then we came to this room, and we've been hiding in the city ever since, planning how to infiltrate the slave market hierarchy. We were hoping Thorne would buy her so she could get some information from him."

"Why the interest in the slave market?"

"Two reasons. First, Zoë's story made me realize how evil and pervasive the trafficking is. Second, I heard that the fire season had begun on Delta Ninety-five, and I thought you might have returned to Ninety-eight right away. Since most unguarded children who come here end up in the slave market, I thought you might have been grabbed by a trader, and maybe by infiltrating it, I might learn where you were, whether on this planet or transported to another."

"It was your only choice," I said, "since the *Dragon* was too damaged to fly."

"Right. Anyway, asking Zoë to be a spy could accomplish both goals—finding you and crippling the market. Even with all my spying experience, it took me months to learn their secrets and to get accepted as a trader, especially since I posed as an Alliance officer. Although most officers look the other way when it comes to trafficking, the official stance is to oppose it, and a few take their jobs seriously, so I had to pretend to be one of the scoundrels. Also, we lost a lot of time going back to the *Dragon* to work on repairing her. When she was finally ready to fly, I was going to delay our plan to send Zoë into the market until after I flew to Delta Ninety-five to search for you. Then I changed my mind. And here's why." She gestured toward the desktop radio. "My radio records all communications traffic in the area and flags messages from Nebula ships."

I grinned. "You heard my message. The one with the bird singing."

"Exactly. That idea had you written all over it." She caressed my cheek. "Well done, Megan."

Warmth flooded my body. It felt so good to hear those words.

"And I heard the scuttlebutt about you escaping with Thorne's slaves, so I guessed that you would return with a passion to smash Thorne's operation again. That's why we decided to go to the next sale, armed with my new reputation as a trader, a strong and lovely young woman who could attract a buyer, and plenty of money from our cache."

"Well, you guessed right. Stopping Thorne is exactly what my friends and I were trying to do." I gave her a quick summary of my story with Oliver and Crystal in the bramble bee cave, our labors on Delta Ninety-five, and our journey back to this planet.

When I finished, my mother nodded toward Zoë. "She was one of the children on Delta Ninety-five. Maybe now's a good time for her to tell her story."

Zoë yawned. "I think we should catch a nap first. We might not get another chance to sleep."

"I agree." My mother stretched out on the mattress with her back to the wall. "There's room for all of us."

I scooted next to my mother and grasped her hand with both of mine, holding the clasp at my waist. Zoë lay on my other side and settled closer than I expected. Her familiarity felt good and strange at the same time. For some reason, I hesitated to like her, but she wasn't going to let me wait. And her plan was working. I liked her already.

I fell asleep immediately. For how long, I don't know. Maybe a few hours. I was awakened by the tingling of my commlink. I pinched it and spoke in a low tone. "Who's calling?"

"Megan," Dirk whispered, his words breaking. "I got caught . . . in a prison cell . . . the *Nebula One*." Static interrupted several words. He had to be near the commlink's transmission boundary.

I sat up. "Where's the ship? We'll come and rescue you."

My mother and Zoë sat up as well, both looking at me.

"Across the river," Dirk said. "In the forest. I sent Perdantus . . . tell you where I am."

"But Perdantus will go to Thorne's place. I'm not there."

"But . . . the plan."

"I know going to Thorne's was the plan. It's a long story." I rose from the mattress. "But I'll get to Thorne's as quick as I can. I have to—"

"Uh-oh," Dirk said.

"What's wrong?"

"They see the commlink."

Metal clanked against metal. Then someone cried out in pain.

I raised my voice. "Dirk, give me something. Are you all right?"

Except for my pounding heart, silence ruled the entire room as my mother and Zoë rose and joined me.

I whispered, "Dirk's in trouble."

28

"Crystal? Oliver? Can you hear me?" After a few seconds of silence, I pinched my commlink, turning it off. "No response. Let's go to Thorne's and meet a bird named Perdantus. One of us needs to follow him to the *Nebula One* to rescue Dirk from a prison cell there. The other two should sneak into Thorne's to find a lockbox that we think holds information about the slave trade."

"Is Perdantus the bird in your coded message?" my mother asked.

"Right. He's smart and loyal. A great ally."

"Then I'll go with him while you two sneak into Thorne's."

"Perfect." I grabbed the parka and handed it to her. "Take it. We'll be warm at Thorne's."

"Agreed." She threw it on and pushed her arms through the sleeves. "Ready."

The three of us hustled out the door and into the night. Once we reached the street, I searched for the smokestacks of the ironworks factory, but darkness blurred the many vertical spires that knifed the sky. Soon, my eyes adjusted, bringing the stacks into focus, dimly illuminated by moonlight.

"Follow me." Jogging slowly to keep from slipping on icy spots, we turned this way and that through the patchwork pattern of streets. Two paths led to dead ends that forced us to retreat and try another. Others narrowed to littered alleys that slowed our pace as we dodged trash cans and unidentified debris.

As we continued, we chatted while puffing white vapor into the cold, dark air. Now was my chance to see if my mother's knowledge matched my theories. "Mama, what's up with the dragon's eye? Why does everyone—Gavin and Thorne and the admiral—want it?"

"There's an ancient tale that says the eye's life energy will give someone power, maybe even immortality. I doubt that it's true, but I guess anyone who believes it would want one."

"But Thorne's a Willow Wind. He's already immortal. Why would he want one?"

She squinted at me. "Immortal? Are you sure?"

"Well, practically immortal. He needs air to survive. Anyway, that's what another Willow Wind told me. Since he's just a bunch of sparkling air, I guess it makes sense. How else could a Willow Wind die?"

My mother looked at Zoë. "Any ideas?"

Zoë shrugged. "Even if I can't kill him, I still want to try to mess up his operation. I'll figure out how when I see what's going on."

My mother nodded. "Good. I know I can trust you."

I refocused on the smokestacks, not wanting them to see my face as I led them onward. The situation bothered me. Was it because Zoë had taken my place as my mother's scheming sidekick? Maybe that was part of it. But hearing Zoë so casually talking about killing Thorne rattled me. She wasn't here simply to infiltrate the slave market; she was here to kill him.

We stopped at the door leading to the furnace room. A sign had been nailed to the front with words I couldn't read. "This is the place," I whispered as I reached for the doorknob.

A bird chirped loudly. "Stop!"

I drew back. Perdantus landed on my shoulder, gasping for breath.

"I apologize for the shout. Thorne has tightened security. The sign on the door says that the entry is protected by an electric field. Any unauthorized attempt to open it will result in a severe shock."

"Whew! Thanks. You were just in time."

"I hoped to get here earlier, but the wind was contrary. Dirk has been captured, and I—"

"Yes, we heard." I set a hand on my mother's arm. "Can you lead her to the ship?"

"Yes, of course." He bowed his head. "I am Perdantus, and I am at your service."

"Anne Willis, Megan's mother."

"Her mother?" He fluttered over to her shoulder. "Well, this is excellent news. I am pleased to—"

"Enough talk. We have to hurry." She kissed Zoë's forehead, then mine. Her lips lingered on my skin as she whispered, "I love you, Megan, and I'm so proud of you." When she stepped back, she looked at Perdantus. "Fly. I'll follow at my best speed."

"Yes, of course." Perdantus lifted off and flew away.

Without looking back, my mother ran into the night. As she faded in the darkness, I slowly exhaled. The forehead kiss was a wonderful reminder of our family bond, but she had also done the same to Zoë. Maybe my mother thought Zoë was a new member of our family, but she was barely more than a stranger to me. And now my mother was gone. Of course she had to rush to save Dirk. My brain knew that, but my heart felt empty. I had my dear Mama for a few minutes, and now we were both plunging ourselves into danger once more. Would I ever see her again?

"Not to interrupt your thoughts . . ." Zoë cupped her hands and blew on them. "Maybe we should try to get in."

"Right." I gave the knob a quick tap with my finger. "No shock. It's probably activated by turning it."

I looked at my bracelet. Maybe I could send electricity into the knob and short-circuit the mechanism. Just as I flexed my biceps to activate the current, the knob started turning on its own. Something buzzed. The door slowly opened outward. Electricity arced from the knob to the metal catch on the jamb. When the gap widened, the arc snapped, clearing the way.

Warm air rushed out. Across the room, the furnace blazed, as usual.

I squinted at Zoë. "Did you do that?"

"Maybe." Giving me a slight grin, she grabbed the door and pulled it wide open. "Let's get warm."

"Uh . . . sure. But hold the door while I get something to prop it open." I walked inside and spotted a stack of crates. "Stay there. I'll be right back."

I jogged to the stack, reached high, and slid the top crate off. Something was in it, but it was still light enough to carry. As I lowered it, a clatter rang in my ears. On the floor, the gun portion of Gavin's flamethrower lay next to the bottom crate.

I set my crate down, lifted the lid, and found the fuel tank inside. I scanned the room. Gavin wasn't anywhere in sight. Why would he hide his weapon, and where could he be now?

After removing the tank and setting it next to the gun, I pushed the crate to the exit. Zoë still stood outside, staring at the open door.

"What're you doing?" I asked.

"Holding the door, like you said."

I slid the crate in place next to the jamb. "You're just looking at it. It's staying open on its own."

"No, it's not." She walked in. The moment she cleared the opening, the door swung behind her and struck the crate, staying ajar.

I blinked at her. "Did you keep it open with your mind?"

She nodded as she walked closer to the furnace. "And I can move things. Small things, mostly. Sometimes I can move bigger objects, but they wear me out."

When we stopped and warmed ourselves near the fire, I touched my locket. "You moved this, didn't you? When you passed by me at the market."

"Yeah. I saw the cord around your neck. Your mother said to be watching for you and that you'd have a locket, so I decided to check."

"We need to talk." I sat cross-legged in the warmth and gestured for her to sit across from me. When she did, I looked her in the eye. "I know you were on Delta Ninety-five with the Ashers. Did Phyllis Asher die of pneumonia?"

Zoë averted her gaze. "How would I know that? We kids left on the ship. The Ashers stayed behind."

I kept my expression slack. Although Crystal was a lot better at detecting lies, even I could tell that Zoë was hiding something, but I couldn't accuse her without proof. "All right. How did you and my mother get together?"

Zoë regained eye contact, though she still seemed hesitant to look at me. "Admiral Fairbanks commanded the ship that picked up the other kids and me on Delta Ninety-five, because we thought the volcanoes might erupt soon. At a transport depot, he split us into three groups on smaller ships heading to sanctuary planets. I was supposed to go to Gamma Five, because I was born there."

I nodded. "Go on."

"At one of the way stations along our route, the captain of the transport ship separated me from the others and gave me to a woman. Never heard her name, but she was older, maybe sixty, and mean as a hornet hound, assuming you know what that is."

"It's like an Alpha One wolverine. I got the picture."

"Well, your mom was spying on the wolverine witch because she's married to a highly ranked Alliance officer. Your mom wanted to make sure Gavin was telling the truth about the *Nebula Nine*'s location and thought the witch might have intel about it. Anyway, long story short, while she was getting the info, she bumped into me, found out that I was being trafficked as a slave, and rescued me. When she learned that I could move things with my mind, she asked me to join her on the *Astral Dragon* to help her rescue you."

"How could you help?"

She flashed a proud smile. "You might've noticed how accurate the *Dragon*'s strike was on the *Nine*."

I nodded. "Pinpoint. Even though the captain took evasive action." I widened my eyes. "You did that? Those torpedoes weigh at least thirty kilos."

"Not in space. They're weightless. I just had to alter their course a bit."

"Okay. That's super powerful." I tilted my head. "What happened to the wolverine witch?"

Zoë shrugged. "We were at a transport station, not the witch's home base. We had to escape in a hurry, and your mom lost track of her. Never picked up the trail again."

My commlink tingled. "Someone's calling." I pinched the flap and waited for someone to talk.

After a few seconds, Crystal's voice came through. "Listen, Thorne, you can stand there all night and demand to know where Megan is, and I'll tell you the same thing. I don't know. I have no idea who bought her. I've never seen that guy before in my life."

"It's Crystal," I said to Zoë. "She's talking to Thorne and letting me listen in."

"What do you know about the dragon's eye?" Thorne said, his voice barely audible. "Why isn't it glowing?"

As they talked, I whispered their words to Zoë rapid-fire, hoping I wouldn't confuse Crystal.

"How should I know?" Crystal said. "Maybe because Megan's not wearing it."

"Yes, that is a reasonable possibility. Perhaps I need her presence to activate it."

"Crystal," I said, "ask him what that means. Activate it for what?"

"Activate it for what?" Crystal asked.

"I suppose it won't hurt to tell you. Since you know Megan so well, maybe you can help me solve the mysteries."

"Sure. I don't mind trying. I mean, you've always been fair to me."

"I'm glad you recognize that."

I smiled. Crystal's act was working.

"I have been using the glowsap," Thorne continued, "to give myself substance. You might have noticed that I am, shall we say, thicker than before."

"I noticed. You're quite a bit thicker. But why do you want substance?"

"It is not so much substance that I crave. It is significance. Substance is a necessary evil to achieve significance. If you are nothing but swirling air and glitter, no one will consider you to be anything more than a bag of wind. I'm sure you heard Megan's buyer call me a windbag."

"I did," Crystal said. "I thought it was rude. You can't help how you were born."

"True, but I can help what I become. The problem with gaining substance is that I will become vulnerable. I will lose whatever form of immortality I possess. And the dragon's eye will give it back to me."

"Oh, I get it. It has to be glowing to give you immortality."

"Correct. I have a book from an old sorcerer that explains how it works. I memorized the incantation that activates the eye's power."

"If you can get substance, what would you look like?"

"A villain I captured. I have been absorbing his physicality—even his brain's knowledge and memories—by using bramble bee poison's destructive effects on him and glowsap's healing powers on me. It's a complicated process, but it is nearly done. Soon, he will be dead, which will be no loss to anyone. The universe will be far better off without him."

"When will you finish transforming?" Crystal asked.

"As soon as possible. Yet, once I transform, I will be vulnerable, and too many people want to kill me. I want to have the eye in hand so I can become immortal again right away."

I sucked in a quick breath. The old story my mother told me about was true! Or at least Thorne believed it was. "Ask him where the power comes from," I whispered to Crystal.

"So you get immortality from the dragon's eye," Crystal said. "Where does the power come from?"

"From the person who makes the eye glow. When my own life essence blends with another's, the combination along with the magic from the incantation will give me immortality."

"What happens to the other person, the one who makes the eye glow?"

"That person dies."

I gulped. If he got his hands on my locket, and if his plan worked, my mother would die.

Crystal's voice spiked. "What? You would do that to an innocent person?"

"No one is truly innocent, Crystal. Not I, not you, not your friends, which is why I forgave you for escaping. And the magic would be doing the work. I would merely be the beneficiary." He laughed. "Don't look at me that way. I am not a monster."

I clenched a fist as I whispered to Zoë the most recent part of the conversation.

"Does Thorne sleep?" Zoë asked.

"Maybe we can find out." I spoke a bit louder. "Crystal, can you let me know if Thorne ever sleeps?"

"I know you're not a monster," Crystal said. "You're just so different, you know, with all the spinning wind and sparks. And like how you never sleep. I mean, it's getting late, and I'm ready to fall asleep. How do you stay awake so much?"

"I do have a nightly dormant period. It lasts only about two hours, and I do it while you are sleeping, which is why you have never seen it."

"Oh, good plan. You don't have to worry about anyone trying to escape while you're dormant."

"And I'm telling you now because the exits are all sealed and protected."

"What time do you usually go dormant?"

Thorne chuckled. "Why so many questions? Do you think you'll be able to attack me during my dormancy? You can't possibly hurt me."

Metal rattled. "I can't do anything chained to the bed. Besides, why would I attack you? Life is better for me here than almost anywhere else I've been."

"Almost?" Thorne asked.

A pause ensued. "Well, I had a life before my parents died. It was good then."

"I know your story—stolen from Gamma Five when traffickers murdered your parents, thinking you might have special powers. Now that you are again with me, life will be good soon. When I become human, I will be like a father to you, not a twisted fart as you called me only hours ago."

"I was mad. You grabbed me like an old sack of dirt."

"I apologize. My anger got the best of me, as well." After a moment of silence, Thorne added, "Truce?"

"I guess so. If you trust me now."

"It seems that we have come to an understanding, so I will say that my trust in you has increased substantially."

The chain rattled again. "Enough to take this blasted chain off?"

"Not yet, but I will tell you that I am going to my study room to start my dormancy."

Crystal huffed. "That's not much trust. Not while I'm chained."

"A little at a time. Good night, Crystal."

"Good night."

After another few seconds of silence, I said, "Crystal, is he gone?"

"Yeah. He's gone."

"You did a great job pulling all that information out of him."

"Thanks. Being nice to that creep made me want to barf. But what good did it do? I'm still chained to a bed."

"Lots of good. Now I know it's safe to sneak in. I'm in the furnace room."

"You are? Blazes! That's great. But the door at the top of the stairs has a new lock on it. Thorne uses a card to get in and out."

"We'll work on it."

"We?" Crystal asked.

"I'm with Zoë, one of the kids who was on Ninety-five with the Ashers. Hold tight. We'll be there soon." I climbed to my feet and helped Zoë to hers. "Let's go. Quiet from here on out."

I led her up the stairs and tapped the doorknob with a finger. Like the other one, it was safe to touch. I shifted to the side and nodded at Zoë, signaling for her to try to open it.

In the light of the furnace fire, she stared at the knob, deep furrows in her brow. The knob turned slightly clockwise, then in the other direction.

Zoë shook her head. "It's not working. Maybe it's an electronic lock. I can't open those."

"Let me try." I wrapped my hand around the knob and flexed my biceps. The collar activated with a tingle that spread to the ink on my arm and sharpened as it ran into my hand. Electricity sparked along my palm and fingers as well as the knob, giving me a worse shock than usual.

After a couple of seconds, something sizzled, then clicked. I turned the knob and opened the door a few centimeters.

Zoë's eyes widened as she whispered, "Claw of the Dragon! What did you do?"

I leaned close to her. "I shorted the lock. I'll explain later."

Zoë held the knob while I grabbed a cooking pot from the stove and propped the door open. Guided by light from the furnace room, we walked through the kitchen. When we came to the lockbox on the counter, I tried to lift the lid, but the padlock held firm, and the box itself wouldn't move at all, likely bolted to the counter.

Zoë stared at the padlock. Within a few seconds, it clicked. She opened the box and picked up a stack of papers from inside. "Nothing else in there."

"Let's take them."

Zoë stuffed the papers under her shirt. "Done."

We walked past the dining room table, turned in the direction the children had gone when they went to bed, and followed a short corridor to the bottom of a stairway. Here, an oil lantern on the wall provided plenty of light to see the stairs.

I set a shushing finger to my lips and tiptoed up, silently begging each stair to stay silent. Behind me, Zoë copied my stealthy climb. When I reached the tenth stair, it let out a squeak.

Wincing, I drew my foot back and waited. Light from the lantern flickered across us, painting our statue-like shadows on the side wall. Now I wished I had hidden my locket somewhere Thorne would never find it.

I untied the cord and slipped it into my pants pocket. After waiting for a few more seconds, I set my foot on another part of the stair and slowly shifted my weight to it. It stayed silent. I pointed at the stair's safe spot for Zoë's sake and tiptoed the rest of the way up.

When Zoë joined me, we walked together through a corridor, another wall lantern lighting our way. Three doors stood closed on the left and three on the right. Straight ahead, a barely open door emitted a constant whoosh, maybe the sound Thorne made while in dormancy. A stench rode the air from that direction, giving more evidence that he was inside.

Metal clinked to the left. I looked that way. Crystal had to be sitting behind one of those three doors, but which one? After a few seconds, the chain rattled from the first door, a bit louder this time.

When I raised my foot to step toward it, Zoë grasped my arm and held me back. She stared at the knob. It turned slowly clockwise until it clicked. The door swung inward, spilling light into the room.

Crystal sat on the lower bed of a bunk, a chain attaching a shackle on her ankle to a metal ring on the bedpost. Still dressed in daytime clothes, she blinked at the light, then smiled and waved for us to enter.

I detached the lantern from the wall, walked in with Zoë, and closed the door behind us. I set the lantern on the floor and, after giving Crystal a hug, knelt at the side of her bed. I spoke as quietly as I could. "Do you know where the key to your shackle is?"

Crystal shook her head.

Zoë sat on the bed, lifted Crystal's ankle over her lap, and stared at the iron band. Zoë's face tensed. Lines dug into her forehead. A few seconds later, something clicked. She opened the shackle and set it on the floor.

Crystal drew her leg back and rubbed her ankle, offering a nod of thanks as she whispered, "Now *that's* a magic power."

Zoë smiled. "You're welcome."

"Did you look in the lockbox?" Crystal asked me.

"Yeah. Got some papers. We'll read them later."

"What're we going to do about the other kids? They're pitiful little things. Greta, the girl in the bed above me, is only six. She said three of them have died from bee stings since she got here, and that was only a few weeks ago. I think Thorne's new system is to toss them into the cave without training and see who can survive. They're scared to death."

I forked my fingers at them. "You and Zoë should go to my mother. Maybe she'll have rescued Dirk by then. If you can't find her, try to figure out where Oliver is. We know the Jaradian's name who bought him, so it shouldn't be too hard."

Crystal pointed at me. "And you're gonna stay and rescue these kids? All eight of them? By yourself?" She shook her head. "No way, sister. It'll be a huge job. I'm staying here with you."

"Same here," Zoë said. "Since Thorne's a swirl of wind, I can't fight him with my powers, but I can help kids get out."

Crystal grinned. "Yeah, tell me more about your powers. What are you, some kind of magic lock breaker?"

Zoë touched her head. "I can move things with my mind. Or stop things. I can even stop someone's heart."

"Really? How do you know? I mean, whose heart did you stop to test it?"

"I . . . um . . . I'd rather not talk about it." Zoë shrugged. "But Thorne doesn't have a heart. I'm no use against him."

"So you *did* stop someone's heart. He must've been a real rat's butt if you hated him that much."

"Crystal," I said. "Hush."

She frowned. "All right. I'll zip it."

Once again silence settled all around. Crystal broke it with a whispered "What's the plan?"

"Is anyone else chained?" I asked.

Crystal shook her head. "I was the only one. Thorne doesn't trust me yet."

"Then let's get everyone out while he's dormant."

"That'll make a lot of noise. He's bound to wake up."

I looked around the room. "Maybe we could cause a distraction."

"Like an emergency?" Crystal locked her gaze on the lantern I had brought in. "Maybe a fire?"

I looked at the flaming wick. "A fire might work, but fire sucks air out of a room. It could actually kill Thorne."

"All the better," Zoë said. "Dead villain. Easier escape."

I frowned but stayed quiet.

Crystal touched my arm. "Listen, Megan, I know you're all about saving lives, but getting rid of Thorne means we *will* save lives, kids' lives, the kids who live here now and no telling how many kids later. They're dropping like flies."

"She's right," Zoë said. "He's a monster."

"I know. I know." I heaved a sigh. In my mind, I had criticized others for rationalizing their killings, including my own mother. But now, facing the choice myself when every other option seemed a lot worse, I couldn't see a way to avoid it. "I guess we might as well go for the throat and start the fire in Thorne's room."

"Or maybe in front of his door," Zoë said. "Less chance of waking him up that way."

"True." I scanned the room again. "Any fuel for a fire around here besides lamp oil?"

"Just bedcovers."

"Bring them. Let's do it before I change my mind." The lantern in hand, I tiptoed into the hall, Crystal and Zoë following, Crystal with her blanket and pillow in her arms. I set my ear close to Thorne's door. The whooshing sound came through again, and the stench was worse than ever. He had to be in there.

Crystal laid her bedding in front of the door and spread it out. I poured lamp oil over the material and whispered, "I'll stand here while you two try to get everyone out quietly. If I hear Thorne come toward the door, I'll light the fire."

Crystal nodded and hurried back to her room while Zoë opened a different bedroom door and peeked inside. Seconds later, Crystal reappeared in the hall leading Greta to the stairs. Rubbing her eyes, the little girl scampered down with slapping footsteps.

I cringed. She was too loud, much too loud. And she was just the first. This wasn't going to work. I had to start the fire now.

My hands trembling, I set the lantern's flame to an edge of the blanket. When the fire caught and began spreading, I hissed, "Crystal. Full alarm mode. Get everyone out of here. Zoë, get them organized as they come down."

Zoë raced down the stairs while Crystal ran to the bedroom across the hall from hers, threw open the door, and called, "Jeremy! Fire! Get out!"

A boy about Crystal's age walked stiff-legged from the room, leading a smaller boy by the hand. Crystal and I ran to the other rooms, opened the doors, and shouted the fire alarm. Soon, the other children filled the hall and hustled toward the stairs.

After we checked the beds for any stragglers, Crystal and I stood at the top of the stairs and looked at Thorne's room. The fire had taken hold of the door and the adjacent walls and now crawled toward the ceiling. Still, he stayed inside. Maybe his dormancy state kept him from hearing sounds. This might be an easy escape after all.

We hurried downstairs and found Zoë huddling with the kids in the dining area, her arms around Greta. "They're scared," Zoë said, "but they're being brave."

I pointed at the door leading to the furnace room and said in Humaniversal, "Go! Hurry!"

"Zoë and I will lead them," Crystal said. "You follow at the end of the line." She took the hand of the biggest boy. "Everyone make a chain!" When we linked hands, with Zoë at the middle and me at the tail holding Greta's hand, Crystal led the procession out the door and down the stairs toward the furnace room.

As I neared the furnace stairway, a moan emanated from upstairs. I halted and released Greta. "Zoë," I called. "Head for the room my mother took us to. I'll be right behind you."

"Don't go soft," Zoë called back, now nearing the top of the furnace room stairs. "Thorne needs to die."

"I heard someone moan. It didn't sound like Thorne."

"Okay. But hurry."

I jogged back to the bedroom stairway and looked up. Smoke coiled down in a slow spin, reminding me of Thorne. Maybe that moan really did come from him. Now that the kids had escaped, should I check to make sure he was dead? Or maybe to save him? The pull from both sides seemed to be ripping my soul in two.

I held my breath, ran upstairs into a wall of smoky heat, and stood in front of Thorne's blazing doorway. The flames licked the door's panel and crawled along the jambs, sparking and curling. The image raised a reminder of the flames in the furnace when the dragon's form took shape in the same twisting pattern.

The Astral Dragon's words returned to mind from when I was lying clinically dead, waiting for Oliver to make a decision. *Life is a gift that must be protected.*

And now I had to make a decision. Was Thorne's life also a protected gift, or had he forfeited protection because of his cruelty? Did he deserve revenge instead of mercy?

Nearly choking now in the smoke, I gritted my teeth. I couldn't let this happen. I had to choose mercy and let the Astral Dragon decide who deserved to die.

I kicked the scorched blanket from Thorne's doorway. Since the fire had burned the jamb, the door stood ajar, illuminated by flames that crackled along the ceiling and surrounding walls.

Using my foot, I pushed the door fully open. Inside, flames roared, burning piles of wadded paper and the legs of a worktable covered with liquid-filled glass jars. In one jar, green liquid bubbled to the top, flowed over the lip, and spilled to the table's surface. Fire crept toward the growing green pool. If it was flammable, I had to hurry.

I scanned the room for Thorne, but nothing spun anywhere. I shouted, "Thorne? Are you here? I'll try to help you escape. We need to get out right now."

I covered my mouth with my shirt, inhaled a smoke-saturated gulp of air, and held my breath again as I listened. Only the fire answered with pops and hisses.

Was I too late? If the fire absorbed him, it might not have left any trace. I bit my lip hard. Had I killed Thorne?

Just as I turned to leave, an explosion erupted from the table. The force sent me flying over the rail and down the stairwell. I slammed into the steps, hands first, and tumbled to the bottom. My head crashed against the floor. Pain ripped through my skull and down my spine.

From above, smoke billowed down. Fire swarmed across the stairs and walls, running fast. My limbs shaking, I pushed up and climbed to a standing position. My lungs burned. I coughed hard, again and again. When I took a step, my knee buckled. I fell once more, this time hitting the floor chin first.

I rolled to my back and tried to get up, but my legs wouldn't budge. I coughed as I struggled to spit out each word. "Oliver . . . help. . . . Dirk . . . Zoë . . . anyone. . . . Help."

As I lay there, dark spots coated my vision, swelling in size. The room spun in dizzying circles while fire and smoke cascaded from above like an erupting volcano. Knowing that I was losing consciousness yet again, I battled to stay awake. This time, blacking out meant certain death. In spite of my efforts, the darkness quickly took over, and everything faded away.

Cold air slapped my face, jerking me awake. I tried to open my eyes, but they seemed glued shut. My limbs refused to move, dangling limply as if someone were carrying me. Every few seconds a foul smell wafted by, then the breeze carried it away until the next invasion of putrid air arrived for another assault.

A whisper came from somewhere, but only in one ear. "Megan, it's Oliver. I hope you left your commlink on. I don't know if you can hear me or not. I guess you're not answering because you can't risk talking, so I'll just talk and let you know what's going on. I'm with Crystal, Zoë, Perdantus, and Quixon in a secret room Zoë says you know about. Dirk keeps trying to call us on the commlink, but there's a bunch of static. We heard enough to figure out that your mother rescued him, but Admiral Fairbanks caught her while Dirk got away. We're not sure where he is now. Maybe he's still at the *Nebula One* trying to help your mother.

"Anyway, we heard your call for help. Crystal tried to go back into the house, but one of Thorne's kids stopped her because the fire was too dangerous. The house burned to the ground, and we're hoping . . ." His voice cracked. "We're hoping you escaped somehow."

"Oliver," Crystal said, "tell her how you got away."

"Right." Oliver's voice steadied. "I got away because Quixon bought me and some other kids from Castol. He used the money your mother bought you with. Then we ran into Zoë and Crystal herding Thorne's kids down the street in the middle of the night. And Perdantus spotted us from the air."

"So now we're back at the hideout," Crystal said. "We're going to take all the kids to the Tauranta temple and ask Melda to watch over them there. The battle storm's over, so we can trust her now."

"Right," Oliver said. "Crystal, Zoë, and Quixon will lead the kids to the temple, and I'm coming to look for you. I'll take Perdantus with me. If I get in trouble, he'll come back to tell Crystal."

Silence ensued. The only sounds came from below, steady footsteps crunching ice, one after another, never changing pace. Now that my mind had cleared a bit, the picture took shape. Someone was carrying me, someone strong enough to do so for quite a while without getting tired. An adult human? A Jaradian? A Tauranta? The recurring odor told me he might be a Jaradian, but the smell wasn't quite the same. Still, my eyes wouldn't open to find out.

A frigid blast of wind pierced my clothes, making me shiver. The footsteps halted. My carrier set me down feetfirst. "Megan, try to stand." It was a human male's voice, speaking Alpha One. "Don't worry. I've got you."

I steeled my legs. They worked well enough to balance my body, but my head pounded with throbbing pain, making it hard to stay upright. I peeled my eyes open and looked at my rescuer's barely visible face. Former First Mate Gavin Foster stood before me, his hands close to my shoulders as if ready to catch me. "Are you all right?"

"Yeah." I lifted my legs in turn. "Yeah, I think so."

"Good. We still have a couple of kilometers to go. If you don't think you can walk, I'll keep carrying you."

Oliver's voice entered my ear. "Megan, it's me. I heard your voice. Man, it's great to know you're alive. Listen. I'm on a city street near the factory. I can tell you're with someone so you might not want to talk directly to me. Try to give me clues if you can."

I tested my legs again. They seemed stronger now. "Thanks, Gavin, but I can walk."

"Good. Let's go."

As we walked side by side, the odor returned, stronger than ever. "What is that awful smell?"

Gavin pointed at his shoes. "I stepped in something disgusting. It won't rub off. Now come on. We need to move. It's freezing out here."

Still trying to clear my vision, I blinked at him. Everything seemed odd. Something was definitely wrong, but my scrambled brain couldn't put it all together. Could I have suffered a concussion? "Where are you taking me?"

"To the *Astral Dragon*."

"To the *Astral Dragon*?" I repeated for Oliver's sake. "Why?"

"Simple. It's warm and safe there. No slavers. No bramble bees. No houses on fire."

"Right. The fire. How did I get out of it?"

"I've been spying on Thorne. Trying to break up his operation. When all of the kids got out of the house except you, I went in and found you unconscious. By the time I carried you outside, the other kids had left the area."

"So you saved me."

"Yeah." He cleared his throat. "Yeah, I saved you."

Normally I looked adults in the eye, especially ones who deserved respect, but I couldn't with Gavin. I lowered my head. "Well . . . um . . . thanks, Gavin. Thanks a lot."

"You're welcome, Megan."

I expected him to add some kind of I-told-you-so comment, that I had misjudged him all along, but it didn't come. I looked around. The lights of Bassolith shone far away. Above, three moons cast more light, allowing a view of the frozen river alongside our path. I needed to give Oliver more guidance, but if we continued toward the *Astral Dragon*, would my commlink broadcast far enough to reach the

Nebula Nine to be boosted back to him? "I see the river on the right, and Bassolith's behind us. Exactly where are we?"

"Between the city and the bay. I'm not sure exactly how far from either one. Why?"

"Just wondering how far from my friends I am."

Without breaking stride, he looked at me. "Any idea where they went?"

"I'm not sure. I was trying to get the slave kids out of the fire, and I stayed to rescue Thorne. But something exploded, and I fell down the stairs."

His brow knitted tightly. "You wanted to rescue Thorne? A slaver? Why? Didn't he deserve to die?"

"Yeah, he did." I shrugged. "I guess I thought he was still worth saving."

"I see. You hoped your mercy would bring him around." Gavin nodded, his lips pressed firmly together. "Maybe so. Maybe so."

I blinked at him. "You're acting weird, Gavin. What's gotten into you?"

He set a hand on his chest. "You think you know me, but you don't. The me you knew before? The dolt who hated you? That was all an act. I have been your mother's ally for a long time."

I lagged behind a couple of steps, having trouble keeping up with his long-legged pace. "Does she know that?"

He shook his head sadly. "Not anymore. She accused me of infecting the ship with a virus, but I couldn't convince her that I didn't."

I jogged to his side and marched at his pace. "Then help me find her, and we'll convince her together."

"I'll do what I can, but if the admiral captured her, she might be dead by now. She had a death sentence. By law, he can summarily execute her."

Aching to know if she was still alive, I stealthily reached to my neck for my locket's cord, but it wasn't there. Then I remembered that I had put it in my pocket. I checked both pockets. Empty. Maybe it fell out when I dropped down the stairwell.

I bit my lip hard, battling the pounding in my head. Could I have put it somewhere else? Or maybe Gavin took it from me. That seemed far more likely. He had done it before.

He halted, withdrew a sheet of paper from his pants pocket, and angled the front toward the largest of the three moons. "The river's frozen, but the ice is too thin to walk on. There's a footbridge not far from here. Now that you're on your feet, we'll get to the ship pretty soon."

"Is that a map?" I said as I tried to get a look at the page.

"Yes." He began walking again as he stuffed the map back into his pocket. "Better to be ready than to be lost. The ship is near a swamp, and I want to make sure I go around it instead of wading through it."

I caught up and again kept pace at his side. "Does the map have a name for the swamp?"

"No, but the bridge is called Addock's Crossing."

"Addock's Crossing," I repeated, again for Oliver's ears.

"I know where that is," Oliver said. "Listen, I'm only picking up some of your conversation. Lots of static. But I think I figured it out. I'm on my way. I'll send Perdantus ahead to scout the area."

Gavin and I crossed the footbridge, a wooden arch over the frozen river. As we marched on, a feeling in my gut amplified. Something was definitely wrong, but my throbbing head still wouldn't let me put the puzzle pieces in place.

Soon, we strode into a slightly upsloping field of wiry knee-high grass. Hoping to secretly talk to Oliver, I lagged behind again. Just as I opened my mouth, Perdantus landed on my shoulder and whispered in his chirping language, "Good. I have found you. I will fly back to Oliver and report your location."

I kept my voice low as well. "Before you do that, fly ahead and see if you can find a space cruiser near a swamp. Let me know."

"I will." He leaped off my shoulder and flew into the cover of darkness. Gavin didn't seem to notice.

I stayed quiet. No sense risking Gavin hearing me talk to Oliver. Perdantus would take care of getting us all together.

After we walked a few more minutes in silence, Perdantus returned and again perched on my shoulder. "There is, indeed, a space cruiser about three hundred human paces ahead. I led your mother to a similar ship, but it was at a different location. Perhaps it is the same one, and it has moved."

"What color is it?"

"It is difficult to tell with so little light, but I believe it is dull silver."

"Not black?"

"Definitely not black. If it were, I don't think I could have located it from the air."

I started putting the puzzle pieces together. The Willow Wind said that my mother landed her ship on the opposite side of Bassolith from where we were now. And Gavin couldn't have flown the *Astral Dragon* because my mother revoked his clearance. And the color was wrong. This silvery ship that lay ahead couldn't be the *Astral Dragon*. "Then Gavin's leading me into a trap. I'll try to sneak away. Go tell Oliver."

"Yes, of course." He flew away to my rear.

I slowed my pace further, putting more distance between Gavin and me. The field offered no place to hide, though it gave way to a forest well ahead. Which would be better? Wait to find a hiding place in the forest or turn around now and run? With my head still throbbing and my legs weak, I probably couldn't outrun Gavin unless I had a good head start.

He glanced back. "Tired?"

"Yeah, but don't worry about me. I'll make it."

"The offer to carry you still stands. On my back if you want."

"No, thanks." I quickened my pace. "I'll keep up."

"Suit yourself."

Now that Gavin had seen me falling behind, he continued glancing at me every few seconds. Trying to bolt in the opposite direction was no longer an option. I could try to shock him, but I couldn't know how effective that would be.

When we reached the forest, Gavin stopped and scanned the tree line. I halted next to him. "What are you looking for?"

"A path through the woods. It's easy to find in daylight, but not so much at night."

Hoping to delay as long as possible, I walked slowly along the tree line. "Is it a dirt path?"

"Dirt covered with fallen leaves. Maybe iced over now."

"I don't see anything in this direction."

"Hmmm." He turned the other way. "Let's look over here."

I ducked into the forest, plunged several paces deep, and hid behind a tree while peeking around the trunk. Gavin pivoted back and set a fist on his hip. "Really, Megan? You're hiding from me? Don't be a foolish child."

I cocked my head. *Foolish child?* That definitely didn't sound like Gavin.

At that moment, my brain cleared, and more puzzle pieces clicked into place—Gavin's long absence, his strange behavior, his persistent odor, his presence at the burning house, Thorne's statement about absorbing physicality. This man wasn't Gavin at all. Thorne had killed him and taken his body. Not only that, Thorne had my locket and planned to use it to take my mother's life essence for himself. I had to stop him.

Thorne stalked into the forest, barely visible in the darkness as he zigzagged around trees toward me. He would be here in seconds. I could either run or fight, but if I ran, that would leave my mother vulnerable. I had to fight.

I flexed my biceps. My bracelets tingled. Electricity arced across my palms and fingers. Hoping to make him do something rash, I stepped into the open. "I figured out who you are, Thorne."

He lunged with his arms outstretched. When he came within reach, I grasped his wrists. Electricity surged into him. He backpedaled, halted, and blinked at me stupidly. Sparks passed across his eyes, as if he were an electronic robot. A moment later, he shook free of his stupor and lunged again.

My calf muscles now supercharged, I leaped straight up, caught a limb, and slammed my foot into his face. He backpedaled again, smacked his head against a tree, and collapsed, motionless.

I dropped to the ground and crept toward him. I had to get my locket back. Yet, although he appeared to be unconscious, stepping within his reach might be a huge mistake. "Oliver," I hissed. "Where are you?"

No one answered. Maybe I was too far from the *Nine* now. But Perdantus had plenty of time to report my location. Oliver had to be closing in.

I cupped my hands around my mouth and called, "Oliver, I'm here."

The wind and trees seemed to swallow my words. When I shouted again, Oliver's voice came through the woods instead of my comm-link: "I'm coming."

Seconds later, he pushed through some underbrush and stood next to the tree where Thorne lay. I wrapped my arms around him and hugged him close. "Man, it's good to see you."

"You, too." After returning my hug, he pulled back and stared at Thorne. "Looks like you didn't need me, though."

"I got lucky."

"I heard a few words a minute ago. Is this guy really Thorne?"

I nodded. "He transformed into Gavin and was trying to trick me into thinking we were going to the *Astral Dragon*. But it's probably the *Nebula One* up ahead somewhere."

"We'll find out soon. Perdantus saw a path through the forest. He's scouting ahead."

Crystal's voice came through the commlink. "You two sound like you're a million kilometers away, but I think I figured out what's going on. Here's my report. The kids are all safe at the temple. Quixon's coming with Zoë and me to the *Nebula Nine*. We're going to fly it to the *Astral Dragon*. As long as the admiral's goons aren't guarding the *Dragon*, we can bring her to pick you up and rescue your mom. I just hope Emerson will help me fly the *Nine*. I know you listed me as an official navigator, but since you won't be there, you never know if he's going to dust off some fossilized rule and not let me fly."

"No worries. He'll let you fly. Just be careful. We'll meet up with you as soon as we can." Crystal didn't answer. Maybe my signal was no longer getting to the *Nine* at all.

I turned to Oliver. "Okay, while we're waiting for Perdantus,

I need you to stand guard while I check Thorne for my locket." I crouched next to Thorne's body and pulled his shirt's plackets open. Just as I suspected, the locket lay on his chest, attached to its leather cord.

My hands trembling, I opened the locket's secret clasp and found the dragon's eye. It glowed with its usual red light. My throat tightened as I squeaked, "My mother's still alive."

"Great. Take it, and I'll whistle for Perdantus."

While Oliver whistled, I reached behind Thorne's neck and tried to untie the cord, but the knot wouldn't give way. Something rustled in the brush. I had to hurry. I dug into the cord with my fingernails. Still no luck. Blazes! Why wouldn't it come loose?

Four soldiers in military uniforms burst through the brush, aiming long-barreled laser blasters, two at me and two at Oliver. I jerked on the cord once more, but it refused to break. One of the soldiers grabbed my arm and hauled me to my feet.

I flexed my biceps, twisted free, and latched on to his wrist, delivering a jolt. He yelped and staggered back. Another soldier whacked me in the nose with the butt of his gun. Blood sprayed. Pain rattled my skull. My knees buckled, and I fell to my backside.

Oliver charged. A different soldier shot him in the shoulder with a laser, drilling a hole through to the other side. Oliver cried out and dropped to his knees. He pressed a hand against his shoulder as smoke rose between his fingers, though no blood flowed. The heat of the laser blast likely cauterized the vessels within.

While the soldiers aimed their guns at us, yet another soldier appeared through the brush. Tall and gray-haired with equally gray bushy eyebrows and mustache, he wore a military jacket adorned with three silver stars, an admiral's designation.

He waved a hand. "Lower your weapons. They're just children."

The soldier I jolted shook his arm. "Beg your pardon, Admiral, but the girl can bite like a bear."

The admiral chuckled. "No surprise. She's the daughter of Anne Willis." As he stared at me, his green eyes sparkled. "So we finally meet, Megan. It's a pleasure."

Something fluttered at the corner of my eye—Perdantus alighting on a limb over my head. I intentionally avoided looking directly at him as I wiped blood from under my nose. "The pleasure's all yours, Admiral Fairbanks."

He withdrew a handkerchief from his pants pocket and tossed it to my lap. "I see that you inherited your mother's acerbic wit."

"And her hatred of brutal tyrants like you." I picked up the hand-kerchief and held it over my nose. "We know you're neck-deep in the child-slave trade."

"Nonsense. I am here to break up the slave trading and arrest all the participants."

"Oh, really?" I said with a sarcastic tone. "How many prisoners have you caught?"

He raised fingers as he replied. "A Jaradian named Castol and a Tauranta named Essen, both of whom we killed when they tried to escape."

I concealed a hard swallow. I had heard it all before. The trying-to-escape story was just an excuse. The admiral didn't need them, so they were summarily executed.

"I also have your mother," the admiral continued, "and now the two of you."

I lowered the handkerchief. "Us? Are you crazy? We busted Thorne's operation wide open. We rescued the kids he enslaved."

"Stole them, you mean. Your mother planned to sell them to the highest bidder. We know for a fact that she was at the most recent market buying children and that you've been helping her."

"What? No, she wasn't. I mean—" I clammed up. Explaining her presence at the market would only make the situation worse.

"And I planned to arrest Thorne, but it seems that he died in a fire."

"No." I pointed at Thorne. "He's right there. He transformed into a human."

The admiral chuckled again. "That gun butt to the nose must have caused a concussion. You know Gavin Foster. He's been your moth-er's ally, and he tried to be a double agent by feeding information to me to get a ransom I put on your mother's head. Worthless information, I might add. Just a puny mouse who couldn't figure out which cat would win. Now he's yet another prisoner to add to my count."

I stared into the admiral's steady eyes, then looked at each of his soldiers as they continued aiming their guns, unwavering, unmoved. It would do no good to tell anyone the truth. I dabbed my nose. The bleeding had stopped. "So what are you going to do with us?"

"Take you to my ship. Since you are now of age, I can have you executed according to the terms of your original sentence. If, however, you cooperate with my interrogation, I will be lenient and fly you to the Beta system where you will be imprisoned on Beta Four." He nodded toward Oliver. "He will be put on trial as an accessory to slave trafficking, but considering that he was a slave himself, I think the court will go easy on him, especially when I personally vouch for him. His potential is much greater than he realizes. Which is why . . ." The admiral glared at the soldier who shot Oliver. "I will make sure that no more harm comes to him."

I looked at Oliver. He looked back at me, his expression baffled. The admiral probably knew about Oliver's Gamma Five birth and maybe the fact that he never got sick. But did he know about the enhancing power of the dragon's eye? Maybe soon we would find out.

The admiral gestured toward one of the soldiers. "Get them up. Two of you carry Foster. And don't let the girl touch you with her hands."

A soldier set a gun barrel at the back of my head. "Let's go."

Oliver growled. "Leave her alone." He stood and reached a hand toward me, his other hand still covering his laser wound. "C'mon."

As I rode his pull, I glanced up. Perdantus continued watching, probably to gather all the information he could before going for help.

When I straightened, the admiral looked at the side of my head. "Well, well, well. What is this?" He pushed a finger into my ear, peeled off my commlink and dropped it on the ground, then did the same to Oliver before turning toward me again. "With whom were you communicating, pirate girl?"

I spat on the ground. "As if I'd tell you."

"Oh, so dramatic." The admiral smiled. "Well, you'll cool your heels in a prison cell while we gather your friends. We'll soon have you all."

The soldiers prodded our backs with their guns. We marched single file through the woods, Oliver leading the procession and the light of dawn illuminating our way. Behind us, the sound of fluttering wings let me know that Perdantus was flying for help.

When we reached a wide, leaf-covered path, we walked along it, Oliver and me abreast, a soldier behind each of us. Now that Oliver had uncovered his wound, I could see his scorched, torn shirt and a black circle on his skin. It had to hurt terribly, but he did nothing more than wince as we walked. His healing powers were probably helping a lot. Yet, after his failure with healing Renalda and since I no longer had the dragon's eye, I couldn't be sure.

I wanted so badly to talk to him, to put our heads together and plan an ingenious escape. With my own head still pounding, worsened by the butt to the nose, I couldn't come up with a plan myself. It seemed like the puzzle pieces had scattered once more.

One fact, however, seemed clear. Admiral Fairbanks knew that my slave-trading accusations against him were true. He simply invented lies to cover for himself. He also believed Thorne was Gavin. Maybe I could use that to my advantage. But how? At this point I had no idea, and since Perdantus was our only means to communicate, I couldn't count on our friends to help us in time.

I sighed. Even if they could find us, we needed more help than a few kids and a half-drunk Jaradian could provide. In spite of the brightening skies, the world seemed darker than ever.

30

We walked out of the forest and into a clearing. A huge silver space cruiser sat straight ahead, its front access hatch making a ramp to the ground. Its wings spanned from the edge of the forest to a swamp on its far side. Although I had seen this ship before, it was in space at the time. In this more enclosed area, it looked much bigger.

The two soldiers carrying Thorne set him down on his feet. Now conscious but unsteady, he hobbled up the ramp with one of them at each side and the admiral close behind. Thorne's voice reached us. "I swear I've been loyal to the Alliance. I brought Megan, didn't I?"

The other two soldiers prodded our backs, forcing us to ascend the ramp. With every step, my head throbbed. Marching into this beast of a spaceship felt like stepping into the jaws of an enormous shark.

I whispered to Oliver, "How's your shoulder?"

"It stings. Mostly healed. How's your head?"

Not wanting him to worry, a lie came to mind—that I was fine— but I couldn't speak it. Not to Oliver. "It hurts, but I'll be all right."

When we reached the top of the ramp, we walked into the ship's anteroom, a massive lobby with reflective, marble-like floors, a chamber they probably used to greet important guests. A ramp at each side led up to the bridge where Admiral Fairbanks stood next to a captain's console seat.

"Max," he said as the two soldiers helped Thorne into a wheelchair, "alert Dr. Wexel that we have a new prisoner who appears to have suffered a blow to the head."

"Alert commencing." The feminine computer voice came from hidden speakers.

"Add three new prisoners to the list," the admiral continued. "Gavin Foster, Oliver Tillman, and Megan Willis. I'm sure all three are in the database."

"List updated," Max said.

The admiral nodded at the two soldiers guarding Oliver and me. "You two take them to the brig. Separate cells, but make sure Megan can see her mother."

The soldiers prodded our backs once more and guided us up the left-side ramp. As we passed Thorne on the bridge, he glared at me from the wheelchair but said nothing. His stare made me shudder. He still planned to use the dragon's eye to gain immortality and kill my mother in the process. But how? He was sure to have a devious plan, and if he wanted to maintain his charade as Gavin, he would probably have to avoid being examined by the doctor. Yet, he was crafty enough to pull it off.

A soldier slid a card through a reader mounted on a wall next to an elevator. The door opened with a noise that sounded like the *snick* of a blade cutting leather. The soldier gestured with his gun for us to get in. When we did, he followed, and the second soldier came after, pushing Thorne's wheelchair. Once we stood in the elevator car, the soldiers kept their weapons aimed, likely fearing my touch.

As we rode upward, I eyed their tense faces. They were worried, a good sign. Since they were nervous about transporting two kids, they probably weren't the bravest soldiers the admiral could have sent. With only these two watching us, maybe I could overpower them with an electric shock, but it had to be big enough to knock them out, which might deliver a jolt to me as well. But if I got the chance, I had to take it.

We exited the car into a large chamber. To our right, a huge window showed a view of the swamp. One of our guards prodded us to walk to the left while the other pushed Thorne's chair behind us. In that direction, a corridor exited the room with four prison cells lining each side. Lamps on the ceiling cast fluorescent light, illuminating the cells. In the first one on the left, a gray parka lay a few centimeters behind the vertical bars.

I ran ahead to the cell. Inside, my mother stood against the back wall with her wrists in manacles, fastened to the wall by chains. I grasped two of the cell's metal bars. "Mama!"

"Megan!" She stepped toward me, but the chains tightened, holding her in place.

I released the bars and flexed my biceps, energizing the bracelets. "Are you all right?"

"Unharmed." She jerked against a chain. "But not exactly all right."

I whispered, "I understand. I'm going to try to get you out." I turned away from the guards, my electrically charged hands hidden in front of me, then glanced back. The guards wheeled Thorne toward me with Oliver a step or two ahead of them. Thorne eyed me. He knew I was up to something, but he stayed quiet.

I flexed my electrified fingers. I had to disable the guards, but could I do it without killing them? Maybe. Maybe not. Another horrible choice approached like a deadly phantom, and my decision couldn't wait.

"Max," a guard said as they arrived, "open cell number two." A door on the right side of the corridor clanked open. "This is your new home, Megan. Get in."

I kept my back toward the guard. "No. I need to talk to my mother."

"You can talk to her from your cell." He grabbed my arm and pulled.

I spun, leaped, and wrapped my legs around the guard's torso and my hands around his throat. He thrashed and tried to throw me off, but I hung on as electricity surged into him.

"Let him go!" the other guard yelled as he aimed his gun at me.

Oliver batted the gun to the side and punched the guard in the stomach. He swatted Oliver in the head with the gun, knocking him down. On the floor, Oliver bit the guard's ankle and locked his jaws in place.

While Oliver's guard tried to shake him loose, my guard dropped to his knees, trembling at the jolts coming from my hands. Shock waves coursed through me as well, but I held on, weakening by the second as I gasped for breath. Finally, the guard keeled over, and I rode his body to the floor. I let go of his throat and watched his spasmodic respiration. He wasn't dead, but he might not last long.

I leaped over to the other guard, snatched the gun away, and set the barrel against his chin. "It's all right, Oliver. I got him."

Oliver stood and spat a stream of blood next to Thorne's wheelchair. "Yuck. I never want to do that again."

Thorne shifted his feet to dodge the blood. "Unsavory, Oliver, but well done."

"Yeah, well, the admiral told them not to hurt me. Otherwise, I might've gotten shot."

"Good point." I stepped back and nodded toward the bitten guard. "Get in the cell."

He walked in and turned toward me.

"Now close it."

"Can't. Only Max can close it. And she won't recognize your voice."

I rolled my eyes. "Well, genius, then you tell her to close it and open my mother's cell."

He sneered. "Fat chance, pirate."

Thorne laughed. "I'm sure a hole in his leg will persuade him."

"Exactly what I was thinking." I shot the laser into the ankle Oliver had bitten. The guard shouted a string of obscenities while hopping on one foot. "All right. I'll tell her." When he settled, he spoke into the air. "Max, close cell number two and open number one."

His door slid closed, and my mother's opened.

"Now tell Max to strip your security clearance from this level."

He sighed. "Max, remove my access to the cell-block level."

"Provide a reason," Max said.

"Code six. Transferring to another vessel."

"Acknowledged. Security clearance removed."

I extended my hand. "I need the key to the chains."

"I don't have it."

I aimed the gun again. "I can burn a hole through your other leg."

He raised a hand. "No. Seriously. I don't have it." He turned his pockets inside out. "See?"

"Then where is it?"

"In the security office."

The elevator's *snick* sounded along with a new voice. "What's all the commotion up here?"

I spun that way. The admiral stood next to the open elevator car, a laser blaster in hand.

My mother hissed, "Shoot him, Megan. Shoot him now before it's too late."

Just as I took aim, the admiral fired. A laser beam sliced across my hand and ripped the gun from my grasp. It clattered to the floor, sizzling. Oliver stepped in front of me, but I shoved him to the side and glared at the admiral. A gash along my thumb smoked, burning like crazy, but I refused to grimace.

Admiral Fairbanks looked past me. "I see that you incapacitated one of my men and locked another in a cell."

I kept my hard stare fixed on him as I flexed my biceps, ready to shock him if he stepped close enough. "Is it still a pleasure to meet me?"

"The pleasure is fading. You are far more formidable than I realized." Keeping his distance, he waved his gun. "You and Oliver get in the cell with your mother."

New tingles ran along my arms, building more slowly this time, but with this Nebula-class ship recharging my bracelets, the power would be ready soon. "And if we don't?"

"I will kill your mother."

I glanced back at the downed guard's gun lying on the floor about two steps behind me. Maybe one of us could grab it before the admiral could fire again.

"Admiral Fairbanks," Thorne said as he wheeled toward the gun. "Let's not make rash decisions." He leaned over the side of his chair, picked up the gun, and tossed it toward the admiral. It slid on the floor and bumped against his feet.

"Good choice, Foster." The admiral smiled. "I'm not surprised that you want to protect Anne. I always suspected the rumors were true. With my bounty reward in hand, you could present quite a handsome lure to a greedy pirate."

Thorne smiled in a boyish way. "I confess that I am enamored with her."

New hot fury roared into my head. Gavin was enamored with my mother? The thought disgusted me.

The admiral chuckled. "Confession is good for the soul."

"Is that so?" Thorne returned the admiral's smile in a sneering way. "What about you? Is there anything you'd like to confess? Maybe how you sold eight children from Delta Ninety-five to slave traders for a tidy profit?"

I caught a glimpse of the guard in the cell. The furrows in his brow gave away more than a little suspicion. Thorne was apparently planting as many seeds of doubt as possible.

"Nonsense," the admiral said. "I rescued those children. They're on sanctuary planets now."

"Really? Including Greta, an eight-year-old you sold to Thorne only a few weeks ago for exactly two hundred forty mesots? I sent a recording of her testimony to an audio vault that will release the file to Judge Philpot if I don't regularly prevent the transmission."

The admiral nodded. "In other words, if I kill you, the judge gets the testimony. A kill switch."

"That's right."

"Very clever."

"Admiral?" the guard said from the cell. "Are you saying Foster's telling the truth?"

"Of course not. Don't be ridiculous." The admiral called out, "Max, open cell number two." When the door slid open, he nodded toward the guard in the cell. "Put Foster in."

The guard exited the cell and wheeled Thorne inside.

The admiral picked up the other gun and tossed it toward the guard. When he caught it, the admiral waved a hand. "If Oliver and Megan refuse to get in, kill Anne."

The guard aimed the gun at my mother. "You heard him."

I shut off the electricity to my hands. As Oliver and I shuffled into cell one, I muttered, "Cowards."

"Max," the admiral said, "close cells one and two."

Both doors shut with a clank. I rushed to my mother and gave her a hug. When I drew back, I looked into her weary eyes. "Are you okay?"

"As good as can be expected." She gave me a smile, though I could tell it was forced. "Keep the faith, Megan. We'll work this out somehow."

The admiral walked to our bars and looked in. His smug expression nauseated me. "Well, it looks like you managed to get locked up together. Congratulations. Now make yourselves comfortable. It's a long flight to the Beta system."

He turned toward the guard, set the gun close to his forehead, and fired. A laser beam drilled through his skull and zipped out the other side, nearly hitting Thorne as it slammed against his cell wall. The guard's eyes rolled upward, and he collapsed on the floor.

I gasped. My mother clenched a fist and whispered, "You're a dead man, Fairbanks."

He crouched next to the guard I had shocked and set a hand on his throat. "Well, Megan, this man is dead. Now you have two murders on your record."

"Two murders?" I lunged forward and slapped a cell bar. "You're out of your mind!"

"Not at all." The admiral rose and walked to our cell. "I will charge you with the murders of both of these guards. And don't bother saying you have witnesses that will testify otherwise. Who will believe a pirate or her allies?"

My mother jerked her chains, making them rattle hard. "I'll submit to a lie-detector test. Will you?"

He let out a tsking sound. "Oh, Anne, are you still hoping that a fair trial is possible?"

She growled. "There was a day when justice ruled the galaxy, but when jackasses like you got power, justice wilted and died."

The admiral laughed. "I would love to stay and hear more of your entertaining moralisms, but it's time for me to find Greta and coerce a denial of her earlier testimony." He looked toward the ceiling. "Max, summon a crew of four to remove two corpses from the cell block, and erase all audio recorded here today."

"Summoning crew," Max said. "Audio erased."

The admiral turned and walked toward the elevator, calling back, "Needless to say, the doctor will not be paying a visit. I will see you again soon."

When the sound of the elevator's closing door reached us, I grabbed the bars and shouted. "Thorne! You rat! Why did you help him?"

He rose from his chair, walked shakily to his own bars, and grasped them for support. "Just a way to stay alive, Megan. From his perspective, I'm a traitor, fit to be shot without batting an eye. I needed to put a bit of a buffer around me. Delay until I can prove my loyalty."

As he looked at me, the locket slipped out of his shirt and dangled in front. In all the chaos, I had forgotten to try again to snatch it from him.

I glared at him. "So you killed Gavin, but I heard Willow Winds couldn't kill anyone."

"True, which is why the last part of my transformation ritual required the death of my victim. Killing Gavin expelled my Willow Wind essence, and I absorbed Gavin's humanness. Yet, fear not. He didn't suffer long."

"You're a monster! I should never have saved your life!"

He smiled in a smug way, reigniting my nausea. "It's in your nature, Megan. You're a life giver, not a life taker."

I shook the bars. "If I could get to you, you might learn different."

"Considering your rage at the moment, I believe you. Nevertheless, I appreciate your effort to save me, your current anger notwithstanding."

Oliver joined me at the bars, also staring at Thorne. "Don't listen to him. We need to concentrate on coming up with a plan." He looked at me and lowered his voice. "You're already working on one, right?"

"Maybe." Setting a hand on the cell's locking mechanism, I flexed the muscle and delivered a shot of current. Nothing happened. I shut the power off and scanned the corridor. The two guards lay motionless on the floor well out of reach, the electrocuted one staring straight up with open eyes. Although he was alive when I left him, his death was my fault. I tried to lessen the shock and just paralyze him for a while, but my efforts weren't enough. My rage must've burst through. I didn't know how to control it yet.

"Megan." Oliver prodded my shoulder. "Hey, stay with us. We can't afford you losing focus."

I shook my head, casting off the mind shadows. "Yeah. Sorry."

"Got any ideas?"

"No." I gave him a mournful look. "I killed someone, Oliver. And I didn't have to kill him."

He pushed his hands into his pockets. "I know. I saw."

"Megan," my mother said, "in the heat of battle, it's kill or be killed. You can't stop fighting to justify every shot you take."

"Yeah, but—"

A fluttering interrupted. Perdantus landed on the floor in the corridor and walked into our cell with something in his beak. He hopped up to my wrist and set two commlinks in my hand.

I wanted to shout, but knowing that Max was probably recording us, I whispered, "The ones the admiral dropped?"

He chirped more quietly than I knew he could. "Yes. The ship's door was wide open, so I flew in. It was a simple matter to search the spaces and air shafts until I found you, though I think I explored every nook and cranny in this mansion of a vessel."

"You're the best." I inserted one link into my ear and gave the other to Oliver. "How is everyone doing?"

Perdantus resumed his quiet chirping. "Emerson helped Crystal fly the *Nebula Nine* to the *Astral Dragon*, but when they boarded, Sonya wouldn't give them security access to fly it."

I nodded. "She's a stubborn one."

"So they're thinking about flying the *Nebula Nine* here instead of the *Dragon*."

"No, no." I pinched my commlink. "Crystal? It's Megan. Can you hear me?"

"Yep. What's up?"

"Too much to explain, but we're in the brig on the *Nebula One*. Don't bring the *Nine*. The admiral can send codes to disable it. It has to be the *Dragon*."

"Got it. Don't fly the *Nine*. No worries. We're on the *Astral Dragon*, and we're picking up the commlink signals here and rebroadcasting them. The receiver's a lot closer to you than it was before, so static's not a problem. And Sonya says she can pick up the signal from a lot farther away than the *Nine* can. Something about your father's spy technology."

"Great. Keep listening." I turned to Perdantus. "During all your flying around the ship, did you notice a security office? It might have had a sign on the door written in Alpha One."

"I did," Perdantus said. "Why?"

"That's where they keep the key to my mother's chains. I need it. It's probably a silver cylinder about the size of a human finger. Since everything here is computer controlled, almost any key you find there will probably sense the lock and open it."

"I will do what I can."

"Also, do you know if there's a maintenance shaft in the ceiling on this level?"

Perdantus nodded. "There is."

"We need to go silent in the cell block. Look for microphone wiring. In the Nebula series, it's green with a white stripe. Break any you can find. But don't break the speaker wires. They're yellow and white. We need to listen to any ship-wide broadcasts."

"Very well. Anything else?"

"Bring the key first. Then cut the wires. Then come back to report."

The *snick* of the opening elevator silenced me. I stepped up to the bars and looked that way. Three soldiers—one big and two medium-sized—emerged and marched toward us, rage burning in their faces. The big soldier held a long-barreled laser blaster, and the two others guided a wheeled gurney.

I turned toward Perdantus and waved a hand. He hopped out of the cell and flew over the men's heads.

The big one swatted at him but missed. "How did a bird get up here?"

"Maybe through one of the vents," another man said. "It'll find its way out."

When they arrived, the big gunman slapped the rifle's barrel against our cell's bars, slamming my hand. I jerked back and sucked a wounded finger.

He growled, "You'd get a lot worse if I was in charge."

"Leave her alone!" my mother shouted. "Or I'll—"

"Or you'll what?" He snickered. "Like mother, like daughter. Bigmouthed pirates, pretending to be brave."

I tightened my jaw. Maybe I could use this guy to get out. "Yeah, well you're pretty brave standing out there with a gun. I'm just a girl in a cage."

He jabbed a finger at me. "A girl who killed two of my friends."

I set a fist on my hip and took on a cocky tone. "So you're afraid of me, huh? A big guy like you afraid of a little girl." I laughed. "That's really funny."

"The admiral said you took them by surprise, shot one of them in the back of the head." He looked at the two other men as they lifted the corpses onto the gurney. "Hey, you guys all right taking them down to the morgue? I want to settle the score with this girl. No one will notice a few more bruises on her pretty face."

One of the other men, gray-haired and leather-skinned, scowled. "Leave her alone, Harvey. She's just a kid."

Harvey prodded my defender's chest with the gun barrel. "A kid who murdered Sherman and Bobby!"

The other man spread his arms. "So now you're going to shoot me?"

"If you stop me from punishing the hellcat, I'll put a laser burn on your butt you'll never forget."

The third man pushed the gun barrel down. "C'mon, Harvey. We all want her to suffer. But shooting Weston? That's just stupid, especially since he's the security boss. He can hack your records and get you busted to latrine duty for a year."

"Well, then, maybe I'll shoot *her*. Call it an accident."

"Let's go," Weston said. "We've got a job to do. The admiral's waiting."

Harvey looked at me for a long moment, then sighed. "All right. She's not worth the trouble anyway." As the two others wheeled the dead men away, Harvey leaned close to the bars and whispered, "I'm coming back for you, darlin'. Alone. No one will protect you then." He strode away quickly and caught up with the others. Seconds later, they disappeared into the elevator.

I swallowed hard, my cheeks as hot as fire. If that creep tried anything, I would fry his brain like eggs on a skillet. Still, in spite of my internal bravado, the threat shook me to the core. Bruising my face might not be the only punishment Harvey had in mind.

The elevator opened once more. I whispered, "Someone's coming." Oliver stepped in front of me again, and this time I let him stay.

31

Weston exited the elevator and walked to the bars, his face flushed as he looked at me. "Hey, um, I know I probably shouldn't help you, but Harvey's not giving up on his ideas, and I can't stand by and let it happen. I got a daughter of my own. About your age."

I stepped out from behind Oliver. "So what're you going to do?"

"Like you probably heard, I'm chief of security. I can lock down this level so tight even the admiral can't get in. Harvey wouldn't be able to bother you."

I narrowed an eye. A tic near Weston's eyelid gave away nervousness. "I get the feeling it's not that simple."

He nodded. "I have to do it at the main console. If I do it here, I wouldn't be able to get out myself."

"Why is doing it at the console a problem?"

"Not for me. For you. The only reason for a lockdown is if the ship's in danger, you know, like a fire, and we have to evacuate the prisoners. During the lockdown sequence, the cell doors open for thirty seconds, enough time for guards to escort prisoners to the stairway. After that, the stairway door locks, and the cells close. Everything's locked tight until I unlock it again."

I raised my brow, hoping to appear cooperative. "That's not a problem. We wouldn't try to run down the stairs before the door locks. We'd get shot."

"No, but I figure you'd want to get out of your cell, which is fine by me because you're not going anywhere, but your mother'll still be chained. When the door closes, you'll be separated."

"You're the chief of security. Don't you have a key to the chains?"

"Not on me. And I'm protecting you, not your mother. I'll feel better about this if she stays locked up."

A flutter drew my attention to the main room. Perdantus stood on the floor at the end of the corridor, a metal cylinder in his beak. I needed to wrap this up.

"Well, I'm in favor of your plan, and thanks for helping. I hope you don't get in trouble with the admiral."

Weston laughed softly and kept his voice low. "It's not him I'm worried about. It's his wife. You're lucky she's not on board. You'd all be dead by now." His cheeks reddening, he turned and walked toward the elevator.

Perdantus leaped out of his way and flew over his head as Weston batted at him. "There's that fool bird again." Then he strode onward and into the elevator car.

When Perdantus flew into the cell, he dropped the key on the floor in front of me. "Those savages think I'm a common beast."

"They're probably an Alpha system crew," I said. "No sentient birds there. Better for us if the guards stay ignorant."

"Quite true. And now I must cut the audio lines."

I picked up the key. "Good. Then come back to us again."

"Consider it done. I assume you will make sure Crystal is aware of our progress." Perdantus hopped out of the cell and flew away.

I reached to pinch my commlink, then remembered that it was already activated. "Crystal, are you still listening?"

"Yep. Blazes, girl, sounds like things are really cooking there."

"They are." I set the end of the cylinder key against my mother's left wrist manacle. The lock clicked open. "And soon you're going to have to fly the *Astral Dragon* into battle."

"Are you kidding me? I nearly crashed three times flying the *Nebula Nine*. If not for Emerson, the ship would be a bent trash can in the woods. And besides, Sonya locked the ship down. We don't have security clearance."

"I know. Perdantus told me. Listen, can you put your ear near Sonya's microphone?"

"I suppose so. Zoë probably knows where it is."

"Then do it. I need Sonya to hear us."

The cell door slid open, as did Thorne's. My mother threw off the open shackle and nodded toward the locked one. "Hurry! Thirty seconds!"

"Can't talk, Crystal." When I set the key to the shackle, it failed to click. "It's not working."

Across the way, Thorne sat in his chair and wheeled himself into the corridor. "Twenty-five seconds," he said. "But that's just a guess. I'm mentally counting."

Oliver knelt next to me and pushed my hands away. "Let me. Maybe a different spot on the shackle."

While he tried, the elevator car's telltale *snick* reached my ears, though farther away than usual. Maybe it had opened on the bridge level. I rushed out of the cell and looked that way. "Someone's coming. This place isn't locked down yet."

"It won't lock down," Thorne said. "Not until the cell doors close. Let's hope Harvey's not coming to pay you a visit."

"Oliver!" I barked. "Get it open!"

He held the key against the shackle, his hands shaking. "I'm trying. Maybe the lock's rusted."

"Fifteen seconds," Thorne said.

Max's voice emanated from speakers in the ceiling. "All crew members report to your stations immediately. We are taking off in approximately thirty seconds."

The ship trembled. I looked out the viewing window. Soldiers rushed up the hatch ramp below us.

"Ten seconds for us," Thorne said.

The elevator hummed. The car was coming to our level. I ran back into the cell, pushed a finger into Oliver's ear, and stripped out his commlink.

"Hey! What're you doing?"

"Putting my mother in charge of the *Astral Dragon*." I pressed the commlink in place inside her ear. "Tell Sonya what to do. Help Crystal fly the ship."

"Sonya," my mother said. "This is Captain Anne Willis. Prepare for takeoff. Put me on speakers so everyone can hear us."

The lock clicked. "Got it," Oliver said.

She threw off the shackle. "Let's go."

Our cell door began sliding shut. Thorne wheeled his chair into the way. The door banged into it and made a grinding sound as it bent the chair's metal frame.

Thorne crawled to the floor inside the cell and nodded at the chair. "Climb over it. Hurry."

My mother, Oliver, and I scrambled over the chair. Once we were outside the cell, Thorne kicked the chair and sent it tumbling into the corridor. The door slammed shut, locking him inside cell one.

I looked toward the elevator. It stopped humming for a moment, then restarted again. A distant *snick* sounded below. The car had returned to bridge level.

I exhaled. "We did it. We're locked in."

"Especially Thorne," Oliver said.

Thorne grasped two bars and climbed to his feet. "It's all right. I'm no worse off than I was before."

The ship trembled harder. Outside, the swamp slowly descended out of view. "No time to waste," my mother said as she marched toward the viewing window. "Sonya, are you ready for takeoff?"

"Affirmative, Captain," Sonya said, now audible in my ear. "And I am broadcasting our conversation along with all voices on this channel throughout the ship, not that the passengers deserve to hear it."

"Cut the commentary. Who's on board?"

"Two dirty girls. I don't consider *dirty* to be commentary. It is a fact."

The *Nebula One* continued rising slowly, likely taking care to avoid strenuous g-forces, a relief for us since we had no chairs to strap into.

My mother gazed out our viewing window, massaging a wrist. "No time for snark of any kind. That's an order."

"Snark level set to zero."

"Good. Now scan low altitudes for the *Nebula One*. The ship's signature is in your database. It's lifting off near a big swamp at this moment."

"*Nebula One* detected, Captain. Estimated time of engagement, three minutes, depending on any changes to the Nebula ship's trajectory and speed."

"Shields up. Execute flight pattern to engage. Everyone strap in. Prepare for battle."

"Battle?" Thorne shouted from his cell. "Are you crazy? Either you'll kill us, or you'll kill your friends."

I touched my mother's arm. "Not if we cripple this ship from inside and force it to the ground. Then we can issue terms of surrender."

"But we're locked in here," Thorne said. "We can't cripple the ship."

"Maybe there's a way."

As I scanned the huge chamber, Perdantus squeezed between two slats in a ventilation cover near the ceiling and flew down to my shoulder. "I believe all outgoing audio from this room has been cut."

"Perfect. No one can hear our plans."

Something thumped at the vent. Its cover popped off and clattered to the floor. A second later, Dirk's head protruded, his face smeared with dirt. "Finally! There are so many vent shafts in this ship it took forever to find the right one."

"Dirk!" I ran to the wall and looked up. "Have you been hiding in the shafts ever since you escaped?"

"Yeah. I ran to the engine room and opened a panel there. I've been trying to find the brig ever since." He squinted. "How did you and Oliver get caught?"

"Tell you later." I flexed my biceps and bent my knees. "Get ready to catch me."

"What?"

I raised my voice. "Reach those wiry arms down and get ready to catch me." I leaped up to him. We grabbed each other's wrists, and he hauled me into the shaft.

I turned around in the tight space and looked down at my mother, Oliver, and Perdantus. "Okay, here's what I'm thinking. First, I'll shut off the gravity engine. Then I can float to the shield generator boxes on the inner side of the hull. Since they're lined with a rubberized covering, I can't short them with my hands, but I can jerk their control cables out."

Oliver flashed a thumbs-up. "Great. We can float here. No problem."

"You can use the braces." I pointed at one of several raised areas on the floor. "You set the sides of your feet against those, and you stay put unless the ship swerves suddenly."

"Got it."

"I'll cut the gravity and come back here and wait to see if they can fix the engine right away. If the gravity stays off, I'll search for the hull space."

I drew back into the shaft, squirmed a one-eighty again, and faced Dirk. "Ready?"

"Yep. I saw the gravity engine. It's blue and egg-shaped, just like in the *Nine*." He rotated—easier for him than for me—and scooted away.

"Any updates from the *Astral Dragon*, Sonya?" I whispered as I belly crawled after him.

"The *Nebula One* has increased its forward speed," Sonya said. "Our time to engagement is now three point five minutes."

My mother broke in. "Increase speed to close the gap to two minutes and stay there. We don't want to spook them yet."

"Acknowledged."

Dirk stopped at a square hole in the shaft's floor. "This drops about ten meters and ends at another horizontal shaft."

"Okay, let's go."

Dirk crawled past the hole, then backed up and lowered himself into the vertical shaft. I copied his moves and followed. Pressing my arms against the sides, I slid down as fast as I could. When I reached bottom, I squeezed into the new shaft and lay on my stomach with Dirk's shoes near my face.

He crawled on. "This way."

As I followed, I passed over a grating. "Stop. Let me see what's here." I looked down between the vent's metal slats. Dozens of crates stood in stacks on the floor against a wall, each labeled "Bramble Bee Sap" in block letters. "They're hauling a bunch of glowsap. It's worth a fortune."

"Worthless to us," Dirk said.

"True. Let's keep going."

He crawled several more meters, stopped beyond another vent, and turned around. "It's down there."

When I arrived at the vent, I looked through it. Below, a blue engine hummed. The size of a rover, it was much bigger than similar engines on the *Nine* and the *Astral Dragon*. Since the crew of the *One* had already turned it on, they expected to be in space soon.

I pried the vent cover off, but it slipped from my fingers and clattered to the floor. I drew back and waited. Only the hum of the engine rose into the shaft. I poked my head down through the vent. No one stood in sight. Because a gravity engine rarely caused problems, the engineers often left it running without supervision.

"Dirk, stay up here and be ready to catch me." I lowered myself feetfirst through the hole, dropped to the floor, and crouched low in case cameras might be watching. To my right, a chest-high, one-person control console stood next to the equally tall egg-shaped engine.

Keeping my knees bent, I used the console as a blind, shuffled to the engine, and set my hand on its metallic surface. Although the motor hummed, it had not yet engaged, probably set to automatic. It would begin gravity sequencing as soon as it detected its own weight dropping.

I reached under the curved bottom edge and felt for the weight-sensing wheel. When my fingers came across it, I turned it fully counterclockwise, shutting it off. Now unable to detect weight loss, the engine wouldn't engage automatically, but I still had to override any manual attempt, and I had to do it without Max detecting me.

I pried a floor panel loose, revealing a braided set of five insulated wires of differing colors that led from the console to the engine. I fished through the wires until I isolated a red one, the control signal wire. As I wrapped my hand around it, I flexed my biceps and activated the bracelet. Electricity flooded my hand and melted the wire's insulation. When the current touched the bare wire, it shot into the engine and the console. The surge stung like crazy, but I held on.

Something popped. I jerked back from the hot wire. The odor of a fried circuit filled the room. Now I had to hope that Max wouldn't—

"Anomaly detected in the gravity engine room," Max said through a ceiling speaker. "Engineer on duty, report there at once."

"Blazes!" I slid the floor panel back in place. Staying low, I shuffled to my landing spot under the ceiling vent and looked up. Just as I flexed to activate my legs, a door on the opposite side of the room slid open.

I leaped and caught Dirk's wrists. As he pulled me up, my sounds masked by the engine's hum, I glanced down. A young dark-haired woman entered and set her fists on her hips as she stared at the gravity engine's console.

Once in the shaft again, I peeked down. The woman scanned the room, sniffing, probably detecting the fried circuit.

Dirk peered down with me. I set a shushing finger to my lips. From below, the woman's voice rose to the shaft. "Hey, Bob, something weird's going on. The console shorted out." She paused, apparently listening to an answer only she could hear. "The engine's running, so we should be fine once we get into space. . . . Yeah. I'll check for rats. See you soon."

"The *Nebula One*'s shields are going up," Sonya said in my ear. "She is turning about."

"Turn on your gravity engine," my mother replied. "Make sure everyone's strapped in and prepare for battle. Then fly into zero gravity. Let's hope Megan took care of the engine."

Unable to risk answering, I crawled toward the upward vertical shaft, Dirk now behind me. As I passed over the vent leading to the glowsap cargo, I glanced down again. At this new angle, something different caught my attention. It looked like a human child trapped in a glass-covered box.

I whispered, "I have to check on something." I pried the vent cover off, leaned it against the shaft's side, and dropped into the room. The crates of sap abutted one wall, and long rectangular boxes lay on gurneys that lined the opposite wall, each box with a human child lying under a glass cover.

At the ceiling, a camera pointed toward the opposite side of the room, rotating slowly. I had to act fast. I strode to the closest box. A naked girl, maybe ten years old, lay inside, her skin gray and her chest motionless.

I whispered, "They're coffins."

A label on the side of the box said, "SS #15. Name: Penelope. Age: 9. Failure code: 7. Expired: Day 28." Underneath the codes, someone signed the label. The name looked like Camille Fairbanks. Maybe the admiral's wife.

I stepped over to the next box where a naked boy lay. His label said, "SS #14. Name: Theodore. Age: 8. Failure code: 7. Expired: Day 24." The same signature was on this label.

As the camera rotated toward me, I quickly counted the coffins, ten in all. I leaped to the vent, and Dirk helped me climb into the shaft. Now breathless, I looked down again. Could those kids be part of the SS Squad? Maybe failed participants? But there was no more time to ponder the questions. I had to hurry on.

I whispered, "Let's go." I crawled to the vertical shaft and tried to squirm upward, but a sudden increase in g-forces kept me planted at the bottom. The *Astral Dragon* had probably taken off toward zero gravity, and the *Nebula One* was giving chase.

Soon, the ship slowed, and the force eased. Seconds later, my body became weightless. I leaped and shot up into the horizontal shaft leading to the cell block with Dirk directly behind me. I propelled myself to the vent hole and into the prison chamber's viewing room.

My momentum sent me flying over my mother and Oliver as they stood on the floor, their feet pressed against the braces and Perdantus perched on Oliver's shoulder. When I reached the opposite wall, I pushed off toward them. My mother caught me and turned me upright. "You did it. Good job." She helped me set my feet next to hers.

I looked at the vent. Dirk lay there, grinning as he braced himself with his elbows. "Easier to stay put up here."

The admiral's voice came through the ceiling speakers. "We will engage the *Astral Dragon* in a few moments. Prepare for battle."

"Looks like they don't mind the gravity loss," Oliver said. "The engine might stay down for a while. You can try to shut off the shields, but wouldn't they see you on a monitor?"

I shook my head. "The Nebula series doesn't have cameras in the hull space. Stupid design, but it works to our advantage."

Dirk called from the vent. "I know the way to the hull space, and I can jerk cables out with the best of them."

"I'll help him," Oliver said. "I'm no use for battle strategy. You should stay and help your mom."

I nodded. "Have you ever been in a hull space with zero gravity?"

"Lots of times. Better than a kiddie bounce room."

"If you like thin air and danger. And if gravity turns back on suddenly, you could fall to your deaths."

"Always hang on to something. Got it." When Dirk slid out of the way, Oliver pushed from the floor and flew into the shaft.

I gazed at the opening, mentally tracking their progress. "I hope they don't kill themselves."

Perdantus chirped, "I will accompany them. I can fly back with a report if they encounter trouble."

I nodded. "Go."

The moment he disappeared into the shaft, Crystal's voice barged in. "We're staring down the *Nebula One*. What do we do?"

I swiveled toward the front. The viewing window drew an outline around the dark form of the *Astral Dragon*. It faced us, about fifty meters away.

"Hold steady, Crystal," my mother said. "Your shields can withstand a lot. We have to give Oliver and Dirk time to take down our shields."

"What about the weakness in the port turret?" I asked. "The admiral knows about it."

She narrowed her eyes. "He does?"

I nodded. "I heard him say so."

A photon torpedo shot into our view and hurtled toward the *Astral Dragon*'s port side. My mother shouted, "Evade!"

The *Dragon* shifted down. The torpedo glanced off the turret and zipped into blackness behind the ship.

"Fire two torpedoes and flee toward Delta Ninety-eight."

Two bright lights exploded from the *Dragon*'s turrets, brilliant pulsing balls that zoomed toward us. They splashed against our window and shook the ship. The jolt sent us flying from our braces and through the air.

Aiming for the floor, I pushed off a wall, grabbed a brace, and set my feet again. When I caught my mother and helped her settle, I looked out the viewing window. The *Astral Dragon* shrank into the background of Delta Ninety-eight, like a black marble as it reflected Yama-Yami's light.

"The *Nebula One* is in pursuit," Sonya said, "but we will have to decelerate to avoid colliding with the planet."

My mother clenched her fists. "So ordered, but we have to delay engagement as long as we can."

"Can we go into orbit awhile?" I asked. "Oliver and Dirk need to stay weightless to get as many shields down as possible."

"Right. Set an orbit course, Sonya."

Thorne shouted from his cell. "You people are insane. You're going to get us all killed."

I replied without looking at him. "We want the admiral to surrender."

"Admiral Fairbanks surrender? You've got to be kidding me. It'll never happen. He'll sacrifice himself, the ship, and the crew before he'd think about surrendering."

"It's the only strategy we have. Nothing you can do about it."

"Is that so? I've been holding off doing this, Megan, because you saved my life, but I'm not going to let you destroy this ship and us with it."

I turned toward him. Thorne stood with his arms protruding between the bars, holding my locket open to expose the dragon's eye. I must have left it open when I was trying to take it back from him. "Thanks for opening the locket for me." His voice rode the air as he spoke in a rhythmic cadence: "*Dragon's eye, filled with power, grant me life from astral towers.*"

"No!" I leaped toward him and flew. When I drew near the cell, he pushed away from the bars. I caught two of them and hung on. "No. Don't. Please."

"It's the only way to stop this madness," he said, floating near the back of his cell. "And when I tell the admiral that I saved his ship, maybe he'll be convinced that Double Agent Gavin Foster really was on his side all along."

I looked at my mother as she continued staring out the viewing window. So far, Thorne's words seemed to have no effect.

He continued in the eerie cadence: "*Magic power, ruby's glow, draw the essence, make it flow.*"

The dragon's eye brightened, casting its glow across the face of Gavin, the mask of Thorne. His eyes shone with a hint of red as if casting a light of their own.

My mother turned toward us. She blinked, her face twisting in pain.

"Mama?" I called. "Are you all right?"

She shook her head. Her legs buckled, and she floated above the floor.

I flexed my biceps, igniting my hands with wildly arcing electricity. "Stop! You have to stop!"

"Or you'll kill me?" Thorne pushed a foot against the floor, pinning himself to the cell's far wall. "In less than a minute, you won't be able to." He resumed his macabre poem. "*Drain the life, down the line, transfer essence, make it mine.*"

I shook the bars, sending the current throughout the door's frame. "You locked yourself in there on purpose, didn't you? So I couldn't stop you."

"Merely a safety precaution. I wasn't going to do it unless you forced my hand. Your plan is suicide. I am helping you survive."

I looked at my mother again. Now she floated with her eyes closed.

I screamed at Thorne. "No, no, no! You have to stop!"

"What's going on, Megan?" Crystal asked.

I shook the bars again. "Thorne's killing my mother!"

"The *Nebula One*'s shields have fallen to eighty percent," Sonya said. "Its bridge is vulnerable. What are the captain's orders?"

I gritted my teeth. "The captain's unconscious. Let Crystal command the ship."

"You do not have the authority to assign Crystal as the commander."

"What authority do I have?"

"You may declare the captain incapacitated and assume command of the *Astral Dragon* yourself."

Thorne gave me an expectant look. "I have one more verse, Megan. This is your last chance to prevent your mother's death."

My voice quaked. "What do you want me to do? Surrender?"

"In short, yes. If you halt this absurd chase, I will appeal to the admiral for mercy for your sake."

"But then the admiral will win. The child torture will go on and on. This is my chance to stop it."

"As you know, I have no pity for the children. They are beasts of burden to me. Your appeal is not persuasive."

"Megan," Crystal said, "ask yourself what your mother would want you to do."

I wept through my words. "No, no, please don't make me ask that question."

Sonya spoke again. "The *Nebula One*'s shields have dropped below fifty percent. If we turn about, our weapons can destroy it, but I cannot proceed without an officer's orders. Megan Willis, are you assuming command?"

"Yes." I sniffed and brushed away tears. "Captain Anne Willis is incapacitated. I, Megan Willis, assume command of the *Astral Dragon*."

"Acknowledged. What are your orders, Captain?"

Still in the prison cell corridor, I looked out the viewing window. We appeared to be in orbit around the planet, the *Astral Dragon* zooming out in front of us. "The admiral has to know his shields are falling. Why is he still in pursuit?"

A barrage of photon torpedoes burst into view, heading for the *Astral Dragon*, bigger and brighter than any I had seen before.

I shouted, "Evade! Take the *Dragon* to the planet!"

The *Astral Dragon* dropped out of orbit. The torpedoes flew past it and sailed into space. The *Nebula One* shifted hard in pursuit, pushing us upward. I held to the cell bars, but my body slanted. Thorne flew to the ceiling and banged his head. My mother shot to the ceiling as well. Her limp body pressed against it as we plunged toward Delta Ninety-eight.

Moments later, the ship righted itself, and planetary gravity kicked in. When we dropped, I set my feet and looked into the main room. My mother lay on the floor near the center. I ran to her and knelt at her side. "Are you all right?"

She gasped for breath. "No. My chest. The pain. So awful."

"Thorne's using the dragon's eye. He's chanting some kind of spell to steal your life essence to become immortal. He says we have to surrender, or he'll finish the spell and kill you."

Tears streamed down the sides of her face. "No. We can't surrender. This is our only chance to stop the slave trading."

"But what about Thorne? I can't stop him from killing you. And if he becomes immortal, we'll never have a chance against the slavers."

She pushed trembling fingers through my hair. "Megan, you can stop him. You can kill me before he finishes. Then he won't be immortal."

I gasped. "What? Kill you? No! Never!"

Sonya broke in. "The *Astral Dragon* is using landing thrusters to hover ten meters above a swamp on Delta Ninety-eight. The *Nebula One* is approaching and is hailing us. What are your orders, Captain?"

"What did Fairbanks say?" I asked.

"He is demanding our unconditional surrender."

"Surrender? But I—"

"Now's your chance to save your mother," Thorne said from his cell. "Surrender, and I will let her live."

She shook her head. "No, Megan. Don't surrender. You know Fairbanks will kill me anyway."

"It's here," Crystal said. "The *Nebula One* is staring us down. Megan, what should we do?"

Swallowing hard, I straightened and looked out the front window. The *Astral Dragon* faced us from about thirty meters away, its landing thrusters blasting downward and throwing swamp water in all directions. "Sonya, do you have voice prints in your database that you could use to alter my voice? I can't let him know I'm commanding your ship from here."

"Affirmative. I advise you to choose a voice quickly. The *Nebula One* has armed its weapons. I am detecting a power source from the firing turrets that is much stronger than usual."

"Just choose a voice for me. A man's would be best."

"Voice chosen. The communication channel is open, and I will send the admiral's responses through the commlink."

I cleared my throat. "*Nebula One*, it seems that you demanded surrender, but I must have misunderstood. I thought you might call to offer *your* surrender." The words echoed to my ear in my father's voice. I gulped. Sonya had made the worst possible choice, the voice of a dead man. I just had to hope the admiral wouldn't recognize it.

"Surrender to you?" The admiral laughed. "I'm sure you saw the enhanced torpedoes you narrowly avoided. Trust me, I won't miss again, not from this range. I, Admiral Fairbanks, repeat my demand. Surrender now or be destroyed."

Trying not to shake, I looked again at my mother, gasping on the floor. Earlier, Crystal said I should ask myself what my mother would want me to do. She wouldn't surrender. I knew that without a doubt. Yet, I also knew what she would want *me* to do. To be Megan Willis, not Anne Willis. The decision was mine alone to make, and I had to make it now.

I tried for a confident tone. "Admiral, do you think I am ignorant of the status of your shields? Although my torpedoes are less powerful, I can blow a cavern in your hull in two seconds. I'll trust my shields to keep my ship intact for that long."

"Who are you?" the admiral asked. "You sound familiar."

My heart raced, but I kept my voice under control. "I am the captain of the *Astral Dragon*. That's all you need to know."

"Max, identify the voice."

"The voice is that of Julian Willis," Max said, "convicted pirate."

"Ah! Julian Willis, back from your supposed death. How did you escape Beta Four?"

My body stiffened. Beta Four? He was exiled? Not executed? I glanced at my mother again. Her eyes were closed, probably unconscious.

I collected myself and spoke with as much calmness as I could manage. "I will keep my escape methods to myself. Suffice it to say that security on Beta Four isn't as airtight as you imagined."

"Perhaps not, but that can be rectified. In any case, regardless of who has the better odds of winning a battle, I suggest that you surrender. I have your wife and daughter on board."

"Are they unharmed?"

"Yes, of course. I am not cruel to my prisoners, though every time I look at your daughter, I wonder if she knows about your cruelty. It would be interesting to see her reaction if I were to tell her about what you and your wife did on Gamma Five."

I froze. He couldn't be lying. Negotiation strategy taught that it's crazy to try to bluff if your opponent knows the truth. The admiral held some awful information about my parents that I didn't know. I needed time to think.

Perdantus alighted on my shoulder and nudged my ear with his beak.

"Admiral," I said, "allow me a moment to consider my options. Sonya, close the channel to the *Nebula One*."

"Channel closed, Captain."

I exhaled. Jumbled thoughts tossed through my mind. I had to settle them. "What's up, Perdantus?"

"Oliver and Dirk are on their way. Gravity is slowing their progress through a vertical shaft."

"I'm negotiating with the admiral, and he punched me in the gut. I need more leverage. Can you lead Oliver and Dirk to a torpedo?"

"Yes, Megan."

"Good. Do it. Have Dirk give Oliver his commlink, and tell Oliver to call me when they get there. I'll explain how to arm a torpedo."

"On my way." Perdantus flew to the vent.

Thorne shouted from his cell. "Are you out of your mind? You'll kill us all."

I shouted in return. "I'm negotiating, you idiot! I need leverage. The admiral will be able to detect the armed torpedo."

"Beware, Megan. You're playing with fire."

"Sonya," I said, "restore the channel to the *Nebula One*."

"Channel restored."

The admiral's voice returned to my ear. "Captain Willis, it seems that my comment about your daughter unraveled your resolve. If you surrender now, I will not breathe a word about your activities on

Gamma Five. If you don't surrender, then I make no promises regarding your daughter's safety. She is, after all, under a death sentence."

I took a deep breath to settle my nerves. "Admiral, if you want me to surrender, then I request that you broadcast our conversation throughout your ship. Unless you have something to fear."

"Your intimidation tactics won't work on me. I will grant your request, though you have no way to verify my compliance."

"I will trust your word, Admiral, though you don't deserve it."

Something clicked at the ceiling, and the admiral's voice boomed from above. "Captain Julian Willis of the *Astral Dragon*, you are now addressing my entire crew."

"Good. I hope they are aware that you just threatened the life of a child."

"They are aware that I will sacrifice the life of any pirate in order to put an end to child trafficking. They know Megan is not a mere child. She probably has more danger potential than you or your wife ever had."

Strangely enough, his words felt good. Being a dangerous pirate in his eyes was a compliment. Still, the impasse continued. I needed to give Oliver and Dirk more time. "What are your terms of surrender, Admiral?"

"You will land your ship, and everyone in your crew will disembark with no weapons. My crew will come out, put all of you in chains, and lead you onto my ship as prisoners."

"To kill us all? What kind of terms are those?"

"No. You will be prisoners and subject to a fair trial. There are now dozens of witnesses to this arrangement."

"Allow me another moment to address my crew privately."

The admiral let out an impatient sigh. "Granted."

"Sonya, close the channel."

"Channel closed."

I looked up, imagining Oliver and Dirk in a vent shaft. "Oliver, do you have an update? I assume you have Dirk's commlink by now."

"I have it, and I'm at the torpedo room. Dirk and I hauled one off a shelf and stood it in a corner, and I see how to arm it and set its timer. Just say the word."

"Can you hear what's going on?"

"Pretty well. Is that you negotiating with the admiral?"

"Yeah. Just listen and arm the torpedo at the right time. Set it for thirty seconds, then get back here on the double."

"Will do. There are shelves against the wall here. It's easy to climb into the vent system."

"Sonya, reopen the channel."

"Channel open."

"Admiral, you think you have a tactical advantage with your new weapon, but you don't realize that its security is worse than what I broke through to escape Beta Four."

"Nonsense. My weapons are completely secure. I think you're stalling."

"Not at all, Admiral. And to prove your lack of security, I am going to remotely arm one of your torpedoes now. It will explode long before you can mount it in a firing tube."

"That's preposterous. You can't remotely—"

"Admiral," Max said, "a torpedo has been armed. It will explode in thirty seconds."

The admiral shouted, "Someone disarm it! Now!" More shouts erupted along with pounding footsteps below our level.

I pressed my ear, shutting off my commlink.

"Very clever," Thorne said. "You bought yourself some time and leverage. You have no intention of surrendering, do you?"

Ignoring Thorne, I knelt again next to my mother. "Are you feeling any better?"

She shook her head, her eyes tightly shut as she gasped through shallow breaths. "Everything's draining . . . from my body. Like there's a . . . a leak with no way to plug it."

Thorne's voice drifted in once more. "No more chances, Megan. I can't let you kill us all."

My mother's eyes opened, red and wet. "Kill me now. It's the only way."

I whispered sharply, "No. I already told you. I can't."

"If you don't, I'll die anyway. I want to die by your hands, not Thorne's or Fairbanks's. Use your electricity before it's too late. Before Thorne becomes an unstoppable monster."

"*Mortal life become immortal,*" Thorne said in a singsong cadence. "You have five seconds, Megan, before I speak the final phrase."

"Okay, Mama. Okay. I can shock your heart and make it stop. But not for long. I'll try to revive you later. Are you ready?"

She nodded, weeping. "I love you, Megan. With all my heart. Forgive me for pushing you so hard. If you think it's wrong to kill, then don't kill. Don't live with a guilty conscience."

"I love you, too, Mama. And . . ." A sobbing spasm broke through. "And I forgive you."

I flexed my muscles, sent electricity shooting into my hands, and pressed my palms on her chest. Her body heaved upward, then fell limply to the floor.

"*Come to me through dragon's portal,*" Thorne said.

Silence descended. Every shout, footstep, and voice quieted. Only the hum of the ship's engines gave any hint of activity. I set my ear on my mother's chest. No heartbeat. No breathing. She was dead.

I leaped up and ran to Thorne's cell, grabbed the bars, and screamed, "You killed her! You monster! You killed my mother!"

"I warned you." He stalked to the front of the cell, an evil grin on his face. "Now it doesn't matter if you surrender or not. Blow up the ship for all I care. I'll survive."

I thrust my hands between the bars and grabbed his throat. Flexing again, I sent a huge jolt into him as I squeezed with all my might. Electricity arced across his face. The fiery shock sent peals of pain up my arms, into my skull, and down my spine, but I couldn't let go. I had to find out if this monster stole my mother's life. If he did, then I had no hope of reviving her, and I wouldn't be able to kill him anyway because of his immortality.

As I looked into his bulging eyes, his cruelty stormed into my mind—his brutality toward the orphans, his murder of Gavin, and his selfish passion to kill my mother. At that moment, I realized that if his spell didn't kill her, and if I spared him and managed to revive her, he would just try again to take her life.

He had to die.

Finally, Thorne's hair caught fire, and hot vibrations in his skin stung my hands. When I released him, he collapsed to the floor, motionless.

I looked at my hands, red and trembling. I had killed him. On purpose. But I didn't have time to think about it.

I snatched my locket from his hand, ran to my mother, and knelt, this time straddling her body with a knee on each side. "Okay," I said, knowing she couldn't hear me, "I think he's dead. Maybe I can revive you."

Using all my weight, I pushed on her chest, once, twice, three times, simulating a heart rhythm. As I continued pressing, I cried out, breathless, "Mama! Come back to me! I need you!"

The admiral's voice returned to the speakers. "Captain Willis, that was an impressive display of power. I'm not sure how you did it, but I now have crew members standing at the ready to disable any torpedoes that you arm."

"No, no, no," I whispered. "I don't have time to answer."

"What's going on?" Oliver asked from the vent, only his head in view.

"I need help." My voice squeaked. "Hurry!"

"Captain Willis," the admiral said. "Shall we continue negotiations?"

Oliver pushed out of the vent, dropped to the floor, and ran to me while Dirk and Perdantus watched from the shaft's opening.

"You revived me this way," I said to Oliver as I rose and tied the locket on. "Do it to her. Use your healing power."

"Okay, but the dragon's eye isn't glowing. I don't know if I'll be a dynamo."

As he took my place and pushed on her chest with both hands, I looked at the gem. Of course it wasn't glowing. My mother was dead. But maybe Oliver's gift had matured enough not to need my enhancing gift. That was our only hope.

Breathing rapidly, I tried to shut out his efforts. I had to focus on my part.

I pinched my commlink. "Admiral . . ." My voice shook badly. "The torpedoes aren't your only concern. Earlier, we disabled your gravity engine and half of your shields. I suggest that you surrender while you still have a chance."

"So you know about the gravity loss and the shields. That is compelling." After a silent pause, he continued. "Here is my proposal. We will land our ships, and you and I will meet face-to-face for a parley. Just the two of us. Shields down. Weapons disarmed. Since we have your loved ones on board, you don't have many options."

I bit my lip. Obviously I couldn't meet with him. I had to think of another dodge. I glanced at Oliver as he continued pressing my mother's chest, sweat now dampening his shirt. I needed to buy more time.

I took a deep breath. "Agreed, Admiral. We will fly to a dry landing spot, and I will meet with you in a few moments. Sonya, close the communications channel to the *Nebula One*."

"Channel closed."

"When their ship disarms its weapons, then lower our shields and disarm our weapons."

"Acknowledged."

I heaved a heavy sigh. "Sonya, Crystal, take us to the closest safe landing, and if you have any ideas about the mess I've gotten us into, I'm listening."

"Acknowledged," Sonya said. "Landing sequence commencing. I have no advice about your mess."

Crystal's voice broke in. "I have an idea. I'll get back to you in a minute."

"Okay. Good." I crouched close to Oliver, my heart thumping as I tried to talk without crying. "Do you . . . do you think I should try to shock her to life again?"

He continued the rapid compressions. "Not sure. We used your shock collar to stop your heart's shaking, then compressions to restart you. I don't know if another shock would work or not."

"The compressions aren't working. I have to try."

"Sure." He lifted his hands and brushed sweat from his brow. "Anything else I can do?"

I took his place and flexed my biceps, again signaling my bracelets to turn on. "Can you think of another way you and Dirk can disable this ship?"

He rose and looked at the vent. "Not with gravity grounding us."

"Then stay here. Maybe we've done enough." Electricity flowed along my inked arms and into my palms, though not as much as before. The bracelets needed to recharge.

Just as I lowered my hands toward my mother's chest, the elevator door slid open. Three men and a woman ran out, two with rifles aimed and one carrying chains. "Don't move, pirate," the woman barked.

I set my hands on my mother's chest and delivered a quick shock. Her body heaved before settling to stillness.

"I said, don't move!" She fired her rifle. The laser zipped past my ear and drilled into the far wall. The hole smoked and sizzled. "That was your only warning."

Trembling, I looked at my hands. Only a trickle of electricity remained. The woman grabbed my arm and hoisted me up. Wearing thick gloves, she began putting similar gloves on my hands. When I tried to jerk away, one of the men held me from behind.

"No! No!" I tried to break loose, kicking and thrashing. "I have to save my mother!"

One of the two men held Oliver, while the other hurried into the cell corridor. Oliver growled, "Can't you see she's trying to save her mother's life? Give her a chance."

"No need," Admiral Fairbanks said as he walked into view from behind a guard. "Anne Willis has a death sentence. If she dies here, the execution has merely been expedited." He dropped the chains and nodded at the woman. "Secure them both."

She fastened the gloves at my wrists with a metal clasp. I broke free, lunged to my mother, and continued pressing her chest, crying again. "Mama! Don't die! You can't die!"

"Restrain her and the boy," the admiral said. "Be gentle."

The woman grabbed my arms, twisted them behind me, and fastened cuffs on my wrists and leg irons on my ankles, then did the same to Oliver.

Tears blurred my vision. Sobbing spasms rocked my body, but I couldn't help it. I had lost my mother. My dear, wonderful Mama was dead.

The admiral lowered himself to a knee and felt her neck.

I screamed, "Don't you touch her!"

Ignoring my protest, he felt her wrist and set his ear close to her chest. After a short moment, he rose and looked at me. "She's gone."

I glared at him, my lips pressed together, though they still quivered. I wanted to shout again, to curse with a million obscenities, but I would sound like a damaged little girl. I had to stay strong. Regain my poise. It might be our only way to survive.

I cast a quick glance at the vent opening. Dirk was no longer there. Maybe I was wrong. He could prove to be another hope, but what could he possibly do?

The man who went to the cells returned, dragging Thorne's body. He dropped Thorne on the floor in front of the admiral. "Fried to a crisp."

"Interesting." Admiral Fairbanks stepped close to me and lifted my locket. It was still open, the darkened dragon's eye exposed. He then looked at my mother. "I'm beginning to see what happened here. You used your electrified hands to escape from your cell, and you wouldn't let Foster out. He used the dragon's eye to kill your mother, but obviously it couldn't make him immortal. Considering the burned state of his body, I assume you killed him in retaliation for your mother's death."

Not knowing what to say, I nodded weakly.

"Therefore, the gem can kill its essence bearer, but it has no power that can be transferred. The legend is a lie. A dragon's eye is worthless—at least this one is."

I sniffed hard. "Not . . . not to me. It's a keepsake."

He closed the locket and let it drop back in place while I contin-ued sucking in spasmodic breaths.

"So, what now?" Oliver asked as he glowered at the admiral.

"I intend to employ a potent bit of leverage." The admiral nodded at the guards. "Bring them along, including Anne's corpse."

The guards pushed us into the elevator, chains dragging at our feet, and squeezed us in to fit everyone. Tucked in the back against the car's rear door, I could barely see my mother as one of the guards dragged her in.

Another sob tried to erupt. I sniffed hard to quell it. Oliver, stand-ing next to me, slid his hand behind my back and into my gloved hand. He spoke no words, but his firm grasp said plenty. He would be with me no matter what.

Perdantus and Dirk came to mind. Perdantus could fly out of the ship as soon as the hatch opened, but Dirk was stuck. Even if I could talk to one of them, I couldn't come up with a plan. I was out of ideas.

When the elevator door slid to the side, one guard dragged my mother out by the wrists while the rest of us walked onto bridge level. The front hatch already lay extended to the ground. The admiral waved a hand at the lead guard. "Leave the corpse here until I call for it."

He nodded and stood by my mother as I shuffled past. Her pale face wore a serene expression, no hint of suffering. Unlike when I screamed at the Astral Dragon over Renalda's death, I just let out a sigh and whispered to her, "Maybe I'll see you again soon."

While the other guards guided us with firm grips, the admiral led the way down the ramp toward the lower-level anteroom. I looked back. At least twenty crew members watched from the bridge.

I spotted Weston. He lowered his head, avoiding eye contact. Apparently he had given the admiral access to the cell block, probably after delaying as long as he could. What choice did he have? What choice did any of these crew members have? It was either do what the admiral commanded or lose their jobs, their careers, maybe their lives.

I faced forward. How many people had the integrity to stand against corruption while risking their livelihoods? And even if they had a shred of integrity, did they really know what the admiral was doing? Maybe I could plant a seed of doubt somehow.

When we reached the floor of the anteroom, I looked up at the bridge again and shouted, "Admiral Fairbanks has fooled you all. He is the head of the slave-trading operation. You're all accomplices to the man who profits from selling children into slavery. Look in the cargo hold. Ten dead children are there. See for yourselves."

The admiral halted and slapped my face. Several gasps erupted from the bridge. The admiral glared at them for a moment before turning toward me again. "How dare you insult the honor of these sacrificial men and women? They would sooner die than to give quarter to slavers. And we confiscated those dead children from a laboratory that was conducting gruesome experiments on them. We intend to return them to their families for a proper burial. Now you, an impudent pirate girl, dare to question their integrity?" He shook a finger at me. "You will stay quiet or I will have you gagged."

I kept my face slack, refusing to wince at the stinging pain in my cheek. I glanced at Weston. He stared straight at me, his brow low. Yet, he did nothing, said nothing. He was just like the rest of them, brainwashed fools or cowards who bowed to lying tyrants, even one who would attack a defenseless girl. Maybe my mother was right after all. They really did deserve to die.

"Now let's go." The admiral turned again and walked down the hatch ramp. Outside, the *Astral Dragon* sat about twenty meters away, its landing feet planted firmly. As I followed the admiral, I blinked at the bright light. Yama-Yami stood at its midmorning angle, casting the *Nebula One*'s shadow across the gap between the two ships. Perdantus stood atop the *Astral Dragon* as if waiting to see how he could help.

Crystal spoke into my ear. "I see you, Megan and Oliver. Our plan is weak. We hope to spark a mutiny. Wait'll you hear Zoë's speech we wrote. She's been practicing it."

"It'd better be a good one," I whispered. "I already tried to do the same."

When we reached level ground, Admiral Fairbanks called out, "Captain Julian Willis, we are here."

The *Astral Dragon*'s hatch opened. As the ramp descended, Crystal and Zoë walked out side by side at a slow pace, both with their hair tied back, apparently trying to look older than they were. They stopped at the end of their ramp, no more than five meters away.

I looked through the *Dragon*'s front viewing window. Someone sat in the captain's chair, probably Quixon pretending to be my father. The *Nebula One* likely had a life-form scanner able to detect someone inside, especially at such a close range. Since he was the closest to my father's size, he was the obvious choice to stay behind for the deception.

"Who are you?" the admiral asked.

"We are Captain Willis's emissaries," Crystal said with a formal air. "We will conduct his business."

The admiral spread an arm toward me. "I have the captain's daughter. Doesn't he want to come out and see her? She's been imprisoned for more than a year."

"Indeed he does, but he is certain that you will order him to be shot on sight." Crystal leaned to the side as if trying to look past the admiral. "Where is the captain's wife?"

"Yes, of course." The admiral waved a hand. "Bring her out."

33

A guard cradled my mother in his arms and descended the hatch ramp at a respectful pace, his expression solemn. When he reached the end, he laid her on the ground in front of the admiral before returning to the ship.

The admiral nodded toward her body. "As a gesture of good faith, I give her over freely without requesting anything in return. Tell your captain that I had nothing to do with her death. His daughter, if she tells the truth, will testify to that fact."

Crystal and Zoë looked at me expectantly. Obviously I had to say something. "The admiral did not kill my mother. Neither did any of his crew."

"Who killed her, then?" Crystal asked, tears sparkling in her eyes.

I opened my mouth to answer, then paused. How could I explain that Thorne was the reason she died, but I was the one who actually stopped her heart and later couldn't revive her? "It's . . . it's hard to say."

"Megan's reticence is understandable," the admiral said. "The circumstances are mysterious. But I will tell you that Gavin Foster, former first mate of the *Nebula Nine*, killed Anne Willis." He looked at me as if seeking confirmation. I lowered my head and nodded, not really wanting to lie. His explanation was close enough.

Something clicked. The cuffs on my wrists loosened. I looked at Zoë. As she stared at me intently, more clicks sounded at my ankles. She had set me free with her telekinetic ability.

I kept my hands in place. I probably had some shock power, but not enough to overcome so many guards. I had to bide my time until the right moment.

Just as Zoë shifted her stare to Oliver, the admiral narrowed his eyes at her. "Wait a moment. Aren't you one of the children we rescued on Delta Ninety-five?"

Zoë nodded. "But you mean captured," she said loudly enough for the crew members to hear, "not rescued."

The admiral's lips twitched. "Captured? Nonsense. Soon after I collected you and the others on Delta Ninety-five, I sent you on a smaller cruiser to a sanctuary planet where you would be safe from traders."

"Safe?" Zoë huffed. "When the commander of that cruiser sold me to a slaver, I overheard her talking about how you're running the whole operation secretly, that you're combing through the children, especially those from Gamma Five, sending some to slave markets and taking others away for a super-secret project. You're using your own crew as an unwitting band of child traffickers. They had no idea until now that they are complicit in sending children to torture, beatings, and death."

My chest swelled. What a speech! But would it make a difference? I glanced back at the ship. Weston stood on the hatch ramp with several others. His face bright red, he spun and hurried back inside while the others stayed and continued watching.

The admiral's facial tremors continued, though his voice stayed calm and strong. "Your lies will have no effect here. Why should anyone believe a murderer like you?"

Zoë stood firm, though her eyes gave away a hint of fear.

"What do you mean?" Crystal asked. "Zoë's no murderer."

"She killed one of her caretakers on Delta Ninety-five." The admiral waved toward Zoë. "Ask her yourself. She has a deadly power that can stop a person's heart. Of course, she's not foolish enough to use it here. It would expose her as a fraud and prove that her absurd accusations against me and my crew are outrageous lies."

Zoë backed away a step, her eyes wide as she shook her head.

The admiral jabbed a finger at her. "Did you or did you not kill Phyllis Asher?"

Her entire body quaked. "I . . . um . . ."

"I thought so. At first I couldn't believe what the other children told me, so to protect you I wrote a different account of Phyllis's death in her husband's journal. But later it all made sense. And why couldn't he write his own account? Because I found him dead, having committed suicide because of his despondency over his dear wife's death, caused by a girl for whom they risked their lives to try to create a sanctuary. She returned their love with murder."

I stifled a gasp. His accusation couldn't be true, could it? I glanced at Crystal. Tears trickling, she nodded, a sign that the admiral wasn't lying. I looked again at the *Nebula One*'s hatch ramp. Some crew members crossed their arms while others nodded as if agreeing with the admiral's defense. Yet, Weston was nowhere in sight.

Zoë's voice shook. "It . . . it was an accident. I didn't understand my power. I got mad at her because she—"

"Ah! You can't control your power or your temper. Anger drives you to kill, proving that you can't be trusted."

Zoë shouted, "No! She was about to whip one of the little girls, and I didn't even know I could—"

"Enough of your excuses. You have condemned yourself with your own testimony." The admiral focused on Crystal. "Tell your captain that I will not negotiate with a murderer. If Julian Willis will not come out here personally, I will return to my ship with his daughter and take her to stand trial for the murders of two soldiers. I am confident that she will be executed for these new crimes as well as her previous acts of piracy."

I concealed a tight swallow. The admiral was calling our bluff. Somehow he knew that my father wasn't really on board. But how?

At that moment, the truth hit me broadside. We armed the torpedo after the admiral told the *Astral Dragon*'s crew that I was on board the *Nebula One*. My father would never endanger my life like that.

I whispered, "Crystal, we're sunk. Abort and make a break for it."

"Just a second," she whispered in return. "Plan B coming up. Get ready to run." She cleared her throat. "Admiral, I will summon Captain Willis and give him your message, but first I need to deliver a message from him."

The admiral's tone took on a pompous air. "And what message is that?"

She smiled in a sassy way. "Drop dead."

Zoë raised a fist and twisted it, her teeth clenched.

The admiral clutched his chest, gasping, "She's . . . killing me."

I shook off the manacles, drew my hands to the front, and tried to jerk the gloves off, but the metal clasps held them in place. While I bit one of the clasps and pulled, a guard lunged and punched Zoë in the face. She staggered and fell. Oliver leaped toward her but tripped on his leg irons and toppled face-first.

Crystal leaped onto the guard who punched Zoë. Locking his torso with her arms and legs, she looked into his eyes. "You must protect the admiral. Take him into the ship and fly away. He's delusional. Get him to safety." She released him and dropped to her feet. "Now go!"

The guard hooked an arm around the hunched and gasping admiral and escorted him up the ramp, both weaving as they climbed. Another grabbed Oliver's arm, jerked him to his feet, and set a handgun against his head as he barked, "March!"

Just as a third guard stalked down the ramp toward me while drawing his gun, the wrist clasp broke. I ripped the glove off with my teeth, sent a charge into my hand, and leaped at him. I clutched his throat, sending a jolt into his body, then jumped back. He dropped to the ramp, stunned as he crawled toward the ship on trembling limbs.

The guard walking up the ramp with Oliver glared back as if daring me to attack. He could pull the trigger far quicker than I could catch up and try to shock him.

I stepped off the *Nebula One*'s ramp and stood next to my mother's corpse. From the ship, the admiral cried out, "Never mind the pirate girl. Shields up. Prepare for battle."

My thoughts swirled. Our plans had shattered. Everything was falling to pieces. I knelt at my mother's side and grasped her hand. Something glimmered on her chest. I leaned close. Her locket lay exposed, the one containing a dragon's eye that glowed with my life's essence.

As I untied her locket's cord, the ramp began rising. My heart raced. I couldn't leave Crystal and Zoë to fight the *Nebula One*. Quixon probably had no experience either. But I also couldn't abandon Oliver—or Dirk, still hiding somewhere on the ship.

I looked back. Crystal helped Zoë stagger up the *Dragon*'s ramp. They would be ready to fly in moments. They could escape.

But Oliver and Dirk couldn't.

I tied the locket around my own neck as I called, "Crystal, send Quixon to get my mother! I'm going to save Oliver and get Dirk, too."

Crystal pushed Zoë at a faster pace. "On it!"

At the same time, Quixon hustled down the *Dragon*'s ramp, calling, "I will tend to your mother."

The ramp rose above my head and sloped downward toward the ship. I supercharged my legs and leaped onto it. As I hunkered low and scrambled down the ramp, Perdantus landed on my shoulder. "When we get inside," he said, "tell me what to do. I am at your command."

Staying quiet, I nodded. I padded on tiptoes into the ship as the hatch closed behind me. Above, at bridge level, the admiral sat in the command chair with his crew seated and strapped in at consoles all around. Everyone stared through the front viewing window, apparently unaware of my presence.

The *Nebula One*'s engines started and let out a loud hum, giving me noise cover. I backed against the wall out of sight of the bridge and whispered, "Crystal, it's up to you to navigate. Use your smaller size to outmaneuver the *Nebula One* by staying close to the ground. The admiral's furious enough to make a mistake. Try to get the *One* to crash into something."

"But you and Oliver and Dirk—"

"Don't worry about us. If we stay low, we have a chance to survive a crash, but you won't survive those souped-up torpedoes. Just get the *Dragon* off the ground and fly away."

"All right. You're the captain. Quixon has your mother, and we're all strapping in now."

"Sonya," I said. "If I can't talk, follow Crystal's orders."

"Negative, Captain. My programming will not allow it. She lacks the appropriate security clearance."

"Then stand down. Crystal will operate the ship without you. Emergency protocol."

"Acknowledged. Standing down."

"What?" Crystal cried out. "Fly the ship alone?"

"I'll help," Zoë said, her voice distant. "We can do this."

From above, the admiral's voice reached my ears. "Take Oliver to the prison level and check him for a communications device."

I whispered, "Oliver. It's Megan. This might be my last chance to talk to you. I'm on board. Fairbanks doesn't know. I'll figure out a way to get to you."

No one answered. Either he couldn't talk without someone hearing, or they had already taken his commlink away. And no telling where Dirk was. Maybe he had been captured as well.

The *Nebula One* trembled and lifted off the ground. I twisted my neck and looked at Perdantus on my shoulder. "Is there a shaft down here anywhere? Something that can lead me to the prison level?"

"Not that I know of. At the bridge level's rear wall, however, there is a door leading to a ladder that climbs to a level between the bridge and the prison. If I cause a distraction, perhaps you will be able to get to the ladder undetected."

"Okay. Let's—"

The ship surged ahead, pinning me against the wall. The chase was on. I looked up and tried to see through the front window, but at this angle, only the sky lay in view.

"Max," the admiral barked. "Shield report."

Max spoke from the ceiling speakers. "Shields are functioning across seventy-eight percent of the hull. Repairs are still ongoing, but the ship's movement will slow the effort."

"Good enough, but we still need to maintain adequate distance between us and any target. Otherwise flying debris might damage our ship."

"Acknowledged."

As the g-forces eased, I pushed away from the wall and looked at Perdantus. "Now."

The moment he lifted from my shoulder, I hustled up the left-side ramp, bending low. Perdantus flew at the admiral and fluttered his wings in his face, squealing and squawking. The admiral batted at him and bellowed, "Where did this fool bird come from?"

While everyone watched Perdantus continue his crazed attack, I sneaked to the rear of the bridge, found the door, and eased it open. Inside, a ladder led through a hole in the ceiling. As I entered and drew the door closed, I peered out through the narrowing gap. One of the admiral's swinging hands finally swatted Perdantus, sending him tumbling through the air. His wings spread, and he flew out of sight into a vent near the ceiling.

I closed the door, holding the latch and easing it into place. It clicked anyway. I cringed and waited, hoping for no response.

"What was that?" the admiral called.

A man answered. "I'll check."

I shot up the ladder to the next level, stepped away from the hole, and scanned the dim area. I stood in a corridor with doors leading to cabin rooms all around, most likely the crew's living quarters. There was no sign of an easy exit, though near the ceiling, a ventilation shaft led through a nearby wall.

Footfalls struck the ladder rungs. I charged my legs again, leaped to the shaft, and pushed my fingers through the gaps in the grating.

Hanging on, I looked down. A man emerged from the ladder hole and glanced around.

Crystal's voice piped in through the commlink. "We're heading into Bassolith, Megan. I'm going to make Fairbanks chase us around buildings, so hold tight to something."

The ship shifted hard. The force jerked me from the vent, and I fell on top of the man, flattening him. I rolled off, climbed to my feet, and looked at him—Weston.

He rose and blinked at me. "I thought it might be you."

Just as I turned to run, the ship swerved again, sending me staggering into his arms. I struggled, but he held me fast. Facing him, I electrified my hands and hissed, "Let me go or I'll fry your brains."

Weston pushed me away. I set my feet in a wide stance, riding the ship's nearly constant swerves, my shimmering hands spread in front of me. "Take me to Oliver."

"You can go yourself." He extended a plastic card. "This'll give you access anywhere."

I discharged my hands and took the card cautiously. Could I trust him? "Why are you doing this?"

"I hacked the admiral's messages and discovered that you're right about his crimes. I sent a message to the Alliance commandant about it." He pointed toward the end of the hallway. "Elevator's the last door on the right. Save your friend. I have to make sure the admiral doesn't destroy the evidence."

I looked at the door. "Um . . . thanks."

Balancing against the swerves, Weston weaved his way to the ladder and stepped down a few rungs.

I called, "Wait."

He stopped and looked at me. "What?"

"I need a key to Oliver's cell and chains."

"You're in luck." Weston fished a metal cylinder from his pocket and tossed it to me. When I caught it, he climbed down the ladder and disappeared.

I ran to the elevator and slid the card through the reader. As I set my feet again and waited for the car to arrive, something bumped the ship, making it lurch. I toppled toward the elevator just as it opened, fell headlong into the car, and rolled against the rear door.

"Admiral," Max said from a speaker in the elevator car, "I detect a weight anomaly in the main elevator."

The same speaker announced the admiral's reply. "Override the controls. Bring the car to bridge level."

I scrambled to my feet, scanned the control panel, and pushed the button for the rear door. The moment it opened, I leaped out. A split-second later, the door closed, and the elevator hummed, fading as the car glided downward.

My knees bent to ride the ship's constant swerves, I looked around. I stood in a short corridor with two doors—one straight ahead and one to my left. Since I had no idea which way to go, now was a good time to check in with the *Astral Dragon*.

I kept my voice low. "Crystal. Update."

"We're not dead yet. He's shooting laser blasts. Some are hitting us, but the shields are working. No photon torpedoes. No idea why he's holding off on those."

"Strange. Maybe I can find out why."

"You do that while I keep dodging. At least I haven't puked yet."

"Back to you in a second." I slid the card through the left-hand door's reader. When it beeped, I turned the knob, hoping my actions wouldn't trigger an alert from Max. I pushed the door open and walked into the room holding the coffins and glowsap.

The swerves suddenly ended. Strange again. "Crystal, what's up?"

"He quit chasing us. No idea why. Now you're flying over the road that leads to the bramble bee cave. I'm keeping close, but not real close."

"The cave? That doesn't make sense . . . unless . . ." My mind whirred. Could the admiral be trying to hide evidence?

"Unless what?"

A gunshot rang out from a hidden speaker. The admiral's voice followed. "If any of you are in league with Weston, I will learn of it soon enough. Mutiny will not be tolerated."

I shuddered. Fairbanks had killed my only *Nebula One* ally.

"I think I got the answer. The admiral's covering his tracks. I have to preserve some evidence. Stand by." I looked at little Penelope through the coffin's glass cover. A glimmer caught my attention. A tiny computer drive on a chain lay on her chest. Maybe it held some valuable information.

When I lifted the coffin lid, air pressure hissed from its vacuum seal. I grabbed the drive and jerked the chain, breaking it. I pushed the drive into my pocket and closed the lid. Now I had to get out of this room without being seen.

I looked up. The shaft opening I had used to drop here earlier was still uncovered. Perdantus flew down from the hole and landed on my shoulder. "I thought you might come here. I brought Dirk with me. He is waiting in the vent shaft."

"Fire!" the admiral said through the speaker.

"Crystal," I hissed. "What do you see?"

"The *Nebula One* shot a photon torpedo. It's heading toward the forest."

An explosion boomed, making the ship tremble.

"Rocks are flying everywhere, Megan. Bees, too. He blew up the cave."

"Return to Bassolith," the admiral said. "Load the enhanced photon torpedoes. All of them."

As the ship turned and accelerated, Crystal's voice spiked. "Now you're heading toward the city! What's that maniac going to destroy next?"

My heart thudded. "The slave market. The kids. The slavers. Any piece of evidence that'll nail him. Those torpedoes can level Bassolith."

Perdantus flew off my shoulder and perched on the coffin. "What can we do to stop him?"

"Not sure. Dirk! Catch me!" I charged my legs again and leaped to the ceiling hole. Dirk's arms jutted out just in time. I grabbed his wrists and rode his pull into the shaft. When Perdantus joined us, I withdrew Weston's key and set it on the shaft's floor and spoke to them both. "Oliver's probably in a cell on the prison level. Perdantus,

I need you to get the key to him and tell him I'm coming soon, and I need Dirk to lead me to the torpedoes."

Perdantus picked up the key with a claw and flew away like a silver streak.

"This way to the torpedoes." Dirk crawled along the shaft. Pushing with my knees and elbows, I scrambled after him. When we arrived at another ventilation hole, he nodded toward it.

I looked down through the open hole, its cover likely removed by Oliver and Dirk when they armed a torpedo earlier. Below, a man with bulging biceps heaved a huge metallic missile from a shelf to a firing tube and slid the tube's loading arm to lock the missile in place.

"Weapons status," the admiral called, his voice coming from a speaker in the torpedo room.

"Just one more." The man lugged another large missile to the tube, loaded it, and fastened a latch that secured the tube. "Finished. You may fire when ready, Admiral."

"Good. We'll be in position over the city in thirty seconds."

With a quick muscle flex, I charged my hands and dropped into the room. My feet slammed the man's shoulders and sent him staggering. When he regained his balance, he charged at me. I tried to grab his arm, but he batted my hand away and punched me with a crushing fist to the chin. I fell to my back, dazed. He pulled a pistol from his belt and took aim. "One dead pirate, coming up."

Dirk landed feetfirst on the man's head, knocking him flat. I scooted to him and set a charged hand on his head, giving him a hefty shock. After shuddering for a moment, he lay motionless, though he appeared to be breathing.

Dirk took the man's gun and slid it behind his waistband. "What next?"

"I don't know. Let me think." I tried to unfasten the torpedo tube's latch, but it wouldn't budge. "It's too tight."

Our momentum eased to a stop, and Dirk cringed. "That can't be good."

Max's voice came from a ceiling speaker. "We are in position, Admiral."

"Fire!" the admiral shouted.

A high-pitched squeal shot from the torpedo tube. Another explosion boomed somewhere outside. Shock waves reverberated and rattled the ship again.

Crystal gasped. "He blew up the ironworks factory!"

"Proceed to the next target," the admiral said, "the temple of the Taurantas."

I whispered, "No, no, no. The kids are there. Crystal, how close are you?"

"I don't know how to lock a weapon on him while he's moving. I'm buzzing around him, but he's ignoring me. I'm just a gnat trying to annoy an elephant."

"Better than nothing." I eyed a torpedo on a waist-high shelf against a wall. A timer dial protruded from the top. It might be our only chance to get out of this. "Just keep him thinking you're going to attack."

"I'll do my best."

"Dirk, help me carry this thing." We picked up the torpedo, one at each end, and shuffled with it out of the room, through the corridor I had been in earlier, and into the coffin room, using Weston's card to get in.

I set the torpedo's timer dial to its three-minute maximum, and we wedged it behind a row of glowsap containers on one of the shelves. According to Oliver, the sap was super flammable. I had no idea if a blast could cripple the ship, but at least it would be a distraction while Oliver, Dirk, and I tried to escape.

"Torpedo activation anomaly detected," Max said from a ceiling speaker.

"Lieutenant," the admiral called. "What's going on in the torpedo room?"

Dirk whispered, "We have to get out of here. Follow me." We hustled back to the torpedo room. Dirk clambered to the top of a set of shelves, crawled into the vent shaft, and reached down. "Hurry!"

I charged my legs, leaped to the hole, and climbed in with Dirk's help. "Thanks. Now to get Oliver." While mentally counting down the timer, I crawled to the vertical shaft leading to the prison level and leaped up about halfway, my legs weaker now. I wormed my body to the top, Dirk following, though several meters behind. When I made it to the horizontal shaft, I crawled as fast as I could to the prison chamber.

I looked out the opening. Oliver was free from the cell and shaking loose an ankle bracelet, Perdantus on his shoulder. I dropped to the floor and hurried to his side. "Two minutes before a bomb blows. We have to scram."

"Where? How?"

"The vent shaft. I can boost you to Dirk, then jump—"

An alarm blared, and the elevator's distinctive *snick* followed. "Someone's coming."

"Hurry!" I crouched at the wall. Oliver climbed onto my shoulders while Perdantus flew into the hole. Using all my remaining strength, I lunged upward while he jumped. Dirk caught Oliver's wrists, but Oliver slipped away and dropped back to the floor.

The elevator car opened. The admiral stormed out with an armed guard. I flexed my biceps, but nothing happened. I was out of power. The guard caught me and held my forearm.

The admiral set a gun to my head and roared, "Where's the torpedo?"

I glared at him. "Can't you follow its signal, Admiral?"

"If you think killing us all is funny . . ." He aimed the gun at my leg and fired.

Pain ripped through my calf and shot to my hip. My knees buckled, but the guard kept me from falling.

As I dangled in the guard's grasp, the admiral shifted the gun back to my head. "Tell me! Now!"

An explosion rocked the ship, making it list violently to one side. Perdantus flew down, landed on the admiral's face, and pecked at his eyes. The admiral batted at Perdantus furiously, but the agile bird avoided every swat.

"Oliver!" Dirk dropped the pistol he'd taken from the man in the torpedo room. Oliver caught it and shot the guard in the shoulder. He yelped and let me go, staggering with the ship's steepening slope.

With the wall now at an angle, Oliver and I scrambled toward the shaft, Oliver supporting me as blood streamed down my leg.

We dove through the hole, Oliver first and me following. We barreled into Dirk, nearly knocking him over. As the three of us crawled at a downward angle, smoke billowed in from the vertical shaft ahead. "We can't go that way," I called. "Go to the hull space. Every Nebula ship has an escape hatch at the top."

"How's your leg?" Oliver asked.

Pain pulsed. I could feel blood streaming down my leg, but we didn't have time to discuss it. "Never mind. Just go."

The moment we crossed the pillar of smoke, shots rang out, and a bird squawked.

I turned and shouted, "Perdantus!" But no answer came.

I grabbed Oliver's ankle, stopping him. "I have to go back."

More explosions erupted. Flames shot up through the smoke, blocking the path to the prison room.

"We can't," Oliver said, coughing. "We'll get cooked. Our only chance is to go to the hull space."

Coughs throttled my voice. "I'm not leaving Perdantus behind!"

Something burst through the fire and fell next to me. Perdantus lolled on the shaft floor, his feathers sizzling. I batted the flames away and set him upright, but he toppled over, dazed and wheezing.

I scooped him up. "Let's go!"

Dirk and Oliver scooted ahead through the thickening smoke. I followed, still angling downward, using one hand to prop myself in front and the other to hold Perdantus. My wounded leg felt like it was on fire, but I couldn't look at it. I had to ignore the pain and keep moving.

New explosions thundered. Cracking noises echoed, like the ship might be breaking apart. A voice buzzed in my ear, probably Crystal calling through the commlink, but I couldn't stop to listen.

Dirk crawled out into the hull space, reached back into the shaft, and helped Oliver and me climb out onto a ramp that spanned a gap between us and the ship's central support. Below, fire spewed from vents, partially veiled by smoke that churned and swirled as it filled the enormous cylindrical chamber, too thick to allow a view of the escape hatch above.

"Crystal," I called, standing on one foot while I held Oliver's shoulder. "Can you see what's going on?"

"Blazes! Literally. The *Nebula One* is spewing flames and sitting on the ground at an angle."

I coughed fitfully as I spoke. "I need you to blow a hole in the *One's* roof. Let some of this smoke out. Hit us with a photon torpedo. The shields should be down."

"Are you nuts? I might kill you."

"We're dead if you don't. Just do it. Try to graze the top. Tell Zoë to guide the torpedo."

"It's not weightless here," Zoë said, "but I'll try."

A moment later, a new explosion ripped through the air. The ship rocked. I braced myself on Oliver while he and Dirk held on to a railing. Light streamed in, and smoke poured out through a massive jagged hole in the roof.

Directly over our heads, a tether line with a hook at the end dangled from the escape hatch, uncoiled by the torpedo's impact. Oliver jumped, but his fingers merely brushed the hook.

"Hold Perdantus." I gave him to Oliver and mentally measured the distance to the line.

Oliver slid Perdantus into his shirt pocket. "Can you jump that high with one leg?"

"I have to. It's the only way out."

"No. I got this." Dirk ran along the ramp and began shinnying up the central support.

"Stop!" The admiral appeared at the opening of the shaft we had crawled through, a handgun aimed at us as he propped himself with an elbow. His face blackened and his hair charred, he growled, "I can't let you escape. You know too much."

Oliver aimed his pistol, but the admiral fired first. The bullet grazed Oliver's hand, making him drop the gun.

"Megan!" Dirk called, dangling upside down with the tether hook fastened to his belt. "Jump!"

I charged my good leg, leaped, and caught his arms. The admiral fired at me but missed. As we swayed, the admiral crawled out of the shaft, stood upright, and fired at us again and again. A bullet zinged past my ear. Another nicked Dirk's sleeve. Oliver lunged at the admiral, throwing fists. Using a foot, the admiral shoved him back and took aim at him.

I latched on to Dirk with my legs, flipped my body, and reached down with both hands. "Oliver! Jump!"

He leaped up and grabbed my wrists. As we dangled, more shots were fired. I forced us into a wider sway, hoping the movement would keep us from being an easy target.

The admiral fired several more times. Finally, the gun clicked, out of ammo. Our line jerked, sending us a meter lower, within his reach. From above, someone called, "I've got you!"

I looked up. Quixon stood on the *Astral Dragon's* retrieval ladder, the bottom extending into the roof hole and our tether line now attached to a carabiner, locked to the lowest rung.

The ladder began retracting, lifting us higher. As we rose, the pendant around my neck slipped from under my collar, dangling like a scarlet strobe. My mother's dragon's eye—pulsing with new strength and infusing it into me. We were going to make it.

The admiral jumped and wrapped his arms around Oliver's legs. The sudden extra weight made my hold on Oliver slip. I tightened my grip, feeling stronger than I thought possible. Yet, even with the dragon's eye–enhanced strength, I couldn't hang on much longer, and Dirk probably felt like my legs were about to crush him.

"Crystal!" I shouted. "Fly straight up! Now!"

We zoomed upward. When we reached the hole, the admiral banged against the edge, broke loose, and toppled onto the *Nebula One's* roof while Oliver, Dirk, and I continued rising.

When the ladder fully retracted, Quixon and Zoë pulled the tether line and drew us into the *Astral Dragon*. The moment I set foot on the ship, I called, "Crystal, get in position to shoot another torpedo at the *Nebula One*. I'll be right there. I want to push the button myself."

"Will do, Captain," Crystal said through the commlink.

Quixon and Oliver guided me to the ladder. I grasped the sides and hopped on one foot to bridge level, then limped to the bridge with Oliver, Dirk, Quixon, and Zoë close behind. Crystal shot up from my mother's console chair and helped me sit.

"Sonya," I said, heaving fast breaths. "Activate. You're back in the game."

"Acknowledged, Captain."

I looked out the viewing window at Admiral Fairbanks as he stood atop the *Nebula One*'s domed roof. Fire and smoke belched from underneath his ship and from every side. After a couple of attempts at sliding down the roof only to be chased back to the top by fire, the admiral gave up, crossed his arms, and glared at us, shouting something inaudible.

"Lock both torpedo turrets on the *Nebula One*," I said as I set the targeting grid. "Aim directly at the man standing on the roof."

"Acknowledged. Torpedoes locked. You may fire when ready."

As I looked at the admiral's defiant stance, I flipped the cover off the firing button and set my finger on it, the same button my mother had used to fire on the *Nebula Nine* and kill Captain Tillman and his crew.

As if summoned by my touch, her words returned to mind. *We have to fight fire with fire. If we don't come at those monsters with guns blazing, they'll kill thousands. Tens of thousands. And they'll keep enslaving innocent children in every star system.*

Beyond the city's skyline, dark smoke rose, the aftermath of the admiral's attack on the bramble bee cave. With Thorne gone, no slave kids were in danger there. Closer in, the Tauranta temple stood about twenty meters from the ship, still intact. We had foiled the admiral's bid to destroy it. The children inside were safe. The danger was over.

The Astral Dragon's words whispered in my mind, as if responding to my mother. *Life is a gift that must be protected. Our feelings are not a factor in that decision.*

As everyone else looked on, I touched my pocket where the computer drive lay. The drive's data and the papers from the lockbox might hold the evidence we needed to put the admiral away forever. He had no ship, no crew, no power. He had failed. My rage and hunger for revenge weren't enough of a reason to put that monster down.

"Megan," Crystal said, "the admiral's practically begging you to shove a torpedo up his nose. Are you going to let him have it or not?"

I flipped the trigger cover back in place. "It's over. Better to make him live in shame than to kill him."

"Are you sure?" Quixon asked. "He's bound to cause more trouble."

Crystal nodded. "Yeah. It'll be hard to pin the crimes on his slippery hide."

"I'm sure. We just need to read the lockbox papers and figure out what's on the drive I found and—"

New flames exploded throughout the *Nebula One*, maybe a fuel tank rupture. The blast burst through the roof and wrapped the admiral in a swirl of flames. His arms flailing, he plunged into the heart of the ship.

"Okay," Crystal said, grinning. "Swallowed by a dragon. That'll do."

I gazed at the fiery hole that had consumed the admiral. I wanted to crack a joke and share the joy of victory. But I couldn't. So many lives had been lost. True, the admiral deserved to die, but not Weston. And what about the rest of the crew? How much did they really know about their leader's crimes?

I let out a long sigh. This was a time to mourn.

Zoë patted me on the shoulder. "You made the right call, Megan. The admiral's dead, his wicked witch of a wife can't do any more experiments on those poor kids' bodies, and you have a clear conscience."

"Yep." Oliver compressed my shoulder. "Now let's get you and Perdantus to sick bay."

I looked at the bulge in his shirt pocket. "How is he?"

"Warm. Still breathing. I can feel him."

"Can you try to heal him? You know, with your powers?"

"I already did." Oliver released my shoulder and peeked into his pocket. "He was nearly dead, but he's perking up now."

"Great." I nodded toward my leg. "Got any healing power left for me?"

He winced but quickly slackened his face. "I can try, but no guarantees. I'm pooped."

"No. You rest. I'm sure I'll be all right."

"I know a good doctor," Quixon said. "Set the ship down, and I'll bring him in. I think he'll even work on birds."

I nodded. "Fine. I'll head to sick bay." I rose and stood on one leg. "But as soon as Perdantus and I get patched up, we have to go to the *Nebula Nine* and get Renalda's ashes, and everyone else's."

"True," Crystal said. "And we have to take care of your mother's body. She's in the sleeping quarters."

Her words hit me like a lightning bolt. Battling an upwelling sob, I breathed a deep sigh. "You're right. Let's sew up my wounds and get out of here."

34

The doctor found that the bullet had passed through my calf without much damage. He bandaged my leg and ordered me to stay in bed for a week—ridiculous, of course. When he left, I began limping around right away. Perdantus recovered quickly as well. Although annoyed by his burnt feathers, especially the odor, he was able to fly.

Oliver helped me hobble to my family's sleeping quarters. Quixon had laid my mother's body on a mattress that took up most of the floor space in the small room. Once we had strapped her down for our upcoming flight, I straightened and looked around.

Nothing had changed since the last time I slept here—bare walls and a nightstand bolted to the floor. My mother always kept things simple, and at that moment I vowed the same. The *Astral Dragon* would honor her memory in every way.

I returned to the bridge and took my mother's seat again at the dual captain's console. Oliver sat in my father's seat, next to mine. Crystal chose my old navigator's chair, Dirk sat next to her at the communications seat, Zoë took the mapping station, and Perdantus perched on my shoulder. Quixon stood with his feet set firmly, insisting that he could balance himself during the short ride to the *Nebula Nine*.

"Sonya," I said, "prepare for takeoff."

"Acknowledged." As the front hatch closed, she added, "Captain Megan Willis."

I allowed myself a smile in spite of my grief. "And feel free to be snarky again. I miss my old Sonya."

"Snark level set at fifty out of one hundred. And I missed you as well, though your hair looks like someone cut it with a chain saw, and your face makes you look like you wallowed in a pile of ashes. Even so, welcome home, Megan."

"Thank you, but maybe you should cut the snark level to forty." I flew the *Astral Dragon* about a kilometer and landed where Crystal and company had left the *Nebula Nine* earlier—in a forest glade, pretty well hidden from view.

After lowering the hatch, we walked down the ramp to the ground while Perdantus flew out and perched on a nearby sapling. When we gathered in the gap between the two ships, Oliver patted the *Nine*'s exterior wall. "So, now what? We have two ships and lots to do."

Dirk's eyes brightened. "My father should be out of jail by now. I want to go home and be with him."

Oliver nodded. "We'll definitely put that on the to-do list."

Crystal sidled close to me. "I'll bet I know what you want to do."

"Doesn't take a mind reader, right?" I squinted at her. "Did you get a read on the admiral when he talked about my father being alive? I mean, was he telling the truth?"

"Yep. I'm sure he believed that your father's alive. Whether or not he really is, I don't know."

"Good enough for me. I'll go to Beta Four and search for my father. If he's there, I'll rescue him from that frozen prison if it's the last thing I do."

Crystal clenched a fist. "Yeah. That's the spirit."

I let my shoulders sag. I didn't feel spirited. Not one bit. Even the anticipation of finding my father seemed blunted, scary. Apparently he and my mother did something terrible on Gamma Five, making him a mysterious specter, someone to be approached with caution.

Not only that, so many other mysteries abounded. How did the dragon's eye get so much power? Was it a blessing to have one or a curse? And what did my great-grandfather have to do with the mysterious gem?

I shook my head to cast away the gloom. "And after that, I have to scour the galaxy for all the slave camps, traders, and bramble bee mines and wipe out the entire disgusting business. We have the papers from Thorne's lockbox, and we'll see what's on the computer drive I took from the coffin, so we have a good start. And I also have to find Camille Fairbanks, the admiral's wife. I think she's behind the SS Squad, experimenting on children in some way. Captain Tillman seemed to think that this squad could cause the deaths of billions."

Crystal set a hand on her chest and blinked, speaking in a sing-song manner. "Then you'll need a faithful navigator to go with you, right, Captain?"

I smiled. "I couldn't survive without you."

"That's no lie. I'd better hang around to keep you from launching yourself into space, burning in a fire, getting shot, and whatever other ways you've already tried to kill yourself. I mean, you've been knocked out, what, five times?"

"I lost count."

"No wonder. Too many concussions. Your brain's coming loose."

"Megan?" Zoë stepped close, her voice quivering. "It sounds like you're going to face some of the most dangerous monsters in the galaxy."

I waved a hand. "No worries. We'll find a sanctuary planet for you before we—"

Zoë poked my shoulder with a finger. "Gotcha."

I blinked at her. "What?"

"I gotcha. Fooled you with my excellent acting skills." She grinned. "I'm aching to mow down some monsters. If you try to go without me, I'll use my mind to make your eyeballs turn inside out."

Crystal punched Zoë's arm. "I'm liking this girl better all the time."

"Same here." I grasped her wrist. "Glad to have you on board. It'll be great getting to know you better."

She grasped my wrist in return. "Thanks, but I'm a lot weirder than you might think. I've been kind of hiding my, shall we say, unusual qualities until I feel like I'm part of the family.

"That won't take long." I released her and looked at Oliver. "I still have an open seat next to mine on the *Astral Dragon*."

He fidgeted. "Yeah. Thanks. But let's talk about it after we . . ." He nodded toward the *Astral Dragon*. "You know. Take care of your mom."

I looked that way and imagined her still lying on our family mattress. The thought of setting her on fire burned a hole in my heart, but, of course, it had to be done.

At a sparse spot in the glade, Oliver, Dirk, and Quixon prepared the pyre and laid my mother on it while I watched, trying to put out of my mind the identity of the person they were handling. That effort failed miserably. I cried myself into a blubbering mess. Each of my friends came by and whispered kind words, but their gestures didn't help. I had lost my dear Mama. What pain could possibly be worse?

During my crying spell, Zoë quietly stood next to me for a while, also crying. She had been with my mother for several months and probably grew attached to her as a new mother. Although I understood her grief, I couldn't say a word. My own grief had swollen my throat nearly completely shut.

When Zoë left my side, she, Crystal, Oliver, and Dirk gathered into a huddle. They spoke in whispers that sometimes grew sharp, but I didn't pay much attention. Maybe they were planning to do something to cheer me up, which would be nice of them, though I doubted it could work. I did catch Dirk saying something about the idea being crazy and Oliver saying he wouldn't be part of it, but they seemed to come to an agreement and ended their huddle.

Moments later, Oliver fashioned an oil-soaked torch, lit the end, and extended the handle to me. I couldn't push my responsibilities away any longer. I gathered my courage, wiped my nose and cheeks, and took the torch.

While the others looked on, I stepped close to the pyre and gazed at my mother's serene face. Tears welling again, I steeled myself and tried my best to steady my voice. "Captain Anne Willis, I commit your body to the sky and your soul to the Astral Dragon. I swear to you in his name that if Julian Willis is still alive, I will find him and release him from his bonds, whatever they may be, and together we will cherish your memory—your wisdom, your strength, your courage, and most of all, your love."

I laid the torch on the wood. The flames caught and spread over her body. Seeing her burn thrashed my heart. I dropped to my knees and once again sobbed. "Oh, Mama! I love you so much! What am I going to do without you?"

Oliver knelt next to me and rubbed my shoulder. "I know it's not the same, not even close, but I'll go with you to find your father. I mean, if that's what you want."

I looked at him through a blur of tears. Tears spilled from his eyes as well. He really did want to be with me, but I knew he was torn. I didn't need Crystal's magic powers to tell me he was hiding his true passion. "You want to get those kids to a sanctuary, don't you? The kids at the temple."

He looked away for a moment before focusing on me again. "Yeah. You never know when the next battle storm's coming, and then the temple won't be safe. The rovers are probably where we left them in the woods, so it won't take long to get the kids to the *Nebula Nine*. Then I'll fly them all to Delta Ninety-five. They'll be all right there with the other kids."

"True." Holding his hands, I rose and lifted him with me. "Dirk can go with you. After you drop the kids off, you can take him home to his father. And don't forget to deliver the crew's ashes to the Alliance for transport to the families, but you'll have to figure out how to do it secretly. Before he died, Fairbanks probably made sure we're all wanted as criminals everywhere in the galaxy. I'm not sure what you should do with Renalda's remains, but I know you'll come up with a good idea."

When I mentioned Renalda, thoughts of Oliver's failure to heal her returned to mind, though his own wounds seemed to have already mended. The inconsistency was another mystery left unsolved.

He grinned. "Should I consider those my orders, Captain?"

I brushed tears away and smiled. "Yes, though Emerson will probably promote you to captain of the *Nebula Nine*."

"I hope I can handle it. My landing skills aren't the best."

As the fire crackled and warmed my body, my heart warmed as well. I would really miss this amazing guy. "Promise me you'll stay in touch. I want to see you again someday. I mean, you know, to hear how things are going for you."

"I promise. I'll look forward to it."

Quixon raised a finger. "And speaking of promises, I promised that I would give you half the proceeds from your slave sale above a thousand mesots. If you'll look in your quarters, you will find the ten thousand mesots minus the paltry sum I paid for the release of some of the children. It's only fair to give you as much as possible, since the money came from your mother, and I have the metasilver. And I also have a new promise—to make sure that Bassolith is rid of every trace of slavery. I will not rest until everyone is free."

I smiled in spite of my sadness. For some reason, this tragic end felt like a new beginning. We had done so much, including cutting off two of the slavery serpent's heads, but there were many more, some possibly even more powerful and dangerous than Thorne or Admiral Fairbanks. Yet, in spite of the size of the task, now I felt like we could actually do it.

Perdantus flew to my shoulder and chirped, "And I shall go with you—that is, if you don't mind. My mate is gone, and I have no close relatives. My home is now wherever I set my heart, and my heart is set on slaying the slavery monster."

I rubbed his chest with a finger. "Of course you can, Perdantus. We'd love to have anyone along who believes in what we're doing."

"And I do, but there is another reason. You females smell so much better than the males, especially the Jaradians."

We all burst out laughing, though the lightheartedness was

short-lived. With my mother burning nearby, the crackling fire seemed to consume any joy we tried to generate.

"Well, Megan," Quixon said, bowing his head. "I will take my leave now and walk home, but I have a question for you before I go."

I nodded. "Then ask it."

"First, let me say that you are the most heroic and courageous person I have ever met, human or otherwise. You are an inspiration to us all."

Everyone clapped, and Dirk added a whistle. My heart warmed once again. Their support felt so good.

"And for my part . . ." Quixon withdrew his flask, twisted the cap off, and poured out its amber liquid, shaking it until the last drop fell to the ground. "I pledge to no longer find my courage in a flask. Your inspiration has infected me as well."

Goose bumps crawled across my skin. I had no idea what to say. Staying quiet would probably be the right choice.

"Also," Quixon continued, "you will need more than mere courage. To accomplish your mission—to free your father and break the back of the slave trade—you will be forced to break the law as well." He looked me in the eye. "I heard about your desire to avoid killing, yet, even though you spared the admiral, you have killed more than once. You will need to decide what your boundaries are so that you will not be paralyzed every time you have to make a choice between life and death."

I looked at the bracelets and the conductive ink leading to my hands, the same hands that killed Thorne and my own mother. Yes, she demanded it, and yes, I had to do it, but I couldn't revive her as I had promised. Forcing back another sob, I met Quixon's stare. "I did kill. I hated it. I never want to do it again. And I know I can't avoid the choice when it comes, but I'm still trying to figure out my boundaries. I can force myself to kill when it means saving an innocent life, but even then I'm not sure it's the right thing to do. Every life is sacred."

"Including the life you're saving. Never forget that."

"True." I averted my eyes. "I'll keep thinking about it."

"Very well. I won't trouble you any further except to ask, are you now going to follow in your parents' footsteps? Are you willing to be known as a pirate?"

I refocused on him. "If being a pirate means breaking unjust laws to set kids free, then I'll do it without hesitation. I will be a pirate."

Quixon nodded. "Well stated. I share your vision and passion."

"Same here," Crystal said, "and to prove that we're pirates, too . . ." She looked at Dirk. "Is it ready?"

Dirk winced. "Yeah, but I still think it's crazy."

"Doesn't matter. We're going to do it."

"If you say so." Dirk leaned over and grabbed an end of a metal rod, the other end resting in the fire. When he picked it up, the fiery end glowed orange, displaying a dragon. "Where did you get this thing, anyway?"

"From Quixon. I've been planning this for a while. It's not exactly the same as Megan's dragon, but almost." Crystal stepped closer and peered at the dragon. "Are her ashes on it?"

Dirk brought the symbol close to his eyes. "It's morbid, but yeah, her ashes are there. Plenty of them."

Crystal pulled her shirt off, exposing a sleeveless white singlet. "I'm ready."

I gasped. "Crystal! No!"

Zoë did the same with her shirt, her singlet dark gray. "I'm ready, too."

I raised a hand, laughing nervously to keep from crying again. "Seriously, you two. No. You don't have to do this."

"I know." Crystal nodded at Dirk. "Do it, before I change my mind."

Dirk pressed the symbol into Crystal's upper arm. As her flesh sizzled, she grimaced, clenched her eyes shut, and moaned. I grimaced with her, feeling the pain of my own branding as if it were happening again.

When Dirk pulled back, vapor rose from the raw wound, a perfect dragon brand. Crystal nodded toward Zoë, her face tight with pain. "Hurry, while it's still hot."

Dirk repeated the procedure on Zoë's arm. She, too, grimaced, adding a wail to her moans. When Dirk drew back again, the dragon brand sizzled on her arm, though not as easy to see on her dark skin. Dirk threw the branding iron to the ground. "I hope you two are satisfied."

"Perfectly." Cringing again, Crystal put her outer shirt over her head, slid one arm through a sleeve, but left her wounded arm exposed. Zoë did the same.

Crystal looked at me with a pain-streaked smile. "Now Zoë and I are carrying your mother's DNA, just like you. We're not just your partners in crime—we're your sisters, pirate sisters. And we decided to call our trio the Astral Dragon Alliance, or just Astral Alliance for short."

As my throat tightened, I swallowed hard. "I . . . I don't know what to say."

"Then don't say anything. It was our decision, not yours." Crystal took my hand and gestured for Zoë to take the other.

When Zoë completed our chain, I gazed at my two new sisters. With their courage, grit, determination, and especially their love, maybe we really could make a difference in the galaxy. I kissed Crystal's forehead, then Zoë's. "Thank you, my sisters. I love you both."

They each kissed my forehead in return.

When they drew back, I turned toward the others. "And I love all of you." As I gazed at my wonderful friends, I knew I had to say more. "Some of us will part company. Some will stick together. But no matter where we go, no matter who we're with, remember this. Whether we're covered with skin, scales, or feathers, we're family. We're bound together by love and a purpose, and that bond will never break. We'll all be together again someday, if not here, then among the stars. Until then, goodbye to those I'm leaving. I will never forget you. Never."

Crystal applauded. "That was amazing. Like it came straight from one of my novels."

"Yes," Perdantus said. "Well done. Your speaking abilities add another magic power to the trio's arsenal. You three young ladies are powerful indeed."

Crystal grinned. "Speaking of powerful young ladies, how do we smell now, oh bird of the sensitive beak?"

"Like burning flesh." Perdantus sneezed. "Since I will be traveling with you, I hope this branding is a one-time event."

"Don't get your hopes up too high. You might think we smell better than the guys, but after a hard day's work with lots of sweating, we stinky girls might change your mind. And, remember, the *Astral Dragon* has only one bedroom. You can't escape our odors."

Perdantus cringed. "Then can we bring aboard a whole case of air freshener?"

CAST OF CHARACTERS
(IN ORDER OF APPEARANCE)

MEGAN RUTH WILLIS—freedom fighter, daughter of Anne and Julian Willis

EMERSON—*Nebula Nine*'s computer system

CAPTAIN TILLMAN—captain of the *Nebula Nine*, father of Oliver

OLIVER TILLMAN—Captain Tillman's son, one of Thorne's slaves

DIONNE—worker on the *Nebula Nine*

DIRK—scullery boy and computer technician on the *Nebula Nine*

ANNE WILLIS—Megan's mother, a freedom fighter, Julian's wife

JULIAN WILLIS—Megan's father, a freedom fighter, Anne's husband

GAVIN FOSTER—first mate of the *Nebula Nine*

DR. COLE—ship's doctor of the *Nebula Nine*

ZOË—girl who travels with Anne Willis on the *Astral Dragon*, aka Andrea, has magical powers

PERDANTUS—silver jay, a master negotiator, Salsa's mate

QUIXON—formerly slave-trading Jaradian

NOLDIC—Tauranta male, Melda's husband

MELDA—Tauranta female, Noldic's wife

BANNIF—Tauranta male, Noldic and Melda's oldest son

HUSK—Tauranta male, Noldic and Melda's second son

DILIPPA—Tauranta female, Noldic and Melda's daughter

ASTRAL DRAGON—deity Megan believes in, aka Draco and Stellar

JUDGE MASON STATLER—judge who sentences the Willises

DORIS—cleaning woman at the court

ESSEN—Tauranta priest

SALSA—silver jay, Perdantus's mate, works for Thorne

CRYSTAL—one of Thorne's slaves, has magical powers

CYNDA—one of Thorne's slaves

THORNE—Willow Wind who uses child slave labor in a glowsap mine

AXLEBACK—Jaradian ironworks foreman

ERDATH—Jaradian bus driver

VONDA—one of Thorne's slaves

BASTIAN—one of Thorne's slaves

RENALDA—one of Thorne's slaves

NORBERT—one of Thorne's slaves

ADMIRAL FAIRBANKS—commander of the Nebula fleet and of the *Nebula One*, Camille's husband

WINTHROP ASHER—settler on Delta Ninety-five, Phyllis's husband

PHYLLIS ASHER—settler on Delta Ninety-five, Winthrop's wife

CASTOL—Jaradian slave trader

SONYA—*Astral Dragon*'s computer system

MAX—*Nebula One*'s computer system

SHERMAN—soldier on the *Nebula One*

BOBBY—soldier on the *Nebula One*

HARVEY—soldier on the *Nebula One*

WESTON—head of security on the *Nebula One*

GRETA—one of Thorne's slaves

PENELOPE—dead girl whose body is aboard the *Nebula One*

THEODORE—dead boy whose body is aboard the *Nebula One*

CAMILLE FAIRBANKS—Admiral Fairbanks's wife

ABOUT THE AUTHOR

Bryan Davis is the author of fantasy/science-fiction novels for youth and adults, including the bestselling Dragons in Our Midst series. Other series include The Oculus Gate, Reapers, Dragons of Starlight, Tales of Starlight, Time Echoes, and Wanted: Superheroes, several of which have been bestsellers.

Bryan was born in 1958 and grew up in the eastern US. From the time he taught himself how to read before school age, through his seminary years and beyond, he has demonstrated a passion for the written word, reading and writing in many disciplines and genres, including theology, fiction, devotionals, poetry, and humor.

Bryan is a graduate of the University of Florida (BS in Industrial Engineering). In high school, he was valedictorian of his class and won various academic awards. He was also a member of the National Honor Society and voted Most Likely to Succeed. He continues to expand his writing education by teaching at relevant writing conferences and conventions.

Although he is now a full-time writer, Bryan was a computer professional for over twenty years. Bryan lives in western Tennessee with his wife, Susie. Bryan and Susie homeschooled their four girls and three boys, and they work together as an author/editor team.

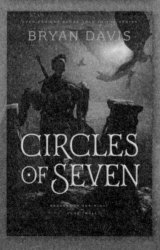

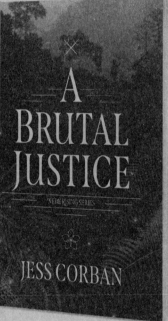

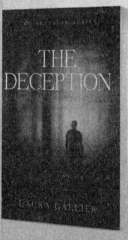

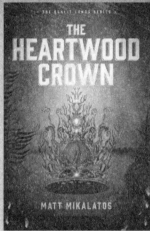

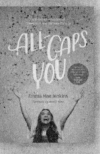